The
FEARLESS
TRAVELLERS' GUIDE
to WICKED PLACES

Pete Begler

Published by Curious Fox, an imprint of Capstone Global
Library Limited, 264 Banbury Road, Oxford, OX2 7DY –
Registered company number: 6695582

www.curious-fox.com

Text © Pete Begler 2017

The author's moral rights are hereby asserted.

Illustrations © Capstone 2017

Cover artist: Manuel Šumberac

Author photo © Miyoshi Barosh

ISBN 978 1 782 02595 5

20 19 18 17 16
10 9 8 7 6 5 4 3 2 1

A CIP catalogue for this book is available from the British
Library.

Printed and bound by CPI Group (UK) Ltd, Croydon, CR0 4YY

For Shannon, Trixie and Piper

You will get lost.
You will be afraid.
You will fail.
You will fight.
You will remember.
You will rise.
And without doubt:
You will find your way home.

MOTTO OF THE
FEARLESS TRAVELLERS

THE
DREAMLANDS

THE
DEEP
SEA

THE
WICKED
PLACES

THE SWEETLANDS

PROPERTY OF THE FEARLESS TRAVELLERS

PROLOGUE

Night was falling. Time to trumpet her call home, but the pure white swan racing across the darkening sky was silent as the bones of the dead.

Bones.

The thought would not leave her now. She had seen them tumble from the dark cloud like bits of snow. Heard them plunk into the silent sea and sink beneath the cold water, leaving no trace. Four of her brothers and three of her sisters had already been eaten by the dense cloud the colour of a rotten plum. There was no song for it. No way to understand it. Never had there been a cloud that brought not shade from the sun, not whispering snow or gentle rain, but death.

The clouds had become wolves, unrelenting beasts, chasing the swans through the sky with silent white paws and cunning noses from which they could not escape.

But I will escape the cloud, the swan thought as she pushed on alone towards home through the vast night.

I must. Two of her babies were awaiting her return.

A long hiss filled the air around her. A trumpet of fear escaped from the swan's long white throat. Now she knew the sound of the vaporous beast that had swallowed her brothers and sisters. It was right behind her!

"Faster," she told herself. "Faster."

She pushed harder, beating her wings until they burned with pain, but it was too late. The sky became muddled with mist. In a few seconds she could see no sky before her and no earth below, only wisps of purple vapour. The smell of the world and all it contained disappeared just as quickly, replaced by the throat-stinging char of wood smoke. Cold enveloped her and snow began to fall, coating her feathers. The flakes, fat and damp, quickly turned to ice and with a *CRACK* they tightened like a chain around her body.

Unable to fly, she began to fall.

I will drop through the cloud and crash into the sea below, she thought, and that would be her end. She would sink into the cold water and see her children no more.

A sharp pain clanged through her breast as she hit. A pained honk escaped her beak, taking her wind. The dark water did not drag her down. It was not the sea, but a stretch of ground. As she thrashed on the hard-packed snow, trying to break free of the chains of ice that bound her, the mist began to clear, and the swan saw the gossamer wisps of white where the sky should be. Her body trembled at the strange magic of it all. She was still within the cloud, yet it was like no cloud she had ever travelled through, for nestled inside was a small snow-dusted forest. And gathered in this small forest was a group of humans. All were female. They wore long dresses and stood before a crackling fire of purple flame as the snow fell around them. Their skin was as pale as her own feathers and their hair raven black or golden as a finch.

The swan was ignored for a moment, but then a tall woman with raven-black hair and piercing green eyes came to inspect. Beside her was a child with dirty feet and a snarling smile. The child plucked the swan carelessly from the ground. She wrapped her nail-bitten hands around the swan's belly and squeezed tight.

"Kitchen or the cage?" she said to the tall woman.

The woman studied the swan for a moment and grabbed her beak roughly. Finally she nodded.

"Put her in the cage."

The child put the swan under her arm and walked towards a tall tree with a large hollow.

"You're lucky," the little girl sneered as she entered the hollow of the great tree. "I was hungry for swan." For a moment all was darkness, then the swan found herself in a long narrow hallway, lit with electric lights and lined with cages. Locked behind the thick bars were animals. Bears, a lynx, coyotes, foxes. All paced in their cages and let out screams of horror as the little girl passed with the swan under her arm.

"Quiet!" she snarled and marched with authority towards the biggest cage of all.

It was vast and filled with birds. Thousands and thousands. All shapes, all sizes, of every type. All frozen in flight. Just floating in the air, wings outstretched. Alive and silent. Among them were some of her brothers and her sisters.

"Here you go," the girl snarled, opening the door and stepping inside. Standing among the birds and just as frozen were half a dozen young women with looks of terror on their faces. With a rough toss, the girl threw the swan into the air. The ice melted! Her wings suddenly worked!

As she opened her wings to fly she let out a long TRUMPET, but instantly she froze again. This time completely. She hung in mid-air with all the others as the door slammed and the sound vanished into nothing.

PART ONE
HOME

CHAPTER 1

In the week since the bruise-coloured cloud had appeared over the tiny coastal town of Mist Falls, three mothers had disappeared. The first while riding her bicycle down a leaf-swept street, the second while sitting in a parked car drinking a cup of coffee, and the last from her bedroom while her new baby napped beside her. Not a single person had witnessed the cloud take the women, but Nell Perkins knew it was true.

Even now, as she piloted her bike along the damp streets, she felt the grim cloud watching everyone from above. One had only to glance up to see that this cloud was different. It didn't float along aimlessly like other clouds, but moved with slow, scheming purpose, and while it had first appeared over the trees wispy-thin, it had grown fatter with each passing day, like a bloated tick filling with blood.

Nell rode carefully, keeping a watchful eye on the leafy shadows on the cracked pavement, making sure to stay within their protection. She tried to tell herself that it was silly. *It's just a cloud.* But another voice inside her whispered for her to stay hidden from its dark wisps, which reminded her of a ball of candy floss lying burnt and alone in an abandoned fairground.

The truth was, this wasn't the first time people had disappeared from their small town. Over the years almost a dozen people had simply vanished. Most were young women, though one was a boy Nell's age called Max. They had just started to become friends when he vanished four weeks ago. He was funny and daring and liked to play the trumpet. They had the kind of friendship built on nothing more than a love of weird jokes and an obsession with chocolate. He didn't vanish in the same way, though it felt the same to Nell. One night he went to sleep and he didn't wake up. He had fallen into a coma. They took him to the hospital, where he was still asleep.

As Nell pulled her bike into the school playground, she had the strangest thought. Maybe the cloud was behind it. Maybe it had drifted over his house while he slept and kidnapped a part of him. The thought sent a shiver up her spine and she quickly locked up her bike. The normally busy playground was empty. A few teachers were hustling the late pupils inside.

"Attention, pupils and staff!" The head teacher's voice crackled over the loudspeaker as Nell entered. "All pupils and staff are not to go to their classrooms. Report directly to the school hall for a special assembly."

Nell's stomach was tight with nerves. The assembly was her chance to tell everyone what she knew to be the truth. The cloud had kidnapped the women and maybe Max as well.

I am going to look like an idiot, she told herself, but it was too late. She had decided she did not have a choice. Nell had seen a crime and the town needed to know about it, no matter how strange it would sound. It had happened quickly and was so weird that even remembering it now caused her heart to beat loudly and her breath to quicken. She recounted the facts as though she were telling them to a police officer.

A few days ago Nell had been at the town library until nearly dinnertime, reading about whales and secretly eating chocolate-covered raisins. Perhaps she would leave that part out when she told it, but, she reasoned, it did show that she was thinking clearly and had an eye for detail. When the library closed, Nell walked outside. The sky was free of clouds and the streets empty of people. She got on her bike and headed home. As she rode she felt a great burst of happiness, like she was the last person on Earth and free to do anything. Summer was coming and she had books to read and the ocean to dash into.

The mist was drifting off the sea, caressing her cheeks and dancing across her lips. Nell liked the briny taste of the salty air. She stopped her bike at the corner of Sea View and Stone Lane Road, and was taking in the view of the waves violently crashing upon the black rocks of the shore, when a high-pitched shriek rang out in the sky. Looking up, she caught sight of a strange purple cloud, rising quickly from behind the large Victorian house at the end of Stone Lane Road.

The horrible cloud rose with a rumble, as if it were an animal Nell had surprised in the act of feasting on a fresh kill. All was still and utterly silent. Nell wanted to turn away, to ride as fast as she could in the other direction, but her eyes were locked on the cloud as it rose higher and higher.

As she stared, Nell wished for several things. She wished to be home, she wished she wasn't afraid, she wished she wasn't alone, and in a few seconds she would wish forevermore that she had closed her eyes. But her eyes were open, and Nell watched as from out of the purple cloud fell a woman's shoe, bright white and dotted with red marks that could only be blood. Alone. A single shoe and nothing more, spit out as if it were a part not worth eating. The shoe dropped slowly, twirling as it tumbled through the air, and without a sound disappeared into a clump of leafless trees.

Without thinking to look for it, Nell raced home, trying to understand how a bloody shoe could fall from a cloud. No plane had flown overhead. No giant bird. There was only one conclusion. Someone was trapped inside the cloud. The secret weighed on her for the next several days, and she told no one. How could she? It was ridiculous. Insane. Clouds don't kidnap people. They don't eat young women. Keeping quiet seemed like the best choice. But when the head teacher announced the special assembly, Nell knew it was about the disappearances, and she knew she had to tell. Suddenly, as she walked through the corridors, she felt everyone's eyes on her, as if they knew she had a secret.

But they look at me anyway, Nell reminded herself. That much was true. On any day Nell Perkins was hard to miss. She was an uncommon-looking twelve-year-old girl, with hair so blonde it almost appeared silver, large amber eyes and a slightly crooked smile that seemed to be hiding something.

But it wasn't the way she looked or her smile or the slightly determined way she walked that made people look. No. People looked because Nell Perkins was well known in her small town for claiming to see things that did not exist.

Not things exactly, but creatures.

"Inner animals", Rose had called them when they first began making themselves known to Nell. They appeared at about the same time Nell's father had become ill and passed away. Most of the creatures had human bodies and animal heads, though others had no human parts at all and could be a frightening mixture of animal and machine. Nell had begun talking to them when she was four.

The first one to speak to her had the body of a man and the head of an elephant. Being so young, Nell didn't think this was unusual. His name was Jim and he delivered the post. Nell would get excited and jump up and down when she saw Jim walking towards the house. His trunk would swish from side to side, his great ears twitching and his white tusks looking fierce and dangerous in the bright sun.

Nell had also discovered that if she blinked her eyes and said her name, the person would return to normal. The mask, which had suddenly appeared, would drop away. Without his inner animal, Jim was quite bald and had a face filled with freckles. As Nell grew older she accepted the fact that almost everyone she knew, except her family, had an inner animal that would sometimes appear to say hello. It was fun for Nell to see who was hiding what. Gentle-looking old women could suddenly turn into alligators; tough men on motorcycles could have the faces of soft rabbits. Nell never talked about her rare skill, for she thought it was normal. Then, during her first day of school, Nell Perkins learned the truth.

All the children were sitting on the rug with eager, excited faces, trying not to squirm. Nell wasn't sure she liked school and longed to be at home in her pyjamas. The boy next to her, a redhead called Tommy Jenkins, was digging relentlessly into his nose with a pudgy finger and the whole place smelled like lima beans. Ms Rook, the teacher, was another story. She was the prettiest person Nell had ever seen. She was explaining that good pupils could win gold stars and sweets by following the rules when suddenly her inner animal appeared. In an instant Ms Rook's pretty face disappeared and her head was replaced, not by the head of an animal, but by the head of a giant doll with a cracked skull and a missing eye. Nell screamed loudly and wouldn't stop screaming as the doll stood over her. Nell was so gripped with terror that her mind felt blank. She couldn't remember how to make the terrible dead-eyed face go away. Other teachers came rushing in to help and their faces were just as frightening. Faces of stone, faces of tangled thorn, and worst of all, a face made of burning flames.

"You're special, Nell. Don't forget that and it will all be okay," her mother told her when Nell explained about the inner animals. For everyone else the answer was simple. Nell had an overactive imagination that encouraged her to see things that weren't there. The cause of her condition, they concluded, lay in the fact she didn't dream. Her nights were dark and dreamless.

"All that imagination has to go somewhere," said Wellington Miles, a famous doctor, who began to study her. He attached multicoloured wires to her head and watched her as she slept. Despite what he said about their non-existence, the doctor's own inner animal was that of a friendly walrus. Nell liked him very much, and he sat beside her for three nights, monitoring her sleep on a large machine and puffing on a pipe, his walrus whiskers twitching.

Nell and her family were told that her condition would diminish over time and she had to learn to live with it in the meantime. It did not diminish, but Nell learned not to tell anyone and to keep what she saw secret. Still there was only one way to make them go away. Nell was forced to say "My name is Nell Perkins" aloud several times a day. This declaration became a curse.

"My name is Nell Perkins."

It left others thinking her strange and her feeling lonely and odd and without much confidence that she would ever be anything but a freak.

"My name is Nell Perkins."

A shy girl who preferred books to people and whose only friend was now in a coma.

Now she was about to embarrass herself again. Nell felt a knot of fear grow in her stomach. As the teachers hustled the pupils into the hall for the big meeting, Nell's breathing began to grow fast. All eyes were on the stage, where the local chief of police was standing with Mr Green.

I can't do it, she said to herself in desperation. *I'm not going to say a thing.*

Nell moved down the aisle and found herself sitting next to Todd Lincoln, a twitchy boy who dressed mostly in army fatigues and bragged about hunting deer. He turned to Nell and whispered, "My dad said the government is kidnapping people for experiments." He twitched and continued, "Have you seen those black vans on the road lately?"

Nell admitted she had not.

"Stay away from them," warned Todd.

"Children!" The head teacher stepped over to the microphone. Mr Green was a trim little man with a beard and glasses, and a booming voice that made it seem as if he was always giving a speech. "There has been a lot of talk going on about recent events. Rumours can be scary things, and as you head out for the summer holidays we want you to feel safe and be safe and make safe choices. The best way to do that is to make sure everyone has the right information, so we asked Police Chief Byrne to give us the facts about these recent events and relieve our worries."

"'Recent events'. How about 'experiments'?" Todd Lincoln elbowed Nell.

The police won't say what it is, Nell reasoned, *because they don't know the truth.* This meant Nell alone held the secret to the disappearances and, afraid or not, she would have to tell them. Her stomach clenched even tighter.

The police chief nodded and stepped forward. He cleared his throat. "Three women have gone missing from our town. These are the facts. In these cases rumours can cause more problems than the actual incidents. All we know is that the three women – Connie Little, Saffron Jones and Lulu Gram – are all unaccounted for. As of yet we don't think a crime has been committed. We have seen no evidence of harm. Sometimes kids can be a great help to police. I want you to think. Do you have any information you'd like to share? Keep in mind this is a serious matter. We are only interested in facts. Things you have seen, not stories or rumours about UFOs or secret experiments."

Before she could stop herself, Nell stood. There were two hundred pupils in her school, and every single one turned and stared.

"Yes?" the police chief said, smiling. Nell felt her hands go clammy. She knew at once standing up had been a mistake. How could she possibly explain? She tried to think of a different story.

Mention a man in a strange mask or a black government van, she thought.

"Have you seen something?" said the police chief.

And out it came. Nell spoke.

"A shoe."

A hush fell over the pupils and Nell knew at once she had said something wrong.

"A shoe?" the chief said to Nell, who was not sure where to put her hands. A wet sweet hit Nell on the cheek and stuck.

The whole room broke out in peals of laughter.

"QUIET!" shouted the police chief. The mob grew silent.

"Sit down," Todd Lincoln hissed, but to everyone's surprise, including her own, Nell did not sit. She plucked the wet watermelon sweet from her cheek and continued.

"The cloud that is hanging above town. Haven't you seen it? The dark purple one," Nell said, growing less confident with each passing second. "It did it."

"A cloud?" the police chief said, still trying to understand what this had to do with a shoe. Nell turned to the crowd and froze at the sight before her. There was a burbling sound of flesh stretching as everyone in the hall transformed. In an instant, Nell found herself staring not at a room of teenagers, but at a room of creatures with human bodies and animal heads. Pigs, hyenas, boars, dogs, cats, all still sitting as they had been moments before, dressed in the school uniform, unaware that their heads were furry and their mouths filled with razor-sharp fangs. Nell's heart began to pound and her face grew red and hot.

"No," she whispered to herself. "Not now." But like it or not, *it* was happening again. She was having a "moment". The entire school was showing their inner animals. She had to make them go away as fast as possible or she would get flustered and everything would come out wrong. But that meant doing what she hated more than anything else: reminding herself loudly who she was.

"Did what?" the police chief said, his head now transformed into the head of a large frog with watery green eyes.

"My name is Nell Perkins," Nell announced nervously, "and the cloud is stealing people. I saw the shoe fall from it. I think there was blood on it."

A shocked and awkward silence fell over the room until

a boy with the head of a hyena shouted, "My name is Nell Perkins and I'm a freak!"

The whole room erupted with laughter and the head teacher whispered something in the police chief's ear. He nodded and frowned. Nell knew what he was saying. "Don't listen to that girl. There is something wrong with her." Nell felt her cheeks flush with shame. As she sat, everyone's inner animals disappeared.

"That was awesome," Todd whispered to her, but she did not agree. She sank into her seat.

CHAPTER 2

The remainder of the last day of school before the summer holidays passed like a blur. Yearbooks were signed, parties were held, but Nell wanted nothing to do with any of it. She stayed in the library reading a book and drinking from a mug of tea, a privilege given to library helpers. When she finally walked out of school at the end of the day, the cloud was nowhere to be seen. The sky overhead was blue. Nell's bike was the only one left in the rack.

"It's okay," Nell told herself, and felt she could handle the ride home. As she rode her bike through the now-bright afternoon, Nell suddenly realized that school was actually finished for the summer. All its pressure and battles were over for nearly three months.

"Who are you?" Nell repeated to herself as she rode. It was the title of her favourite book. It was beyond favourite. Nell was obsessed with the science-fiction story about a small town that was stricken with a virus that gave everyone amnesia. Suddenly, in the course of one day, everyone forgot who they were, what they liked and how they were supposed to act. Friends. Enemies. Parents. Kids. Everyone was given a second chance to be whoever they wanted to be. The closest Nell got to that actually happening was the first day of the summer holidays. Today. She could be anyone she wanted now.

Nell let out a scream of joy as she wheeled her bike into her front garden, past the antique sculptures of circus animals that rested here and there on the grass.

Nell's mother, Rose, was walking out of the front door.

"Darling!" she shouted at Nell.

As always, Rose looked slightly unreal to Nell. Her deep green eyes, milk-white skin, copper-red hair and the old-fashioned clothes that she collected and always wore made her look as though she had fallen out of a deep past of enchanted forests. It was rare that Nell and her brothers even called her "Mum". She was Rose. But what was most unreal about her to Nell was that she seemed never to be afraid.

"Who are you?" Nell smiled, staring at Rose with wide-eyed confusion as though she could not recognize her. Nell had got into the habit of pretending that she had amnesia and everyone and everything was a mystery. "Kale? I've never heard of it," she'd say when the green vegetable appeared on her plate. "Make my bed? What's a bed?" she'd remark when the command to clean her room was issued. Even Nell knew the joke was getting a little tired but still she couldn't stop. Maybe she wanted it to be true. Maybe she hoped that she really could forget who she was and become new again. And Rose sometimes played along, but lately she gave the same response.

"You could never forget who you are, Nell, and you shouldn't want to. You are your own person and that person is fantastic." Today was no exception. She sighed and repeated that Nell could never forget and the book itself was wrong.

"It's not wrong. It's a virus," Nell snapped, suddenly finding herself flaring with anger. "Anyone can get it."

"Impossible. It's ridiculous," Rose shot back. "No parent in that town could get that virus."

"Anyone can get it," Nell repeated.

"Memory doesn't just live in your brain, Nell. When you're a parent, it fills up your entire body. It becomes your body. And that means a mother could never forget her child ever, no matter what. Now," Rose said with a smile, "Look at these beauties. I found them at a car boot sale in Newberg."

Rose was an antiques dealer and was always buying and selling interesting things. Lying in the bed of the truck was an enormous vintage kite made of metal rods and cloth that was painted with birds of all types.

"This is a hurricane kite," Rose said. "It was made to fly in the fiercest winds to signal to boats in the sea and police on the ground that you were still alive. It even has an anchor." Attached to the centre of the kite was a cord of thick leather that ran to a wooden spool. On the top of the spool was a metal hook shaped like a lion's paw.

"The hook was wrapped around a tree or a metal pole and, once attached, could weather any storm," Rose said, giddy with excitement. "Best of all, it is hand-painted. The artist is quite famous. Only three of these are known to exist. I have a buyer in Wickerton who will give me cash if I bring it right over."

"Now?"

"Yes. Now. Your brothers are at Jack's house and won't be home until supper. It is the perfect way to start your summer holiday."

"All right," Nell said. She hated going on deliveries with her mother. The truck was a piece of junk. The radio didn't work. The roof leaked when it rained and during the summer it always smelled like wet fur. But as much as she hated the deliveries, the truth was she liked to spend alone time with her mother. Nell considered her mother the bravest person she had ever met. She had seen her face down stray dogs that had tried to attack them and speak her mind to the largest of angry men. Whenever Nell was with her she felt safe, and right now, with the rain falling, she needed that feeling.

"Really?" Rose said, not sure if she was joking. "You want to come?"

"Yes," Nell chirped. She opened the truck's passenger door and climbed inside. An antique, hand-cranked record player sat on the front seat. Nell had seen many pass through her house, but this one was particularly beautiful. The cone where the sound came out was made of golden glass and shaped like a lily.

"A 1929 St Oiseau gramophone," Rose said proudly.

"Does it work?"

"Find out. Turn the handle and when it begins to move, place the needle arm on the disc." Nell followed the instructions, watching as the disc began to spin. Gently she lifted the arm and placed it on the record. The needle touched the fat black disc and the scratchy sound of a violin drifted out. Soon a woman began to sing in French, her voice haunted and lonely.

"Isn't it fantastic?" Rose said as the truck pulled out into the street. But Nell was hardly listening. All her thoughts were on the storm rumbling in the distance. It was coming.

They began to drive through town. A small thimble of green thread with a needle stuck out of it lay on the dashboard. It rolled back and forth as they drove. Rose didn't care but the rattling as the thimble tumbled helplessly from side to side was driving Nell crazy. She liked things in their proper place. As Rose turned a corner the thimble rolled towards Nell and she snatched it and buried it in the pocket of her hoodie.

The truck didn't get very far before the storm caught them. By the time they had reached the back road that ran along the woods and meadows at the far end of town, the rain was pounding down so hard it became impossible to even see out of the windscreen. All at once the truck began shaking. *THUMP. THUMP. THUMP.*

"Hold on," Rose said, as the engine rattled and wheezed. Smoke began to pour from the bonnet, and within a metre, the truck slowed to a stop. With a final *THUMP*, it died.

"What happened?"

"It's fine," Rose answered. For several minutes Rose tried to start the truck without any luck, until finally she admitted the truth.

"The engine's dead," Rose said. "A fine time for it to die. Poor thing."

The rain was clattering fiercely on the roof as though an army of monkeys were trying to smash its way in.

"Call a tow truck," Nell said.

"Of course. You're as smart as you are brave." Rose took out her phone and stared at it with a furrowed brow. "No service."

Nell gazed out of the window. This road was empty and there were no houses around, only a large, weed-covered field with an abandoned factory at the far end. It was a lonely turn-of-the-century building, made of white bricks and leaded glass. Rose thought for a minute. All was silent save for the rain drumming on the roof and the wind rattling the windows.

"We can hide out in the factory until the storm passes. It will be safer. If the road floods," Rose said.

"But someone will come," Nell said hopefully. "The police?"

"I don't think we can wait, sweetie," Rose said, her eyes on the water rushing along the road. Suddenly, a flood seemed very likely. In a heartbeat, Nell and Rose were out of the truck. Quickly, Rose untied the kite.

"Get the gramophone."

Nell grabbed the gramophone out of the front seat. As she closed the door, a fierce blast of wind shot past them, thin and contained, like a great invisible arm. In an instant, the truck was lifted from the ground and flung hard against a tree on the other side of the road, with a shattering of glass and crushed metal.

"The truck!" Nell yelled, but what she meant was *that was not right*. It wasn't normal, and it was all terribly frightening.

Nell threw herself into her mother and instantly felt her mother's arms surround her. Rose held on tightly. She kissed Nell's head and murmured, "It's okay. I have you." With her mother's arms wrapped around her, Nell felt safe and couldn't hear the wind or feel the rain on her cheeks. Both of them stood there for a moment thinking the same thought. It had been so long since they had hugged each other.

Finally they let go, and Rose laughed, saying no matter what happened, the day was a success.

"I have got a hug from the unhugger."

The unhugger was what she called Nell, for when she had turned eleven, Nell had decided she was too old for hugs.

"Let's walk," Rose said, her voice steady, nodding to the factory across the meadow.

"But the truck," Nell said.

"Let's not worry. Let's just walk. Nothing to worry about!" Rose said, and started moving across the weedy meadow.

Nell followed. She held the record player in her arms and Rose carried the large kite.

"Isn't it fantastic!" Rose yelled. They were both bent low, taking hard, thudding steps, walking slowly into the wind.

Each struggling step made Nell's mother's smile grow even wider.

"No!" Nell yelled. "It sucks!"

But Nell's fear only made Rose laugh. *What must that be like?* Nell wondered. *To walk through the world never afraid. To always feel right and never want to forget who you are.*

"It's so beautiful!" Rose shouted.

"What?"

"You are. The storm is. Life itself is. All of it. As long as you are not afraid. Though," Rose hesitated, "I don't like the look of that cloud." Nell followed Rose's frozen gaze upwards. Her heart sank. The bruise-coloured cloud had returned for her. The very same one that had dropped the shoe had appeared over the treetops as if it had been following them all along.

"That's the cloud," Nell said. "The cloud that kidnapped all the women."

"What are you talking about?" Rose said.

"It's after us." Nell lurched forward, nearly slipping. The needle fell onto the record. They heard the scratchy sound of the violin, and the woman's voice sang out. And, as the music played on, the cloud began to rumble.

Even though now would be the time to run, they couldn't. Nell and Rose could do nothing but stare at the cloud above them, frozen in horror at what it was doing. It was changing. Transforming into something wicked. The cloud's purple smoke twisted furiously in hundreds of small rumbling whirlpools until it had shaped itself into a giant skull.

"I am Nell Perkins," Nell said, hoping it was only a moment. "And that is a normal cloud."

"It's not," Rose whispered, and Nell knew for sure this was really happening. And it was wrong. Very. Very. Wrong.

27

"Run," Rose commanded. "Run, Nell. Run and don't stop! Don't look back. Just go!"

In an instant they both took off, darting as quickly as they could across the wet field. A crack of lightning shot from the skull-shaped cloud, slashing down into the grass before them. Rose tripped and the kite was ripped from her hands. The spool of wire hit the ground and wildly unfurled. Nell put down the record player and ran to help her mother up, but was knocked over by the massive hurricane kite as it swooped past.

The kite, borne up by the mad wind, turned, swirled back and charged to deliver another blow. Nell turned. The metal lion claw of the kite's hook came straight for her head with a *whoosh*. She might have caught it in her hand, but instead, and to her everlasting shame and unhappiness, Nell ducked.

The claw passed above her head and hit Rose hard in her stomach, snagging her belt. She yelped in pain and struggled to pull the claw off her as the kite, flying high overhead, changed direction. It circled swiftly back again and again and again, wrapping the leather cord around Rose like a cowboy lassoing a calf.

Rose desperately tried to break free of the cord coiling up her middle. She was staring up at the cloud, her eyes wide in horror at what she saw inside. In desperation, she yelled to Nell a warning, but the shriek of the wind made hearing impossible.

"What?" Nell yelled. She tried to reach her mother but could not. The closer she got, the more the wind pushed her back. Blocking her. All Nell could do was watch as the hurricane kite rose higher and higher into the air, tugging the leather cord that now bound her mother's arms tightly to her side. With a powerful yank, Rose was lifted off the ground and pulled skywards towards the base of the massive floating skull.

"Mama!" Nell screamed as her mother was reeled up, rising towards the cloud like a fish on a line. "Mama!"

It was a word Nell had not said since she was a baby, but suddenly she felt like a tiny child, set adrift in a great and terrible sea, as the only person in the world who made her feel safe was taken.

"Goodbye, my love," Rose answered, refusing to show her fear. Her head disappeared into the cloud with a final scream as she glimpsed what awaited her inside.

"Mama," Nell wailed helplessly, eyes on her mother's body dangling from the cloud, her legs kicking in protest.

Nell threw up her arms and jumped. She knew it was ridiculous but couldn't help it. Couldn't stop. If she stopped it would be over. If she stopped she would be alone. Who would look after her and her brothers? How would she tell them their mother was gone?

Nell jumped and jumped and jumped. Jumped as if she could jump to the cloud and pull her mother down.

"Come back," Nell whispered helplessly as her mother's shoes slipped inside the cloud. "Please! Come back."

Nell jumped again and slipped on the wet ground, hitting her head on a rock. The last thing she saw before her eyes closed was the skull-shaped cloud rolling away with her mother inside, moving slowly and lazily across the abandoned field, like a just-fed crocodile sinking back into a dark river.

CHAPTER 3

Nell awoke hours later, wet, freezing and alone on the damp field. The wind and rain had stopped and night had fallen. A small yellow feather lay across her trainers, bright as a slash of sunlight. As she reached for it, her hand hurt. She put it in her mouth. It tasted of the strange metallic tang of blood. Above her, the night was aglow with stars, white, hot and twinkling. It was as if the storm had never happened. And this made things worse. At least the cloud would be part of a chain of events. Nell could explain the strange cloud that had arrived in their town to steal people, and the army could use planes or helicopters to find it and fight it. But now there was nothing in the sky. All that remained was the cold, wet wind that slipped beneath Nell's hoodie to chew at her skin.

Nell shivered, and all at once she knew she couldn't stay, didn't want to stay. The record player sat on the ground, its large speaker cone the only flower in the dead field. Nell picked it up. The square box was awkward to hold with her wounded hand, but she couldn't leave it. Rose would kill her. Rose! It all rushed back to Nell with bared fangs. But they were just memories, and that was all. The truth was she was alone. Alone in the dark of a wet field.

"I'm alone," she murmured to herself. And with that fact clear, there was nothing else to do now but walk home. Nell picked her way slowly across the large meadow, her trainers squishing in the mud mockingly until she found a deserted road.

Nell looked around.

"Where am I?" All of a sudden Nell felt very lost. "Have I been down this street before? No. I haven't." This wasn't the way home. Her body tensed with the mistake. Without a doubt, it was the wrong direction.

"Perfect!" Nell screamed. Her voice echoed in the emptiness. The shout was answered by a muffled thump of feet touching down, soft and delicate, onto the wet tarmac. The noise could only mean one thing. Something had landed behind her. As slowly as she could, Nell twisted her body to face it.

Standing across the street under the sputtering light of a broken street lamp was a creature that didn't belong. For it wasn't an animal of land, but of the darkest sea: an octopus the size of a large dog. Nell almost laughed. It wasn't an octopus. Not really. How could it be? No. She was staring at a large statue of a sea creature. But what a statue! It was black as a cave in the most desolate trench in the Atlantic. Two egg-yellow eyes, immense and still, watched Nell with unwavering intensity.

The octopus blinked, and Nell felt a shiver up her spine. Now the fact was clear. It wasn't a statue. The creature, as if to prove to Nell he was very much alive, began to move its thick tentacles. The long arms wriggled like vipers, kicking the dead leaves from the ground and swirling them around the beast's head like an evil crown. Nell knew what was happening.

"It is an inner animal," she told herself. It wasn't an octopus but a person. Nell lifted her head and stated, "I'm Nell Perkins and I'm walking home." Nell blinked.

The inner animal remained. The octopus was still an octopus. Nell took a breath and, nodding her head bravely, she looked straight into the beast's vicious mustard eyes and spoke again.

"I'm Nell Perkins and I'm walking home." It helped to be honest. "I was with my mother and she was kidnapped by a cloud." Her voice became less confident and quieter as she continued. "I need to go home. My brothers. They've never spent the night alone before."

That was clear enough. That should do it. The thoughts would vanish. The moment would end. Maybe the person would even offer her a lift home once he or she changed back. Nell blinked. The octopus was still the octopus. Now Nell did something she had never done before. Something she had vowed she never would. But tonight certainly was a night for vows to get broken. She explained to the person whom she couldn't see that she was having a moment.

"I'm Nell Perkins and I know this sounds really weird and it's kind of hard to explain, but sometimes I see things that aren't always there. You see, I'm looking at you and I see an octopus. I know it sounds completely stupid and you are actually just a person who has come outside to check on the storm. These things usually pass, but for some reason it's not passing, and I need to get home." Nell smiled and continued, "So maybe you could just go back inside."

A drop of blood fell from Nell's wounded hand and hit the ground. The octopus's eyes watched it fall, following it the entire way down. A normal person would never be able to see a drop of blood falling from across a dark street.

"This isn't a moment, is it?" Nell whispered suddenly as the octopus transformed. A large, wolf-like muzzle pushed its way out of the creature's round head with a wet, dripping sound.

When the transformation was complete, the strange monster with a wolf's head and octopus's body opened its new mouth, displaying a powerful jaw of tiny, razor-sharp teeth.

Nell and the octopus stared at one another in the desolate street, both knowing what was going to happen next. All other possibilities had been laid aside. The world had narrowed into a singular act. The octopus with its new wolf-like muzzle was going to attack. Nell wanted to run but was frozen in fear, and suddenly something even stranger than facing an octopus on land happened. A swirling ball of golden light passed through the beam of the streetlamp and landed in the road between her and the monster, settling on the ground soft as a snowflake.

It was a small bird, with warm golden feathers and a bright red head. Delicately beautiful and no bigger than an apple. Two warm amber eyes shone out of the small golden bird's ruby-coloured head and looked curiously at Nell, as if it had been suddenly blown off course by the wind and was surprised to find itself in the middle of the street between a girl and a monster instead of among the clouds.

"It must have got lost in the storm," Nell said in wonder to the octopus, as if they were joined in the miracle of the lovely thing that had landed before them. The monster's gaze fell upon the small, delicate creature. Its head twitched, and Nell was sure she heard a grunt of disgust.

"No," Nell gasped, suddenly realizing that the monster had switched its attention to the bird and wanted to eat her, not because it was hungry, but because of the pleasure it would get in destroying something so perfect.

"Get," she said and gave a swift kick to a rock that skidded across the pavement. The small golden bird tweeted in protest, swirled into the air and disappeared into the night.

The octopus watched the golden bird fly away. Seeing its meal gone, it growled in terrible anger. Its tentacles began moving in wavy slithers, and suddenly the creature leapt into the air and began to fly towards her.

"You can't fly!" Nell babbled as though the octopus had broken the rules. But it could. And it did. Nell gasped and took off, clutching the heavy record player in her hand as she ran. Every nerve in her body sparked with fear as the octopus's giant shadow glided over her own. Eight tentacles strained to grab her. She could smell it now, an ancient brackish odour that made her gag. Even worse than being bitten by those tiny razor teeth was the thought that when it attacked, the octopus would be on top of her, the slimy suckers against her skin, the disgusting stench in her face.

Soon, it became clear she couldn't outrun the beast. This wasn't a job for her, she thought nervously. It wasn't what she did. *I read books! I stay quiet and let the moment pass and then think about what I would do after someone else takes care of scary things.*

Rose was the brave one. Rose would fight back. But Rose wasn't here, Nell thought. It was up to her. Nell's mind raced through the possibilities until she realized she had only one choice. The record player would have to do for a weapon. One shot was all she would get. If she missed, she would be done for. Dead. Nell stopped short and, with her whole body trembling, turned to face the snarling octopus swooping down for her.

CHAPTER 4

The octopus headed for Nell like a black missile that had never, not once in its entire life, missed its target. Nell's body seized up in fear, and she dropped the record player at her feet. She was no longer thinking of how it would hurt when she was bitten or how the tentacles would wrap around her. Instead a single sad thought blared in her head: *If I die, I'll never see my mother again.*

The octopus sped down the empty street. Suddenly, a golden ball of light blasted out of the treetops and hit the octopus square in the eye. Blood splattered, and the creature tumbled to the ground with a pained shriek. The great black monster stood up, furious and confused, his slime-soaked body pulsing in anger. Dancing around his head was the golden light that had shot out of the darkness. Nell saw at once that it was not a flaming bullet, laser gun or blast of magic, but the bird, the little golden bird with the bright red head. It had returned to save her. Flapping around the monster's face, the little bird continued to defend Nell until, giving up, the octopus flew off in a fury of howls and disappeared into the darkness of the night.

Nell's small golden saviour landed right before her and shook its feathers proudly.

"Thank you," Nell said in surprise. For the first time since the storm began, Nell felt calm as she watched the bird clean itself in a puddle.

"Where is your home?" Nell said to her new friend and held out her hand. The bird turned, cocking her head as if pondering the question.

"It's all right," Nell said gently. "Come on."

Without hesitation, the bird jumped onto Nell's palm. She was not much heavier than a powdery handful of fresh snow. Her red head didn't move in that jerky bird fashion, but turned steadily and looked down at the specks of blood on Nell's palm, as if inspecting them with grave concern.

"I'm fine," Nell whispered, as though talking to an old friend.

The bird wasn't sure and rubbed her head on Nell's palm and tweeted. Nell liked the little bird, and even more she liked being alone with her in the darkness of the strange night. She felt safe and even hopeful, as if the little bird was going to sing into her ear all the answers of the universe.

The bird turned its head towards the sky cautiously and Nell felt a jolt of fear. The cloud. She didn't want to look up and see it floating above her. But it wasn't the cloud the bird was watching. The storm had picked up again and a sharp blade of lightning cracked through the darkness. Nell's body tensed, waiting for the boom. She hated thunder. Hated it worse than lightning. Her eyes flashed to the little bird. She wanted to say "Don't worry", though she was worried, but before the words could reach her lips a clap of thunder exploded. Nell jumped and the little bird was startled. With a frightened leap it flew from Nell's hand in a golden flash and vanished into the darkness.

"Wait." Nell's body trembled with the sudden separation. "Come back," she said again. But her shouts were met with the hiss of the rain.

"Lost in the storm?"

Nell looked up to see a strangely dressed man who seemed to appear out of nowhere. The man was standing in the middle of the street, his body still as a statue. Above his head, he held a dark blue umbrella that was lit from within, bathing him in a column of blue neon light.

His name was Duke Badger. Everyone in town knew him, though no one was brave enough to ever talk to him, as his temper was fierce and easily provoked. He owned a little shop called Sparktondale Supplies. What they sold inside was a mystery as the shop was never open. Badger's hair was neat and combed in the old-fashioned style of a fancy gentleman, but his face was rough with a thick moustache and full beard, which looked like they were from another time – but whether it was far in the future or deep in the past was impossible to tell, for it seemed to be both. His trousers were made of rugged grey wool stuck into tall combat boots.

Most striking was the long, black leather trench coat that he wore in all seasons. It was tightly fitted and it hugged two powerful arms that ended in large hands with knuckles covered in tattoos. On one side of the jacket, above his heart, was a small patch. Though it was dark, Nell could see it perfectly, for it was sewn in a reflective gold-and-silver thread that made it glow. The patch showed an ancient ship's steering wheel with a full moon of bright sterling in the centre and a golden pinecone in the centre of that.

The weird rain stopped again. The instant it did, Badger swung his arm, and with a *whoosh*, his umbrella closed tightly and disappeared into a nearly invisible quiver on his back, leaving only the curved handle visible above his shoulder.

"A cloud–" was all Nell got out. Her lip was beginning to tremble. She didn't want to cry.

Badger stared at Nell for a moment, his eyes the colour of ancient stones. While he stared at her, Nell felt calm, as though this man understood and was a match for a murderous cloud. Finally he nodded grimly.

"A skull-shaped cloud?"

Nell nodded, surprised that he knew. He actually knew.

"It took my mother."

Suddenly, from out of the darkness leapt a lean black cat with bright green eyes. The cat landed with perfect silent grace on Badger's shoulder. Badger took no notice of it.

"What is your name, girl?"

"Nell Perkins."

"Nice to meet you, Nell Perkins. I am Duke Badger, and I am sorry to tell you this. The cloud didn't take your mother."

"It did. I swear it."

"No, your mother was taken by the ones inside the cloud. The Dark Daughters."

Nell felt a shiver go up her spine at the sound of the name. "The Dark Daughters?" For a moment, and it felt to Nell like a very long moment, no words would come. Nell thought of Rose being lifted by the wire into the swollen purple belly of the cloud, her pretty feet dangling helplessly. *How could there be people inside?* she wondered. "Who are they? Why do they want my mother?"

"You could say that they are witches and they are on the hunt," Badger explained. "That's what this whole storm is about. This storm is a hunting party. If your mother was taken by that cloud, I am sorry. But listen, don't go looking for that cloud. Trust me on this."

"Don't go looking?" Nell said confused. "I have to go. That cloud. Those Dark Daughters," Nell said and the words made her feel cold and terribly alone. "They can't have my mother."

"You're a brave girl." Badger smiled, and Nell felt her cheeks blush slightly and wanted to point out that she really wasn't brave, her mother was brave, but he continued with such force that she grew quiet. "If the cloud took your mother, she's already gone. She is no longer in Mist Falls."

"Where is she?" Nell asked.

"The Wicked Places," Badger said solemnly.

"The Wicked Places?" Nell said. "What are the Wicked Places? Where are they?"

The rain began again with such sudden violence that all noise was drowned out. Badger slid his umbrella from behind his back. He moved his arm with a powerful swing and opened the umbrella with a mighty THWACK that echoed into the night. With a hum, the canopy came to life, shining down a warm shaft of blue light, and Badger, cat still on his shoulder, disappeared into the deepening storm, grimacing each time his left foot hit the ground.

CHAPTER 5

Nell walked home as the rain clattered around her. In her arms she held the record player. It was heavy and probably ruined and Nell thought she should throw it in the bin, but she couldn't. What would Rose say when she came home and found it missing? When Nell finally entered her house, the lights were on, the television was blaring and her brothers were asleep, both of them still fully dressed. George, the youngest, was on the couch, sitting straight up, arms folded as if he were having an argument with the night itself. Nell untied his shoes and removed them.

He was nine, a wisp of a boy with a lightly freckled face and dark black eyes that were constantly judging the world around him and finding it not good enough. George had decided that despite his smaller size, he was the one in charge. He liked to give orders and have them met quickly.

Her other brother, Speedy, was sleeping half on the coffee table and half on the floor. He was almost eleven and was a large boy, almost as big as a grown-up. His hair was constantly tousled, his eyes always large in fascination, his smile wide and goofy, and his big mitts of hands always sticky. But most of all he was, as everyone who met him agreed – except for his brother George, who wouldn't give anyone credit for anything – one of the kindest people in the world.

The rain had grown harder. It crashed against the window like handfuls of pebbles. Never in her life had Nell been so tired. She sat down on the fat chair facing her brothers, wanting nothing more than to close her tired eyes and sleep, but she couldn't. Not yet. She needed to know how she was going to explain everything to them. How do you tell someone their mother is gone? Try as she might to sort it out in her head, the day had been too much, and after mumbling "Gone", she fell asleep.

The night passed in an instant. Nell's sleep, as always, was dreamless and even as she heard the noises around her and felt her brother's fingers repeatedly poking her skull, she wanted to stay in that dreamless quiet place forever. Even asleep, she knew once she woke a terrible truth was waiting for her.

"Hey!"

Nell opened her eyes. The room was flooded with morning sunlight and George was standing over her, his arms crossed in fury.

"Where is she?"

George was smart and, seeing the condition of Nell and the record player, he had rightly determined, just as Nell knew he would, that something terrible had happened.

"Don't worry," Nell said. "Let me explain."

"She's making pancakes!" Speedy said, standing up, yawning and scratching his belly. "She got up early to get us blueberries because today is my birthday."

"Today is your birthday. Right," Nell said awkwardly. She had completely forgotten. This was going to be even worse than she'd feared. "Happy birthday," she said meekly.

"Thanks, Nell," Speedy said with a smile. "Now. Tell him about the blueberry pancakes," he added, confident that his mother's disappearance was related to breakfast. "It's okay. I know I always get a special birthday breakfast."

"I told you. She's not making pancakes!" George snarled. "It's something else. Something bad."

Nell decided she would tell them in a calm and smooth manner.

"Look. The thing is. Well." The words were coming out in a jumpy sputter. She couldn't stop them now. "Facts are," she continued. "It's just that. Last night. Yesterday, actually. Something happened."

Both boys grew silent. They sat on the couch and listened as Nell told the entire story. The storm. The skull-shaped cloud. The way Rose was dragged up into its belly and disappeared. After it was over the boys just sat in silence trying to understand. *Say something!* Nell thought. *Call me names!* The sound of the rain clattering on the window filled the room. In the silence between the drops was the truth. Their mother was gone.

"We're going to find her," Nell said, trying to sound in charge. In her mind it sounded like the voice of a scared puppet. Pretend and nothing more.

Both of her brothers jumped up. Speedy looked at Nell, his usually kind and happy eyes wet with tears. "What are we going to do without a mother?"

"I messed up," Nell said quietly, knowing there was no defence she could offer. She should have caught the kite when it came towards her. Instead she had ducked.

Nell took a deep breath and looked at George. She couldn't dwell on that. "Listen, George, listen. We don't have time to sit around and be upset. We have to go out and find that cloud."

"You're right," George said, his mind formulating a plan. "We need to go and find a cloud. Just one more question?"

"Yes," Nell said.

George curled his little hand into a fist.

"Where do you want it?"

"What?"

"I'm going to have to punch you."

"Punch me?"

"I need to get revenge. I can't think of anything else until I get revenge. So, if you want me to help you, I am going to have to punch you. Where do you want it?"

Nell looked at her brother, his small fist curled in fury. She needed him on her side. They were going to have to work together. And if this would help, she would do it.

"My face, I guess," she said quietly and closed her eyes. George held up his fist. He pulled it back to punch and hesitated.

"I'm going to do it," he warned.

"I know," Nell said, opening her eyes. "Do your worst."

"Here it comes," George said, but did not move.

"I'm ready," Nell said.

"You're tricking me!" George whined.

"It's not a trick. I swear. Go on, hit me. Get your revenge."

"But– but– you're always scared of getting hurt."

"I am scared. But I need your help. So get it over with. Hit me."

George's fist began to shake. "Promise me we'll find her, and I'll let you go," he squeaked as if something was caught in his throat.

"Will you help me?"

"Yes," George said softly, tears streaming down his cheeks.

43

"Then I promise. We will find her."

George dropped his fist and threw himself into his sister's arms. Nell held him tightly as his little body shivered with large, gulping sobs, and all she could think was, *Oh no, I am in charge now. I am in charge now, I am in charge now.*

After a messy birthday breakfast of alternately well-done and doughy pancakes, cooked by Nell, the three Perkins children sat in the living room and Nell explained their plan. They would head into town and find Duke Badger.

"That's the plan?" George said incredulously. "Duke Badger, the guy with the cat?"

"He seems to know about this stuff," Nell reasoned.

"He's kind of…" Speedy paused, searching for the right word. An extremely positive boy, he didn't like to say anything bad about people, but his brother had no such problem.

"Crazy!" George interrupted. "Everyone knows that."

"He will help us," Nell said, but thought to herself it was a lie. Badger had no reason to help them. Besides, he didn't seem to like anyone, and children even less, but still a voice inside told her that Duke Badger was the person they needed.

CHAPTER 6

Nell and her brothers walked through the rain towards the small alley at the edge of town where Badger had his shop. They had no umbrella. The cold water attacked their clothes, dripping down their necks and plastering hair to their faces. Nell was not thinking about the water, but about failing. She had made mistakes before, had messed things up, made ridiculous choices, including a homework-themed birthday party, but this was something different. She was in charge. If she failed they would never see their mother again. She imagined the word "failure" carved in metal, attached to a long pole and lit over a fire until it glowed orange. She pictured the incandescent brand pressed against her forehead with a sickly sizzle. *Failure*.

"Where is everyone?" George said.

Nell looked up from her feet. The streets were deserted and it seemed as if the entire town had picked up and left.

"You don't think the cloud could have got them?" he added.

"No," Nell said, shaking her head. "I mean, I don't know."

"You should know," Speedy said, but not meanly. He meant that Nell always had an answer. Nell could be relied on. Not now. Now she was lost.

"Maybe everyone was changed into snails?" George said.

That did seem possible. The tiny molluscs had come out in the rain and were now everywhere, their small brown shells and straining yellow-green bodies inching slowly across the pavement.

"Careful," Nell said, grabbing George by the shoulder. He hadn't been looking and was about to step on one. George jerked backwards, slipped on the wet pavement, and landed face-first on the front lawn of Mist View, the town's only hotel. Once it had been a grand mansion, but it was now a rundown, paint-chipped hulk of a building that no one visited.

George stood up and brushed off a snail that had got stuck to his lips. It fell to the pavement unharmed. This only made him angrier. He raised his foot to stamp down on it in a rush of revenge.

"Please don't!" cried a soft voice that sounded panicked and embarrassed to be crying out. The children turned. Rushing down the wooden stairs of Mist View was a young mother and a nine-year-old girl. Both wore long, dark-red raincoats, hats and green boots, all of which had a sophisticated foreign look that Nell instantly admired. The woman held a small tin bucket, and the child carried a very tall bucket that was covered in black silk.

"We can't let a single one get away," the woman said as she reached down, picked up the snail and dropped it into her bucket. "Even a smashed one."

"I wasn't really going to do it," George said, slightly embarrassed. It wasn't a feeling George had very often, but this wasn't an ordinary woman he was talking to. They all felt it. This woman, with her raven-black hair, milk-white skin, large, kind eyes, green as the first burst of spring grass, and lips the colour of strawberry jam, was special, almost royal in her bearing. So beautiful was her face that it was hard to look anywhere else.

And as lovely as the woman was, the child beside her was not. She had a sour face and hard, mud-coloured eyes. Her tiny, ragged teeth looked as if they had never been brushed. Nell knew what it was like to have a beautiful mother and feel less than beautiful. She smiled at the child, who turned her head away quickly as if slapped.

"You don't find snails this plump where we come from," the woman said, and then, as if remembering, added, "I am Freyja Skoll, and this is my daughter, Fenrir Skoll. We call her Fenn. We are visiting from what you call in English the Land of Ice."

"Iceland?" Speedy said. Freyja Skoll nodded and asked the children for their names.

Nell couldn't stop staring, the words trapped in her throat. Finally she murmured, "I'm Nell Perkins, and these are my brothers, Speedy and George."

"It is my pleasure to meet you. We are here on holiday and came to visit the falls of your lovely town. It reminds me of the town where I was born. A town high in the mountains, known as Vazencrack."

"Pretty name," Speedy said, obviously lying. "Bet it means something real nice."

"It means Bloody Mountain," Fenn said, sneering.

"Or not." George shrugged.

"It seems we are stuck here by the weather until tonight. But if you don't mind my asking, why in the world are you walking around this town when everyone else has left? I'm sure you know a terrible storm is coming, and powerful storms bring all kinds of trouble. Where are your parents?"

"Witches," Nell blurted out, surprising even herself. It felt as if the word had just been plucked from her brain without her permission. After saying it out loud, it felt real. Real and true.

"Witches?" The woman's eyes grew large and her smile wide as she broke into a peal of warm laughter. Then she said with some authority, "There are no witches here."

Colour rose to Nell's cheeks. "I saw them, I think."

"You saw them?" Freyja shuddered and became serious. "You saw witches?"

"Not face to face," Nell explained. "But they have been kidnapping mothers, and ours was taken last night." At the sound of the word "kidnapping", Freyja Skoll's gaze on Nell sharpened. "There was this cloud."

"A cloud? What kind of cloud?"

"It was shaped like a skull." The words hung in the air until an alarmed chirp rang out from inside Fenn's covered bucket, shattering the silence.

"Quiet!" Fenn snarled and smacked the bucket with her small fist.

"*Fenn!* Do you have any kindness in you?" Freyja asked as if they both knew the answer, and the answer was no.

Carefully, Freyja Skoll lifted the thin black silk that covered the bucket, and Nell saw at once that it wasn't a bucket after all. It was a miniature birdcage of antique black metal, and between the bars was a familiar face: the golden bird with the red-crowned head that Nell had met the night before. The instant it saw Nell, the bird began to chirp and flap its wings in excitement.

"It's okay," Nell said softly, and to the surprise of everyone the frantic bird grew calm.

"She likes you," Freyja Skoll said.

"She saved my life," Nell said proudly.

"I don't doubt it. She is a brave one. She got free yesterday, unlocked the cage on her own, and flew straight out the window of the hotel. Smashed the glass. We thought we had lost her, poor thing. But she came back this morning, happy as can be. Saved your life, you said?"

"She fought off a monster!" Nell said.

"A monster?" Fenn whispered, her eyes widening in fear.

"What's her name?" Nell said, not wanting to frighten the little girl.

"Her name is Gleipnir," Freyja Skoll said, and when she did, Nell felt herself beginning to have a moment. It came fast and hard as a punch to the stomach, and instantly, the achingly beautiful head and neck of Freyja Skoll vanished off her shoulders.

"I'm Nell Perkins," Nell managed to mutter calmly, though her heart raced at the ghastly sight of the headless body standing before her. Speedy put his hand on his sister's shoulder and gave it a friendly squeeze. He knew what it meant when Nell said her name. Nell looked up at her brother's kind eyes. It did the trick. She whispered, "Thank you," and turned back to Freyja. Her head had returned in full.

"Why Gleipnir?"

"Gleipnir is the name of a magic rope that can never be broken."

"A rope?" Nell said. The confusion in her voice made the beautiful woman nod. She continued her explanation.

"This little bird wants to be home, you see. From the moment it came to us, it has tried to escape. It is almost as if there was a rope tied around its heart and connected to the heart of another bird far away. Most birds forget who they are the moment they are in a cage and being fed, but this one

49

cannot be broken. The rope only she can see and feel draws her home."

"Let it go then," Nell said. "Let it fly to her family."

"She tries to escape, I'll pluck her wings," Fenn snarled.

Freyja smiled as if she understood Nell's concern. "I know you must think we are awful but I'm afraid we can't do that. This bird is special to us. She'll soon forget who she was. The rope, as it were, will be broken."

A taxi pulled up before them. "Our ride is here," Freyja said, sounding sad to leave her new friends. "Let us not say goodbye, for I am sure we will meet again."

"Can I say goodbye to the bird?" Nell asked quietly, for all she could think of now was the bird and how she wouldn't see it again. A pang of sadness echoed inside her.

"Of course," Freyja offered kindly. "You two did have quite an adventure."

Freyja took the cage from Fenn and held it up so it was at Nell's eye level. The creature's small hazel eyes were wide and pleading and seemed almost human. They held Nell's gaze as though desperately wanting to tell her something. Several times, the bird flicked its red head down in a swift bow. Nell returned the bow, and when she did, she noticed something she hadn't before. Painted on the bird's tiny toes were letters. They read S-T-I on the left and N-K-Y on the right.

Freyja cleared her throat, politely. It was time to go.

"I could watch her for you," Nell blurted suddenly, overcome with the feeling of not wanting the bird to leave. She put her hand on the cage.

"Watch it?" Freyja said, confused.

"Please," Nell yelled, her voice tinged with panic. Freyja, startled by Nell's intense voice, pulled the bird away, and when she did there was a great tugging at Nell's heart. The boys felt it too. It was a terrible feeling.

"Just for an hour," George said quickly.

"It's my birthday," Speedy added desperately.

"I'm sorry, children," Freyja said coldly. "Our car is here."

"Please!" Nell said desperately, grabbing Freyja's arm. "Please! I want her to stay with us."

Freyja's eyes flashed with a rush of anger that made plain the fact that she wasn't a person who was used to being grabbed. A vicious slap stung Nell's hand. The blow felt like the sharp crack of a whip. Nell let go as if bitten.

"You hit me?" Nell whispered, flashing hot with surprise.

"And I will again," Freyja said crisply. "You need to mind yourself, young lady. I will not have my sleeve grabbed."

Her voice was so confident and sharp that Nell felt it was her fault, that she was the one who had done something terrible. She looked up to apologize. Freyja's head had disappeared once more. Nell wanted to look away, but she didn't, watching instead in frozen horror as the headless body stepped into the taxi with the bird. The door slammed shut, and the taxi sped away down the empty street.

The rain began again at once, as if to punish them. Hard streams of water chimed coldly on the tarmac. For a moment, the three children stared at each other in the falling rain, water streaming down their faces, and said nothing. All felt a vast pit of emptiness inside, as though they had seen something terrible happen but could not say exactly what. They simply couldn't put into words why they felt so bad, yet the feeling remained.

Finally, Speedy spoke. "Did you see the bird's feet? Its nails were painted with letters. Well, yesterday, I painted Mum's nails while she was sleeping."

Speedy and his mother loved to play pranks on each other. Once Rose glued a moustache on Speedy while he slept. Another time, Speedy put a live goldfish in his mother's bedside water that she tried to drink in the dark.

"What did you paint?" Nell asked, already knowing what her brother would answer, as a stream of dread quickly coursed through her body.

"I painted a letter on each toe. S-T-I-N-K on one foot and Y-T-O-E-S on the other. Stinky toes. It was a joke," Speedy said, feeling guilty.

"That wasn't a bird in Fenn's cage," Nell whispered, and as she said it, she knew without a doubt it was the truth. She looked her brothers straight in the eyes, first George and then Speedy, and said, "That was our mother!"

CHAPTER 7

The word "mother" hung in the air like the haze of gun smoke. Once again, silence overtook them. Nell knew the faster they found Badger the better, and pushed her brothers forward towards the centre of town. Things would make sense when they saw other people. The world would take a familiar shape and not be the strange thing Nell couldn't make sense of. Without speaking, she led her brothers down all the familiar streets, but when they reached the high street, they all stopped. The always busy stretch of shops was empty. Completely and utterly deserted.

"Where is everyone?" Speedy moaned.

"They're gone," Nell said, looking around at the abandoned streets. Not a person was in sight and all the traffic lights were out. The ground rumbled. They turned their heads and what they saw made their blood run cold. At the end of the street, big as a parade float and shaped like a skull, was the bruise-coloured cloud that had stolen their mother. It turned in their direction and began to move towards them.

"Run!" Nell said. She dashed forward with her brothers close behind. They needed shelter. Nell tried the front door of the hardware shop. Locked. Inside, the lights were dim. Nell ran to the next door, a coffee shop. It was dark inside, but she yanked at the door with all her strength. Locked. The howl of the wind drowned out all sound, and it was a few seconds before the children heard someone calling them.

"Here!"

Nell looked up to see Duke Badger standing in front of Joe's Diner, holding the door open for them. He was, Nell noticed, without his cat. The children ran inside under his arm, and Badger locked the door behind them. The lights were on, and the place was bright, clean and empty.

"Dark Daughters!" Nell said, hardly able to get the words out.

"It's all right. We can weather it," Badger said. He limped through the diner, his dead foot echoing off the floor with loud clanks as if his combat boots were made of iron. Outside, the cloud rumbled, and the sound rattled the windows. Finally, Badger pointed them to a back booth, and while they sat, he went behind the counter to the big, old-fashioned silver coffee urn. He held down the lever, watching intently as a hot stream of black coffee flowed out of the spout and into three cups. A boom of thunder rattled the window.

"Where is everyone?" Nell asked.

"Storm scared them off and should have done the same to you."

"We need to find our mother," Nell said. Badger nodded, taking in the information.

"Some things are better left lost," Badger said. "Searching can lead to all sorts of dangers." He placed the three cups of black coffee in front of them.

"Thank you," Nell said politely. "We don't drink coffee."

"Now's as good as any time to start," Badger said. "Go on, just doctor it up with some sugar and cream. And take a few sips." He nodded for them to hurry.

They didn't move, so he explained, "The ones hunting you, they hate coffee. They avoid it, especially when sweet. The smell repulses them. They'll steer clear of this booth when they get here, and if you have it on your lips, all the better."

"When they get here?" Speedy asked, pouring an endless stream of sugar into his mug and mixing furiously.

"All those snails. I imagine they'll want to cook them up."

"In here?"

"Yup."

"Then why in the world did you bring us here?" Nell asked, feeling she had been tricked.

"Can't run from them like you were. They're the best hunters, bar none. You run, they'll chase. They can't stop themselves. Children's blood makes them crazy. All you can do is hide, hold tight and let them pass through."

"Let them pass through?" Speedy said, looking at Nell. He took a big gulp of coffee until his face twisted in disgust. "That tastes like dirt," Speedy admitted.

"Spoiled dirt," George added, taking a sip and shuddering.

Thunder exploded outside. The coffee cups on the table jumped. Badger regarded the children with steady eyes. Nell imagined he got a lot of information from his eyes. Not just the way things looked, but the way things were. He was the type of person who looked at something and could not only see what was there but what was missing.

"Boys," he said. "What are your names?"

"Sorry," Nell said. "This is Speedy and this is George."

"Mr Perkins to you!" George added.

"Listen, I know you kids are scared. And you're smart to be. But the fact is this: what you call witches are going to fill this place in a minute or two, judging from the sound outside.

But if you do as I say, they ain't going to see us or hear us, because I always carry this."

"It'd better be a hand grenade," George said.

Badger reached down into his shirt and pulled out a leather necklace.

"Jewellery!" George said in horror. "What do you have as a backup? Some lipstick?"

"Hey," Badger snarled. "You want to live or you want to talk?"

George said no more, his eyes now riveted to the glass vial dangling from the end of the necklace. Beneath its slender glass was a violent, churning mist like a storm on a dark sea.

"What's that?" Nell asked.

"It's a few icicle shards from the cliffs of a place known as Vazencrack."

"The Bloody Mountain," Nell said, repeating the name of the town where Freyja Skoll was from. And when Nell said it she realized it had been whispering in her mind since they had met the horrible woman.

"That's right," he nodded. "I won it in a poker game and hoped the day would never come that I'd have to use it. But here it is. As long as we are touching it, or touching what it is touching, no one will be able to see or hear us until the ice melts – and it will melt. A few pieces like this will give us twenty minutes at most."

Suddenly a crack of lightning plunged like a jagged knife into the street right outside the door. The force of the blast rattled their teeth and made the hair on their arms stand.

"They're here!" Badger said, his voice clear and steady, making sure Nell and her brothers understood. One mistake, and they would be doomed. "Keep one hand on the table at all times!"

Badger removed his necklace and popped the cork. The shriek of a fighting cat sprang out as a plume of blue mist escaped from the vial. With a tip of his wrist, a few small pebbles of bright blue ice poured out of the glass and skittered onto the table, glowing with a phosphorescent moonlit colour that didn't seem of this world. Unlike any other stone they had ever seen, which all rested in eternal silence, these small pieces spoke. Furious elfin voices, whispering things you didn't want to hear.

"Look!" Nell pointed to the napkin dispenser that sat on the edge of the table. They all watched their reflections in its shiny chrome as suddenly she, her brothers and Badger faded from view, becoming completely invisible. They could see each other, but in the reflection, the booth they were sitting in was now empty.

"It's working," Nell said in wonder.

"Just in time," Badger answered as the cloud arrived.

A fat slap of smoke hit the window. Small tendrils of fog, the colour of rotten plums, slithered silently up the glass as if looking for a way to enter, but found none. For a moment, it seemed the cloud would just pass. Nell's heart was beating wildly.

"It's not coming in," Nell said hopefully. "They're passing overhead."

"Let's see now," Badger answered. Ink-coloured rain splattered on the window. Small black blobs hit the glass and skittered up and down, jumping off and returning like insects. But what kind of insect would be out in a rainstorm?

"Flies," said Badger, answering the unspoken question as the front door slowly creaked open. Nell felt her heart thump wildly. She remembered her mother's scream and didn't want

57

to see what had been inside the cloud that had made her yell so horribly. A drop of sweat rolled down George's face, and Speedy nervously bit the back of his thumb. There was a creak as the door pushed open a little wider, and a tiny ring of smoke wandered in tentatively as if it were a lost child.

"That it?" George said with a scoff. "Kinda pathetic, really."

Badger shook his head. That wasn't all. That wasn't even close. With a *BANG*, the door swung open wide, and a massive wall of purple smoke with a dark liquorice smell rolled in like a train pulling into a station. With a *whoosh*, the smoke approached their table as it filled every centimetre of the diner.

"Whatever happens, keep something touching the table," Badger instructed. As he spoke, he was engulfed in the thick fog of smoke until he disappeared. Nell and her brothers glanced at each other for a final time as they faded from each other's view.

All around the children, hidden by the dark fog, was a sudden riot of noise. First was the clatter of antique boots walking across the floor. This was followed by the sound of bodies settling into seats, the clang of cooking pans being taken down, and the excited voices of women.

"Place stinks of coffee."

"This whole town stinks."

"Once these snails hit the pan, you ladies will smell the smell of home," a familiar voice shouted.

"That's Freyja Skoll," Nell said, then gasped that she had spoken.

"They can't hear you," Badger reassured her. "As long as the ice holds, we are invisible and silent."

"I don't want anything those disgusting children touched," Fenn sneered haughtily.

"And Fenn," Speedy added.

"Nell," George asked quietly, not wanting to show he was afraid, but beginning to sweat, "I think your arm might need a rest. I can help you hold it up with my shoulder if you want," he squeaked. Nell understood. She lifted one hand off the table and put her arm around her younger brother, pulling him in close.

"It's okay, George. They can't hear or see us."

Slowly, the smoke began to thin, and what was hidden became clear. The diner was filled with witches. They were all young women, some not much older than Nell, of different races as though they had come from everywhere on Earth, and surprisingly all were strikingly beautiful. Each wore a long antique dress of deep velvet, all the colour of burnt logs, and the skirts were decorated with tiny buttons made of bone that ran up and down the sides. Around their waists were tightly cinched red belts from which hung silver-handled daggers. It was a terrible sight, but one they could not but help stare at as if their minds needed extra time to convince themselves that all of this was indeed real.

The witches were busy gossiping: all, that is, except for the young Fenn, who sat on a stool, staring directly at the table where Nell and her brothers sat.

"Why is no one sitting at that table?" she asked Freyja, who was behind the counter working the hob.

"She can see us," said Speedy as Fenn stared at them with her button-black and wholly merciless eyes.

"We're fine," Badger reassured them. He spilled some coffee on the table. "So far, so good."

"Why don't you go over to the table and see," Freyja instructed her daughter as she scooped up a lump of lard and threw it in a huge cast-iron frying pan. The lard hit the metal and sizzled.

"All right," Fenn said grudgingly and jumped off her stool. She walked across the floor, reached the table, and stood right over them. The small girl with her ragged hair and jagged teeth smelled of vinegar and rot. Her eyes, hard and black as a night starless and cold, studied the table suspiciously.

Nell felt her own heart beating wildly. Fenn was staring RIGHT at her now. The look held no mercy, no love of anything but destruction. While she couldn't see Nell and her brothers, her confused face said something was not right. But what? She turned to Nell, nose to nose with her.

"Breathe," Badger said. "Go on, girl, give her some coffee breath."

Nell puffed up her cheeks, puckered up, and blew a stream of air at Fenn, whose face twisted in disgust.

"Coffee!"

Freyja laughed a laugh that said *I told you so*. "That's why no one is sitting there," she said.

"It's disgusting. This whole town is disgusting," Fenn said, then turned away and walked back over to her stool. "Let's burn it all to the ground!"

As Fenn reached the counter, she reached down behind it and pulled up an antique birdcage. Inside was a small yellow bird with a red head.

"Mum!" The word escaped from Nell's lips. Freyja Skoll turned in their direction and Nell was sure she had heard. The beautiful witch's cold eyes lingered on Nell.

CHAPTER 8

"That bird in the cage is your mother?" Badger said.

"I'm sure of it."

For a moment, Badger didn't speak. He stared across the diner at the bright little yellow bird in the cage. The bird stared right back, knowingly. Badger turned to Nell and her brothers, his voice firm.

"This is the plan," he said like a doctor about to give a shot with an absurdly large needle. "Let her go," Badger said. "Forget about your mother."

"Forget her?" Nell felt her stomach sink. Of all the plans Nell had imagined that Badger might devise, that was not one of them.

"Even if we could sneak our way over and take her and make it out alive, it's too late. That is a spell that can only be broken by one person, and getting to him is impossible."

"EAT UP, LADIES," Freyja sang out. Nell and her brothers all turned to Freyja, who had a wide smile on her face. She was dipping a ladle into the large pan on the hob, scooping up a stew of snails in blackish goop and pouring the mess onto plates that a young witch with white hair was delivering to the tables.

"We have hunted well and have a long journey home!"

The witches let out a wicked cheer and began to sing a horrible chant.

"Crack the bones. Bitter fruit.
Howling moon. The demon's lute.
Across silver waters. On insane mares.
The Death Dreamer hears our prayers.
Return, return to Vazencrack.
Our Bloody Mountain calls us back."

The song was over. The steaming plates were served. What happened next scared Nell and her brothers more deeply than anything they had yet seen. For it was at that moment the witches' faces changed. Slowly, horribly, their faces stretched outward and became bird beaks. The beaks were black and sharply pointed, like ravens'. The witches didn't use utensils but stuck their fingers into the hot muck, pulled out snail shells, and cracked them in their pointed beaks, slurping the meat and crunching the shells with delight. Speedy's and George's open jaws told Nell that she wasn't having a moment. This was as real as real could be.

"No. No," Nell said, almost to herself, and then before she could think of what she was doing she began to rise. "I don't care how many witches there are. I'm not going to forget our mother."

"Sit down, Nell," Badger said firmly and calmly, but his darting eyes made clear that they were in a dangerous place from which they may not escape. "First off, these aren't witches we are dealing with. These are the Dark Daughters."

"Dark Daughters?"

"They are an ancient tribe of Nightmares, always women and always beautiful."

"How can a nightmare be a woman?" Nell asked. "A nightmare isn't a person. It's just a dream – a bad dream. Right?"

Badger shook his head. "The first thing you must know is life is bigger and greater than you have ever imagined. To understand what I am about to tell you, you must accept that things you think you know completely, things you have seen all your life, are only the tip of what is truly there. Days and Nights are different from what you suppose; they are deeper, and bigger, and aren't bound by the turning of the clock. Which means Dreams and Nightmares aren't the stories you see when you sleep," Badger explained. "Dreams and Nightmares are the people who live in a world that is right beyond our own."

Badger reached over and grabbed the salt and pepper shakers. Carefully he shook some salt into one of his large palms. They were strong hands and looked both young and old at the same time.

"Nell, pour some pepper in my other hand, please." Nell lifted the pepper and sprinkled some in Badger's outstretched palm. Badger slapped both his hands together and began to rub. A soft golden light began to flow out of his palms. Quickly he turned his hands over and flicked them open. Suddenly a bright flash blasted from them and they were staring into a curtain of shivering golden light that rose from his hands. Silver ink the colour of moonlight spread out across the curtain, drawing an ancient map. It showed a vast sea where hundreds of small islands floated.

"Look quickly: this will only last a few seconds. What you're seeing is a map of the world, unseen by the so-called awake world. This is the Dreamlands. It is a land of islands, some tiny and some immense, all floating in a sea so vast that its end has never and will never be charted. One side of the world is known as Sweetland and the ones who live on that side are known as Dreams. Across the sea is a dark and often frozen place known as the Wicked Places. There live the enemies of Dreams, known as Nightmares."

Badger slapped his hands together. The map flickered for a moment and grew gloomy as the sky during a thunderstorm. A new set of islands now dotted the map. They rose out of a terrible sea. Just looking at it made the children feel lonely and small. The map began to fade and in a moment vanished completely.

"How did you do that?" Nell asked.

"It is nothing, an old traveller's trick, but tricks won't get your mother back."

One of the Dark Daughters who was rushing back and forth serving steaming snails stopped at the booth where Nell and her brothers sat with Badger to catch her breath. Up close, her beak was terrifying, sharp as a knife blade. She turned away from the table and leaned her back against it to rest, placing her hand down on the tabletop behind her for support. The moment her pale hand touched the table, invisibility began racing up it. In a few seconds, her hand had disappeared completely. Badger, Nell, Speedy and George all froze in horror. All the young Dark Daughter had to do was look down at her hand, and she would know what was happening. They would be through.

"Easy," Badger mouthed silently.

"Birchvain! Here. Now!" a gruff voice commanded, and the instant the Dark Daughter picked up her hand, it became visible once again.

"The thing you need to know about Dark Daughters is this," Badger continued, gripping a knife. Nell hadn't even seen him take it out. The stealth with which he had done it was slightly alarming, and Nell knew at once that Duke Badger had seen things, terrible things, and had been in places where fights often ended in death. "All Nightmares," Badger explained, "have one thing in common. All of their power comes from the dying side of the Night, what they call *devilartkia*, the dark magic of forgetting, confusion and destruction," Badger explained.

"*Devilartkia*," Nell repeated, and the word filled her with a pang of deep sadness.

"Dark Daughters are masters of *devilartkia*, which means even if you could travel into the Wicked Places and survive and somehow find the only one who could change that bird back into your mother again–"

"She is still our mother," Nell pointed out.

"Have it your way. Even if you could find him and your mother did get changed back into a person, the *devilartkia* would remain inside her. Your mother would be cursed with it. She would never remember you."

"Not remember us?" Speedy said in horror.

"Her memory will have been wiped clean. You will be nothing to her but a bunch of kids she's never met."

"Maybe not them, but she'll remember me!" George said confidently.

"Who is it?" Nell demanded. "Who can help her?"

"It doesn't matter, because you cannot and will not go to find him," Badger grunted without a drop of sensitivity, and he looked deep into Nell's eyes. "The one and only truth of the matter is this. Even if you could survive. Even if you bring her to him and he could change her back, it wouldn't matter. All of you will be forgotten."

"Don't be stupid," Nell said, surging with sudden anger.

"Excuse me?" Badger remarked with surprise at Nell's burst of temper.

"Do you have children?" Nell asked, trying to sound calm.

"No. Absolutely not."

"Well," Nell explained slowly and clearly, as if she were speaking to someone who had no idea what he was talking about, "if you did, you'd know this one fact. When you're a parent, memory fills up your entire body. It becomes your body. And that means a mother could never forget her child ever. No matter what."

Nell looked over at Rose, who was standing in her cage, and the idea of how to save their mother became clear.

"I'm sorry, Nell," Badger said kindly, but Nell wasn't listening.

Suddenly she remembered the thimble she had taken off the dashboard of Rose's truck right before the storm and slipped it into her pocket. Her heart began to race as a plan took shape. She reached into her pocket and pulled out a thimble of green thread, and looked up. "As long as we are touching something that is touching the ice we will be okay, right?"

Badger nodded. "That's right."

"So all I have to do is fasten the end of the thread to the table and slowly unroll it until I reach my mother, then keep going until I reach the door."

Badger's eyes lit up. He smiled at Speedy and George. "Is your sister always this smart?"

"Yes," Speedy said.

"She's not that smart. I'm smart," George said. He then pointed out, "She needs to put the thread on the floor. If she holds it up, anyone can walk through like it's the finish line of a race. It will break, and poof! She's Dark Daughter meat."

"He's right," Nell realized.

"Like I said, I'm smart."

They discussed the finer points of the plan, and when the moment seemed right, Nell found the fattest spool of thread, dipped the end of it into the small puddle forming beside the ice, and unrolled the thread to the edge of the table. Speedy, George and Badger all pressed their thumbs onto the thread to hold it steady.

"Don't let go," Nell said. She pinched the thread between her fingers, pulling out a metre of slack. This gave her room to manoeuvre. She slipped off the edge of the booth like a scuba diver sliding from a boat into the water. She was still unseen.

Nell needed to roll the spool clean and straight across the floor. It had to reach right under the cage. She watched anxiously for a clear shot. One of the waitresses was headed right for her; when she passed, Nell would have her moment. The waitress came closer. Nell readied her finger, and when the Dark Daughter passed, she flicked the spool. *Whoosh!* It was a fantastic shot, unrolling across the floor in a tight line and coming to rest at the foot of the stool beside Fenn.

"Awesome!" Speedy yelled. Nell nodded in relief but did not turn around. She needed to be fast. The thread was spread out like a tightrope before her. All it would take was a simple walk. One foot in front of the other.

"Go on," Badger urged her. "You got it. Just keep your feet on the thread. If you fall off, you'll be visible."

Nell put one shaky foot out in front of her. It shivered as she gingerly touched it down on the thread. She sighed and took another step.

"That's right," she encouraged herself. She glanced up. Rose was watching her with bright brown eyes.

"I'm coming," Nell whispered to the little bird.

CHAPTER 9

Nell walked carefully. Another metre, and she would be there. But suddenly her plan came to a screeching halt. A massively tall Dark Daughter jumped up from her booth holding an empty bowl. Aside from her black beak, her skin was bleached white, her eyes a sharp green.

"THESE BOWLS ARE PUNY!" her voice shouted in fury. Nell twisted her head and almost fell off the thread. Her arms waved, and she jerked her body straight.

"Sit down, now!" Fenn commanded.

"Give me yer bowl. You don't need such a big bowl, you little roach!" she screamed and mashed her bowl on the floor. Instantly, a spray of razor-sharp shards slid across the floor towards the thread. Nell's whole body strained as she watched the shards pass over the thread. It took her a moment to realize the line had not been cut. She was still invisible. Nell let out her breath.

"Tavsi," Freyja said quietly from behind the counter. Of all the Dark Daughters, she alone had not changed, but remained a woman, her bearing royal, her eyes merciless. "Is there a problem?"

The tall Dark Daughter raised her beak proudly and squawked at Freyja Skoll. "You're favouring Fenn. The little roach don't need a big bowl. I'm seven hundred years old, and

I've caught more mothers than anyone here. I deserve a big bowl."

"All are fed according to their needs. Sit down, my dear," Freyja said in the calm voice of a teacher. "Sit down before you do something you will regret."

"I want the girl's bowl," Tavsi growled and took a step forward. Freyja walked out from behind the counter, wiping her hands on her apron.

Nell was now in the centre between the two Dark Daughters, who were standing on either end of the diner, facing each other like two gunslingers about to duel.

"I aim to do something, Freyja Skoll." She slid her knife out from her belt. "I aim to get Fenn's bowl."

"All right," Freyja said. "You are free to try." Freyja reached behind her head into her hair and pulled out a long silver needle. As she did, her beautiful hair tumbled down around her shoulders. Tavsi spun her knife in her hand until she held it tight by the blade.

Nell was stuck between the two women.

"All here know the truth, Freyja Skoll," Tavsi said grandly as if she had been waiting many years for this moment. "You will fail. The Red Egg will never be broken open!" Tavsi raised her arm back to throw.

"I'm sorry you think so," Freyja Skoll said kindly.

"I know so. I am three hundred years older than you. In my time I've seen many a queen try to break open the Red Egg in the hope of ruling the Dreamlands. All were young, pretty and smart, just like you. And, like you, all felt themselves smarter than the rest. They took us hunting for mothers into the land of Daylight. They would tell us they had cracked the ancient code and found the secret ingredient to make the spell that would break the Red Egg open once and for all," Tavsi snorted grandly. She looked around the room, fixing her haughty eyes on all the Dark Daughters before landing on Freyja Skoll, who listened patiently.

"Just like you, Freyja Skoll, these queens boasted that they could outwit Ravenhead. They would promise to lay the Bird Dreamer on the death slab in the main hall of Vazencrack and, with a twisted knife, unleash his flaming soul. The Bird Dreamer's soul, a blazing inferno, bright as ten suns, would do the rest, they would say. The flaming soul would awaken the Plague Dreamer from his dead slumber. He would stand. Rise up. And then all of the Dreamlands would hear his scream as he raged across the land. The Dreamlands would finally be ours. But it never happened for them and it will not happen for you!"

Nell's eyes flashed to the cage. Rose was watching every move as if she could see her coming. She began to chirp wildly, urging Nell on.

"Quiet," Fenn snarled, slapping the birdcage with cruel violence.

"Fenn," Freyja Skoll said. "Leave your bowl and the bird, and go and sit by Birchvain Root until I am done."

Fenn turned her eyes towards Tavsi, and defiantly scooped her hand into her bowl and pulled out the fattest snail. She put the shell in her beak and cracked it loudly, letting the sauce drip down her face.

"You'll be sorry, Fenn," Tavsi snarled to the small Dark Daughter as Fenn walked past her haughtily. The rest of the Dark Daughters watched with intense eyes. No one dared speak or take a side.

"You may start the count," Freyja said, raising her thin needle.

"One…" Tavsi intoned and took a step to the left and then to the right. On the other side of Nell, Freyja mirrored her movements.

"Two…" Freyja answered and took a step to the right and then to the left. Tavsi followed step for step.

"Run!" Nell heard her brothers screaming, but she was stuck in the middle between the two fighters. She didn't know which way was safe. Either way might mean getting caught between the flying weapons. Not knowing what else to do, she reached up and pulled the hood of her sweatshirt up around her head as though it would protect her.

"Three!" Tavsi screamed. And with that, both Dark Daughters threw their weapons. The knife and the needle whistled as they cut through the air. From the back of the knife trailed a blaze of flame, and from the back of the needle, a delicate flurry of snow.

Both instruments of death flew towards Nell, and as they did, Nell ducked as directly above her head the two weapons met each other in mid-air, tip to tip. There was the horrible sound of a train crash, and an explosion of bright orange sparks followed as the weapons collided. They didn't fall or even lose speed. Freyja's thin steel needle simply shattered Tavsi's blade as though it were a sheet of new-formed ice and hers were a stamping foot. Unstoppable, the needle continued on its course, shooting straight towards Tavsi's stunned face. Before she could jump out of the way, the weapon hit her right between her eyes, and Tavsi Drey's entire body became a solid block of ice – all except for her eyes, which were very much alive. They gazed around, wide with anger.

Nell was stunned. All the Dark Daughters watched in stunned silence as Freyja Skoll walked over to inspect Tavsi, the sound of her boots filling the diner with their loud, hollow echo. *CLICK. CLICK. CLICK.* As she passed, Nell knew this was her moment to rescue her mother.

"Now," she said to herself. "Three steps, and you're there." Nell ran along the thin thread until she reached the counter. She reached down, steadying her trembling hand with a breath, and plucked the spool of thread from the floor. Carefully, she unrolled it, slacking out the line. If it broke now, all would be lost. Trying to keep her hands still, she placed the line of thread on the counter and sat a heavy sugar shaker on top to keep it in position. She turned to the cage.

"Hi, Mum," she whispered. A flash of doubt raced through her mind. What if she opened the door and the bird flew away? It didn't matter now. She had to try. "Can you come with me?" she said to Rose as she opened the tiny door.

Sensing her freedom had come, the little yellow bird hopped onto the counter and looked around curiously. She was free. Her chest puffed out. She shook, opening her wings.

For a moment, Rose turned away, looking towards Fenn. Nell's heart sank. Fenn had jumped out of the booth and was walking towards the counter. She stuck her little hand in her bowl of snails and, staring at the icy statue of Tavsi Drey, began to eat loudly.

"Come on," Nell pleaded, and the bird turned away from Fenn and back to her. "Please. Please, Mum. You have to come with me."

Rose's eyes stared into Nell's and then, like the ping of a bullet, the bird flew straight into Nell's hoodie, burying herself under Nell's hair, beside her neck.

"I got you," Nell said tenderly. Nell turned to move but suddenly lost her nerve, for all around her walked the Dark

Daughters. The tribe gathered around the icy statue of Tavsi Drey.

The sight was terrible to see. The witch's eyes gazed out of her frost-caked face, silently begging for help. Freyja explained to the others that she would not feel her victory was complete until Tavsi had a proper punishment. With that, she began to sing the witches' chant and, unlike the harsh, riotous cheer of the crowd, her voice was sweet and gentle as a mother's lullaby.

"*Crack the bones. Bitter fruit.*
Howling moon. The demon's lute.
Across silver waters. On insane mares.
The Death Dreamer hears our prayers.
Return, return to Vazencrack.
Our Bloody Mountain calls us back."

Sweet as it sounded, Freyja's voice had a dark magic in it. The haunting song caused all the windows of the diner to crackle with frost. One of the lights froze and shattered. And then something even stranger happened. At once, Badger and all the children were no longer looking out of their own eyes but out of Freyja Skoll's eyes, and all were thinking her thoughts. The image of a great dark tidal wave flashed before them. The ocean was not made of liquid but of insects, black and buzzing. The horrible sea blotted out the light in the sky, sucked the air from their lungs, and separated them from one another.

When Freyja was done, the images disappeared, but the feeling did not. A deep sadness filled the children's souls, as though they had been flung into a deep hole from which they could never climb out. Around the diner, all the witches were trembling, some openly weeping. Freyja smiled at them and sighed.

"The song is over, and we have seen what our dear friend will miss once the Red Egg is broken open." She was face to face with Tavsi, close enough to kiss her. "Goodbye, Tavsi Drey. Your time in this life has amounted to nothing. All your spoils shall be divided among us, your house will be burned, your relatives banished. All who dare to speak well of you henceforth will suffer the same fate. Saying the name Tavsi Drey will be punishable by death."

Raising a finger, she touched it to Tavsi's beak, and *whoosh*, the fat witch's entire body shattered into a thousand tiny pebbles of ice, which spread across the floor.

"The walrus is dead!" Fenn squealed in wicked delight and jumped from the counter to inspect.

"On the counter," Badger commanded. Nell turned. Her brothers were standing in line on the thread behind her like a team of circus performers sharing a tightrope. The thread was now attached to the counter and ran back to the table like an electric wire. As long as the thread didn't snap, the entire counter all the way to the door would hold the spell and keep them invisible. But, for some reason, Badger wasn't with them. He was still sitting in the booth as if stuck.

"Hurry," Badger said, urging Nell on. "The ice is melting. You have only a few minutes left. Make it to the door and run."

"Aren't you coming?" Nell couldn't believe it. Why was he still sitting there?

"I can't," he grunted. "Could never make it across that string with my leg."

Nell's eyes flashed to Badger's leg, and what she saw made her freeze. She saw an inner animal. But unlike other inner animals, this one was attached to Badger like a chain, wrapped around his leg from his ankle to his knee. Its shape was a giant centipede, very much alive and made of smoky black iron and slick with oily goo. Each segment of the snarling monster's rivet-lined body was thick as a cannon ball, and its long row of razor-sharp legs dug deep into Badger's flesh, holding it in a vice-like grip.

Nell gasped. Without saying anything, she carefully scurried down from the counter and walked back across the string.

"Nell!" George yelled. But Nell waved for him to keep quiet.

"That bug," Nell said, reaching Badger.

"You can see the Shacklepede?" Badger asked in surprise.

"If you mean that monster on your leg, yes," Nell said, faking calmness. She bit her lip to avoid the horrible face she wanted to make, because now she could also smell it and it smelled awful.

"You're lucid, Nell!" Badger said between clenched teeth, his eyes wide with awe.

"Is that a good thing?"

"A very good thing. It means that you and your brothers might even live through this, but first you have to go. Leave me here," Badger grunted, his eyes flashing to the table where the shard of ice was melting away.

"But they'll see you."

"They'll see all of us if I try to go. I am too clumsy with this bug on my leg. I will fall off, the string will break and all of you will be taken and tortured."

Nell grabbed his hand. "I'm not leaving you."

"Let me go, Nell."

"No."

Nell knew she didn't have much practice being brave – that was her mother's department – but her mother was gone now, turned into a bird, and these evil women had caused it all. So, fixing Badger with her toughest glare, she said clearly, "Unless you come with me, I'll hold on until the ice melts, and we will all be taken away together!"

Badger thought for a moment and realized Nell meant what she said. He stood. Nell watched the bug react to Badger's movement, wriggling quickly, its fang-sharp legs digging into Badger's tortured flesh. He bit his lip against the searing pain, took a breath, and began to walk. Nell could see now how much effort it took to lift the fat metal bug.

"Seventy pounds," Badger grunted, understanding what she was staring at. Sweat began to wet Badger's brow as Nell led him by his large hand along the thread. With each heavy clomp of his leg, their bodies teetered. At any second they might be knocked off and made visible.

"Almost there," she said, her eyes flashing to the door.

"I am fine," Badger snarled. Slowly Nell led Badger to the door of the diner where her brothers waited, and all of them slipped outside to freedom.

Chapter 10

As the Perkins children stepped through the door into the rain, Badger wasted no time. The instant they were outside, he began limping as fast as he could down the street.

Only Nell could hear the heavy clang of Badger's steps. The noise of crashing metal was broken only by the high-pitched squealing of the Shacklepede greedily feeding. Badger banged the metal head of the monster repeatedly with his hand and gritted his teeth against the fearsome pain.

"How can we get it off?" Nell whispered as she walked alongside Badger. It felt as if it were her own leg that was trapped beneath the beast's gorging fangs.

"There is a key. It is in a place that the Shacklepede prevents me from reaching, but I think you might be able to get it for me, Nell," Badger said. He smashed his hand again on the metal monster. "And if you can free me, I can help you find the one who can turn your mother back into a person – but like I said, she won't remember you."

"She will," Nell said quickly, not wanting to get into another argument. "I'll try and get the key," she added, trying to sound as confident and brave as possible. She even jutted her chin out a little to give the impression that nothing would stop her. "I mean, I will. I will. I'll do it."

Just then, a violent blast of glass and metal cut through the storm as a fireball exploded out of the windows of the diner. Rising through the crackling flames was a thin plume of hissing purple smoke. The vapour climbed three metres into the air. Then, with cold, machine-like precision, it stopped and began to rebuild itself into a skull-shaped cloud.

"They're coming," Speedy yelped as he stared at the forming cloud.

"They'll be looking for their bird," Badger said.

"Why?" Nell asked desperately. "Why do they want our mother?"

"Mothers are the most powerful beings in all worlds. They give life. Traditionally the Dark Daughters like to use their souls as a basis for many spells, though the practice has been made illegal."

"Their souls?" Nell said.

"Don't worry. We won't let them have her, will we? But right now we have to get out of here before the Dark Daughters arrive. We have time. The snails dull their senses and they will not be able to move fast. If we're lucky and you can get that key for me, I'll be free again, and we might just make it out of this town alive before they are ready to attack."

At this, everyone began to walk faster, until they were nearly running.

Soon, they found themselves in front of Badger's shop. The inside of the window was shaded with a blood-red curtain on the outside. Stencilled in crisp cursive were the words *Sparktondale Supplies* and, in smaller letters, *Goods for the Fearless Traveller*.

"Maybe it would help your business if people could read your sign without a magnifying glass," George said.

"Those that need to know will find out," Badger grunted, unlocking the door and leading them into the shop, then closing the fortified door behind him. The shop was lined with dark wood walls on which umbrellas, unlike any the children had ever seen, hung, fully opened, in velvet-lined cases like works of art. Each umbrella was a different colour, and from inside the canopy of each one glowed a matching light.

Resting on a purple pillow on a glass counter was an umbrella that was open wide and rose straight up from the pillow, unsupported by hand or stand. The wood of the shaft was carved into two interlocking snakes, and the canopy was the deep, dark blue of the hours before dawn. The children fell silent just looking at what was clearly no ordinary umbrella.

Badger lifted it from the pillow and wrapped his tattooed fingers around the wood. A warm blue light flowed down from the canopy, and just to stare at it made the children feel that, standing inside that light, nothing could or would ever harm them. With an electric crackle, the light of the canopy snapped off as bright streams of energy shot up the snake-shaped handle, racing for the ferrule, the pointed tip, above the canopy, which began to glow with a lethal blue flame. Nell knew at once this wasn't just an umbrella, but a weapon. Badger swung it around his head with a powerful *THWACK*, and it closed tight, transforming into a thin sword whose sides gleamed with a razor's edge and sparked with a high-voltage current. Badger handled it with the skill of a seasoned fighter. With another crisp movement, the weapon was slung behind his back, resting inside a previously invisible quiver.

"That's some umbrella," Nell said.

"You have no idea," Badger replied through a clenched mouth, and it was clear now that the more he moved in any way, the tighter the metal monster attached to his leg gripped. There was an annoyed yowl as Badger's cat, Pinch, trotted in and jumped on the counter, taking in the children with her intense yellow eyes.

"That's Pinch," Badger said. "And she's hungry. So don't interrupt me until I feed her, or we'll all be in trouble."

Nell reached out her hand to pet her, and the cat yowled in fury.

"Do not try to pet Pinch," Badger instructed, reaching below the counter to a mini fridge and pulling out a tray of cheese cubes and crackers, placing it before her. "She does not like to be treated like a cat."

"Good doggy," Speedy said with a smile. The cat yowled louder, and Speedy apologized. "Sorry."

With a great wiggle of her small body, Rose pushed her way out from inside Nell's hoodie and landed on the counter.

"Mum," Nell gasped, afraid of what the cat might do. Rose, ignoring Nell, hopped beside the cat and began to peck away at a cracker. Pinch flashed her a surprised look, but did not scare her away, sharing her plate with the brave yellow bird.

"If we can get the key and you can get that thing off your leg, do we have far to go to find the person who can help?" Nell wondered.

"What thing?" Speedy asked. Nell looked at Badger and he nodded, indicating it was okay to share what only she could see.

"Badger has an inner animal on his leg that makes it impossible for him to take us to the person who can help Mum. But if we can help him get it off, he will help us. We have a deal, right?" Nell asked Badger. "We help you and you'll take us to the person who can help change Rose back into human?"

"He's not a person," Badger said. "His name is Ravenhead."

"They mentioned Ravenhead," Nell said, "the Dark Daughters. They needed to capture him for their spell. To break the Red Egg."

"It is ridiculous," Badger snarled. "It is not a plan. It is a nursery rhyme that every Nightmare learns as a child." Badger repeated it slowly:

"Collect mothers,
Break the egg,
On the death slab lay Ravenhead.
Eclipse potion down his throat,
Bird Dreamer's soul, blazing bright,
Plague Dreamer awakes,
Endless Nightmares,
Wicked delight."

"What kind of nursery school did they go to?" George asked.

"The Dark Daughters," Badger continued, "are mischief-makers. Thieves. Cut-throats with a few skilled warriors among them, but never have they been able to capture a Dreamer. Especially one as powerful as Ravenhead," Badger said and shook his head as if the thought of it was impossible, "and the recipe for the Eclipse potion has been lost to time. If it ever existed at all."

"Back up," George said. "You keep saying Dreamer. Our mother is a BIRD, understand. We need to change her back to a person. We don't need a dreamer to help her. We need a do-er!"

"I think what George means," Nell said, shooting her brother a glaring look, "is, what actually is a Dreamer?"

"Oh yes," Badger said as if he had just realized Nell and her brothers knew very little of what was common knowledge to him. "The Dreamers are the rulers of the Dreamlands. Only they can unmake a spell of transformation made by a Nightmare."

"The Dreamlands?" Nell said slowly, as if saying it slowly would make Badger realize his mistake. It didn't. There was no mistake.

"Yes. The world of Dreams and Nightmares. That is where we must go."

"You're kidding?" Nell said in disbelief. "The Dreamlands? Is that even real?"

"It is as real as can be if you can get there, and you can only get there if you have a Fearless Traveller to guide you."

"And what," George sighed loudly, "is a Fearless Traveller? He's been waiting to tell us all night. Come on, big guy, tell us about your little club."

"Little club?" Badger said in astonishment and stared at George with hard eyes, studying the youngest Perkins until George realized, as he often did, that he had crossed the line.

He cast his eyes down and mumbled an apologetic "Sorry."

"A Fearless Traveller," Badger said proudly, "is part of a loyal order of Dream warriors who have sworn an oath to live their dream life travelling through the islands of the Dreamlands, from the Sweetlands to the Wicked Places, to help those in need and bring them home. But," Badger admitted, "Fearless Traveller or not, I can't enter the Dreamlands with this Shacklepede on my leg. Until I get the key and unlock it, I am stranded here, and without me so are you."

"Where is the key?" Nell glanced around the shop, hoping the key was stuck on a high shelf or behind a case he could not reach. Now she wanted to save him from his wretched torture nearly as much as she wanted to free her mother.

"Do you know the bat tree?" Badger asked.

Nell, George and Speedy shot one another knowing glances, and all mumbled "Yes" nervously, for every child in the area knew of the oak tree that loomed over a rarely used playground on the edge of town. The playground was rarely used because of the tree, which was named for the hundreds of creatures that called it home. During the day, the bats, plump as large pears, hung in the tree, only to wake when the moon appeared. They would rise up into the darkness in a screeching frenzy, swirling like a dark tornado to hunt in the woods and along the banks of the falls.

"The key is waiting in the high branches. With your help, I think I can reach it."

"Guess what is *not* hidden in that tree?" George said, his voice dripping with sarcasm. Without waiting for an answer, he screamed, "Bats!"

"In the tree?" Nell repeated, feeling her stomach drop. For if there was one thing she hated more than bats, it was heights. "I'm not really much of a tree climber," she said as Rose leapt from the counter and into her hoodie, snuggling beside her neck.

"Maybe you are. Maybe you aren't. But it's not the climbing that matters. What matters is the seeing. Seeing what is in the tree and finding the key: that is what you can do for me, Nell."

"Me?"

"Yes. You saw the weight that binds me to the earth. Most don't. You can see things that others ignore."

"I don't like to," Nell admitted.

"Why not?"

"It's weird," Nell said, feeling shy. While all her life she had felt different and her mother had constantly reminded her that being different was a gift, Nell did not see it that way. In truth, what she wanted more than anything was to be the same as everyone else. "And scary," she added. "I hate it," she said finally.

"Actually, it is the most natural thing in the world. In the Dreamlands it is simply called being lucid. Everyone has the ability to do it: to see the truth. Most people ignore it. They train themselves from an early age to only see that which suits them. Some people, like you, cannot help but see the truth. Which means you are just about the only one who can do both – see what is hidden to most of us and climb the tree that stands in the way of me being free."

Badger opened a silver box on the counter and pulled out a small book. The cover was made of soft, tough leather, like the reins of a horse that had been ridden for years through rushing streams, over snow-capped mountains and burnished in the flames of battle. In bright golden letters, the cover said:

THE FEARLESS TRAVELLERS' GUIDE TO WICKED PLACES

The children stared at it in wonder. The book was no ordinary book – that was clear. It was an object of deep mystery and great power.

"What's that?" George said.

"This," Badger explained, slipping the book inside a nearly invisible pocket above his heart, "is the book written by those who see the truth all the time and stare into it no matter how scary it is. It is all a Fearless Traveller needs in any situation. You ready to head out?" Without waiting for a response, he opened the door, but then froze at what was waiting before them.

The skull-shaped cloud, with its dark swirls of burnt purple smoke, was floating right before the door, blocking their exit. While it was still only halfway formed, it seethed with menace. It was breathing. A foul breath blew into the children's faces and, with each exhalation, the cloud emitted a low, violent growl. They were trapped.

"You don't happen to have a back door?" Speedy asked politely.

"No. We'll have to scoot past. George first."

"He means you," George said, jabbing his brother with his elbow.

"I'll go first," Nell volunteered.

"Whatever you do," Badger whispered, "try not to make any loud sounds or look into it."

Nell nodded. Taking a deep breath, she stepped through the door and pushed herself as far back as she could against the shop window, like she was on a ledge. The rumbling cloud was only centimetres away, and now she could feel the frigid cold of it on her skin. Instantly, as though tossed into an Arctic lake, her lips turned blue and her teeth chattered.

"So cold," she whispered. But worse than the frost caking her skin was the burnt, rotten smell watering her eyes and stinging her nose. For a moment, she couldn't walk.

"Go on," Badger said, touching her hand. "We're right behind you."

"Okay," she whispered. Looking at her feet, she took one step and then another. Thinking she had reached the end and desperate to be warm again, Nell glanced up, gazing directly at the dark smoke. A swirl of smoke parted, and she found herself staring straight into the face of a young woman, her eyes wide with horror. Nell knew her at once. Her name was

Saffron Jones. She worked in the local library and was one of the mothers who had gone missing. Speedy was especially fond of her, as she had a baby whose nickname was also Speedy. Whenever he went to the library he would say, "How's Speedy?" and she would reply, "Great. How's Speedy?" and he would ask again and the game would go on and on and she never lost the smile on her face.

"Help me," Saffron whispered in pain as she began to transform. Dark black feathers raced up her face. A pointed yellow beak replaced her nose and mouth. And her body shrank until she was no longer a young woman, but a blackbird. Saffron flapped her wings wildly, trying to escape, but it was as if she were caught in a great wind, and in a blink, she was sucked into the darkness of the cloud.

"NO!" Nell yelled. Cobra-fast, a dozen arms shot out of the cloud, grabbing Nell all over her body, each hand cold as a corpse. Her voice rang out in terror as the strong hands dragged her towards the darkness of the cloud.

A mighty *THWACK* rang out as Badger whipped the umbrella off his back and swung it. There was a trailing flash of laser-thin, burning blue light, and the arms shattered into smoke. Nell was free. With another crisp *THWACK*, the umbrella was once again in its quiver. Badger pushed Speedy and George along, and they all slid past the cloud and down the street.

"They have Saffron Jones!" Nell yelled.

"What?"

"Inside the cloud. They have Saffron Jones," Nell said. Speedy turned and rushed back towards the cloud. Badger stood in front of the boy and held him back, but it was a struggle, for he was large and strong.

"Ms Jones!" he yelled.

Nell took her brother's large hand and the fight went out of him.

"Maybe if we can save Rose – maybe we can also save Ms Jones, right?"

Badger answered with a slight nod and added bluntly, "I'm not going to promise anything, but we're not going to have much chance with either of them if we lose you, that's for sure."

"Okay," Speedy whispered, as the cloud let loose a snarling growl.

"Get going!" Badger screamed above the din. "Head to the bat tree. I'll be along behind you."

CHAPTER II

Without another word, Nell, George and Speedy continued to run, pushing onwards, ignoring the burning in their lungs and the soreness of their feet. The rain had stopped and the streets were deserted and silent, save for the patter of their footsteps on the tarmac. In the quiet, Nell heard the alarmed tweet of the bird hidden beside her neck and ran faster.

"Stay there," she whispered to her mother. If Rose flew away now in the confusion, who knew what would happen. In a few minutes, Nell and her brothers were at the dark edge of town where the streetlights ended, and as they came upon Camden Park, they all stopped as though they'd reached the edge of a cliff.

The fat ash-coloured clouds hung heavy over the abandoned playground. Empty swings creaked back and forth in the wind of the growing storm. As if to acknowledge their arrival and remind Nell of the danger before her, the red glow of the sun had broken through the grey clouds and was shining directly on the tall leafless tree, solid and grim, that rose impossibly high in the centre of the park. Black, teardrop-shaped sacks shivered like drips of dark blood from the finger-like tips of each skeletal branch.

"Who put all those bags in the tree?" Speedy said.

"Those are not bags. Those are the bats," Nell said, her voice quivering with the dread that was now rushing through her entire body. "Thousands of bats."

In a few minutes, Nell would have to climb between the sleeping bats to find a key. But, for some reason, worse than the bats was the sight of a large tangle of balloons in the tree's topmost branches. They were dirty with age and shivering in the wind, and they filled Nell with a pinching sadness. They were so alone. Alone and abandoned. *Just like us,* Nell thought.

"I want to go home!" George said in protest. "I want to go home right now!"

"See those balloons?" Badger said, limping up to them, his jaw clenched tight against the pain. Pinch was perched on his shoulder. In his hand, Badger held a thin brass telescope. "Inside there is the key."

He handed Nell the telescope for her to use. It was smooth with age and heavy, despite its slim size. Nell lifted it to her eye, and suddenly she found herself having a moment. For as she stared, the bunch of dirty balloons transformed, and Nell saw she was no longer looking at a tangle of balloons but at a giant birdcage that was dangling in the wind on the highest branch of the tree. The black metal dome was over a metre high and made of thick iron bars. Inside the cage was no bird but a ragged boy, sitting silent and cross-legged. His dark hair hung across his forehead, covering his eyes.

"There's a boy in there," she said.

"Not a boy, a Sleeper," Badger grunted against the pain of his Shacklepede. "Here is your first fact about the Dreamlands and the most important. Every human being is also a dream being. Inside your human body lives your dream body. In the Dreamlands, it is called your Sleeper."

"Dream body?"

"People think they go to sleep at night, but they don't. What happens is their Sleeper awakes. You close your eyes, and your Sleeper leaves your human body behind in bed and travels to the Dreamlands. The Dark Daughters must have poached that boy before he made it. Could be they're punishing him. Could be just wickedness. Either way, if he isn't freed soon, he will die. And when a Sleeper dies, the human body that it belongs to soon follows. One cannot exist without the other."

"Can't you help him?"

"I tried to free him a few weeks back, but was outnumbered by Dark Daughters and defeated. For that, I ended up with this Shacklepede on my leg, and he was given the key to my punishment, which I cannot reach."

"How do you know he still has the key?" Nell asked.

"It is attached to his body." Badger adjusted the telescope and handed it back to Nell.

Looking through the eyepiece, she could now see more clearly. The boy was turned away from her, but his hand was visible. It was not a human hand but one made of the same black metal as the monster that was bound to Badger's leg.

"The hand is attached to his arm by a leather harness. Inside the hand is the key," Badger explained. "He simply needs to snap his hand off and give it to you."

"Why?" Nell asked.

"So you can throw it down to me, and I can get this beast off my leg."

"No. I mean, why'd they make his hand the key?"

"It's *devilartkia*," Badger said, shrugging. "Confusion is a powerful weapon. He doesn't even know his real hand is missing."

"How can I break the spell?"

"Confusion is a powerful spell but so are calmness and clarity. Somehow you need to help clear his fog, make the boy remember who he truly is."

"How?"

"I don't know, Nell," Badger said, almost sounding flustered, as though he had talked enough. "There is no one way nor do I have a potion. There is only kindness. You are just going to have to feel it at the moment. Improvise. Be lucid. See and feel the truth. That is power in its own right. Start there. Use that."

A lone bat let out a high-pitched screech that rang through the air.

"We have to hurry," Badger urged. "The bats will be waking soon, making your climb a bit less pleasant."

"What he means by that," George interjected, "is that it's about to get sucky, sucky, suck town."

"Thanks for explaining," Nell said to George, who flashed her a thumbs up.

Without wasting any more time, Nell and her brothers gathered at the bottom of the tree.

"It's easy," Speedy said. "Just like climbing a tree."

"Like you know," George huffed. "You've never climbed a tree in your life."

"'Cause I'm scared of heights! Aren't I, Nell?"

"Shut up!" Nell said nervously. "Please, just stop talking about it."

"Right," Speedy said. "Sorry."

The wind had picked up, bringing with it a wet, bone-chilling mist. Speedy lifted Nell up, and she grabbed the first branch and hoisted her stomach against it. A crack of thunder exploded in the sky, and instantly, Nell slipped and hit the ground with a thud. Pain rattled her head, and Rose tweeted.

"You all right?" Speedy asked.

Nell stood up. She tilted her head and looked up at the massive bat-filled tree waiting for her and without warning she ran. Ran away as fast as she could. Stamping through the wet grass of the playground, past the swings and the slides, the huff of her breath ringing in her ears. Nell didn't even realize she was running until she had crossed the muddy baseball diamond and reached the edge of the woods where she stopped. She bent over, sucking in air in large draughts. Nell kept her head down. She could hear her brothers calling for her to come back but she didn't move. She had run away! Now they all knew. She was scared, a coward, and shouldn't be in charge of anything.

Nell reached her hand into her hoodie and felt for her mother. Gathering the small bird in her fingers, she pulled her out and inspected. The little golden bird warbled a sharp song as if to say "What are you doing, Nell?" and, hearing the distant rumble of thunder, Rose flew back into the hoodie and snuggled beside Nell's neck.

"What am I doing? I'm not climbing that tree. That's what I'm doing," Nell said to Rose and watched anxiously as Badger trudged across the field one heavy thud at a time. His face was tight with pain. Each step a new torture.

I'm mean, Nell thought as she saw him struggle. As awful as she felt, her fear was raw and real. She simply could not move to help him. Nell was frozen on the spot and decided that she would never move. Not now. Not ever. She had done her part in the diner and got Rose back, but that was all she could manage. No bat tree. No Dreamlands. She was done.

Badger reached Nell, and before he could yell at her for being a coward, she blurted, "Don't tell me I CAN do it because I can't. Grown-ups always say that. 'Don't worry, you can do it.' They say that and they give you a thumbs up. I hate the thumbs up. It's stupid. Don't ever give me one. You know what grown-ups won't tell you? Sometimes you can't. Okay. I can't. That is the truth."

Nell braced herself to be yelled at. To be told she had no choice. That she COULD do it. But Badger was silent. The large man said nothing, and the only sound was the whistle of the wind. Finally he reached into his pocket and unexpectedly took out a chocolate bar, snapped off a piece, and handed it to Nell.

"I like chocolate," Nell said in the quiet surprise at not being yelled at.

"Me too," Badger agreed, chewing thoughtfully and then added, "Maybe that's true. Maybe you can't do it. But, tell me, Nell, why can't you?"

The chocolate was soft and delicious and reminded her of the way she had planned to spend the summer, lying around eating chocolate and reading books. But now she was here in the middle of a mess that was her fault. She had ducked. Her mother was kidnapped by Dark Daughters and changed into a bird and now she had run away. All of it for the same reason.

"I'm not brave and I never will be. I'm afraid."

"Of what?"

"Of everything. Of bugs. Of bats. Of heights. Of clowns. Of needles. Of blood. I'm even scared of coconuts. The hair, I guess."

Badger chuckled at that. "I agree coconuts are weird. I've seen lots of brave acts in my time, Nell Perkins, and here is what they don't tell you. The bravest people I know are all scared. Life is scary and the Wicked Places even scarier. But what makes people do brave things is not because they have no fear. The bravest people are scared and do what they need to do anyway. You're going to fail, Nell Perkins."

"I am afraid of that too."

"Good. Welcome it. Know it will happen because it will happen. Everything won't be okay. You will fail. But I think you'll keep going anyway until you get to where you need to be."

"Why?"

The rain had started again, falling soft and gentle. Badger pursed his lips and let out a lilting whistle. Nell felt a rustle beside her ear as Rose popped out, flew around her head, and landed on Badger's outstretched palm.

"That's why," Badger smiled.

Nell and Badger studied the bright yellow bird with the red crown. Rose opened her wings and proudly shook herself out. Then she turned, looked Nell directly in the eye, and sang a bright happy song. For a moment Nell and Badger did nothing but listen. Two people in the falling rain, the taste of chocolate in their mouths, listening to a bird sing.

* * *

"Lift me up," Nell said to Speedy. She had returned to the tree right after Rose finished her song. Badger had said no more but followed behind her. She did not mention running away to her brothers. This time she grabbed tight, digging her nails into the wood, and pulled her stomach flat against the branch. With a huff, she pushed herself to her feet and grabbed on to the next branch. As the rain crashed around her, Nell grunted and pulled herself up once more. Her forehead smashed against something slick and pointed that felt like a bag of chicken bones.

"Bats!" Nell yelped in disgust. The sleeping bats were everywhere, their tiny chests rising and falling as they gibbered restlessly on the verge of waking.

The fear of the bats waking spurred Nell on, and she climbed as fast as she could. Each step was harder than the last as the wind tried to pluck her from the branches and the rain made every surface slick. Fatigue was overtaking her. The tree was impossibly tall and the branches set just wide enough apart that every level was treacherous and demanded a fresh burst of energy.

"Just a little bit more," Nell said to herself, unsure of where to look. Down was the hard ground, to her left and right were the sleeping bats, and up above, the metal cage that was now clanging madly in the rising wind.

Finally, her hands gripped the branch right below the cage. Nell pulled herself up with all her might until she was right beside the small prison. The boy was sitting cross-legged, for there was no room anywhere else, and her legs ached in sympathy for him.

"I'm here," Nell said to herself, still unsure of what she needed to do. "Just look. Look and feel."

A clap of thunder shook the tree and was followed by a brilliant blast of silver light that shattered across the sky, blinding her. Out of the hot silver glare, a silhouette appeared in the cage, and as it took shape, Nell found herself looking directly into the face of someone she knew very well.

"Max?" she said in disbelief. He was an interesting-looking boy, with pale skin and large, dark eyes that stared back at her with an intensity that made Nell feel nervous and suddenly shy.

"Max?" she repeated, needing to say his name. It had been so long since he had slipped into the coma and been taken to the hospital. She had visited him once. Seeing him so quiet and still in the bed was terrible. And he was here. Now. Right before her. *It's not really him. It's his Sleeper,* she reminded herself.

"Who are you?" he said suspiciously.

"It's Nell," Nell said, unsure if he was joking. He always was funny, with a great sense of humour, but that appeared to be gone now. He stared at her blankly, and it was clear he didn't know who she was. She wanted to weep, but held back, and asked in a quiet voice, "Don't you know me?"

"No," he whispered coldly, rubbing his metal hand. Nell instantly thought of the book she had read and loved and felt sick. A town with amnesia now seemed beyond horrible.

"I'm trapped," Max admitted, sounding as though he'd given up any hope of escaping.

"I know," Nell whispered. Taking a breath, she looked her old friend deep in his haunted eyes and shared with him the reason she was in the tree. "I need your hand."

"My hand?"

"Yes," Nell said directly, trying to make the request seem as logical and reasonable as possible.

"How can you have my hand?"

"Well. Thing is … it comes off," Nell said, trying to sound full of purpose and not afraid. It was a lie. She was terrified.

"My hand comes off?" Max sneered as if it were the most ridiculous thing he had ever heard. "Does yours come off?"

"No," Nell said honestly. "But yours does." She pointed to the antique buttons that attached the hand to a leather harness that ran along the upper part of his arm. "Just see those buttons. You unsnap them, and the hand comes off."

Max studied the buttons as if he had never seen them before. "But I play trumpet with that hand."

"I know," Nell said, and despite the danger and the strangeness of the situation, she was happy to be talking to Max about something familiar. "You tried to teach me once."

"I did?"

Nell put her fist to her lips, puffed up her cheeks and blew, moving her fingers as if playing the trumpet. A wet *BARAPP* sounded.

"That sounds awful," Max said, shaking his head primly in horror. Though he didn't seem to know it, the gesture was one Nell had seen many times, and it made her smile.

"It was," she continued, feeling that somewhere hidden behind his confusion he remembered. "Thing is," she said tenderly, breaking the news to him, "your hand isn't there any more."

"It's not?"

"No. It's not. Some really bad people took it from you. And that hand on your arm – the metal hand – it doesn't belong to you."

"What? How?"

"You're asleep. This is a dream, Max. A really bad dream. You know how things are in dreams. Things are different."

"I'm not giving you my hand," he snapped.

"I know it's confusing, but this is a dream. All of this. And your hand – it isn't really a hand."

"It's not?"

"Things are different in a dream," Nell repeated.

A piercing screech shot through the air. The bats were beginning to awaken. Nell knew she had to get him to see that his hand was not just a hand but something else. Suddenly an idea came to her. She gave a tiny whistle and felt Rose beginning to flutter her wings. After another whistle, Rose poked her head out, and with Nell's encouragement, jumped onto her outstretched palm. Max's eyes lit up.

"This is my mother," Nell said.

"Your mother?"

"You remember. Rose."

"Rose," Max mumbled. He had always liked Rose, and she felt the same way about him.

"Things are different in a dream," Nell repeated again, and as he looked at Rose, a change came over Max's face. His eyes widened in terror, and he looked around in shock.

"NELL!" he screamed, grabbing the bars. "NELL! HELP ME! *GET ME OUT!*"

"I will!" Nell promised, her heart racing, but her words were nearly drowned out by a gale of high-pitched shrieks. Max's screams had woken the bats. Hundreds upon hundreds leapt from their branches and swirled around the tree, trapping them inside a tornado of dark, rapidly beating wings. Nell screamed, trying to knock them away from her face.

"Get away," Max said, trying to protect Nell by banging the bars of his cage.

"THE KEY!"

Above the din of the storm, Nell could hear Badger's voice, and she remembered what would save them.

"Please, Max," Nell said. "I need your hand. If you give it to me, my friend can free you."

"All right." Max nodded. Working gingerly, he unsnapped the two buttons that kept the hand attached to his arm and slid the metal hand off, revealing a stump that was crisscrossed with ropy scars. The sight of the stump shocked them both to silence.

"My hand," Max whimpered, his eyes wet with tears. He shook the tears away proudly and snarled at the horror of it. Now he remembered. "This woman and this little girl. They did it. They chopped off my hand with an axe."

"Throw it down," Badger yelled, and Nell tossed the metal hand, watching it fall through the dark cloud of screaming, swirling bats towards the ground. Badger was ready. With perfect precision and power, Badger removed the closed umbrella from his back and swung it around his head. The edge, sharp as a sword, pulsed a bright blue as he sliced the falling hand. In a blinding flash, the hand vaporized, leaving a smoking skeleton key on the ground before Badger's boots.

Sensing what was coming, the Shacklepede growled and began to dig its legs in tighter. Badger howled in pain and, scooping the key from the ground, lifted it above his head and brought it down hard directly into the keyhole-shaped slit on its slimy head, and with a roar, gave it a turn. Instantly, all the life went out of the monster, its eyes darkened, and it fell to the ground with the clank of broken machinery. Duke Badger was free.

Wasting no time, Badger swung his umbrella around his back again. It opened with a mighty *THWACK* and a blue light flowed across his body. Pinch jumped onto his shoulder, and Badger, now leaning back on his heels, began to spin like an Olympic hammer-thrower. Round and round, gaining speed. Suddenly, with a yell, he was lifted into the air, the umbrella rocketing him up through the dark night towards Nell.

As Badger got closer to Nell, Pinch leapt from Badger's shoulders onto the tree, alighting on a branch beside the girl. The midnight-black cat yowled and wasted no time racing back and forth, swatting bats away with her paws. In a few moments, the bats, sensing defeat, swirled away into the darkening sky as Badger floated down and landed on the branch beside Nell and Max.

"Thank you," he said to both of them.

"Help me," Max said, shaking the cold bars to the cage with his one hand.

"I aim to," Badger said, smacking away a few stray bats like flies. He turned to Nell. "Nice work, Nell Perkins. Now, say goodbye to your friend. I'm going to open this cage, and the second I do, the spell will be broken and, as he is in a coma like you say, his Sleeper will continue on to the Night Train and be taken wherever it was going when it was caught."

A rapid squealing clang of metal on metal rang out. The Shacklepede was racing towards them, its hundreds of thin, razor-sharp insect legs skittering effortlessly up the tree, red eyes blazing. With a leap, it threw its iron bulk onto the cage in a spray of snarls. The branch that was holding the cage creaked and, as Max screamed, it snapped.

In an instant, the heavy cage was plunging towards the ground with the Shacklepede on the outside and Max inside.

"MAX!" Nell yelled as her trapped friend plummeted towards the hard earth.

Badger leapt off the branch after the cage. He fell, arms tight to his sides, his body slicing through the air. Reaching the cage, Badger swung the tightly wrapped umbrella over his head. In a flash of sizzling blue light, it hit the side of the cage, sending up a great spray of sparks. Max's Sleeper flickered as it filled with light and then, with a *whoosh,* his ghostly body shot like a flare into the night and disappeared into the dark clouds. The Shacklepede peeled away from the cage and fell into the trees below, its squeals and hisses trailing behind it as it disappeared into the woods. A hollow clang followed as the empty cage hit the ground and crumbled to dust.

Badger, still falling, spun his umbrella again. It opened with a THWACK and he floated down softly towards the ground. Nell gazed out across the night. She could see all of Mist Falls. Everything was still and silent as a napping cat. Nell had the feeling that she was looking at something she might never see again.

PART TWO
THE DREAMLANDS

CHAPTER 12

Night had fallen, and the air had grown colder and colder. They were walking through deep woods. On Badger's shoulder sat the black cat, Pinch, silent and alert, yellow eyes searching.

"Where are we going?" George moaned.

"He already told you, George. We are looking for a place to cross the Dreamlands," Nell said.

"I want him to tell me again that the cat will know the spot, because maybe you all missed that," George said. "'The cat will know!' I mean, come on, people! He's trusting a cat!"

"We heard it," Nell said, beginning to lose her patience. They were all exhausted and cold and, above all, scared. Badger didn't seem well. He talked little now, only breathing heavily in short grunting breaths, for even though he was free from the Shacklepede, the pain in his leg was still clear with every step.

Nell blew into her hands, trying to keep warm, but she wasn't thinking of the way the cold stung her cheeks or the noise of the blasts of wind, which sounded like bones rattling in chains. All Nell was thinking of was Max. Seeing her old friend had made her realize how much she had missed him and how lonely she had been since he'd left. But even worse was the fact that Max didn't remember her at first, and Nell knew that Rose's spell was far deeper and much stronger, for she had been completely changed. Maybe it was true. Maybe, even if they made it to the Dreamlands and found the one who could change her back, Rose would look at Nell and her brothers and see only strangers.

"You all right?" Speedy asked when they stopped to catch their breath.

Nell forced a smile. It was up to her to be strong. "She's going to remember us," she told her brothers.

"Of course she will," Speedy said. "You're talking about Rose."

A forbidding rumble, like that of a low-flying plane, shook the woods around them. The children held their breath and pushed themselves against tree trunks as Badger had instructed. The roar, part mechanical, part beast, grew louder, and all watched, frozen in silence, as the skull-shaped cloud passed over the treetops. At its base was a giant green lizard's eye that beamed a probing searchlight across the freshly fallen snow. Badger had his fingers to his lips, making it clear that any noise would be their end.

The seconds passed like hours as the light swept back and forth, like an animal crazed with hunger. Finally the cloud moved on, continuing its hunt. When it did, the cold tapered off, and above them the moon shone bright and full in an otherwise empty sky.

Suddenly Pinch began to yowl softly.

"Here?" Badger said.

The cat yowled again. The spot had been found.

"Gather round," Badger snarled, as if they were wasting time.

From a small leather knapsack, he removed a squat metal cylinder. On its side was a sticker that read *Property of Fearless Travellers*. He jammed it into the dirt.

"What's that?"

"Beacon Ten Unveiler," Badger explained and took out a match from his pocket. "Once lit, it penetrates the Veil that hides the Dreamlands from human eyes. Its light will reveal the closest station." Badger bent down on one knee. He struck the match on the tip of his boot. It blazed orange. With delicate care he lit the Unveiler. There was a sizzle, and a ferocious spray of silver sparks streamed into the air.

"Stand back," he commanded. The cylinder began to vibrate, and with a *whoosh*, several balls of burning silver shot into the night and burst overhead, sending a shimmering net of sparks hissing across the sky and illuminating two hands the size of mountains. The glowing hands floated high above in the dark sky. They were pressed against one another, backside out and not attached to a body. Nell and her brothers had never seen anything like them before.

"Hands," Speedy muttered in awe.

And so they were. Nell was sure of it. There was no doubt they were as real as the ones she washed her face with every morning. They seemed kind, though, with a soft and gentle look of a tender person. All at once Nell felt like a tiny child playing peek-a-boo with her grandmother.

"It's okay," Nell said to her brothers and to herself. She knew at once there was nothing to fear.

"And so it is. That's the Veil," Badger said as another ball of light shot like a roman candle from the Unveiler and raced through the night.

"Behind it your journey into the Dreamlands begins."

When the ball hit the hands, they swung open like heavy gates, revealing what lay on the other side. As quickly as the hands had appeared they were gone. In their place stood a towering building of dark iron floating like a cloud high above the trees. The celestial structure was round and lined with tier after tier of sweeping arches like pictures Nell had seen of the Coliseum in ancient Rome. The roof was domed, and at its apex was a golden sculpture of a palm with a pyramid in the centre, and inside the pyramid, an eye. Below the hand, in curvy, blood-red neon, were the words "Night Train Transit Authority Way Station 689: Mist Falls".

"Is that real?" Speedy asked, for the building looked at once both solid as stone and as fleeting as a smoke ring.

"As real as real gets," Badger made clear. "That, children, is Mist Falls Station. Inside, we will board the Night Train and travel to the Dreamlands. But first we must reach it and cross the Veil."

All this time a steady stream of thick white fog had been flowing from the Unveiler. It spread along the ground and lapped at their feet like ocean waves. In the near distance a small bell began to clang, and from out of the darkness materialized a red and white rowing boat. Shrouded in the shivering mist, the driver remained hidden. The children were anxious to see who was piloting the ancient craft. The boat came towards them slowly, floating just centimetres above the snowy ground. Each time the oars moved, they let out a scraping creak, which was followed by a thud as they hit the earth.

Thud. Creak. Thud. Creak. As regular as the ticking of a clock.

As the boat got closer, the mist cleared and the children saw that sitting inside the rowing boat was a sea turtle as tall as Badger. He wore dark trousers and a long woollen scarf. A lantern hung from a reed-thin pole, which rose up from the front of the boat. The lantern shone a light on the turtle's deeply carved face and knowing, bloodshot eyes. With a few more powerful strokes, the turtle piloted the boat before Nell and her brothers and then stopped.

"Does anyone else want to tell him there's no water?" George whispered. The turtle said nothing, acknowledging them only with a slight nod. His eyes rolled towards Badger's leg, as if looking for the Shacklepede.

"I'm free," Badger snarled, and he instructed the children to climb inside the boat. Nell went first, finding a space on the smooth wooden seats, the once-bright paint now faded by time. Speedy and George climbed in next, followed by Pinch and Badger. When everyone was seated, the huge turtle began to row with gentle but authoritative strokes, and without the slightest jolt, the rowing boat sailed through the dark night towards the doors of the station. As he worked the oars, the ancient reptile hummed to himself. The turtle's voice was so old, deep and utterly serious that at first the children couldn't recall how they knew the tune he hummed, for there were no words, but they all felt they had heard it before.

"I know that song," Nell said.

"Life is but a dream," Badger chimed in, unlocking the secret.

"That's 'Row, Row, Row Your Boat'?" Nell gasped in recognition.

"If he sings 'The Wheels on the Bus', I'm jumping," George muttered.

"Is this where the song comes from?" Nell wondered.

"This is the boatman's song, written by the Boat Dreamer before time began. It is not only a song, but also a powerful incantation that lights the way," Badger explained, nodding towards the lantern at the front of the boat. As the turtle sang, it glowed more brightly, as though it were connected to his voice. Higher and higher the rowing boat rose. Nell noticed the air was different up here. Soft and silky, it slid across her face in gentle, soothing waves, as though she were walking through a tunnel of invisible curtains.

"The Veil," she whispered.

As they drew closer to the station, more and more rowing boats appeared out of the dark clouds, illuminated by their own glowing lanterns. Oversized animals piloted all the boats, and all were carrying human passengers. Most of the humans were dressed in pyjamas, but still many were dressed in ordinary clothes.

"So they're all Sleepers?" Speedy asked.

"Yes," Badger said. "And while you can't remember it now, your very own Sleepers have ridden these boats every night of your lives."

"I'd remember this," Speedy said, taking in the soft air with happiness. He loved being outside.

"Your Sleeper remembers, but your normal human body cannot," Badger explained.

The turtle pulled the rowing boat up to the main entrance, and Badger ushered the children out of the rowing boat.

"Thank you," Nell said to the turtle. The ancient animal slowly bowed his head with great dignity and silently turned the boat around as the lantern on the front dimmed. The small craft vanished into the darkness.

"Let's go," Pinch said suddenly.

"She speaks?" Speedy asked.

"He's a girl?" George stammered.

"Girl?" Pinch said. Unlike Badger, whose voice was gruff, the cat's voice was regal and female with a distinctly upper-class accent. She shook herself vigorously and began to grow until she had transformed from a small cat into a fully grown black panther with bright yellow eyes and snarling jaws. She continued with an angry sneer. "How dare you!"

"Listen, runts. You're looking at a queen," Badger said.

"Former," Pinch said grandly.

"Former queen," Badger amended. "She gave up her throne and all that went with it long ago when she became a Fearless Traveller."

"She's not your pet?" Speedy asked.

"She is my partner," Badger explained.

"I caution all of you not to forget it! I am no pet!" Pinch insisted.

"Sounds like a long story," George said, and then, as he did with all people who were charged with looking after him, from teachers to babysitters to bus drivers, he made clear some important facts. "So here are the rules. One, I don't like long stories. Two, I don't do explanations. And three, I hate paying attention. Got it?"

"Got it?" Badger snarled at the nerve of the child.

Instead of saying something rude, George gazed at Badger and said quite honestly, "My mum and my teachers and the bus driver and most people who work at shops say I can be pretty annoying sometimes. Don't blame yourself. It's not your fault."

"Why would it be my fault?" Badger snarled.

"I said it wasn't. But," George said holding up his thumb and forefinger like he was measuring something tiny, "you're a bit bossy."

"I'm what?!"

"You heard me."

"Just stop talking and start moving," Pinch commanded.

"Sorry, Your Majesty," Nell said.

"Pinch is fine," the panther said, though it was clear she appreciated being referred to by her old title. She shook her head with an aristocratic flourish and added, "You children are awake and will see what most people only see with their Sleeper and never see with their human eyes."

Speedy jumped before everyone and held up his large hands, blocking the way. "Nell first."

Nell smiled at her brother's kindness and with a deep breath, walked forward. Slipping through the door, she found herself in a descending passage with smooth, curved walls that were lined with small hollows in which candles burned and flickered. The air beneath was cool and hushed like the muffled silence at the bottom of a swimming pool. As Nell approached the glow of honey-coloured light at the end of the tunnel, she felt her mother cooing in her ear.

"It's okay, Mum," she said.

The long, dim corridor opened up into the grand hall of a train station. The walls were made of snowy marble, and the ceiling was an enormous dome of stained glass that depicted fantastic animals made of stars. Food stands and fancy shops lined the main level, though it was hard to see much, for the station was lively with a bustling crowd that made Nell's eyes grow wide and her jaw drop. It was more like a parade than a station. People, animals, machines and strange monsters, some quite tall and others quite frightening, walked among everyday objects that were not only enormous but also completely and utterly alive.

"Inner animals," Nell said to herself. The hidden aspects that she had seen since she was small were now all out in the open.

The rest of the group arrived behind Nell, speechless as they watched in quick succession a towering tin of soup, a peach fit for a giant, and a metre-tall box of matches float past, hovering just above the ground. Many of the creatures transformed before them. One moment they were humans in pyjamas, and the next they had morphed into strange creatures. Many of the animals that were rushing about were wearing human clothes of all styles and types. While most walked around upright on two legs and clothed, some, like Pinch, preferred their fur and remained without additional garments.

"But…?" stuttered Speedy as a giant light bulb glided by, followed by a silvery laptop as large as a billboard and a single brown boot as tall as Nell.

"Is it just me," George whispered, "or did things just get weird?"

"Weird," was all Speedy could manage as an eyeball the size of a car rolled past them.

"Good day," it said in a gruff Russian accent.

"Majorly weird," Nell added, suddenly face to face with a hippo wearing a frilly Victorian dress.

The hippo opened its massive mouth. "Out of the way," it said in a panic. "I'm late for school, and I have a test that I haven't revised for."

The whole experience was both wonderful and unsettling, and Nell felt her heart beat wildly. For a moment, she felt filled with confusion.

"Where are we?" Nell mumbled at Badger as she watched a flock of winged strawberries fluttering overhead and a three-metre-tall baby being pushed in a tiny pram by two tired-looking parents. Badger smiled knowingly, for it is one thing to be told you are headed into the land of dreams but quite another to begin the journey.

"We are in Mist Falls Way Station #689, one of the nine hundred and seventy-five Way Stations that connect the Land of the Daylight to the Dreamlands. Around you are Sleepers who have just arrived, and Dreams and Nightmares who are travelling between islands. All are waiting to board the Night Train. The Way Station can be a dangerous place, so stay near me and try not to get lost. If you do, keep away from the Nightmares. Many are slave traders, and humans fetch a good price."

"Nightmares? Like that guy?" George said, nodding to a corpse-pale young man in colonial dress and a wig that was draped in spiderwebs. In his hand he held a candle with a flame that was not a flame at all, but a tiny and beautiful young woman made of fire.

"Nope," Badger said. "That young man is a Dream. Looks are deceiving. Nightmares and Dreams come in all forms."

"That helps," George sneered sarcastically.

"How can we tell the difference?" Speedy asked anxiously.

"It starts with a feeling. A feeling that beneath the world that you see is another world. Soon you begin to see beneath the appearances of the world and see the truth of what is. It is called being lucid. Anyone can do it. Some need practice; some people, like Nell, can do it from the moment they are born. You've been doing it your whole life, haven't you?"

"Yes," Nell whispered, feeling slightly embarrassed that Badger had discovered her most hidden secret so easily. "I call them inner animals," she added.

"That is a good name. What you are seeing are dream bodies. Sleepers or disguised Dreams or Nightmares. Here it will be a little trickier than at home, but with some practice you will easily see through the confusion and get to the truth." Badger pointed his umbrella at a pretty young woman who was walking towards them. She was wearing a party dress and leading a small golden fawn beside her.

"What do you see, Nell?" he asked.

Nell saw nothing unusual. "Just a woman," she answered. Though she did like her shoes and wondered if she was rich.

"Look again," Badger said, "but this time relax. Don't try so hard. When you try you think and, naturally, you judge and that ruins it."

Nell studied the woman and this time didn't think about what she was wearing or how rich she might be. The moment she stopped trying to work it out, everything around the woman and the fawn grew dim, so that the two shone bright as if under a spotlight. In the new light, the woman transformed. She wasn't a human at all, but a horrible goblin with lizard skin, egg-yellow eyes, pointed ears and jaws ripe with snarling fangs. The fawn beside her morphed into an equally demonic beast, with dripping mouth and sharp red eyes.

"Nightmare," Nell said, frozen in fear as the goblin passed.

"That's right," Badger said, cracking a faint smile. "Forget what you think you see and try to see what you feel."

"Nightmare!" Speedy shouted and pointed at a towering giant that was walking towards them. The hulking creature was four and a half metres tall and had the body of a plump, well-attired human man, and the hands and head of a panda.

"That is not a Nightmare," Badger said respectfully. "That is a Dreamer."

"A Dreamer," Nell said. "Like the one we are going to see?"

"Yes," Badger said.

"You don't usually see them on the Night Train," Pinch added.

"Are they bad?"

"Some are good. Some are bad," Badger said, bowing his head as the giant strolled past. "They are the rulers of the Dreamlands. They are the architects, artists, inventors and creators of everything you will see, feel, hear, touch and taste in these lands," Badger said, holding up his finger for silence. His eyes darted through the station. Nell sensed a growing danger. Rose must have felt it as well, because from inside the hoodie, she began to tweet.

"Keep the bird quiet," Badger whispered, his eyes scanning the distance.

"I can't control her," Nell admitted.

"You'd better learn how," he said. With the stealth of a striking animal, Badger removed his umbrella from his back and held it pressed against his leg, where it changed colours, becoming nearly invisible.

He turned to Nell and whispered cautiously, "The Dark Daughters are here."

CHAPTER 13

B adger wasted no time. He led the children through the bustling crowd to the centre of the station where a line of passengers had formed behind a velvet rope to wait to board the train. At the head of the queue was a tall column of white mist that reached nearly to the ceiling and churned with a steady mechanical rumble. Nell suspected that hidden inside the mist was the door to the train platform. A deep bell began to chime throughout the station, and the tall column of churning fog slowed and slowly dissipated.

"What's happening?" Speedy asked.

"The shaping begins," Pinch snarled.

The two giants who had been hidden by the mist were now visible for all to see. They stood on either side of a round raised platform, facing each other. The first giant was a massive human man, six storeys high, dressed in an antique blacksmith's uniform. His long red beard stretched half the length of his leather waistcoar, and from his sleeveless work shirt poked two enormous muscular arms, one of which held a colossal sledgehammer. Behind his leather goggles were penetrating green eyes filled with the unflinching focus of a true artisan. Across from him, and nearly as tall, was not a man but a snow crane, silent, still and completely elegant.

"These are Station Dreamers," Badger explained. "When a Sleeper arrives at a Way Station, the Station Dreamers ready them for their journey on the Night Train."

"Ready them?" Nell asked with a nervous flutter in her stomach. "How?"

"They decide if the Sleeper will spend her time in the Dreamlands as a Dream or a Nightmare."

"They can turn you into a Nightmare?"

"They must." Badger nodded and continued. "I'm sure you've woken up and said, 'I had a terrible nightmare or a beautiful dream.'"

"Yes," Nell nodded.

"Well, the truth is, you don't have Nightmares or Dreams. You become them."

"You're joking," Nell said, though since she never remembered her dreams she couldn't be sure.

"I'm afraid not. This is the way it is. In the Dreamlands you are changed for what is needed."

"Needed for what?"

"For the Dream."

"Whose dream?" Nell said, trying to keep up.

"The Dream. The one Dream. The only Dream. Because while it feels like we all have our own dreams every night, the truth is we are all in the same Dream."

"The one appearing as many," Pinch said, licking her paws.

"Stretching from the Sweetlands to the Wicked Places. It is all one Dream. A single Dream we all share."

"I'm not keen on sharing," George said, looking around, feeling uneasy about having all these things cluttering his dream. "Are you sure about this?"

"Yes. HE'S SURE!" Pinch snarled.

"Just kitten," George said with a shrug. Pinch stared at George. "Kidding," he mumbled weakly and turned his attention to Badger.

"Think of it as a game of pretend. When you go to sleep, your Sleeper leaves your body and travels here and you are given your part to play in the never-ending game. Every night that part is chosen by the Station Dreamers – Dream or Nightmare. You may play the same part for years or be given a new part every night."

"Like a play?"

"Yes. Sort of. We call this part your shape." Badger motioned to the parade of strange creatures: the man with the apple for a head, the ghostly woman the colour of a dying sunset, the oversized animals and futuristic androids with white plastic faces like kabuki masks.

"What if you don't want your shape?" George asked.

"Most don't," Pinch said. "Everyone wants to be someone else."

"Because most don't know what Fearless Travellers know," Badger added.

"Which is what?" Nell said.

"It is possible."

"It's possible?" Nell repeated.

"This place runs on possibility. That is what makes it so fantastic. ALL shapes can be changed," Badger explained. "That is the gift of being you."

"Me?"

"All of you. Being a human. Having a Sleeper. Your lives are an endless dance of possibility. For the Dreams and Nightmares who are born, live and die here, it is impossible to change."

"How much does it cost to change who you are?" George said.

"You can't buy yourself into something different. It's not about money. You change your shape by the actions you take and the choices you make. You become what you do. Be brave when you are afraid, make the right choices even if they are hard, take the right actions even if everyone is against it. Do that and you'll become exactly who you need to be."

"How long does that take?" Speedy asked.

"Could take a night, could take years. Depends on how fearless you are. Bravery is the key to becoming who you need to be."

A hammer blast shook the hall, and orange sparks swirled upwards like pods on the wind. A pair of neon signs buzzed to life above the two archways positioned across from each other on the topmost tier of the rotunda. One said "Nightmares" and the other said "Dreams".

"It begins," Badger said, as a young man in pyjamas walked sleepily up the three steps and onto the round marble platform. He was busy looking at his phone and didn't seem to even know where he was. Suddenly, he looked around and caught sight of the giant. A gasp of terror escaped from his mouth as the giant's hammer came down upon his head with a mighty thud, obliterating the young man completely.

The Perkins children expected a pool of blood, and a man flattened like a crushed drinks can, but the man was still there – except now he was dressed in a suit and had the head of a chimpanzee.

Instantly, and with mechanical precision, the crane grabbed him gently but firmly in her long yellow beak. As she lifted him into the air, her pure white downy feathers changed into a coat of tiny bright lights and little bells, flashing a rainbow of colours and joyously chiming. Turning crisply, she deposited him under the neon sign that read "Nightmares", and once again her feathers turned pure white.

"He's going to be a Nightmare?"

"The Station Dreamers have chosen," Badger said. "He will be a Nightmare until he is shaped again. Like I said, how long that takes depends on him. How brave he is. Remember: change awaits those who seek it. It's possible."

The Station Dreamer turned towards them, his massive fist gripping his iron hammer. From inside her hoodie, Rose, sensing Nell's fear, let out a nervous song.

"It's okay, Mum," Nell said. And then, "Are we really going to be shaped?"

"Maybe," Badger said honestly, his eyes studying the giant's hammer. "Truth is, I can't really tell you. I deal in Sleepers. I've never taken fully awake human children into the Dreamlands before. Maybe you'll be shaped, maybe you'll be crushed; either way, there's no avoiding the hammer. You can't get on the train any other way. But I am pretty sure it won't hurt too badly."

There was another CLANG as a hammer came down and Rose flew out of Nell's hoodie.

"Mum!" Nell shouted. She turned and took off after her. Walking through the station towards them was a Dreamer. Like the others she was a giant. The giant woman's beautiful gown and entire body were made completely of mirrors. Nell knew at once she did not like her. The woman had the look of a cruel queen. Her mirrored face was cold, haughty and indifferent. Around her stood a gaggle of tuxedoed servants who didn't come higher than her knee. They ran alongside and were busy polishing and dusting her mirrored dress.

"Mum!" Nell yelled again as Rose flew directly into the

Mirror Dreamer's side. Nell expected Rose to smash against the mirror, but instead she disappeared. Without thinking Nell leapt after her. Her hands hit the side of the Mirror Dreamer and vanished as if she had dunked them into a lake. Nell tried to get free, tried to pull away, but could not. She felt a hard tug.

"No," she screamed and watched her own face, eyes wide in fear, as her entire body was pulled towards the Mirror Dreamer's skirt and was sucked inside.

For a moment all was bright light. She was blinded by the glare and then she heard someone calling to her. It was Badger.

"Here," Badger yelled, but where he meant by "here" was impossible to determine, because now there were millions of Badgers and, Nell realized, millions of Nells, Speedys, Georges and Pinches as well. They had multiplied. All of them had been split into an infinite number of themselves in all shapes and sizes.

"Where am I?" Speedy moaned. Nell felt her brother's warm breath on her cheek, and the illusion was broken. She turned and grabbed his large sweaty hand and squeezed it tight. They had not multiplied but were in a land of mirrors.

"Just breathe," Badger instructed. "You'll find yourself soon enough."

After a few deep breaths, the world before them became clear. It was countryside, and a lovely one at that, filled with tall, leafy trees, a lazy river and a sloping meadow of wildflowers, but every surface was made from a mirror. Everywhere you looked you saw your face. Nell saw it in the blades of grass at her feet and in the trunks of the trees beside her. Rose appeared.

"Come here at once," Nell said sternly. Rose tweeted happily as if telling Nell to relax. That it was not a big deal.

Typical, Nell thought. *Never afraid.* Rose flew around her head a few more times and then disappeared inside Nell's hoodie.

"Where are we?" George asked.

"We are inside the Mirror Dreamer," Badger replied.

"Inside? How?"

"Dreamers are worlds unto themselves," Badger explained. "Travelling inside them is risky but sometimes necessary. Once inside a Dreamer, it is easy to lose yourself. It is hard to tell what is real and what is not real. What you fear will find you, but remember there is always a way out. A simple door. Discover it and you will once again be where you belong. But listen to Pinch now. She will get us out."

"Hands on me!" Pinch commanded. "Keep one hand on me at all times. If you get scared or confused, don't run. Just take deep breaths and be still. Stillness will free you."

"Yeah, that sounds great and all for you," George said, "but if I get lost, I'm running."

"George!" Nell scolded, lifting her hand off Pinch to shake her finger at him. It was Rose's gesture, not hers, and she didn't know why she did it, but she did.

"Nell!" Pinch yelled.

Feeling she had to make her point, Nell said to George, "You'll do what you're told."

"You're told! You're told! You're told! You're told!"

The words echoed loudly, coming from a million of Nell's mouths, splashed across a million different surfaces – trees, clouds, grass, barns. Nell's head began to spin. Who was she? Where was she? She glanced up. An infinite number of Badgers were holding up *The Fearless Travellers' Guide*, reading: "Up over the next rise is a gate to freedom. You can't miss it."

"Gate?" Nell asked. Her voice sounded far away.

"Of course," Badger smiled. "Follow me."

"Shouldn't it be a door?"

"Door?" Badger's voice grew cold and familiar, and all at once Nell was no longer looking at Badger but at the master of *devilartkia* herself.

"Hello, Nell," Freyja Skoll said. Nell's eyes darted across the mirrored landscape, searching for any sign of Badger and her brothers, but they had vanished. Instead, everywhere she looked she saw the queen of the Dark Daughters and her ragged little child. Fenn held a jagged knife in her hand, and her tattered dress fluttered in the wind. Freyja Skoll stood beside her, still as a statue. In her hand, she held a long, pointed needle. Testing the end, she slid it into her pale finger and a drop of dark, cherry-coloured blood bubbled to the surface.

"You can't escape us. We are the Dark Daughters," Freyja Skoll explained, holding up the needle, which now appeared everywhere, a drop of blood quivering on its tip. Nell was too frightened to speak. "Now give Fenn my bird, before I lose my temper!"

"She's not yours," Nell said, finding her voice. "She's my mother."

"You're confused," Freyja Skoll said, her voice gentle and understanding. "Now give me my bird, or I will cut out your heart and Fenn will eat it!"

Fenn snarled, showing her tiny pointed teeth, which looked quite ready for the job.

Without thinking, Nell began to run, but everywhere she ran, she saw Fenn sliding towards her on every surface. Suddenly, a flaming needle whooshed past Nell's face, shattering the side of a mirrored tree. Rose was tweeting wildly in her ear, and then she remembered Badger's advice to be still. It was just like seeing an inner animal. She had to remember that she was fine and she could handle it. Nell stopped, making her body as rigid as she could.

"I am Nell Perkins, and I am still," she whispered, as was her habit when her heart pumped out of her chest. In that instant, a simple wooden door that she had not seen before swung open on the side of a tree. Light poured from the door and a strong hand reached out, grabbed hold of her hoodie, and yanked her. Nell tumbled out of the Mirror Dreamer's dress and found herself standing on one of the crowded outdoor train platforms of the Way Station. Badger, Pinch and her brothers were there. Her whole body was shivering and sweat dotted her face. Her brothers threw themselves around her, hugging her tightly.

"One second you were there, and the next second you were gone," Nell said, confused.

"We searched for you for hours," Speedy said.

"And you know how I feel about hiking!" George added. "Hate it!"

"Hours? No, it was only a few seconds, and Freyja Skoll was there," Nell said.

"If she was, you wouldn't be here," Badger grunted. "The Dreamlands, from the Sweetlands to the Wicked Places, are all realms of confusion," Badger told them. "Inside time gets twisted. Hours might pass like minutes, and minutes like years. It is only by the Mirror Dreamer's grace that you found your way out. Luckily she deposited us on the platform so we could fetch you out."

Nell felt a shiver at her brush with what surely would have been death. Across the platform, the Mirror Dreamer was watching her. Nell whispered, "Thank you" to her, and she bowed her head with silent grace.

CHAPTER 14

Nell scanned the platform. Being outside in the crisply cold night air and looking up at the immense sky, it became clear for the first time that Nell was no longer in the world that she had thought, up until a few days ago, was the only one that existed. She was in the Dream World. A rush of excitement filled her and Nell gazed around in wonder trying to see every bit of it. To take it all in at once.

The sky here was different. It was an immense cobalt-blue that wasn't tranquil, but shifted slowly like the ocean. And floating in the darkness were billions of bright stars and comets that raced across the expanse, leaving sizzling golden trails in their curved wakes. Nell and her brothers were on the edge of a new world, and at any moment would be on an ancient, mystical train, travelling deep inside a place most people never saw with eyes open.

A deep bell began to toll, and all talking on the platform died away.

"All of you straighten up and look respectable. No fidgeting," Pinch whispered, like a teacher warning her class. "The Night Train is arriving."

As the bell tolled, the mist around the platform began to disappear. "Where is the track?" Nell asked anxiously.

"There is no track."

"No track!" George screamed. "Trains have tracks. They're the bread and butter of the transportation world."

"You're not in the world any more," Badger said. "You're in the Dream World."

"If there is no track," Nell asked with a growing dread, "where does it stop?"

"It doesn't," Badger replied with a great booming laugh.

"I repeat. You are crazy!" George screamed, and he told Nell that he had better hold her hand in case *she* got freaked out.

Off in the distance, Nell could see a long ribbon of blue flame, bright as a streak of lightning. It raced across the sky in a graceful slither, filling the air with the electric sizzle of a lit fuse. The children were silent. Rose had poked her head out of Nell's hoodie, and even she watched in wide-eyed awe.

Something is coming, Nell thought. Something great and powerful. Nell had the strangest feeling. *I've been here before.*

Their awe vanished and was replaced by a shivering fear as the band of light, like a missile finding its target, turned and headed straight towards them. The hum grew louder, chattering their teeth and jangling their every nerve.

"Steady," Badger instructed, not taking his eyes off the oncoming light.

"You stay steady!" George shouted, trying to run, but Nell held his hand tight.

The Night Train's headlights grew softer as a horn blast filled the air. Now the children saw it clearly, and what they saw made them gasp. Flying at them with immense speed was not the front of a train but simply the head of a woman. Not a sculpture, but an actual face that reached from the wheels to the top of the train. It was a good four and a half metres high and very much alive, but above all it was the kindest, wisest and altogether most beautiful and loving face they had ever seen.

The skin of the woman – in fact, the entire body of the train – appeared to be flawless polished chrome, but then the chrome pulsed and changed, becoming the dark bark and green moss of an ancient tree. It pulsed again, and the outside of the train was made from the roiling waves of a dark sea. It pulsed again, becoming the skin of a snake. It pulsed a final time and was made not of metal but of glowing neon.

"I am the Night Train. Welcome aboard." Her voice was soft and loving, and Nell wasn't sure if she had heard it in her ears or in her head. With a final deafening horn blast, the train passed over them like a frothing wave crashing upon their heads. Within the blink of an eye, Nell and her brothers were no longer on the train platform, but inside the train walking along the aisle of the carriage.

The interior of the train was a fancy jewel box of a space, garlanded with twinkling strings of coloured lights and seats plush with cushions of soft purple velvet. It hummed with activity: a knight in golden armour strolled in through the doors from the next carriage with his dragon, followed by an astronaut in a spacesuit.

"Look!" Speedy said, pointing. Over the normal row of seats was a long, hand-carved wooden shelf that stretched the entire length of the carriage on both sides. The shelf was not for bags but contained an identical row of tiny seats, and in those seats were passengers who were not people or animals, but insects – ladybirds, grasshoppers and elegant praying mantises. Most were wearing clothes and acting like people – talking on phones, playing cards, reading the paper.

"Just because they wear clothes doesn't mean I can't stomp on them, right?" George asked.

"Sit," Badger snarled, pointing to a booth beside a window. The children settled into the booth while Pinch sat upright in the aisle. Seated behind them were two apple trees with calm, ancient faces rising out from their brown bark. The trees stared at Nell and nodded politely.

"What do you think?" Badger asked Nell.

"It's fantastic." Nell smiled, starting to feel relaxed. You could not help but feel safe inside the train. Nell looked outside. Beyond the window, twinkling silver trails of starlight raced alongside as they vaulted faster and faster through untold vastness.

Enormous, glittering animals made completely of stars suddenly appeared and then disappeared into the darkness as if they were slipping in and out of curtains on a stage. Coyotes, hawks and a pair of elks, large as cruise ships, leapt past the window. It looked as if they were scattering, running from something even more enormous. Suddenly Nell saw what they were running from.

"What is that?" she gasped breathlessly. She wanted to scream – not in fear, but in complete joy. For it was a whale made of stars, with a long, twisted tusk on its forehead. His light was deeper and brighter than the other animals, and looking at it filled Nell with a surging feeling of utter happiness.

"That is the Star Dreamer," Badger said as the creature slapped its tail, sending the darkness around it rippling like water, and dived into its depths. As it disappeared, Nell leapt to the window, stung by the loss.

"WAIT!" she yelled and suddenly realized her skin was itchy. She began to scratch the back of her neck. "Are you itchy?" she asked her brothers, but then realized she didn't care, for even more overpowering than the itchy feeling was the smell that began tickling her nose, as though trays of food were being carried past.

So sweet, Nell thought. *I need a bite. I need some right now. I'm so hungry. I want to crunch it. To gobble it. Where is it?*

Nell's eyes darted towards the door. She saw nothing, and this made it worse, as though it were being hidden from her. Anger surged through her. Her teeth tingled with the thought of snapping down and ripping into a tasty bit of meat. The hunger was driving her mad. She had to have it. All of it. And anyone who tried to get in her way would feel her teeth.

"Nell!" Speedy yelled.

Nell turned to her brother and was overcome with confusion. A large black bear was sitting beside her, dressed in her brother's clothes. Nell gasped in surprise as a growl cut through the air. In George's place sat a human-sized rat wearing his clothes.

"What's happening to us?" the rat said in George's most quiet and terrified voice.

"I'm just having a moment," Nell answered. Never in her life had she seen her brother's inner animals. In any other moment the shock might have stopped her in her tracks. George was a rat. Speedy a bear. It would have been a terrible and wonderful thing to see. But at this instant all Nell could think of was the delicious smell. Beneath Nell's sweatshirt, Rose was fluttering wildly. She lifted her hand to calm her mother and gasped in horror. Her hand was no longer a hand but an animal's paw, covered in sleek silver fur and tipped with curved, razor-sharp claws.

"You are not having a moment, Nell," Badger said. "You

don't have moments in the Dreamlands." He was still sitting in the seat across from her, watching her and her brothers change into animals, his face completely calm.

"But they're animals," Nell said.

"So are you," Speedy answered.

Frightened, Nell jumped up. In the reflection of the train window was a fox with silver fur wearing her hoodie and her jeans.

"I'm dreaming," she blurted. "I don't have an inner animal."

"No. This is happening," Badger explained, his brow furrowed as if the answer to a difficult maths problem were finally coming to him but not quite there yet. "I didn't know what would happen bringing humans onto the Night Train, but now it makes sense. You weren't shaped in the station so you are being shaped now." He knew what to do at once. He reached into one of his pockets. In a moment he held out his fist and opened it. Inside his palm were three small, ordinary-looking stones. "These are spirit stones. Take them, and you'll come back to yourselves."

Speedy reached out his large bear paw and George his rat hand, but Nell did not. The instant the boys took hold of the stones, they returned to their human forms. Nell was still standing, a silver fox, amber eyes darting furiously, nose twitching. Turning back into Nell did not interest her at the present moment. What interested her now was eating.

"But what's that smell?" Nell growled, her voice deep and crazed with hunger.

"Take the stone," Badger now insisted firmly.

"It's her," Nell said, suddenly knowing where the smell was coming from. The scents of the train sorted themselves instantly, like marbles rolling into holes, until only one smell remained: the scent of bird flesh. Quick as the slash of a knife, Nell batted the stone out of Badger's hand. It flew across the train and clattered into the aisle. Nell unzipped her hoodie, which disappeared at her touch, her last bit of humanness gone.

Rose, sensing danger and smelling a fox, gave a tweet of alarm and flew, desperate to escape. Nell, thinking of nothing but her need to crunch and gobble the bird, dropped to all fours and darted after her mother.

"NELL!" Speedy screamed.

The train erupted into chaos as Nell sprang after Rose, chasing her down the aisle. Her brain seemed split in two. On one hand, everything was happening in slow motion. Nell was aware of herself as a fox on the hunt, felt all her senses a hundred times more powerfully than ever before, urging her on with an ancient hunger. Her vision was crisp and clear. Even as she ran, darting quickly between riders, slipping under seats, weaving between legs, she could see the strands in the fabric of the clothes all around her, hear the squeak of seats as people leapt away from her, and see the drumming rain of spilled drinks. In an instant, Nell learned how to sort through the ocean of sensation that now flowed through her in one unified rush. She wanted to stop, wanted to change back to Nell, but didn't know how. It was as though she were locked in a room, and on the other side of the wall she could hear the sound of her brothers screaming for her. Nell wanted to answer them but couldn't, for there was another voice inside her as well. A dark voice, which didn't just speak, it commanded. *Crunch the bird. Crunch it between your sharp teeth and eat it all. You need it!*

"I need it," Nell repeated, her voice a deep growl.

Rose flew wildly through the carriage, and the silver fox was dashing fast, not going straight for her, but passing behind in quick diagonals. Nell pushed the small bird forward like a seasoned hunter, exhausting her, confusing her, until she fled towards the window and hit it hard. Rose tumbled to the floor, stunned and helpless. Nell saw her moment to pounce! The thought flashed across her mind that she should stop, that eating this bird wasn't right. But the dark voice snarled a command: *EAT!*

The dark voice needed to be followed. Nell couldn't stop, didn't want to stop. And with a growl, she leapt for the trembling bird.

Nell's jaws were open wide, her sharp, glistening fangs ready to crunch the shivering bird where it lay in the aisle when, like a flash of light, a great panther darted into her path. With a butt of her black head, the panther knocked Nell's jaws shut. Nell tumbled down the aisle, and before she knew it, Badger was kneeling before her, his strong hand on her throat, pinning her to the floor. Nell snarled and snapped, a wild animal mad with rage.

"I got you, my skittery pigeon. I got you," Badger said with deep tenderness and absolutely no fear. With his free hand, he placed the spirit stone between her fierce amber-coloured eyes, and right away Nell returned to her human form. Badger removed his hand with care. Nell stumbled up slowly as grief, fear, confusion and embarrassment burst upon her all at once. A few passengers were staring, but most seemed oblivious to what had just passed. Two angels in shimmering gowns with swan-white wings folded neatly behind them smiled warm smiles of reassurance, but were otherwise perfectly still.

Speedy and George rushed over. Speedy threw his arms around Nell and buried his head in her shoulder as George punched her gently several times with a mixture of fear and slight sympathy. No one could talk, but it didn't matter because Nell wasn't even paying attention to them.

"Where's Mum?" Nell asked, her eyes desperately searching the carriage.

"Over here, child." The voice was so loud and deep that it seemed to cause the entire train to rumble. It belonged to one of the apple trees seated behind them. In his branches sat Rose, half-hidden among the leaves. Nell turned to her mother and froze, embarrassed by what had happened.

"Call her," Badger insisted. "Call her now."

Nell hesitated, gripped by a sudden fear. "But what if she doesn't come?"

"She will. I promise you."

"What if she thinks I'm going to eat her?"

"You normally eat live birds?"

"You know what I mean."

"Call her, because if she doesn't come to you, this mission is over. You know that, don't you?"

Nell did. If Rose was scared of her, they could never carry her to meet Ravenhead, could never change her back into their mother and return home as a family.

Standing in the centre aisle of the Night Train, Nell held out her palm and gave a nervous, cracked whistle. With a lilting trill, Rose leapt from her perch in the branches of the apple tree and flew over the passengers, a bright flash of gold and red feathers, slipping between knights and angels and animals to land on Nell's outstretched hand.

Nell could hardly put into words how awful she felt that, after all they had been through, she had nearly eaten her. "I'm sorry."

"Don't be," said Badger, giving Rose a pat with one finger.

She tweeted happily. "Mistakes happen to all travellers. They are the stones of the path of every journey. You will fail."

"That's loser talk," George said.

"But, Nell," Badger continued. "You will rise."

They returned to their seats. Nell held Rose gently in her cupped hands, her red head and bright eyes staring out happily. The feel of her mother's tiny heartbeat fluttering quietly against her fingers settled her jangled nerves.

"How could I try to eat her?" Nell said, almost to herself. "My own mother."

"You are not your shape and your shape is not you," Badger explained. "It is only how you appear at the moment."

"But why?" Nell said, frightened at how easy it was to forget, to slip into a dark place and do the worst things in the entire world. "Why are we shaped and sorted in the first place?"

"Why? There are a million theories, but Fearless Travellers believe that you are shaped and sorted for one reason only" – Badger lowered his voice – "to remember."

"Remember what?"

"To remember who you really are, unleash your true shape. Only when you find your own truth does the confusion of this world drop away. After that you can travel anywhere without doubt, rise when you fall, and, most of all, find your way home."

"Shape," George said, smacking his hand against the wall to make sure he had everyone's attention. "You want to talk about shapes? I'm a rat!"

"Looks that way," Badger said and added with a chuckle, "rat boy."

"No!" George shouted. "No way."

"Listen, kid," Badger said. "You could have been a slug or a flea or a clam, but you're not. You're a rat – one of the smartest, toughest, strongest creatures ever. They can't be tamed, can escape anything, eat anything and survive where everyone else dies, and best of all – and I know you'll like this part – they scare the hell out of people."

As Badger talked, George brightened. "I'm a rat!" he said, warming to the idea.

"I'm a bear?" said Speedy in wonder.

"Now that makes sense," George said. "Especially when he uses the bathroom. If you know what I mean." Speedy gave his brother a punch and turned to his sister.

"And Nell, you're a–"

"Shut up," Nell said, cutting him off. "For one second, just be quiet." Even though Badger was trying to convince them it was okay, she didn't want to think about it, now or ever.

"There is nothing wrong with your shape, Nell Perkins," Badger said. "It is perfect."

"I almost ate my mother!" Nell fumed at the thought that it could happen at any time. "Any second I could turn back. I could do it again. I could be a killer." Nell suddenly felt like an innocent person being sentenced to a long stretch in a fetid prison.

"You did what foxes do," Pinch said simply, as though Nell were being ridiculous.

"I didn't do anything. It did. It took control of me."

"Because you are awake in the Dreamlands. Your shape is fighting to take control of who you are. But the cure is easy, Nell. When you feel yourself starting to change, just touch one of these spirit stones. Simple as that, you'll be back to yourself," Badger said, handing each of the children half a dozen small stones. They put them in their pockets.

"What if we lose them?" asked Speedy, who had a long history of losing anything important.

"Don't!" Pinch replied.

"I already did," Speedy said sheepishly, looking around for his stones.

The darkness outside began to fade, replaced by the morning sunlight, and out of the formless darkness a world came into focus. The train was racing over an ocean of the most beautiful, clear blue water Nell had ever seen. It seemed as if you could look straight to the bottom, but there was no bottom. Colourful fish, giant turtles, dolphins and moon jellyfish flitted by. Floating on the ocean beneath a crystal-blue sky were islands of the deepest green. They were thick with ancient trees. On some of the islands Nell could make out coloured houses nestled in the hills.

"The Sweetlands," Pinch purred softly. "The land of sweet dreams." Nell and her brothers all had their faces to the window now. The world before them was endless and bathed with golden light, soft and warm. It was the light of the playground and the light shining through butterfly wings. It was the shimmer on a lake waiting for you as you flung yourself off a dock into the cold velvety deep. It was the flashes of brightness reflecting off a chrome counter in an ice cream parlour on a boiling summer day. The warm and inviting light covered everything, and looking at it Nell knew it had always been this way and it always would be.

A long, low horn sounded, alerting passengers that the train was approaching a station.

"Get ready," Badger said. "Crypt approaches."

CHAPTER 15

The speed of the train was increasing. The children could feel it in their whole bodies. Rose began to rub her soft head against Nell's cheek like a gentle nudge to ask the question all were thinking.

"Why aren't we slowing down?" Nell asked. Then with a little quiver in her voice, she added, "We can't pull into the station at this speed."

"Trust the train," Badger grunted.

All felt a tightening in their chests. Ears popped and stomachs dropped. The train, it seemed, was plummeting.

"What's happening?" Nell said, finding it hard to even speak.

"I hope you have insurance!" George screamed.

"We're…" was all Badger could get out, for the next moment, the children found themselves standing in the middle of a great red sand desert, a brilliant blue sky dotted overhead with clouds. The train was nowhere in sight.

"Here," Badger finished.

"I don't like that," Speedy said. "I like a train station where you stop, get off, go to a vending machine sort of train station. Don't you, Nell? The vending machine kind."

Nell didn't answer, for she was riveted to what she saw at the end of the desert. Rising in the distance far into the sky was not a city, but a tightly closed rosebud, tall as a mountain. The green sides of the towering flower bud vibrated in the waves of heat. Badger and Pinch shot each other a concerned glance. Something was wrong.

"What is it?" Nell asked, staring at the colossal flower bud.

"That is the city of Dreamdon," Badger huffed.

"That's a city?" Speedy asked, rubbing his eyes. "Because all I see is a closed-up flower."

"I thought we were going to Crypt," Nell said, "to see the Bird Dreamer."

"That was our intention, but the Night Train doesn't always take you where you want to go, but places you where you need to be."

"Seriously," George huffed, "that is no way to run a transportation system. And besides, we are not even there. I mean, at least stop IN the city!"

"That is a city, a great and unforgettable city," Badger answered, turning to the children. "And like all truly great cities, it is part magic and part magnet. It will soon open up, take hold of us and draw us in. We will be part of it whether we like it or not."

For a moment, nothing happened; they were just standing in the hot sun of a desert staring at the green head of a closed rosebud. The faint scent of roses tickled their faces as the ground began to rumble beneath their feet. With the sound of a great exhalation, the bud began to twist slowly open, the massive green walls bowing down, stretching languidly across the desert floor and revealing a golden city glimmering inside.

"Whoa!" Speedy said, echoing what they each felt.

The skyline before them wasn't just the skyline of one particular city, but that of every great city from the beginning of time. Before them lay streamlined skyscrapers of polished chrome, spiralling towers of sea stone and intricate golden pagodas. These rubbed against columned temples of carved marble, castles that were encased in their own mists and buildings from a far-off future made of flickering neon beams of light. And all were woven together in one perfectly balanced shape, as though the golden city weren't a collection of buildings but a single living entity.

They had just a moment to take the city in from a distance, for the next instant, they were being pulled towards it. Their bodies tingled. Their eyes grew wide and in an instant they were inside it, standing on a bustling street corner with grand buildings looming over them.

"Now that," George said happily, "is service."

"Welcome to Dreamdon," Badger said and swung his arms wide proudly. "Capital of the Sweetlands."

"It's beautiful," Nell said. And so it was. The sun was warm, the air crisp and clean, and the world smelled of a delicious combination of frying bacon, maple syrup, wood smoke and freshly cut grass. The pavement was wide and lined with lush trees in full bloom, which dappled the bright sunshine and cast a net of delicate shadows across the concrete. Rising between the thatch-roofed pubs were swooping modern buildings of curved silver. Rambling, wooden row houses with metal porches rested beside stately mansions. Flying cars shared the street with horse-drawn carriages, racing cars, bicycles and flying surfboards.

Nell, Speedy and George tossed their heads this way and that, interrupting each other with points and shouts and shoves as they tried to share all that was happening around them. The only word that seemed suitable was "Whoa", and they used it over and over again until Badger gave a sharp whistle and pointed down the street.

"Quickly," he commanded. "We must find out why we are here in Dreamdon and not in Crypt."

Rose was tweeting wildly.

"Is it all right if I let her out?" Nell asked.

"Can you trust her?"

"Of course I can," Nell said confidently, but inside, she was worried. Rose was wriggling. She wouldn't be cooped up any longer. "All right," Nell said. "Hold on."

Nell undid her hoodie, letting her bright, silver-yellow hair tumble down, and out from the strands popped Rose. Her head moved side to side, taking in all the sights, and with a happy song, she flew around the small party several times and then landed on Nell's shoulder, where she stayed quite happily.

"Follow me," Badger said, quickly leading the children through the growing crowd of creatures strolling down the street. At the next corner, the crowd was so thick, they could no longer move. Pinch snarled and cleared the way as Badger hustled the children to the very edge of the pavement and peered out. Across the street, the glut of crowd was the same, as though a parade were happening.

A thundering trumpet blast filled the air. From around the corner came an old-fashioned marching band made up of humans and oversized animals. All the marchers wore crisp red uniforms and held bright brass instruments to their lips. On their heads rested top hats made of burning orange flames.

"The News Dreamer approaches," Badger said to Pinch.

"Is that good?" Nell asked.

"I don't know yet. But if nothing else, it will tell us why we're here."

BOOM! BOOM! BOOM!

The street shook with earth-pounding footsteps. The sound was unmistakable – something massive was walking their way. Every creature in the crowd turned its head towards the approaching noise. Following behind the marching band came an enormous, pale horse, large as a parade float. Tendrils of smoke swirled around the frightening creature, which seemed to be a living, breathing shadow.

Riding on the horse was a giant tin sculpture of a man in a three-piece suit, and riding on the sculpture, on a small platform jutting from its forehead, was a distinguished-looking man. The man sat at a modern news desk like a reporter on television.

"Good evening, and welcome to the Nightly News," the man said, his clear newsreader voice ringing out into the crisp autumn air. "Our top story. Ravenhead declares war on the Dark Daughters!" Suddenly, the suit of the tin sculpture flashed to life with hundreds of images as if the fabric were made of video screens. Terrible footage of war and explosions and flying birds of all types covered every centimetre of the sculpture in a horrible collage. The images then cut to video of the beautiful and merciless face of Freyja Skoll, who was standing in a snow-swept plain beside an octopus with a wolf's face. The octopus was the size of a horse and saddled for riding. Nell recognized the creature at once. It had tried to attack her the night her mother had been taken by the cloud. That it belonged to Freyja Skoll made Nell hate her even more.

The News Dreamer's voice rang out sharp and clear. "The Bird Dreamer claims that Freyja Skoll, the headless queen of the Dark Daughters, has been stealing birds, a claim which she denies."

"Headless," Nell whispered in surprise. Of course. Nell had seen her inner animal. A shiver went down her spine at the thought that the woman's beautiful face didn't actually exist.

"She lost it years ago," Badger whispered back. "Her whole life and this war are about getting it back," he continued and nodded to the screens.

"Stealing birds! That is simply ridiculous," the thousand faces of Freyja Skoll, blared from every video screen, scoffed with the polished calm of a trained politician. "Everyone knows that the Treaty of the Veil, signed after the Lullaby War, prevents the Dark Daughters from performing our traditional hunts. This slander does not suit the Bird Dreamer in the least. I promise you, no Dark Daughter has left Vazencrack for two hundred years. Our days of hunting are over. We are a peaceful tribe of Nightmares dedicated to health and craft."

"LIAR!" Nell screamed. She held Rose in her cupped hands, the bird's tiny body trembling as she began to tweet. Nell pulled up her hoodie and placed Rose beside her neck, where she settled down. Around her, people shushed Nell as everyone was focused on the video of Freyja Skoll.

"But that said," Freyja Skoll continued, her voice now dripping with menace, "if the Bird Dreamer wants war, he will have it. And rest assured, we have not been idle over the last two hundred years since the Lullaby War ended. We have weapons beyond reckoning. Weapons that will wipe the Dreamlands clean of the Bird Dreamer and every beak and feather at his command!"

Freyja Skoll disappeared, and the video screens flashed to images of a man with the head of a raven. He was sitting cross-legged at the top of a leafless tree that rose from a foggy graveyard.

"Is that Ravenhead?" Nell asked, suddenly feeling frightened. Even on a screen, Ravenhead was terrifying to look at. His eyes seethed with a cruel intensity, and his feathers were dark as tar.

"That is one of his many forms. His most powerful form is that of a pure black raven, and that form can't be captured on camera. Pray you never see him like that. They say one glance will cause you to burst into flames."

The News Dreamer began to announce again, and the screens flashed to a graphic of a boiling cauldron.

"Despite Freyja Skoll's claims that she has done nothing wrong, last night at the stroke of midnight, Ravenhead officially announced a Ghost Stew in Crypt to celebrate the beginning of the war. The Night Train has suspended service to Crypt, so Ravenhead is paying for a single charter of his own train. They are calling it the Death Express. This will be the only train available for those who want to travel to Nevermore Hall and witness the first Ghost Stew in a generation. Dreams and Nightmares from all corners have been desperate to find a token for the train, with some tokens fetching millions of pounds."

With that, the screens on the sculpture went dark, and the giant horse began to walk again. At once, the crowd began chattering and breaking apart, all filled with dread and terrible excitement at the oncoming war.

"This way, children," Badger said and hurried the children into a small café to escape the jostling crowd.

CHAPTER 16

A s they passed through the fogged glass doors of the café, the children suddenly found themselves in a lovely forest grove. Thick birches, oaks and magnolias spread out over the space, their branches entwined to make a canopy, from which paper lanterns hung, softly glowing.

Groups of people sat around long, hand-carved tables eating food and drinking coffee. A band played. Musicians strumming banjos and guitars stood on a small stage as a woman sang a waltzing country song. A scruffy young man in glasses rode up to them on an antique bicycle. He was barefoot and wore rolled-up jeans, a green velvet waistcoat with no shirt underneath and a wide-brimmed hat with a large feather sticking out.

"You folks eating?" he asked.

"I only eat at places where people wear shirts," George snorted.

"I am," Speedy shouted, and then clarified, "I mean, I am eating. Not wearing a shirt, which I am. I am wearing a shirt. I mean, I'm eating."

"All right," the man said slowly, not sure what to make of them.

"He's hungry," Nell explained.

"Then he's in the right place."

The scruffy young man led the children to a table made from a giant mushroom that was surrounded by deep, soft chairs into which they all gratefully collapsed. Nell was thankful to be out of the crowd. Badger recognized a man standing at the bar and left the children with Pinch. As he walked towards the bar, Badger whispered to a waitress, who nodded, and next thing the children knew, she was placing steaming cups of hot chocolate and a plate of éclairs and hot rolls before them. Her brothers dived in and ate with gusto, but Nell was not hungry. Instead, she broke off a piece of a roll, broke it into tiny pieces, and placed it on the table for Rose, who flew out of Nell's hoodie and began to peck at the crumbs.

"What's a Ghost Stew?" Nell asked Pinch.

"A Ghost Stew is the Potion Dreamer's spell. Dreamers come in and out of this world. They don't die, but they pass on to another place. The only way to bring them back is by making a Ghost Stew. Only the Potion Dreamer knows who will rise from his pot, and the Dreamer he brings out of its dark depths can change the course of events for good or evil."

"Why does everyone want to go?" Nell asked.

"Free food," Speedy said. "Who wouldn't want to go?"

"Beats hanging out in this dump," George complained.

"Dump?" Nell said. "You're in the most fantastic city ever, and you're eating éclairs."

"No sprinkles." George humphed. "An éclair without a sprinkle is a snobby roll."

"Is he done?" Pinch said. George nodded that he was finished complaining, and Pinch continued. "The reason all want to go to the Ghost Stew is this and this alone. Powers and wishes are bestowed on those who watch. It can change a Dream into a Nightmare, a Nightmare into a Dream and all into Dreamers. They are sacred events that happen only once every hundred years or so. Each one is legend."

"So we can't get there," Nell said, realizing the situation they were now in. "I mean, the only way to see Ravenhead now is to get to Crypt, and you need a token that is impossible to find."

"Not any more," Badger boomed. He was standing over them, a mischievous grin on his face. "According to my sources, there is one token left for the Death Express, and I know where it is."

"The token shop?" Speedy said, licking his fingers.

"Two minor Dreamers are fighting to win the last token in all of the Dreamlands."

"You're not serious!" Pinch said, knowing full well where this was going.

"I didn't finish. It is the Moustache Dreamer. He is fighting the Typewriter Dreamer, who, if you remember, owes me a favour and might let me take his place."

"No!" Pinch said. "Duke. No!"

"I'm doing it. It is the only way."

"What is?" Nell said desperately.

"I will fight the Moustache Dreamer and get the token. We will never make it to Crypt otherwise."

"You're going to do that for us?" Nell said, feeling humbled that this man whom she hardly knew was willing to fight for their family.

"Once this war starts, it might drag on for hundreds of years. You won't have another chance to see Ravenhead after tonight. So if we want to save your mother, we go to Crypt, or return home with her as a bird," Badger explained.

"He'll be killed," Pinch snarled at Nell. "You want to live with that?"

"No," Nell said to Badger. "We can't let you do it."

"I don't remember asking either of you for permission," Badger said gruffly. "My vow is to help those who asked for my help. I'm not stopping because I might get killed. You want out, Pinch? There's the door."

For a moment, all were silent. Badger and Pinch stared at one another intensely, neither giving ground. The tension was thick and terrible.

"Please don't fight," Speedy moaned. "I hate it when people fight. I mean, you can fight someone else–"

"Someone with a moustache," George interrupted.

"–but not each other," Speedy commanded.

"The Moustache Dreamer always circles to the left," Pinch said knowingly. "You must fake right and then go left."

"Thank you." Badger nodded, understanding this was her way of giving in.

"Crosstown Chowder!" the scruffy young man said. He had returned holding a small wooden bowl on which a long loaf of warm French bread was balanced. In his other hand, he held a thick hunting knife. He placed the small bowl on the table.

"Spoons?" Speedy asked.

The scruffy young man didn't answer. Instead, he held up the bread and the knife and, working with confidence and artisanal skill, sliced through the bread lengthwise. Steam escaped from the inside, and crusty golden crumbs sprinkled down.

"Who's your friend?" the scruffy young man said, nodding at Rose as his hands continued to carve something fine and delicate out of the bread's bottom half.

"It's my mum," Nell answered.

"Right on." Unfazed, the scruffy young man nodded, and in a few more whittles of his knife, held out what looked like a tiny ladder and a canoe, both made out of the bottom half of the bread. He placed the ladder against the side of the bowl and the canoe inside the broth, where it bobbed on the surface.

"There you go. Crosstown Chowder," he said and placed a fresh sprig of rosemary on the canoe, anchoring it to the side of the bowl.

"Thank you," Badger said and, reaching into his pocket, pulled out several bright orange bills. The scruffy young man took the bills gratefully, placed them in his waistcoat pocket, and walked away.

"Nell, you first," Badger said, nodding to the tiny ladder that rested against the side of the bowl.

"I'm not hungry."

"This is not for eating, but for travelling. Crosstown Chowder. It is the fastest way to Neptune Beach, where the fights are being held."

"What?"

"Come on. Into the soup. Up the ladder, and when you get inside, hold both sides of the canoe. They tip easily."

"Into the soup?" Nell asked.

"You heard him," Pinch said. "Climb aboard; that canoe will soon get soggy and be worthless."

Nell looked at them both and suddenly began laughing, and soon her brothers joined in. "You're joking," she said. "For a moment I thought you were serious." She gave Badger a tender pat on his arm.

"I am."

"But—"

"Anything is possible to those who know how to use the Night. So just place your hand on the rungs and move quickly."

At once Nell knew this wasn't a joke; this was the

Dreamlands. Thinking it best to hide Rose for whatever was about to happen, she placed Rose inside her hoodie and turned to face the tiny ladder. Her fingers trembled as she touched the tiny rungs, and instantly she began to shrink. In the blink of an eye, Nell had shrunk to the size of a sugar cube. She was now standing on the table beside the large bowl, her hand on the tiny bread ladder that from her new height seemed as thick as though it were made of wood. She glanced up at her brothers, who were staring down at her like giants and, seeing no other choice, she climbed up the rungs of the ladder, up and over the edge of the bowl, and into the canoe carved from a loaf of bread.

As she settled into the canoe, Speedy and George followed, shrinking, scurrying up the ladder and climbing into the boat beside her.

"You okay?" Nell asked.

"I hate soup," Speedy answered glumly.

"Take a bite of the boat," George suggested.

"You'll do no such thing," Pinch said, leaping into the canoe, followed by Badger, who held tight to the sprig of rosemary.

"Spoon's here," Pinch said. They all glanced up. Standing over them was a spoon the size of a man. But now, since they were all the size of insects, the spoon appeared as tall as a skyscraper. Two bright eyes stared out from its silver face.

"Where are you going?" the spoon asked, his voice smooth as polished silver.

"Neptune Beach," Badger answered. The spoon nodded, then drew back and blew a long breath between his puckered lips. The powerful wind fluttered their clothes, churned up the broth and rocked the boat.

"Cut it out," George shouted. "I know some really tough forks!"

"What's he doing?" Nell said.

"He's doing what spoons do. Stirring things up," Badger said. "And delivering us."

All around them, the broth began to swirl in a swift circle, forming a whirlpool. The canoe rocked up and down as the current raced past. Badger eyed the centre of the whirlpool. He removed the sprig of rosemary, and the canoe shot out into the rushing rapids, curving around the side of the bowl towards the whirlpool.

The churning broth was in complete control of the small craft, sucking them towards the centre. Nell looked at her brothers. Both were silent and looked frightened. Like them, she had her hands clasped to the side of the canoe as a fine rosemary-scented mist sprayed all around them.

"Deep breath!" Badger shouted as the small craft reached the innermost ring of the whirlpool and tipped downwards into the abyss. "In case we capsize."

With a great tug, the boat shot deep down into the centre of the swirling liquid. Nell couldn't understand it. The bottom of the bowl, with its ancient painted face, was clearly visible. All they would do was smash into the bottom and be flung around in the soup and drown. Crashing waves and a great howl of screams filled Nell's ears. The canoe shot sharply downwards. Broth churned around them on all sides in a perfect ring, and for a moment, the small boat seemed not to be touching anything. It seemed to be floating through space. With a wallop, the front of the boat hit the bottom of the bowl, smashing straight into the mouth of Neptune.

But instead of crashing, the canoe passed into the mouth.

There was a wink of darkness, then a rushing breeze and slash of light as they realized they were no longer in a bowl of soup at all, but had somehow passed through to the outside world. They were now in the bright sunshine of the daylight.

"WHOOOO!!!" Speedy screamed in delight, as he was the first to realize where they were. The canoe was now sliding along the tracks of an old-fashioned wooden rollercoaster that looked out over the sea. With bracing speed, the canoe shot around the track, banked up a few great curves, and after a final plunge, slid to a stop where a bored-looking cheetah wearing an amusement park top and dark sunglasses sat on a stool, slurping a fizzy drink. He lazily pointed a clawed thumb towards the exit. "Watch your step," he mumbled, a phrase he clearly repeated without enthusiasm a thousand times a day.

"Here we are," Badger said. "Neptune Beach."

"Can we go again?" Speedy said.

"No!" Nell blurted loudly.

Nell and her brothers trailed Badger through the gates onto the boardwalk, still blinking at the bright sunshine. Nell's legs were wobbly, and her heart was beating furiously. Somewhere an accordion was playing. Carnival music drifted across the wide boardwalk. A warm, honey-coloured light shone over everything as though it were one of those endless, perfect, lazily happy, quietly tender, end-of-summer days that are always the most beautiful.

"I like it here," Nell said with a languid yawn, wishing they could just rest for a moment.

Most of the buildings on the boardwalk had turrets and porches and stained-glass windows. All were painted in pastel colours, old and faded from the sun and the sea. The boardwalk was filled with broken bits of sea glass that shimmered radiantly. The smell of the summer was everywhere – candy floss, popcorn, pizza and ice cream mixed with salty sea spray, the perfume of sunscreen and the dark scent of sticky tar. All together, it had a deep, beckoning power. Nell wanted to run into the ocean, to build castles in the sand, to bite on a candy necklace and feel the warm sun on her cheeks.

"Come on," Pinch snarled, butting her head against Nell's side.

It wasn't until then Nell realized she had stopped walking and was staring out longingly at the sea.

"Like I said," Badger cautioned, "the Dreamlands are places of confusion as well as beauty. It's especially easy to get lost here at the beach, to drift along in a sweet, soft summer that never ends."

The way he said it made Nell think that he had lost some time on this very beach. Then Nell thought of the one person who loved the beach more than any other place in the world.

"Mum would love this place," Speedy said, putting into words exactly what Nell had been thinking.

"Yeah," George agreed. "Take her out." Nell was already reaching her hand inside her hoodie. Rose came fluttering out, and with a happy chirp flew up into the sky and sped across the boardwalk, diving down and nibbling on fallen sprinkles and bits of smashed ice cream cones. She continued to fly close by, darting around their heads and then upwards, as if excitedly pointing things out. Rose loved to point things out, and Nell looked around, trying to take it all in.

"Promise we'll take her to the beach," Speedy said.

"What?"

"When this is over. After we cure Mum. We'll all go to the beach."

"Yes," Nell said. "I promise."

CHAPTER 17

The fight for the token that Badger was now determined to win was being held in Atlas Yards, a massive building that rose up at the end of the boardwalk. The name came from the fact that the structure, the dull green of oxidized copper, was shaped like the famous Greek Titan, holding the world on his back.

"Atlas," Nell remarked, recognizing the mythological hero. "It's funny," she said to Badger as they walked along. "I hadn't expected that things in the Dreamlands would be named after the things in our world."

"In fact, it's the opposite," Badger replied. "Everything on Earth is named for something in the Dreamlands. Everything you have seen, all that has ever been made, was created here first. This is where ideas come from."

"So the idea to brush your teeth comes from here?" George asked innocently.

"Yup," Badger said.

"Well, then maybe you should spend more time here," George screamed happily and darted out of the way of Badger's boot. The crowd was growing thicker as they reached the building. People, animals, monsters, robots and all manner of oversized objects and creatures were milling about eating, drinking and entering the doors at the base of Atlas's giant toes. A sign on the door read:

TOKEN TURMOIL!

CHALLENGER BEARDSLY WILCOX, THE MOUSTACHE DREAMER

TAKES ON

JACKSON KEROUAC, THE TYPEWRITER DREAMER

PRIZE:

THE LAST TOKEN FOR THE DEATH EXPRESS

"Listen," Badger instructed the children. "It's going to be crowded inside the Yards, and rough. We need to get to the dressing room so I can talk the Typewriter Dreamer into giving me his spot. If he does, I can get a shot at that token."

A clanging iron bell sounded, and the crowd began to push roughly towards the door in a great swarm, carrying Nell and her brothers along with them like twigs in a rushing stream.

"You kids try to stay with me," Badger shouted as he and Pinch slipped through the entrance. Instantly one thing was clear – sticking with anyone would be impossible. The crowd surged through the turnstiles into the outer corridor of the arena, and

Nell lost her brothers. Through the mass of bodies, she glimpsed Speedy's big head, already far away, searching for her.

"Nell!" he shouted desperately through the glut of moving bodies. "NELL!"

"Over here!" she called back, but the roar of the crowd muffled her voice. With a jolt, a tall man in a slick suit and the hairy pinkish head of a pig barrelled into her.

Nell was knocked down with a thud. She hit the floor, and Rose shot out of Nell's hoodie with a frightened *cheep*.

All around Nell's face was a pounding rush of shoes, boots, paws, cloven hooves, clanking robot feet, clawed talons, spike-covered wheels and more. Nell tried to push herself back up to her feet, but kept getting knocked down again by bodies and knees, her face repeatedly pushed into the floor, which stank of spilled beer and peanut shells.

"Ow! Stop! Hey!" she cried.

A few metres away, Rose was tweeting wildly, jumping up and down on the floor, trying to get out of the path of pounding feet.

"Stay still," Nell called to her, fearing that Rose would be crushed. Gently, she reached out her hand to signal to her mother, but it was no use – the hurrying crowd was too thick, and Nell repeatedly had to pull her hand out of the way to avoid it being trampled. An octopus tentacle slapped wetly on the ground before her, the wriggling limb nearly touching her lips before it moved on with a wet pucker that churned Nell's stomach. She knew what octopuses meant. She had faced one down the night her mother had been taken. They belonged to the Dark Daughters. When the tentacle moved, Nell saw Rose. She gave a quick whistle, and the bird let out a happy tweet and skittered towards her.

"That's right," Nell said. "Over here."

Suddenly, a brown woolly paw grabbed Nell by her arm and lifted her up to her feet. In an instant, Nell was standing face to face with a worn brown teddy bear, slightly taller than her.

"That's a way to get the stuffing knocked out of you," the teddy bear said, laughing, and then continued into the crowd.

Nell whipped her head around, frantically looking for Rose, but there was no sign of the bird any more. Most of the crowd had disappeared into the arena. The corridor was nearly empty, which made the truth even clearer. Her mother was lost.

"No," she said, desperate. "No."

Dread filled her stomach. Had Rose been stepped on? Was she hurt? Every bad thought possible flooded in, but Nell knew she had to stay calm. Taking a deep breath, she regained control and wandered the corridors of the arena until she found the fighters' dressing room and stepped inside.

Badger was talking to a very tall man whose head was an old-fashioned typewriter. The Typewriter Dreamer wore a pair of horn-rimmed glasses on his eyes, which were above the typewriter's keys. He and Badger were just finishing up their conversation.

"I'll go square it with the promoter," the Typewriter Dreamer said as he headed out the door. Then he added, "Good luck."

Badger began to loosen up for the fight. He swung his arms across his body and twisted his neck. "If you're here to wish me luck, I don't need it," he said, smiling with confidence. "Go and find your brothers and Pinch. They have seats in the fifth row." He turned to see Nell and saw her face was stricken with worry. "What's wrong, Nell?" he asked.

"I lost her," Nell whispered.

"Lost who?"

"Rose," Nell said. "In the crowd. I messed up. First I tried to eat her, now I've lost her. I'm useless!"

"Listen, Nell. You are going to make mistakes. Every Traveller does. We're in the dream. Mistakes, they're just part of being on the journey. You should welcome them. They are nothing to fear. Every mistake is an opportunity to adjust your approach, to do whatever you are doing again but better."

"Easy for you to say. You don't seem to make any."

"I might be making one in about five minutes," he said, smiling. "But your mother is brave and she's smart and she is alone out there. She'll find you."

"My mother?" Nell said, shocked. "You called her my mother."

"Guess I did," Badger said kindly. "Now, hand me that Minder." Badger pointed to his tightly closed umbrella, which was standing straight up on the table.

"Minder?"

"We call them Minders. They're more than just weapons. They're shelter, protection, and they never let us forget what it is that we're here for."

"The umbrellas remind you? Is that why you call them Minders?"

"We call them Minders because they make others mind their business."

Nell reached out and grabbed the wooden handle. She expected to feel something, but there was nothing special about it, just a smooth, wooden handle.

"Go on," Badger encouraged. "Try to open it. Just swing it around your head and stay loose."

Nell stretched out her arm and swung it over her head like a lasso, expecting a satisfying *THWACK*, but nothing happened other than her doing a half twirl and tripping face-first onto the floor.

Badger laughed and helped her up. "That was terrible," he said.

"I'm not good with weapons," Nell said hotly, her face reddening.

"You just need to understand how it works."

"Can you tell me? Or is it a secret?"

"There is no secret. The Minder works by tapping into the Night and unleashing it."

"The Night? You mean the dark?"

Badger took the umbrella from Nell and swung it around his head. Blue sparks of energy raced up the spine, and Nell could feel the heat of it and hear the electric hum as it passed by her.

"In the Dreamlands, the Night is not a time of day or the absence of the sun. In the Dreamlands, the Night is power."

"Power?"

"Pure dream energy – endlessly mysterious, boundlessly beautiful, full of vast terror and infinite kindness. It is the source from which all of the Dreamlands is created. Unseen, it flows through everything and brings it to life."

With a powerful THWACK, the umbrella opened. A rush of blue light beamed down. Badger spun and the umbrella closed just as quickly. A spray of orange sparks shot from the tip and drifted down like rain.

"This IS the stuff dreams are made of!" Badger thundered.

A man in a suit stuck his head through the doorway.

"Fight time in five," he said. Badger nodded and told Nell to find her seat.

"Good luck," Nell said, and before she knew it, she was giving Badger a quick hug.

"I'll be fine," he assured her, patting her head.

"Me too." Nell smiled and then raced out the door, across the hall and into the arena.

The shape of the building on the outside seemed to have nothing to do with the arena on the inside, which was a deep bowl of a building that descended row after row until finally reaching the floor, where a boxing ring waited.

Nell searched for her brothers, but didn't see them anywhere. She called out for them and then for Rose, but there was so much talking, cheering and barking shouts from vendors selling hotdogs and peanuts that it was hopeless.

"Sit down," a large rhino snarled from behind her.

"Excuse me," Nell said, truly startled at the pure hatred in the creature's voice.

"You heard me. Sit down. You're distracting me."

"I'm looking for my mother," Nell answered. Her body suddenly felt hot and her voice had a slight growl. "My name is Nell Perkins," she said, trying to keep the change from overtaking her. "My name is Nell Perkins," she repeated, "and I'm about to sit."

"Then do it," the rhino said and spat on the floor at Nell's feet.

From the rows all around her came more bullying shouts for Nell to sit and, with no other choice, she found an empty wooden seat next to the large rhino and parked herself. Down on the floor, a bright spotlight appeared, and a little man in a tuxedo entered the ring. The crowd began to shout.

"Ladies and gentlemen. Are you ready for the Turmoil for the Token?" he said, his voice stretching out each word.

The crowd cheered in anticipation.

"Tonight's winner will get the last token in all of the Dreamlands for the Death Express. That little coin will take him and four guests on a one-way trip to Crypt to witness the first Ghost Stew in one hundred years. Everyone who witnesses the blessed event has a chance to change their shape forever. Who knows what wealth and power await them?"

More cheers exploded. The entire arena was shaking with the noise.

"And, might I add, may the Potion Dreamer brew up a Dreamer that makes the Dark Daughters think twice about going to war! But if they do want to fight, we all know the Dreamlands *will be ready!*" This was met with even louder cheers.

"Surely you've seen the beards and moustaches. Every Sleeper has one these days. That is the work of this fine fighter. So now, let's give a warm welcome to an up-and-comer, Beardsly Wilcox, the Moustache Dreamer!"

As the crowd thundered with applause and a fair number of boos, Beardsly Wilcox walked out with gleaming confidence. He was bare-chested, wearing only old-fashioned trousers that came down to his knees and square black boots. His massive arms were covered with tattoos. His hair was neatly divided down the middle of his head in a thick parting, and he wore one of the most fantastic moustache-and-beard combinations Nell had ever seen. The moustache was as wide as an eagle's outstretched wings, with a crisp handlebar curl on either end, and the beard flowed down to his belly. But it wasn't *just* that it was large. It was also the hair's glowing colour. Each strand gleamed fiery orange and golden red, like a river made of late-autumn leaves. Beardsly flexed his muscles, yelled to the crowd, climbed on the ropes and did a backflip.

"And tonight, we have something really special … a

substitution! Tonight! Fighting for the Typewriter Dreamer is Duke Badger, Fearless Traveller!"

The crowd began to boo and jeer as Badger strolled out as if he had all the time in the world, nonchalantly swinging his umbrella by the handle. It was a bizarre sight, for Badger looked like a child next to the Moustache Dreamer, who towered over him and was plainly double his size.

The announcer made a few announcements about fairness, and then the two fighters each took a step towards the centre of the ring and raised their fists. With a bell, the fight began. Nell was expecting the two fighters to go at each other like boxers, but they did not step forward. Instead, bright, crackling bolts of electricity shot slowly up from the top of the Moustache Dreamer's head and hands, crawling upwards as it filled with surging power.

"Look at those bolts," growled the rhino next to Nell. "He'll kill 'em with one blow."

"His bolts?" Nell asked the rhino.

"Of course. Ain't you never seen a fight before? It's how they do it. With bolts of pure lightning."

The Moustache Dreamer shook his massive head in pity at Badger, who did nothing, standing still as an oak tree in a summer breeze.

"Don't be afraid," the Dreamer boomed. "I'll kill you quickly and painlessly. How do you like your death? Over easy or over hard?"

In a flash, Badger swung his umbrella. The transition from stillness to rapid movement was so sudden and graceful that it felt like a gunshot. With a *whoosh*, Badger's umbrella was out, and white-hot bolts of energy shot from its pointed ferrule in an unwavering line.

The Moustache Dreamer stumbled back for a moment, blinded by the light's intensity, and then, realizing he had a real fight on his hands, turned towards Badger, ready to destroy. The bolt of energy flowing from his head hummed.

The crowd was rapt, watching in silence as each of the white-hot bolts of energy slithered and danced around, and then, at the same moment, the two fighters attacked. The Moustache Dreamer jerked his head downwards, directing the pulsing current at Badger, who, using both hands, countered with his umbrella.

The two fat bolts of sizzling electrical current zoomed across the ring and collided with a tremendous crack and hiss. The two white bolts flashed a thousand colours, and a mushroom-shaped cloud of sparks, bright as Bonfire Night fireworks, soared towards the rafters. The crowd gasped.

The Moustache Dreamer groaned and hit the floor with a slam, sliding across the canvas, and both bolts disappeared. The crowd went wild. The fight was on.

The Moustache Dreamer leapt to his feet and roared at Badger. A new collision of bolts began.

CRACK! ZAP! SIZZLE!

The light was blinding in its ferocious brightness, and Badger was a master. He opened his umbrella to block, twirled on his heels to soar upwards, closing the umbrella with a *THWACK,* and attacked from the air with humming bolts of electric power.

Above the roar of the crowd came a loud and echoing "CA-CAW!"

Nell turned her head away from the searing flashes for a moment and spotted a woman in a beautiful black dress a few rows down. The woman was standing on her seat. Her hair was a stark white and, instead of a mouth, she had a long, dark raven's beak.

"Dark Daughters!" Nell gasped in horror.

The woman, as if hearing her, turned to Nell and addressed the crowd. "Attention, fight-goers. There is a little yellow bird with a red head that belongs to the Dark Daughters! We have come to claim her!"

The Dark Daughter threw back her head and from her beak let out another resounding "ca-caw" that echoed through the arena. The crowd froze, chilled by the haunting sound of a bird in terrible pain, and then watched in terror as the young Dark Daughter opened her beak and, from it, let loose a spray of shadowy black ribbons. There were thousands of them, slinky and dark, shooting powerfully out and spreading over the crowd.

"Oh no," Nell gasped, for she realized what they were. They weren't ribbons at all. They were slimy octopus tentacles.

"What's that?" the rhino sitting beside Nell grunted. Nell knew exactly what it was and couldn't believe it.

Nell shouted. "Get out!" She grabbed the rhino's huge arm.

"The wha–" the rhino tried to say, but he didn't finish, because a slimy black tentacle shot towards them like a flying spear and, with a wet smack, hit him between his eyes. His body turned into a quivering shadow and he was pulled, like dust into a vacuum, into the tentacle's suckers.

The entire arena was now engulfed in chaos as the stampeding crowd dispersed in every direction, pushing and shouting in pure panic as they tried to escape the slithering tentacles shooting endlessly from the Dark Daughter's beak. Great explosions rattled the arena, as the fight in the ring grew more intense. Panic overtook Nell. She dashed along the aisles looking everywhere for her brothers. Where were they? Yet suddenly, above all the noise and confusion, Nell heard the sound of her mother's tweet, clear as the whisper of a kiss on her ear.

"CHEEP. CHEEP. CHEEP."

"Mum!" Nell yelled, searching desperately through the crowd for her mother.

Down below in the centre of the ring was the little golden bird with the red head. She was standing between the feet of the Moustache Dreamer. Sizzling bright light leapt from his head and met the jagged blue bolts firing from Badger's umbrella. Nell feared that in the blinding light of the fight the small bird was impossible to see, and even if Badger did see her on the ground, he couldn't reach for her without risking death.

As the crowd sped up the stairs for the exits, Nell darted down towards the ring, pushing and jostling her way through the stampeding mass. The Dark Daughter noticed her movement against the crowd. Tentacles continued to shoot out of her beak. She fixed her eyes on Nell and sent a spray of slithering tentacles towards her head. Nell dived. The tentacles made a throaty roar as they passed, centimetres from her face. They dripped with slime and smelled of the sea.

Nell moved quicker than she had ever moved in her life, leaping over seats, scurrying between bodies and moving with the speed and grace of an animal. By the time she reached the floor, the entire ring was surrounded in a crackling, white-hot web of electricity, so vivid that each flash was blinding. Rose was in the centre of the ring. Nell called for her mother, but her mother didn't move.

"Rose!" she called again. Still, her mother stood her ground. Another collision of energy exploded, knocking Nell to the floor. She pushed herself up.

"Please," Nell called to Badger, but he was lost in the adrenaline of the fight and ignored her. There was no way around it. She'd have to step inside the ring to rescue her mother.

Taking a deep breath, Nell lifted the ropes and slipped inside the ring. A fierce crackle tossed her again to the floor. The heat inside the ring was as intense as a blazing oven. Sweat gathered on her face, and the smell of fireworks, acrid and electrical, brought tears to her eyes. Nell struggled to get up and, bending low, hurried over to Rose. The small bird saw Nell and let out a happy string of cheeps.

As Nell reached down to pick up her mother from the ground, the Moustache Dreamer stamped forward, his heavy shoe, shaking the ring. Startled, Rose leapt up and darted straight into the Moustache Dreamer's thick beard and disappeared.

Nell was so surprised that she lurched after Rose and collided with the Moustache Dreamer, smacking straight into his beard. Nell didn't bounce off or hit the floor but was sucked inside the Moustache Dreamer's beard. The first few seconds were dark and tickly like an old sweater, but she passed through the woolly curtain of beard and suddenly found herself tumbling through the air.

CHAPTER 18

For a moment, all Nell heard was the whistling of the wind. She was falling. Falling fast. Falling hard. The wind that rippled all around her was painfully cold. Her silvery hair tumbled out of her hoodie and streamed upwards. Tendrils of mist crossed her face and slipped away. Nell was plummeting through the sky of a dark and endless night. No land was visible below. And the sky, while infinite, was not empty. It was littered with large wooden schooners with tall sails, and they were engaged in a cannon battle. Bright orange explosions zinged through the air and crashed into the sides of the ships.

Nell had often wondered what people who fall or jump from high places think about as they plummet through the emptiness towards their deaths. She always imagined that with nothing to grab hold of and no way to stop falling, they had deep and important thoughts. But all she thought was this: "I'm in a beard."

Then from the darkness she heard someone call her name.

"NELL!"

Nell turned to find Badger diving towards her from high above. Keeping his arms pressed tight against his side and his body rigid as a knife, he cut through the air quickly and was soon right beside her. In one motion, he grabbed Nell around the waist and, holding her tight, spun, opening his umbrella with a *THWACK*. A warm blue light enveloped them, and they drifted slowly down.

"I'm in a beard," Nell said breathlessly, and then added, "The Dark Daughters."

Badger understood her fear and reassured her. "Your brothers got out safely. Pinch protected them."

Nell glanced down. Waiting below was a rolling ocean, black as the mouth of a great beast, and rising out of it was a large object shrouded in mist. As they got closer, it became clear that it was no iceberg but a massive old-fashioned ocean liner. Badger landed gently on the deck and, with a *whoosh*, the umbrella was closed and put once again in the quiver on his back. The ship's horn blew a deafening blast that made Nell cover her ears. Badger's eyes searched around until he nodded at her that all was safe.

"The fight was interrupted, but we still have a chance to get the token," Badger said.

"How?"

"I am not sure. If anything happens, if we are separated, remember, you are inside a Dreamer. Just like before. Just like the Mirror Dreamer. There is a way out. Find the door, and I will see you on the other side."

They both heard a chirping bird song.

"Rose!" Nell shouted.

Nell and Badger dashed along the boat's deck after the sound. They clattered down wooden stairs and hurried down a long ship corridor until they came upon Rose in a sitting alcove. The little bird was perched on a side table, pecking at a fruit bowl. She looked up and gave a happy tweet in recognition. Nell held out her hand, and Rose flew down and landed in her upturned palm.

"I thought I'd lost you," Nell said, tears welling up at the corner of her eyes. "But it's okay now." She gave her mother a kiss on her bright red crown. "We're close. We just have to get this token, and then we can get to Crypt and meet Ravenhead. He'll help you," Nell said, talking as much to herself as to her mother.

"Follow me," Badger said and led Nell to the end of the corridor and into a large, well-appointed stateroom lit by gas lamps. The flickering light of the gas lamps illuminated a few large, bearded men and left others hidden in shadows. All the men were well armed.

Now Nell saw the Moustache Dreamer. He sat at a gambling table, dwarfing everyone else in the room. Beside him was the most hideously frightening person Nell had ever laid eyes on. He was a tall man with the mismatched clothes of one who'd been robbing others for years – top hat, long coat, animal fur draped around his shoulders and heavy boots. The man's face was painted the yellowish-white of rotten milk and crossed with dripping streaks of bright colour. His bright orange hair was stringy with grease and fell to his shoulders in ragged strands. Most frightening was the green slash of his painted mouth that was full of pointy, gleaming white teeth and a black tongue. In front of the man sat a fat cream pie, piled high with whipped cream that he had been about to tuck into when Nell and Badger entered. He gazed up from the pie. Seeing Nell, his eyes narrowed with disgust as if his meal had been ruined by a foul odour.

"Ain't scared of clowns, are you, little girl?" he said, his voice like sandpaper.

Nell was too frightened to speak and shook her head slightly that she wasn't.

"Then you're stupider than you look," he snarled, scooping up the pie quickly and throwing it with vicious speed and power. In an instant, the fluffy pie hit Nell square in the face, temporarily blinding her and sending whipped cream everywhere. Laughter exploded across the room. Nell's cheeks felt hot with shame and surprise. As she wiped the crust from her face, her body began to itch, her nose filled with a powerful beckoning scent, and a searing hunger gripped her belly as she transformed uncontrollably into a silver fox.

All at once, the pie didn't matter, nor did the clown or the token. Nothing mattered expect for the bird. Nell's fox eyes zeroed in on Rose and, with a snarl, she leapt after her mother, chasing her through the room with snapping, snarling jaws. A voice nearby told her to stop, come back, remember who she was, but her urge was too powerful, her craving too great. Badger was calling her name, but all sounds were easily blocked out except for one – the tiny drum of her mother's heartbeat. The bird slid over the table, and Nell dashed under it, catching the scent of blood from many animals and creatures soaked deep in the leather of the clown's boots.

A flash of yellow flickered in the corner of her eye. Nell's mother was in her sights now. Rose rested on a tabletop, confused by the chase and looking around for the fox, her body trembling.

KILL! Nell thought, and she leapt, her fangs bared and slick with saliva.

With a *smack*, a hard stone hit her in the eye, knocking her off her course, and as she hit the marble floor, she tumbled as if caught in an ocean wave, transforming again into a girl.

The room was filled with more ridiculing laughter. Badger gently lifted Nell to her feet, placed a hand on each of her shoulders, and inspected her. She was slightly dazed and deeply embarrassed.

"You'll get yours, Shivers." Badger turned and snarled at the clown, who waved his pale hand casually in response, as if dismissing a servant.

"I could gut the girl like a fish and feed her to my dogs if I wanted, and I most likely will. Not you or anyone can stop me."

"Not here you can't," Badger said, and with a swift *THWACK*, his umbrella was out and crackling with electric current. "Unless the rules have changed. And if they have," he said, nodding to the armed bearded men hiding in the shadows, "let's get this thing going. Take your shot."

"Give up your Minder, Duke," the Moustache Dreamer said calmly, but Nell could tell he was clearly nervous about the fight. "The rules of play remain. Every player is guaranteed their safety until they exit my domain. No weapons allowed," he said, nodding at the clown.

"Fine," the clown said. "But that means the girl must play dice and gamble her treasure."

"What?" Badger grunted.

"You brought her. She is here," the clown explained, removing a curved dagger from his boot. "She must play. If not, I am allowed to do what clowns do." He honked a horn that dangled from his dusty coat.

Badger turned to Nell and explained their dire situation. "There is no choice. We must play or he will attack us."

"But I didn't bring any treasure," Nell said.

"My friend Freyja Skoll says different," the clown said, sneering. "She says you have a bird that belongs to her, and she is willing to pay me big to get it back. Almost worth as much as that token I'm going to win."

"It's not a bird," Nell said, quaking. "It's my mother."

"Even better."

Nell turned to Badger, whose eyes were scanning the room, counting the armed men and calculating the odds. They weren't good. He took Nell aside and explained.

"Don't make me give up Rose," she whispered.

"We could try to fight our way out, and if it was just a bunch of Dreamers and some Nightmares, I'd take the chance – but that is a clown, and it's not wise to mess with them."

"But you're a Fearless Traveller," Nell said hopefully.

"That's true, but that isn't any clown, that's Venom Shivers. He's an ancient Nightmare whose father was the Poison Dreamer. He has all the power of a Dreamer but none of the goodness. Simply put, he is insane, and a better fighter the Dreamlands has never seen. The game will be true, and Beardsley won't take Rose away from you if he wins. So it's really three against one. It's a chance, but it's all we got."

"All right," Nell agreed, holding Rose tightly in her hand. Her small bird heart was beating fiercely. Nell kissed her head and then looked the clown straight in the eye and whispered, "I'll play."

"Weapons?" the Moustache Dreamer said. Badger handed him his umbrella and the knife in his boot, and the clown began to unload a large and bizarre array of blades, pokers, and fiendish fighting tools that included a whip with a live rat's head on its tip.

"We are playing dice," the Moustache Dreamer said when all the weapons had been taken from the table. "The rules are simple. Each player wagers and rolls one die, and then we go around and roll the second. The highest score from the two rolls wins all wagers. In the case of a tie, either player can withdraw his wager. Now everyone, ante up."

"I do not have anything to wager," Badger admitted.

"What about that umbrella of yours?" the clown said, licking his lips with his blue tongue.

"You know a Fearless Traveller would never give up his umbrella," Badger said.

"I'm sorry, Duke," the Moustache Dreamer said. "You have to wager to play."

"We could give you something," the clown offered.

"What?"

"I have a lot of treasure. So I'll spot you. Thing is, you only get it if you lose."

"If I lose?"

The clown smiled and took off his top hat. He laid the hat on the table and reached his hand in. A guttural growl bellowed from the bowels of the hat, and he cursed against it, fishing for the prize that lay beneath the rim. With a shout, he grabbed hold of something inside and slowly pulled out a goo-dripping Shacklepede. The creature snarled and screeched, its hundreds of tiny legs wriggling.

Badger's face drained of colour, and he took a step back. This delighted the clown.

"Don't you want to give your old friend a hug? No? All right, here's the deal. You can play in the game, maybe win the only token that now exists for the Death Express. But if you lose, the winner – I'm thinking it's going to be me – can decide to return this bad boy to your leg."

"No," Nell said, unable to take her eyes off the flailing legs of the monster. She turned to Badger, grabbing his arm. "Don't. I won't let you."

Badger ignored Nell and snarled at the clown defiantly. "I'm in."

The clown laughed with joy and honked his horn. With a kiss to the oily creature's metal crown, he placed the Shacklepede back in the hat and the hat back on his head.

The Moustache Dreamer held up a small glowing coin. On either side was a glowing skull that pulsed like a beacon.

"You took the token?" Badger said in disbelief and disgust.

"Didn't want it to fall into the wrong hands," the Moustache Dreamer said apologetically. "But I didn't run off with it. You have a chance to get it fairly. One token for the train known as the Death Express. It will take you and up to four guests to the Ghost Stew. It is currently valued at nine million pounds of pure gold and wanted by the powerful, headless queen of the Dark Daughters."

"May I see it?" Shivers said, his ice-blue eyes staring at it with unblinking intensity.

"I don't think that is a good idea," the Moustache Dreamer remarked and placed the coin all of the Dreamlands wanted on the table. "Venom? We all know what you want, but what do you have?"

The clown lifted up his hand. It was pale and powerful and crisscrossed with ropy scars. The nails were ragged and chipped. A true showman, he waited until he had everyone's attention and then turned the hand towards his own face and reached it into his mouth, working his fingers around his teeth. With a vice-like grip, he grabbed his teeth and began to pull at them. Pain twinkled in his eyes, and tears streamed down his painted cheeks as he continued to pull with great growls.

Nell's stomach hurt just to witness what he doing. He was pulling out his own teeth! Streams of blood bubbled over his lips and dripped from his chin until finally, with a wet *pop*, the clown screamed and the light above the gambling table shone down on his hand, which was now holding a blood-streaked set of fangs. He delicately placed them on the table. Nell stared in horror at the gaping holes where his teeth had been.

"One set of clown teeth," the Moustache Dreamer said with a faint tremor of disgust in his voice. "Able to pierce the hides of the thickest Nightmares, suck the souls from Dreamers and chew any known substance to dust. One of the most prized weapons in all of the Wicked Places, they will shrink or expand to fit any size jaw."

The clown wiped the back of his hand across his mouth and smiled. A new set of small pointed fangs grew from his gums. They were white and perfectly shaped, but had a baby-like quality, unlike the fierce set of fangs that sat gleaming on the table.

"Now you," Venom said to Nell. "Put the bird on the table."

"She won't stay," Nell pleaded.

"Put her on the table!" he snarled.

Nell gave Rose a final kiss and placed her on the wager table. The Moustache Dreamer clapped a beer mug over Rose, propping one side up with a matchbook so she could have some air. Inside the cup, Rose chirped wildly and tried to fly away, but she could not move her wings.

"One yellow bird with a red head."

"She's my mother," Nell corrected.

"One mother," the Moustache Dreamer repeated.

A young woman wearing a dress and sporting a very full and real handlebar moustache walked over. She was holding a small wooden box carved in the shape of a whale. She opened the box, and inside was a beautiful set of gleaming white dice. The Moustache Dreamer thanked the girl and removed the dice from the box. She closed it crisply and disappeared into the shadows.

"One set of whale bone dice, carved by the Gambling Dreamer. They are impossible to tamper or cheat with so, rest assured, what you roll is what you will see. If your die falls off the table, your score is zero. Any questions before we begin?"

"Yeah," the clown snarled, "when are you going to shut up and start?"

All the talking in the room died away as the Moustache Dreamer shook his first die and tossed it onto the table. It rolled crisply and landed on a one. "Nuts," he groaned.

Badger was up next. Giving Nell a reassuring wink, he shook the die in his hand and gently tossed it onto the table. He rolled a three.

Nell's stomach clenched up at the sight of the tiny number. She glanced at the snickering clown, who honked his horn with glee and perfumed the air with the scent of rotten eggs and slow decay.

"Let me show you losers what a winner looks like," he said, swiping the die from the table and tossing it with the arrogance of one who was already holding his prize. The die rolled across the green felt and came to rest.

"Two," Badger said with a slight smile.

"What?" the clown yelled in disbelief at his awful roll. "It's a trick!"

"Two," Badger repeated with pleasure. "The number after one and before all the rest."

"Now you, Nell," the Moustache Dreamer said politely, handing Nell the die. Her hands were sweaty, and her heart was racing. Trying to still her shaking hands, Nell wiped the die on her sleeve and glanced at Rose trapped under the glass. With a deep breath, she pulled her arm back and threw. The die hit the table hard and rolled over and over and sped towards the edge of the table.

On and on the die rolled like a boulder down a mountain, but finally it stopped on the lip of the table. The die showed the six most beautiful circles Nell had ever seen.

"I won," she yelped in excitement. "I won!"

"Not yet," the clown growled.

"Two rounds," Badger reminded Nell. "But you're leading, Nell. Good work."

The Moustache Dreamer was up once more. He shook his hand and rolled. The die tumbled and landed on a four. Nell's heart leapt. He was out! The game was down to three players now, and one of them would win the token. Badger took the die. He blew onto it for luck and threw with a poised and graceful hand. The lone die spun across the table and landed on three once again. He had a total of six. He grimaced.

"It's all right," Nell said, her confidence growing. It was now between her and Venom Shivers. The clown took the die in his hand. He stuck out his long blue tongue and ran it along the die, then rolled with a shout. The die tumbled along the table violently and landed on a six.

"Eight!" Nell shouted in excitement. The clown had eight all together. She had six. This meant that if Nell rolled any number above one, all would be okay. She would either tie with the clown and get her wager back or win it all.

"Any number above one, Nell, and we're home free," Badger said.

Nell nodded. She picked the die up and wiped it off on the sleeve of her hoodie. Before she threw, she brought the small square of bone to her lips and, with her eyes closed, whispered into it. "Please," she said, thinking of her brothers and mother.

A feeling of calm came over Nell. Everything would be okay. She knew it. Holding her breath, she threw the die with a strong, steady throw. The little cube tumbled this way and that over the green felt and came to rest in a puddle of light on the centre of the table.

"*ONE!*" the clown shouted, jumping up in victory.

"What?" Nell said in shock.

"That makes seven all together. One less than eight. I win."

Nell couldn't believe it. She looked at the table. There was her die, resting with a single dot staring back at her like the cruel eye of a shark. "No," she said, her eyes welling up with tears. "NO! NO! NO! NO!"

She had lost her mother to the vilest person imaginable. A Nightmare. A true Nightmare, and he was going to deliver Rose directly to Freyja Skoll. Nell's skin began to itch, and she felt herself beginning to transform into a fox, but Badger was there when she needed him. He wrapped his strong arms around her trembling body and placed a spirit stone on her head, and she remained Nell, though sadness and anger rushed through her body.

"Oh yes," the clown said and, with a great flourish, he picked up the glowing token, gave it a wet kiss and placed it in his pocket. Suddenly, five armed men were standing around Badger and Nell, crossbows pointed at Badger's heart. The clown peeled Nell away from Badger, tossing her to the floor roughly. Badger lurched forward to defend her, but without his weapon, there was nothing he could do.

"Time for your prize," Venom Shivers said to Badger. He honked his horn, sending a green cloud into the air. The smell twisted Nell's face. With great flourish, the clown removed his hat and held it between himself and Badger.

"Come out and play," he whispered into the hat, and with great relish, he reached his hand in and lifted the Shacklepede out. The metal creature was squealing in frenzy.

"Double or nothing!" Nell shouted, getting up from the floor.

The clown swivelled around.

"One toss. Me and you," Nell said bravely. "Winner takes all."

"But you lost. Meaning you are a loser. Meaning you have nothing left to wager."

"Myself," Nell said suddenly.

"*No*, Nell," Badger commanded. "You can't. Absolutely not."

"Yourself?" the clown said with a nod, as though the thought hadn't occurred to him. "Interesting. You understand clowns are slave traders?"

Nell nodded nervously. She had blurted the offer before she had really thought about it. Her heart was pounding, but she didn't care what happened. Not now. The only thing that mattered was that the clown couldn't put that monster back on Badger's leg. He wouldn't survive it and, even worse, the clown would take Rose. Rose would be with him and Nell would never see her again. All of it was beyond horrible, but letting him win, Nell thought, that was giving into hopelessness.

The clown was staring at Nell, studying her with a puzzled look. He said, "We occasionally – actually, more than occasionally – drink human blood."

"Yes," Nell said softly. "I understand."

The clown clapped his hands together. "This is fun."

"You don't have to do this, Nell," Badger insisted. "I promise we will find a way to get Rose back, and I can handle the Shacklepede," he continued, but his face twitched slightly at the thought. "I can."

"It's too late," the clown snarled. "She offered, and I agreed."

"The game is Shoot Out," the Moustache Dreamer announced. "One roll. Highest number wins all wagers. Winners first."

The Moustache Dreamer picked up the die and handed it to the clown. The clown took it in his hand and shook it vigorously, letting out a long howl. He let the die fly, and it tumbled across the table, landing on the number five.

"FIVE!" he screamed happily.

"Only six beats a five," the Moustache Dreamer said, picking up the die and handing it to Nell. "Winner takes all."

There was a shattering of glass. All heads turned. Rose had broken free of her makeshift glass cage and was fluttering around the room, furiously tweeting.

"Mum," Nell called, and with a bold tweet, Rose landed delicately on Nell's shoulder.

"You all right?" Nell asked, petting her and kissing her. Rose tweeted brightly in response. Nell studied her bright red head and wondered if this was going to be the last time she ever saw her. "I'm sorry," Nell whispered. "I'm a terrible daughter."

Rose threw her head back, but instead of tweeting, she let loose a beautiful song that made everyone freeze. The sound was as soft as a hand-knitted jumper and delicately sweet. All at once, Nell was reminded of a faraway place, of lying next to her mother on the daybed of their back porch on a summer afternoon as crickets chirped and the trees rustled softly. In her memory, Rose was stroking her hair and singing her a lullaby.

She remembers me, Nell thought. *She remembers.*

The song was cut short as the clown snatched Rose from Nell's shoulder and held her tight in his strong, pale hand.

"Leave her alone!"

"Roll!" he snarled. "Roll. Right. Now."

Anger was surging through Nell, and she rolled the die, not taking her eyes off the clown's ice-blue eyes. The die tumbled across the green table and came to a stop.

"SIX!" Badger shouted.

"What!" the clown roared.

"*Six!*" the Moustache Dreamer repeated. "Nell! You won!"

A mighty *THWACK* rang out and Badger was beside Nell, his umbrella at the clown's throat. In the distraction, he had plucked his weapon from the table, and now he was ready to use it.

"Our prizes," Badger said to the Moustache Dreamer, who handed him the token.

The clown was dumbfounded.

"My mother," Nell demanded. The clown was still so shocked to have lost that he just opened his hand, and Rose leapt up and sailed over to Nell's shoulder, where she landed.

Nell looked at the clown's blood-streaked teeth resting on the gaming table.

"Go on," the Moustache Dreamer encouraged her. "You won them."

Nell shook her head. "Take your teeth," Nell said to the clown kindly.

He looked at the pointed teeth sadly, and then a rush of anger overcame him.

"Next time I see you, little girl, you will be sorry," the clown snarled. Scooping up the set of teeth, he threw them at Nell's face. They opened wide, the fangs gleaming. Badger batted them away with his umbrella and, with a *crunch*, they sank into the wall of the ship.

"You should learn some manners," Badger said to the clown, and with a swift turn, he punched him hard on the nose. The clown tumbled to the floor, snarling like an animal.

"Never give a clown a gift," Badger said to Nell. "To them, kindness is an insult."

"All right," Nell replied as the Moustache Dreamer leaned over. With his enormous hands, he reached into his beard and cleared away some hair, revealing a wooden door. The door opened. For a moment, they were bathed in a hot white light and suddenly they found themselves outside, standing in front of Atlas Yards. Speedy, George and Pinch were there waiting. There was a flurry of hugs and excitement, and finally Nell broke the news. "We got it!" Nell said. "We got the token."

"Your sister is a very brave girl," Badger said, giving her a pat on the head.

"Tell us something we don't know," George said.

"The train leaves in twenty minutes," Pinch said, cutting the celebration short. "We must go, and go now!"

CHAPTER 19

B adger led the way, and they moved quickly through the city. They walked down long avenues and twisting alleys until they came to a lonely street that ended at a wall made of round river stones. A plain wooden door adorned with a skull, so faded it was barely visible, stood in the centre of the wall.

Badger gave a knock. After a moment, a tiny man in a saffron-coloured monk's robe opened the door. Stepping outside, he closed it behind him and tugged to make sure it was locked. When he felt satisfied no one could rush their way in, he turned to Nell. His face was made completely of fruits and vegetables, all of which were delicious-looking. His nose was a large pear; his fat cheeks rosy apples, his eyebrows fluffy stalks of celery, his moustache two curled green chilli peppers and his beard a rich tangle of blackberries and raspberries.

"Holy banana!" George said in surprise when he saw the monk.

"Do you have a token?" the monk asked.

"Here it is." Nell held up the token, which glowed brightly.

"Very good." He smiled, showing a whole row of gleaming pomegranate seeds. Lifting a large keyring from his belt, the monk unlocked the door and led them inside. They walked through the gate to find themselves on a curved beach surrounded by massive, moss-covered boulders, shimmering with dew. Unlike the warm, sunny sand of Neptune Beach, this was a cold and rugged coast. A damp ocean breeze slapped their faces and fluttered their clothes.

Nell and her brothers turned back to the entrance they had just walked through and saw that something had changed. The garden gate was still there, but it was now far in the distance, rising alone from a patch of moss, like the ruin of a now-forgotten city; everything else – the wall, the streets, the buildings – was simply gone.

"Come along," the token-taker said with a wide smile.

They followed the monk as he led them along a path of well-worn wooden planks. Beneath the slats, the ground was made up of multicoloured stones and speckled bits of sea glass. As they walked, Nell marvelled at the beauty of the gleaming rocks.

"Pretty nature," the token-taker confided to Nell, as if he were seeing it all for the first time and delighting in its beauty. The path ended at a tall building made of driftwood that sat on the edge of the roiling ocean. The water was rough, and great, tumbling blue waves of surf crashed in shimmering bursts upon the vast carpet of rocks, sending up a salty spray that tickled their faces and chilled their bones.

"Inside now," the monk said, laughing. They followed him through the door made of seashells into a small, pale-pink room that was lined with wooden shelves upon which hand-carved wooden bowls sat.

"Take a bowl. Empty your pockets of any paper, wood, plastic or metal. No jewellery or coins. Anything that is flammable must go. Have no fear. It will all be waiting for you when you arrive in Crypt."

"The train gets quite hot," Badger explained. "And there is always a chance of combustion."

"You mean the train could blow up?" yelped Speedy.

"Not the train," Badger corrected.

"Not the train," Speedy muttered, pretending he understood what Badger meant. He suddenly realized. "You don't mean—"

"Exactly. He means *you* could combust," Pinch interrupted. "But don't worry. They've been doing this for millions of years, and it hardly ever happens."

"I'm always the 'hardly'," Speedy said, worried.

The monk instructed them to follow him through another door marked "Departing Train". The train platform that awaited them on the other side was a long pier of rough-hewn wood that stretched out over the crashing sea. The platform was already half-filled with birds. Unlike Rose, these were human-sized birds with deeply coloured feathers and sharp beaks, and all had a look of wickedness about them. Hawks, buzzards, owls, falcons and crows, these were birds of Nightmares, creatures one finds looming in dark branches in lonely woods, circling high in starless skies above abandoned stretches of deserted road, and pecking on windows of unfamiliar, cobweb-dusted houses.

Nell didn't think anything could surprise her now, but she thought the pier certainly didn't look like a train platform. At least the others had tracks below and benches to sit on. Not the pier, which was empty except for an evenly placed grid of burnt black circles. It was as though a campfire had been made and set, made and set, over and over again in two neat rows.

"Sit," the monk instructed, pointing to the circles. A squirrel in an orange monk's robe was walking up and down the aisle. He was about George's height and was handing out small white towels from a wicker basket to the birds that were milling about their spots, whispering to each other. No one had sat down yet. The birds, who from the looks of it had taken this train many times before and knew the drill, took the rags in their talons and were carefully wiping off the black circles before sitting down to wait for the train to arrive.

The squirrel walked up to Nell and bowed slightly. "Clean, better," the squirrel said.

Nell shook her head politely. "I'm going to stand, thank you," she said. The squirrel looked at her as if he didn't understand. Badger turned to Nell and explained. "You can't stand, Nell."

"I don't mind. The train will be here any minute. I can wait until then."

"This is the train."

"What?"

"This is the train. And that is your seat."

"Oh," Nell said, her face reddening. "Of course."

"And before you sit, you must clean the seat," he said, nodding towards the squirrel who was patiently waiting, but growing agitated since he had many other passengers to serve. Nell politely took the rag, bent over, and began to wipe the black ashen dust from the circle, which she discovered was made of thick glass. Underneath the layer of cinder dust was an intricate, beautiful pattern of humming electronic lights that Nell knew was called a mandala. The colours were bright and the design complex, but also perfectly balanced. When she was finished, Nell sat cross-legged upon the cold glass and instructed Speedy and George to do the same.

"You promised if we came with you into Dreamlands there would be no cleaning up," George moaned.

"No, I didn't."

"Did."

Badger and Pinch had got up and crossed the pier to talk to a large blue heron that they knew. Nell was watching the conversation when her eyes found the twitching fingers of the hand racing towards her at tremendous speed. It was a human hand, and it wasn't attached to a body. It had a dirty, ragged look, as if it had been living on the streets.

"Go away," she muttered, trying to escape the feral thing. As she stood it leapt. It struck like a snake, leaping in furious silence for Nell's chest. The force of the blow knocked her on her back, and the hand crawled across her chest and grabbed her hoodie, yanking it furiously.

"Get off," Nell screamed in horror and confusion. Why was it attacking her?

The fight was a blur of noise. Rose chirped wildly, and then there was a high-pitched squealing as George joined the fight.

The change into a rat happened in a flash. Suddenly the colourful world around him paled. All was grey and shapes lost their sharpness, but it didn't matter because he could smell each and every single thing. Smell guided him. It moved him forward. The hand, a blur of skin and twitching fingers, smelled of the street and the sea. It had travelled far to get here. As all this was going through his rat brain, George was moving nimbly and silently towards it, and with a leap he had the hand in his sharp teeth. But the hand was powerful and not easily stopped. It ripped itself away from George, hit the ground and shook off the blood. Instantly it leapt again, this time wrapping a finger around George's throat. With a loud yell, the monk arrived with a broom and swung it wildly, separating the two. The hand fell backwards, rolled onto its fingers, and scurried away. George dived after it but was stopped in his tracks when a spirit stone, thrown by Badger, smacked him between the eyes. In the blink of an eye the rat returned to the shape of a boy.

"No fighting," the monk said. "No fighting on the train."

"You all right?" Nell asked. George nodded, slightly dazed. Nell thanked him and, seeing that he was fine, checked on Rose. The little bird peeked out of her hoodie and jumped into her palm, gazing around as if looking for the attacker.

"What was all that about?" Nell said to Badger as he reached her.

"I've just learned some bad news," he admitted. "There's a bounty on Rose."

"What?"

"Freyja Skoll wants her back and wants her badly, according to my friend over there." Badger nodded to the blue heron. He was a fine-looking animal in a well-tailored suit and stylish derby. The heron returned the nod and winked.

"Why?" Nell asked. "What is her obsession with my mother? You said they use mothers in their spells. Why my mother?"

"I don't know the answer, but we are in luck. She is your mother, but she also is a bird now and with the Ghost Stew coming, Ravenhead will do anything to keep a bird, any bird, from Freyja Skoll. Pinch has sent word to an old friend of ours by the name of McShank. He is the gatekeeper at Nevermore Hall, Ravenhead's house. He is expecting us."

"So we can see Ravenhead?"

"McShank owes me," Badger said. "We will get in as soon as Ravenhead arrives. He is en route, as we are." A train whistle blew. "Here we go. You have nothing to fear. If you do start to get scared, don't worry, it happens. Just take a few deep breaths and you will soon feel calm again. Let go of any thoughts."

"Done!" Speedy said.

"Good. Now take your seats and get ready for the ride of your life."

"What's going to happen?" George said nervously. "Is this thing going to ride along an invisible track or something?"

"Or something," Badger said.

"Tell us," Speedy said. He didn't like surprises.

"Now, what fun would that be?"

"What about Mum?" Nell said, petting her tiny red head with her fingers.

"Keep your mother inside, close to your heart."

The boys each gave Rose a kiss, and with a final whisper from Nell, she was put safely inside the hoodie. The train whistle blew again, louder than the first time, and a great, expectant silence fell over the pier. All the large birds, along with Nell, her brothers, Pinch and Badger, were now sitting as still as possible on their circles. Around the pier, the ocean was roaring as the waves crashed wildly into the pylons below.

Nell found the smell of the ocean calming. She took a long, deep breath and filled her lungs. As she exhaled, a soft hum reached her ears, and Nell discovered her bottom was warming up. Glancing down, Nell saw that the mandala she was seated upon was beginning to glow brightly. The heat was not bothersome. In fact, it was quite pleasant, like slipping into a perfectly warmed bath. The sensation quickly spread as the glow from the mandala climbed up, until a bright column of golden light encased Nell completely. She turned and saw that her brothers, Badger, Pinch and all the large birds – in fact, every passenger – were each now sitting in their own tube of golden light.

An ear-shattering roar filled the air, and with a tremendous tug, Nell felt her body lift from the pier. In an instant, all the riders of the train blasted off, rocketing up into the sky, each rider enclosed in his or her own individual column of light.

The blast-off had blinded Nell at first. It took a moment for her to make sense of what was happening and then another to adjust to her flight. Instinctively, her body straightened out, her arms went to her sides, and her head lifted up. And, like that, she was flying, zooming across the endless sky. Her whole body vibrated with the unbelievable speed of it.

Nell turned her head. All around were other passengers rocketing alongside her, sheathed in their own columns of light. On one side was Badger and on the other were Speedy and George. All looked at one another and screamed in complete delight and utter excitement.

"We are comets!" Nell yelled in joy. "We are comets!"

And so they were. Soaring comets unfurling across the vastness of the sky, leaving sparkling ribbons of light trailing metres behind them. The blue sky ended quickly, and they reached the edge of it. Passing over the side, they found themselves in deep space, where a vast, glittering field of planets and stars surrounded them.

On the horizon, a tiny light appeared, brighter than the rest of the stars. Nell knew at once it was this light that they were headed towards. It was lovely and warm inside her cone of light and, to make it even better, Rose began singing, excitedly trilling a simple melody, her sweet noise filling up the cone.

Nell felt her body being pulled downwards towards the Earth once more. As she did the sky became a lighter blue, and in moments they were flying over a cold and dark ocean. Nell could feel the salt spray on her face. Her entire body tingled and she wanted it never to end. With her brothers beside her they zigged and zagged through a series of small islands. They slipped between trees and wound through canyons of tall red rocks and were once again on the water. In the distance was an island unlike the others. It was treeless and made of black rock, and rising from it was a massive diamond made of mist and light. A sign hovering about the island spelled out "Crypt Station".

"Crypt Station!" The announcement rang out, and with machine-like precision all the separate comets came together and formed two uniform lines. Instinctively, everyone's bodies bent into a seated position, and every rider's individual light joined together to form a train shape. As the train of light zoomed towards the massive diamond-shaped station, it blew its horn, which sounded like the gong of an infinite bell.

"We are pulling into the station," Badger said. He was seated next to Nell. She nodded. There was another gong and a blinding flash as they entered the side of the diamond. This was followed by the deep darkness of a tunnel. All around them, the train of light took a solid form, becoming black metal. Nell found herself sitting on a simple iron seat in an antique locomotive, chugging along a track. So quick and complete was the transformation that for a moment Nell wondered if it had happened at all. The train squealed to a stop, and everyone sat for a moment, shaking their heads in disbelief.

"Welcome to Crypt," Badger said.

Nell and her brothers were still unable to speak. Their legs felt weak, and their minds were mush. Everyone mumbled a few *wows* to one another as they followed Badger out of the train into a wooden room that matched the one they had entered on the beach. There they were met by an antelope in a monk's robe that handed them their baskets and shoes.

"Wait a minute," George said, looking at his basket and finding his voice, outraged. "I'm missing a fifty-pound note!"

"What are you talking about?" Nell asked.

"There was a fifty-pound note in my basket. And now it's gone," he said accusingly, narrowing his eyes at the unblinking antelope.

"Watch it, boy," Badger said. "This is not a place to go accusing anyone of anything. These folks have been doing this since time began, and things don't go missing."

The antelope looked at George with a hard, searching stare and then with a curt wave, as though it were not possible and needed no discussion, sent him off. George looked at the antelope for a moment and finally shrugged.

"You can't blame a guy for trying," he said with a smile.

CHAPTER 20

Walking up the stone stairs of the station, the children found themselves in the city of Crypt. Nell immediately loved it. The buildings had shapes that were familiar: skyscraper, cinema, shop, but all were made of materials that were startling. Each one was built not of brick or stone but of intricately woven branches of wood, leaves, vines, straw and coloured wool that seemed untouched by human hands. It was as though here in Crypt, birds' nests were built not in the shape of bowls, but in the shape of everything a modern city needed. And instead of pavements, there were flowers – bright, colourful ones of every kind growing in straight patches on either side of the street. You couldn't help but walk on them, but once trampled underfoot they sprang back again. In the distance and sometimes in the cracks between the buildings you could still see and hear the sea.

"It's wonderful!" Nell said. "This place is beautiful, don't you think, Mum?" Rose was on her shoulder, gazing around in satisfaction.

"Kind of girly, if you ask me," George complained and kicked a daisy.

"No one did ask you," Speedy snapped and sniffed. The air smelled fantastic, and he was breathing it in large gulps. "I love flowers."

"All bears do," Badger said, patting Speedy's shoulder. "But don't fall in love with it too much. Crypt changes very quickly. From street to street, you never know what you're going to get. Ain't that right, Pinch?"

"The streets to Nevermore will soon be impassable," Pinch said. She sniffed the air, her fierce eyes narrowing on Nell. "So I suggest we hurry."

"You love saying that, don't you?" George asked. "I mean, you really love those words in that combination. It's like your perfect sentence. If you had like a top-ten list of favourite sentences, it would be like number two."

"Are you done?" Pinch snarled, swishing her tail in irritation.

"Don't you want to know what number one is?" George said, equally annoyed that the panther hadn't taken the bait and had ruined a perfectly good insult.

"I know what it is," Pinch said confidently.

"Really?" George said, not believing her for a second. "All right. I'll play. What's your favourite sentence of all time?"

"George tasted better than I thought," she said and showed her massive fangs.

Badger laughed, and George's eyes grew wide. He looked at Pinch in shock and finally whispered, "I think we'd better hurry."

"Agreed."

With that, the small band followed Pinch as she made her way along the avenues of Crypt. As Badger had warned, the city quickly became increasingly grim. The flowers turned to weeds, and the buildings were made of dark, thorny brambles. The sun was setting, and as they drew closer to Nevermore, it was clear they had stumbled into the middle of a fiendish party.

The streets were overrun with monstrous birds, each as large as Badger, and music poured from all directions. Every half block, a new band of birds landed, instruments in hand, and began to play until the sky was pulsing with one vast, wicked song. As the sun sank and darkness fell, the music grew wilder and the antique lampposts that lined the streets snapped to life with an eerie green glow.

"Where is Nevermore?" Nell asked Badger, feeling less safe with every step.

"Close," he said, removing his Minder from his back and swinging it above his head like a whip. With a resounding *THWACK*, the umbrella opened wide. From beneath its domed canopy, the reassuring blue glow shone down. Birds squawked and shuffled away from the bright column of illumination.

"Under here," Badger said. Nell and her brothers huddled close beneath the umbrella and peered into the sea of nightmarish faces that surrounded them. The great collage of birds – owls and egrets, seagulls and terns, ragged roosters and woodpeckers with crazed eyes – watched their every step. Rose stayed on Nell's shoulder, chirping out warnings to the birds around her.

"It's okay, Mum," Nell said. "Relax."

"It really doesn't look okay," George squeaked.

"I'm with George," Speedy said.

The group walked quickly, turning one last corner, and finally caught sight of Nevermore Hall. The castle was made of blood-coloured stone and was built in the shape of a massive, leafless elm tree. Surrounding the castle was an expansive, weedy lawn, enclosed by a large iron fence. Two immense snowy owls, white as spirits, guarded the gates. They gazed out over the crowd with unblinking enormous eyes. Behind the owls on a large pile of tinder was an ancient iron cauldron, big enough to boil a herd of elephants.

"The Ghost Stew," Nell said.

"Let me guess," George said, staring at the towering black cauldron. "You can't eat the Ghost Stew, because it eats you."

"Only after it kills you in the most painful manner," Pinch said, licking her paws.

George turned to Speedy and shook his head in disbelief. "Is it me, or when she licks her palms calmly and says that, it's way scarier?"

"Way scarier," Speedy answered.

"You wait here," Badger told the children. "I'll tell McShank we're here."

"And we're hungry," Speedy said.

"Really?" Nell said. Sometimes her brother's desire to eat in even the most stressful circumstances astounded her.

"I can't help it. All this talk about stew."

"*Ghost* Stew," she made clear.

"It has the word 'stew' in it."

Badger went to the fence and talked to the owls. The ghostly birds nodded, and, after conversing in a serious manner, one flew into the castle to relay Badger's message. After a few minutes, the door at the base of the tree-shaped castle opened, and out walked a little man with bright copper-coloured hair, green velvet clothes and silver shoes.

"Leprechauns. We're trusting a leprechaun?" Pinch snarled under her breath.

"McShank owes us," Badger said and turned to the children to give them a warning. "They are a very sensitive lot. If McShank asks you if you trust him, you say yes, understand?"

The children nodded as the leprechaun scurried down the lawn, passing the mountainous cauldron with a worried look. He stopped at the edge of the fence and, standing on a stone so his head poked above the iron spikes, waved them over.

"McShank," Badger said in a greeting that was neither friendly nor angry but a bit of both. The small man was shivering with nerves, as though what he was doing was quite wrong, and for a moment he couldn't speak.

Nell had a dreadful feeling that what he was about to say would be about her.

"What is it?" Badger asked.

McShank shook his head and held his hand to his jaw as if in pain. "It's my tooth," he groaned, speaking out of the side of his mouth in a thick Irish accent. "It's rotten."

"Sorry to hear that," Badger replied as though he couldn't care less. "You want me to pull it?"

"No!" McShank yelped, his eyes wide at the thought.

"What are they stewing?" Pinch asked suspiciously. "Smells powerful."

"It is." He added in a whisper what he clearly thought was a big secret: "Ravenhead is not wasting time. He means to attack the Dark Daughters tonight!"

"Did you speak to him?" Badger said, trying to get him to the point. "About Nell?"

McShank nodded. "Yes, and he said he would be happy to break the spell and return the mother to her proper form. Can she can come inside and bring the bird…"

"I can," Nell said, feeling a rush of excitement.

"But," McShank continued, holding up his child-sized hand.

"But what?" George said.

"But she must come alone. "

Nell felt her stomach clench. "Alone?"

"There are many in the castle. Some of those have problems with Fearless Travellers; some have problems with human children. It is for your own protection. But don't worry, miss. I'll be with you the whole time."

"I don't trust him," Speedy admitted loudly.

"Me neither. Don't go," George said, suddenly throwing himself to her side.

"Don't trust me?" A look of agony came over the leprechaun's face. "Did they say they didn't trust me?"

"Joking," Speedy said and elbowed his brother. "Right, George?"

"Totally. So that it is clear, we trust you and your weirdly tiny hands. But Nell is not going with you. All settled. Your hands are weird, and Nell stays."

"I have to," Nell said, nodding. She knew with every fibre of her being that, as horrible as it sounded, it was true. She had to go alone.

Badger nodded in agreement. From his boot he pulled a knife handle and snapped his wrist. An umbrella shot from one side and a curved handle from the other.

"Take this," he said and pulled a cord, thin as a bowstring, from the tip and fixed it to the base of the handle. Badger held it taut, and Nell slipped it across her chest. "It is my spare."

The umbrella clung tight against her back, and she reached her hand over her shoulder to feel the weapon's ancient wooden handle. A shiver rushed through her body.

"Go on," Badger encouraged. "Take it out."

Nell gripped the handle and pulled. A hum filled the air as the thin umbrella slid out slowly from the quiver.

"Remember, all you are doing is calling forth the Night that waits inside you. Go on, Nell, unleash it!"

Nell held it for another moment, wondering if anything would happen, and, feeling Badger's eyes on her, swung the umbrella around her head quickly. Just as she feared, nothing happened – the umbrella did not spark to life, but remained lifeless and cold. An ordinary umbrella. "I can't," she said.

"Of course you can. The Night belongs to you. Use it!"

"But how…" Nell murmured, unsure of how to proceed.

"Take a chance," Badger advised. "Embrace the unknown. Be a mad one. Don't ask permission. Leap into the darkness. Be free. Welcome the mystery and I promise the power of the Night will be yours."

Nell took a deep breath and closed her eyes. She felt the umbrella in her hand.

"I can do this," she whispered to herself. Suddenly she remembered being at a lake a few years ago and swinging off a rope into the cold, dark water. Over and over she recalled the moment when her hands let go of the rough rope and her body hung in the air unattached. Free.

Nell felt her body relax, and suddenly, in the distance, she heard a rumble racing towards her. She didn't move or try to wish it away – she let it come. A surge of power tingled through her body. She had found it. More precisely, she *was* it.

She swung the umbrella again, and this time it gave off a loud and satisfying THWACK, opening crisply and cleanly. Nell's heart beat rapidly.

"Open is for protection. Closed is for fighting," Badger explained. "Now close it. Just flick your wrist."

Nell gave her wrist a slight flick and, with a *whoosh*, the Minder closed up again, thin as a long sword.

Badger reached into his chest pocket and pulled out a bar of chocolate in a golden wrapper. "If it takes a while and you get hungry, you might want this," he said.

"I want it!" Speedy said.

"You know the Fearless Traveller rule," George said. "When you bring snacks, bring enough for everyone."

"That's not a rule!" Pinch said. "Nell is going in alone. It might be a while before we see her again."

"Why?" Nell asked anxiously.

"This is the Dreamlands. Things happen," Badger said. "So please. Take this and trust we will be here when you are done."

"Take it because it's magic?" Speedy asked hopefully.

"It is chocolate, and that is magic enough. In the cold darkness it will remind you of the sweetness of the Night. Sometimes a little reminding goes a long way."

"All right," Nell said, slipping it into her pocket.

Next, Badger pulled out his *Fearless Travellers' Guide* and handed it to Nell. "This has the answer to all questions. Knowledge hard won by the bravest of the brave."

"Thank you," Nell said and turned to go. Badger stopped her.

"There is one more thing," he added. Speedy and George watched Badger like a hawk, waiting to see what fantastic weapon he would hand to Nell, but all he did was look deeply into her eyes.

"Our motto," he said.

"A motto?" Speedy shook his head in protest. "No way, man. That's our sister and our mother we're sending in there. You have to do better than some old words."

"Go on," Nell said to Badger. With each passing second, she felt more nervous about what lay ahead. The streets were filled with the calls of countless giant birds.

"These aren't ordinary words but a map. A map that has led lost souls through the worst and most wicked places for as long as Fearless Travellers have travelled through the Dreamlands."

Nell nodded and Badger spoke slowly, carefully and quietly, letting each phrase ring out like the chime of a bell.

"You will get lost.

You will be afraid.

You will fail.

You will fight.

You will remember.

You will rise.

And without doubt:

You will find your way home."

"That's a lot of stuff," George complained. "Does she have to go through all that?"

"Say them," Badger instructed. "You must say them."

Nell repeated the words. "You will get lost. You will be afraid. You will fail. You will fight. You will remember. You will rise. And without doubt: You will find your way home."

A feeling of warmth rushed through her body. Her breathing slowed and her vision felt clear. All fear had left her. She was ready. She smiled.

"Do you feel it?" Badger said.

"Yes," Nell said quietly.

"You are ready," Badger said with a nod.

"Come now, miss," McShank said. "Ravenhead, he's waiting."

Nell gave everyone hugs and let her brothers pat Rose one last time. Then the small golden bird fluttered around and took a position on Nell's shoulder.

"Be strong," Pinch encouraged.

"Nell," Badger said. "Remember while you walk into that castle by yourself, you do not walk alone. You are under the protection of the Fearless Travellers and, whatever happens, we will find you and lead you home."

"I know," Nell whispered.

"That is a promise," Badger said. "But you will be fine. Don't forget, there is more inside you than you're using."

"It's what's inside of me that I'm afraid of," Nell said, feeling the three spirit stones in her pocket. Without them, she could turn into a fox and eat her mother.

"Just remember who you are, and if that fails, use the spirit stones. Now go."

Nell said no more but followed McShank along the path, past the massive cauldron to the door of the castle.

CHAPTER 21

The large steel door opened, and Nell followed McShank into the tree-shaped castle. There was a resounding clang as the door shut behind them. To her surprise, Nell found herself gazing at an enormous circular room as grand as any palace. Crystal chandeliers hung above floors of bone-white marble, and the walls were lined with twigs and bones and shards of coloured glass, all perfectly woven together in complex, dazzling patterns. This was the home of a king. Nell felt a rush of hope. Without question, this was the right place and the right man – though he wasn't a man, or a bird, or even an ordinary Dream. He was the Bird Dreamer, and there was no doubt that the journey had been worth it. Looking around at such a grand place, Nell felt certain Ravenhead would break the spell and set her mother free, and they would return home together. What's more, Nell knew the first thing they were going to do.

"We're going to the beach," Nell said to Rose, who was on her shoulder. "And I don't care if it is the middle of the winter when we get back."

Rose tweeted happily.

"Nice how she understands you," McShank commented.

"She's my mother." Nell shrugged, as if it weren't strange.

"You must take care of your mother," McShank advised, passing a set of tall silver doors. "By the way, never ever ever take the lift in a Dreamer's house. It is the realm of the Lift Dreamer, and she is a tricky one indeed. The lifts don't go up and down but through realms and realities beyond reason. There is no telling where you might end up. You get on one floor and get off the last place you want to be."

"Stairs are fine," Nell said and followed McShank up a tall, winding staircase.

"I'm sure you'll find Ravenhead frightening. All do," McShank chatted as he scurried up the stairs. "I myself still find him scary. It is true. He is a king and a killer and most of all, scary. Terrifying, in fact. And horrible. But most of all scary. Very scary. Very, very scary."

"Can you please stop saying that?" Nell whispered.

"My point is, I'll be with you. You trust me, don't you?" McShank yelped, holding his mouth in pain. Every few seconds, his cheeks would twitch as if being struck by swift kicks from the inside, and his eyes would widen in agony.

"Your toothache is getting worse, isn't it?" Nell asked, not realizing she had ignored his question. She kindly put her hand out and touched his tiny cheek with concern. His skin was cold as a dead fish, and touching it repulsed her. Instinctively, Nell jerked her hand away with a quiet gasp, and then felt slightly rude, but McShank smiled apologetically as if it were his fault.

"I'm in terrible pain," he said sadly, stopping on a landing. "Could you give me a hug?"

"A hug?" Nell said, feeling awkward.

"Would be a great comfort," he said.

Nell nodded. The little man threw his arms around her and hugged her tightly for a second and then let go. Finally, after many more flights of stairs, they came to a door. McShank opened it and motioned for Nell to walk through. The long corridor was filled with the noise of a party. Suddenly, McShank shoved Nell into the hall with a blunt push.

"Hey!" Nell said, turning back to the door.

McShank waved his little hand. "Goodbye, girl. Goodbye forever," he said sadly and slammed the door in Nell's face and, with the click of a heavy bolt, locked it behind him.

"What are you doing?" Nell shouted. She tugged uselessly at the handle, which would not turn. Rose pecked at the door, her wings fluttering madly. Nell put her ear to the wood. She could hear McShank's footsteps running down the stairs. The truth was clear now. They were alone.

"Just us now," Nell said to Rose, who had given up and alighted on Nell's shoulder.

Nell gazed down the empty corridor. An oversized wooden door stood on one side of the long hall and a chrome lift door on the other. Behind the wooden door, a party was in progress, and the sound of clinking glasses, talking and laughter seeped out.

"Here we go." Nell straightened her hoodie, touched the handle of her umbrella for luck and knocked on the door.

Nothing happened. Rose tweeted.

"Of course I can do it louder," Nell said. She was about to smack the door when a rumbling voice, loud as a clap of thunder, called from inside.

"Enter!"

The time had come, and Nell wasn't sure she wanted it to. The voice was so deep and so loud that it was hard to imagine the type of bird it could come out of. But he had said it, and Nell was sure she didn't want him to have to repeat himself. So, her stomach fluttering, Nell put her hand on the heavy door and pushed it open.

The room Nell entered was thin and impossibly long. It had no ceiling, and the night sky shone above. As long as it was, it was narrow and cramped, filled with one large table made of rough sticks woven together like threads in a nest. Seated at the seemingly endless table, dwarfing the chairs they sat in, were birds of all types, each one at least two metres tall. There were herons, cockatoos, eagles, ospreys, vultures, turkeys, robins, mallards and all sorts of scaly winged monsters of Nightmares – dragons, griffins, massive bats and flying serpents.

All were full of raucous joy, stuffing their beaks and drinking from large bejewelled goblets – all except for the astonishing Ravenhead, who sat half-hidden in a haze of smoke at the far end of the table.

"Your Minder, please," said a hawk, who was guarding the door. Nell removed the umbrella, quiver and all, from her back and handed it to the hawk, who bowed his head.

"Go on," he said, pointing to Ravenhead. The smoke had dissipated, and now the Bird Dreamer at the end could be seen in full. If the other birds were large, he was enormous. Moreover, he was unmoving, apart from the revelry, like some mysterious obsidian statue carved in the smoky depths of the world at the beginning of time. His stillness made Nell pause.

Sensing her hesitation, he lifted his wing grandly and waved her forward. There was an awkward moment. The table took up so much of the room and the birds were so large that Nell couldn't make her way behind the chairs without being crushed. She imagined that the birds never walked along it anyway, but entered from the sky above.

Realizing she had no other choice, Nell put her hands on the edge of the table, pulled herself up until she was standing on top of it, and began to walk down the centre. The table was lined with a feast. Spread out across it were elaborate golden plates piled high with mounds of fruits and nuts, and insects fried and sautéed with berries. Plates of seeds and breadcrumbs bursting with meat and fish sat beside stews swimming with worms. It was hard to walk without stepping in the food and, try as she might to avoid it, Nell's sneakers squashed into a cherry-red jelly mould that had flies embedded in the goo.

"Sorry," she mumbled repeatedly, feeling the birds eyeing her as if she were a new kind of dessert being served, though aware she belonged to Ravenhead and was for his beak alone. None made any move towards her.

Rose perched on Nell's shoulder, looking out as if from the prow of a ship. She puffed out her yellow chest and chirped warnings at all the watching birds. Nell wished she felt as brave as her mother, but at the moment she didn't and couldn't bring herself to raise her head. Instead, to keep calm, she just watched her own footsteps until she came to a final plate directly before her and realized she could walk no further. She had reached the table's end.

Lifting her head, Nell saw she was standing in front of the great and terrible Bird Dreamer, the one responsible for populating all Dreams and all Nightmares with birds of each and every kind. On the table before him was a rectangular wooden case that looked like it contained an instrument.

Nell stood before the enormous Ravenhead and felt naked, a tender morsel ready to be pecked in two by his sharp black beak. And once she was cut, she'd never be the same. His eyes said as much. Coffin-black and half a metre high, Ravenhead's eyes seemed to be able to see her heart beating, and beat it did. Nell's heart pounded so furiously, she could hardly hear anything but its chugging thump. The great bird said nothing for an entire minute, but then, with a slight nod, he simply said, "Hello."

From the moment she had begun her walk across the table, Nell had felt her skin tingling. Distantly at first, the itch had now turned into a fierce burning. The smell of birds dizzied her senses. Hunger gripped Nell's stomach. She watched in horror as a few silver hairs poked through the skin on the back of her hand.

Oh no! No! I'm changing into a fox!

Nell reached into her hoodie pocket for a spirit stone, but there were none. She quickly padded her hands through both pockets. The horrible truth became stunningly clear.

He took them! she thought. *McShank stole the stones when he hugged me. The little creep!* Nell's body was hot and shivering all at once, trying to change. A howl was trapped in her throat. A small fox among giant birds. They would definitely kill her. She looked up at Ravenhead, who watched her with silent, knowing eyes, as if waiting to see whether she would transform.

Rose, sensing her fear, dug her tiny feet into Nell's shoulder, threw back her head, and burst into a warbling song. *Remember who you are, Nell,* she seemed to sing. *Remember who you are.*

"I am Nell Perkins. And I have come to ask for your help," Nell said, blinking and stamping her feet on the table. Plates shook. The silver fur on her hand dissolved. The smell vanished. A wave of relief swept over her.

"Greetings, Nell Perkins," Ravenhead said, his deep voice serious and direct. "You are not a Dream?"

"No, sir," Nell said. "I am a girl, and I'm awake."

"Awake? How did you find passage to the Dreamlands?"

"I had help. Two Fearless Travellers, Duke Badger and Pinch, a black panther."

"Badger," Ravenhead repeated as if it all made sense. He stared at Rose and let out a crackle sound from deep in his throat. Rose, knowing the calls of birds, flew off Nell's shoulder and landed in her upturned palm.

"And that is no bird, is it?"

"No, sir."

"It is your mother, isn't it?"

"Yes, sir, she was kidnapped and changed by the Dark Daughters. It was all my fault. I'm a terrible daughter."

The giant bird lifted its black wing and gently swept a feather across Nell's face. It felt like a hot breeze in July, just before a storm. It smelled of ancient caves, of spiderwebs, of moss and evening dampness. But there was tenderness in its touch, and the message of reassurance was clear. He was here to help.

Nell let out a breath and looked the impossibly large bird in his enormous black eyes.

"She is a kind and beautiful mother. Isn't she?" the bird asked in his ancient rumble.

Nell was surprised at the question but assured in her answer. "Yes, sir."

"Kind and beautiful is the stuff of dreams, Nell Perkins. You were right to bring her to me."

"You can change her back?" Nell asked.

"Reversing *devilartkia* is no simple bit of magic. It is dangerous, but fear not, the spell will be broken."

"Really?"

"Of course, child." He laughed a loud, booming laugh. "I am Ravenhead. But it is not something your eyes can see. It is secret, for Dreamers only. I hope you understand. So leave your mother here."

"Leave her?" Nell said.

"This is powerful magic. Too dangerous for a human to witness. You wouldn't survive. I am sorry, but that is the only way."

Nell didn't want to leave Rose, but she understood there were rules to things and she had to respect them.

"All right," she agreed.

"Down the hall is a room where you can rest and have some food. I will send for you all when it is done and your mother will be human once again."

"Thank you," Nell said, feeling a little unsteady that she had reached the end of the road and now had to leave her mother behind. For a moment she stood there and did nothing, unsure of what to do.

"Say goodbye," a large red cardinal whispered in a raspy voice, as if Nell had overstayed her welcome.

Nell nodded. She lifted her palm, where the little bird sat, so that they were eye to eye. Rose bent her little red head, and Nell rubbed her against her cheek.

"We made it," Nell whispered to her mother. "We came all this way and made it, just like I promised. But I have to leave you here."

Rose made a tiny warble in protest.

"Ravenhead is going to help you. He'll change you back, and we can go home. And guess what? I'll hug you. That's right. The unhugger will give you a really big hug."

Rose tweeted meekly a few more times. There was fright in her voice, and Nell couldn't stand it. "It will only be a few hours, Mum. I promise," Nell said.

Rose gave a few more sad chirps, but Nell shook her head and put her down on the table and watched with a sick shiver as Ravenhead laid a giant black wing over her. She wiggled out, her red head a slash in the sea of black feathers, and stared at Nell with frightened eyes.

"It's okay," Ravenhead whispered to Rose, who was now protesting wildly.

Nell knew it was best not to look back now but instead to turn and make a quick exit. If she looked back, Rose might try to fly to her. Nell's heart thumped in her chest. This was awful. It wasn't what Nell had expected. She had read many books about wizards and magicians and had thought that a flash of a wooden wand and a burst of light would do the trick. She also knew enough not to question the authority of a king. But before she could let herself walk away, she did have one question.

"Will she remember me?"

"Remember you?" Ravenhead repeated, sounding confused by the question.

All the noise in the room died away. Every eye was on Nell, making her feel nervous again. Nervous and small, as though she had shown someone her diary and that person had read it out loud and laughed.

"I was told that sometimes spells like this make you unable to remember anything," Nell said, unsure.

Ravenhead did not answer. Instead, his cold dark eyes searched Nell's face for a moment, and finally he asked Nell a question. "What do you think?"

Nell didn't have to think. She knew the answer, for it was the flame that had burned inside her every moment since the storm had stolen her mother.

"I think," she said, steadying herself, "I think that a mother always remembers her child, no matter what."

"Then that is what you should think," he said, his voice icy, and turned away briskly to talk in low tones to a large vulture.

That was a strange response, Nell thought, and she felt her temper flare. She wanted to point out that Ravenhead hadn't answered the question. But although she was angry and nervous, Nell understood that the meeting was now over, and she wanted desperately to leave. Never in her life had she wanted more to get out of a place. With an unsettled feeling that something was not quite right about it all, she sped back along the table, stepping through the piles of food. *Just go to the room,* she told herself. *Wait an hour. It will all be fine.* Reaching the edge, Nell jumped off the table and turned to the door. As she landed on the floor, she heard a frantic chirping rise above the party noise. Nell turned back quickly, and what she saw shook her to her core. There was Rose sitting in front of Ravenhead, but now she was locked inside an all-too-familiar antique birdcage.

"That's Fenn's cage," Nell mumbled to herself in confusion. Somehow she had delivered her mother back to the birdcage she had rescued her from. *Why did Ravenhead have Fenn's cage?* Nell's head spun. For a moment, time stopped. Ravenhead disappeared, and sitting in his place was Freyja Skoll, the queen of the Dark Daughters. Sitting there as clear as could be.

Nell blinked, and Freyja Skoll returned to her bird form, but Nell had seen through her disguise. That wasn't Ravenhead.

How could I have been so stupid? Nell wondered as panic overtook her. *How could I think that I could actually save my mother?* She wanted to run, wanted to save Rose. She turned and stumbled, falling hard to the dirty ground littered with bones, peels and ash. No birds reacted. All had turned away and were facing Ravenhead.

Before Nell could rise up, a hand wrapped itself around her ankle, gripping hard. "No!" Nell gasped in pain and then horror as she noticed that the hand was not attached to a body. It was the hand that had attacked her on the train platform! Nell struggled against it as she was dragged towards the darkness beneath the table.

CHAPTER 22

While Badger, Pinch, Speedy and George waited outside the fence for Nell to return, the crowd of birds was growing larger, louder and more restless.

The castle door opened, and from out of the shadows walked a lone, reed-thin giant with a human's body and a coyote's head. George watched him, intensely worried about what he would do. The man radiated a sly menace and walked as though he could and would do anything he wanted.

"Who's that?" George whispered.

"That is the Potion Dreamer," Badger answered.

At the sight of him, all noise ceased, save for the rush of the wind coming from the Potion Dreamer's suit, which was made of blowing sand. Endlessly, the red grains slipped off him and drifted into the dark, but the suit never lost its shape. In each of his thin hands he held two stones. He slid one stone across another. The rough scrape echoed loudly into the night and an orange spark was squeezed out. The Potion Dreamer nodded as if he were surprised by the spark and enjoyed it. He slid the stones together again and again. Soon a spray of sparks danced across the night. They fell upon the kindling beneath the towering cauldron. There was a great roar as all the wood caught fire and, in an instant, a small inferno blazed beneath the pot. After setting the flames, the Potion Dreamer removed a wooden flute from his suit pocket and began to play. A moaning, eerie melody escaped from the instrument and danced across the sky, working its magic on the brew inside the pot. First there was a rumble and then a loud, ear-shattering explosion.

"Birds of Dreamland," the Potion Dreamer announced. "Welcome to the Ghost Stew. Tonight we wake a Dreamer from the Dreamless place and bring him or her back to life."

A chorus of caws filled the sky as another explosion of flames shot up from the depths of the great cauldron, and a geyser of purple smoke followed, spilling over its side and spreading across the lawn. The smoke swirled around the Potion Dreamer but did not touch him, as though keeping a respectful distance. But all else, the lawn, the great cauldron, the towering castle, was quickly becoming hidden behind the smoke thick as a purple fog.

Suddenly, Speedy saw a familiar figure moving through the smoke. It was McShank, and he was alone. "Hey! Mr McShank! Where's Nell?" Speedy asked, but McShank kept running and disappeared between towering puffs of purple smoke.

Speedy knew something had gone terribly wrong. Nell was in trouble. He tried to scream, but all that came out was the violent roar of a bear. He looked at his hands, and at the sight of the large, powerful paws now in their place, he knew he had transformed.

His eyes searched the purple smoke for the leprechaun. It was impossible now. Everything was hidden. Snatches of feathers, glimpses of beaks, tips of talons: everything appeared for a moment before the smoke swallowed it once more. Speedy swung his great bear head, eyes refusing to focus. But all at once, Speedy knew it wasn't eyes he needed, but his nose. He sniffed quickly and felt something he had not felt before. The world took on a different shape. It took on the shape of scents. Everything was outlined in smells. And now among the endless scents of birds and Nightmares burnt and terrible, he found McShank. McShank's small cloud of scent was outlined like a ghost. It was made of grass and clover, melting gold and sweaty fear. It moved across the lawn in quick tiny steps. Without thinking, Speedy sprang after him, crashing through the metal fence and dashing through the smoke.

Birds scattered in all directions.

Nell, he thought. *I must find Nell.* With a snarl, he reached McShank and grabbed the little man's coat in his jaws.

"Leave me be!" McShank screamed, but as much as he struggled, he could not break the grip of Speedy's massive jaws. Speedy shook him furiously from side to side to subdue him, and then he carried the limp leprechaun through the smoke and back to the fence where Badger, Pinch and George waited.

"Nice work, boy," Badger said as Speedy released McShank from his grip.

"You rocked it," George added.

"You're not as useless as I thought," Pinch said and slapped a spirit stone onto Speedy's back, transforming him once again into a boy.

"Thanks," Speedy said proudly.

Badger snatched McShank roughly by his collar and yanked him to his feet. Badger's eyes were hot with anger and his body tense as if it were a struggle not to smash the little man to bits.

"Where is Nell?"

"I had no choice," McShank moaned guiltily. "Freyja Skoll was going to wipe out my whole family if I didn't. All my brothers. My darling mother."

"You don't have a mother!" Badger yelled.

"True. That part was a lie."

"What is Freyja Skoll doing here? Where is Ravenhead?"

"The Bird Dreamer is gone."

"Gone? Ravenhead? Impossible!" Badger snarled.

"Freyja worked some deep spell on him. He's asleep and can't be woken."

"How?"

"We stole his trumpet."

"You did what?!" Badger said with a growl.

"I know. It is awful, a terrible crime. With the help of the Potion Dreamer, we put him under a great sleeping spell, and without his trumpet, Ravenhead cannot be woken."

"The Potion Dreamer has chosen a side," Badger said, trying to take in this information. From his worried look the boys could tell the news was grim.

McShank nodded. "It is all for the mothers," he whispered, as if it was too awful to say. "The Dark Daughters have been collecting the mothers. Slowly. On the sly. No Dreamers would stand for her stealing mothers. Rules are rules, but Freyja Skoll found a way around it. She's been changing all the mothers she kidnapped into birds. Once she changes them, they're easy to steal. She's been paying the right people, getting the right favours. Change a mother here; steal a bird there. The only problem was that every time Freyja Skoll took a mother and made her into a fake bird, a real bird would die, 'cause birds and mothers are connected. A bird's song and a mother's kiss are one and the same. Ravenhead was fooled for a long while, but when he found out, he was furious. He was going to get his vengeance and destroy her whole tribe. But Freyja beat him to it. She has Ravenhead's trumpet, and it's the only thing that can wake him."

McShank smiled. "Be proud, boys. Your mother is the last one she needed. Now she can throw your mother's soul into the potion and mix it with Ravenhead's blood. He'll become a blazing sight then. Every feather a flame. Brighter than the moon on the most brilliant night. He'll fly right into the Plague Dreamer and awaken him."

"Where's Ravenhead now?" Pinch asked, glancing around. "He's not dead yet. If he were, there would be no birds left. Where is the body?"

"That can wait," Badger said.

"Can it?" Pinch shouted as the cauldron let loose another explosion. "Unless we find Ravenhead, we're all done for."

"I said, that can wait," Badger made clear, though in truth he knew that Pinch was right: that they needed to find Ravenhead and try to rouse him. But his first vow was to protect Nell and lead her home, and even though all of the Dreamlands now lay in the balance, his vow came first. "Where is Nell, McShank?" Badger demanded.

"What did you do to our sister?" Speedy roared, turning suddenly into a large bear again.

McShank quivered.

"Easy, boy," Badger said, glancing around at the birds, some of whom were taking notice of the uninvited animals in their midst. Pinch clapped a spirit stone on Speedy's arm, and he became a boy once again.

"Where is Nell?" Badger repeated.

"My tooth," McShank answered weakly. Sweat poured

from his brow, and his whole body began to shake as his mouth opened wide and a thick green vapour poured out.

"Gross," George said.

Suddenly the little man's body buckled, and he heaved over and spat a large black tooth into Badger's hand. The tooth smelled fouler than a rotten egg, and Badger dropped it as if it were a bomb.

"A CRACKER!" he yelled, and with a mighty THWACK, Badger opened his umbrella with one hand and grabbed Speedy and George with the other, yanking them under the blue column of light pouring from the underside of the umbrella.

The black molar shivered on the dying grass. With a reverberating CRACK, the tooth split open and out walked a team of six tiny black horses with glowing yellow eyes. Behind them, they pulled an equally tiny, ornate funeral carriage that looked like a toy for a demon child.

"What's that?" George asked.

"Mares. Quick-growing mares," Pinch said. "Don't touch it!"

The carriage was driven by a thin ghost in a funeral coat and was lined with windows. What was inside, behind the windows, was a terrible thing to see. Lying there on a slab of cold marble was a raven, stiff on its back.

"Ravenhead!" Speedy said. "Is that him?"

"Where is she taking him?" Badger asked.

They all watched helplessly as the little driver cracked his whip. The horses surged forward and did as their name suggested. Instantly they grew, along with the carriage, expanding quickly and massively until horses and carriage were all nine metres tall and dwarfed all the houses around them. The mobs of birds scattered as the mares raced away, charging down the street in a fit of whip cracks and shrieks, and then lifted off skywards with the force of a jet, flying high overhead and disappearing into the bruise-coloured clouds.

"She's taking Ravenhead to Vazencrack," McShank said sadly. "But it doesn't matter, because the Ghost Stew is hers. Don't you see? The Ghost Stew isn't Ravenhead's. This is Freyja Skoll's Ghost Stew. Once it comes out of the pot, none of us will make it out of here alive. That was the whole plan. Invite all who would stop her, every bird in the Dreamlands, and trap them forever."

"Who are they conjuring?" Badger asked tensely.

McShank didn't answer, as if speaking it would make it arrive faster. He shook his head vigorously. "Please. We have to leave," he gulped in a panic. "Once she rises out of the stew, we won't live. We'll fall inside it, and I don't want to be lost in there."

"Who is in the stew, McShank?" Badger repeated.

"The Maze Dreamer," McShank whispered, his eyes wide with fright.

George's heart beat furiously. Badger's brow was furrowed slightly, and Pinch's fur stood on end. Something horrible was about to happen – they could all sense it. A tear ran down McShank's cheek as the chanting of the Potion Dreamer rang through the hot air and the Maze Dreamer, one of the oldest and cruellest Dreamers who has ever wandered the dank fogs of the Wicked Places, floated up from the roiling bowels of the Ghost Stew.

CHAPTER 23

"Shh!"

Nell lay flat on the floor beneath the table. Sharp talons, twisted claws and wrinkled bird feet dangled from chairs on either side of her as far as her eyes could see. The human hand that had dragged her under the table was now pointing to a dark-haired boy who was flat on his stomach a metre away. The two children looked at one another in shock.

"Max?" said Nell.

"Quiet," he whispered in warning. He was wearing jeans, a leather overcoat and a dark wool jumper that showed only one hand. The other was missing, just as it was when she had left him in the bat tree. Over his stump, the jumper was sewn closed.

All around them, large bird feet scratched restlessly on the wooden floor; others curled their mustard-yellow claws, snatching scuttling insects as they passed, yanking them up to waiting beaks.

"How did you get here?" Nell whispered.

"A train. A train with a woman's face on the front."

"The Night Train. Before the train. How did you find the entrance?"

"Entrance? I don't know. I used to be in a cage, but I'm not in the cage any more."

"I saved you," Nell said.

"You did?"

"Yes."

"Thank you," Max whispered, deeply grateful. "I feel kind of bad I don't remember."

"It's all right," Nell said. "What *do* you remember?"

"Well, I was on a train–"

"The Night Train," Nell said.

"Yeah. I was on the Night Train with Lefty, riding along with the weirdest group of creatures ever, and suddenly the train sped up. There was a flash of light, and here I am."

"That means you're supposed to be here," Nell said, feeling somewhat reassured. "The Night Train takes you to where you are supposed to be in the dream."

"I'm supposed to be here with you?"

"I guess," Nell said quietly and then asked, "Who is Lefty?"

"My hand," Max said as if it were the most normal thing in the world to have your hand as a separate being outside your body.

"Yours? But he tried to attack me!" Nell said.

"You sure?" Max asked.

"Yes!"

"I mean, was he attacking you or dragging you? He does a lot of yanking when he wants to get someone's attention," Max explained.

"Oh," Nell said thoughtfully. It made sense. After all, the hand hadn't hit her but grabbed her hood and yanked.

"Where are we?" Max asked.

A large worm fell through a crack in the table, and a hawk talon, sharp as a tiger's claw, snatched it before it hit the ground. The movement was so fast and filled with such precise violence that both Max and Nell felt ice shoot through their veins. Their necks could be next.

Nell caught her breath and said, "We're in Ravenhead's castle. And these aren't birds."

"Dark Daughters!" Freyja's voice rang out above them. Max and Nell snapped their mouths shut. "In a moment, the Ghost Stew will begin. Before we take flight and return home, let us rejoice with a toast. Let your masks down for a moment, and let us drink the Milk of the Wicked."

All around Max and Nell, the bird feet transformed, curling into spiked black leather boots. The ragged feathers shivered as if blown by the wind and changed into silken dresses, and Nell found herself face to face with a pointed pair of bark-covered shoes.

"Anything else I should know?" Max whispered.

"Just one thing," Nell said. "If they catch us, they will kill us."

"Ravenhead has been defeated!" Freyja Skoll shouted. "We have his trumpet. He cannot be awoken."

All at once a cheer went up and all the Dark Daughters began a joyous chant.

"Collect mothers,
Break the egg,
On the death slab lay Ravenhead.
Eclipse potion down his throat,
Bird Dreamer's soul, blazing bright,
Plague Dreamer awakes,
Endless Nightmares,
Wicked delight."

"Well, ladies," Freyja quieted them. "We all know the song. Known it since we were little ones. But to generations of Dark Daughters, a song was all it was. Yes, maybe you could collect mothers. Many queens hunted them. Maybe you could even break the Red Egg. But the recipe for the Eclipse potion had long been lost. Some even suggested it never existed. Until, hidden in the darkest caves of Vrawlitz, I found it."

A gasp went through the crowd. There was a murmur of disbelief. Freyja cleared her voice and swept her eyes across the table, and the noise fell to silence. In the gentle voice of a schoolteacher, she spoke, saying the verse slowly.

"Two parts burnt cedar,
Ten parts marigold ghost toasted,
Dust of tiger eye
In an elephant skull roasted.
Mix a wedding of poppy blood and viper fang,
Vial of monkey paw soaked in lightning clang.
Now add
Gleipnir, Gleipnir,
The sacred rope.
Crush one part in,
Smash all hope.
Bird Dreamer's soul, blazing bright,
Plague Dreamer awakes,
Endless Nightmares,
Wicked delight."

A chill passed through the room, and all around them, snow began to fall, blowing in soft swirls beneath the table. The delicate crystals of powder-white ice dusted the floor and clung to Nell's and Max's eyelids. When the song was over, there was another cheer and the frantic sound of a single bird cheeping in terror.

Freyja waited for the voices to quiet and, fixing her bright green eyes on all assembled, proudly continued. "In this little cage is Gleipnir. Transformed into a bird to avoid detection."

A gale of laughter went up.

Freyja continued. "We found her in the land of Daylight, after our hunt. We were readying our return when there we saw a young girl and her mother walking through the rain. Through the confusion I could see them clearly. Connected to one another by an invisible rope, a bond forever unbreakable. Gleipnir. We only needed half and in truth I wanted the other, the young girl, but this one got snagged on the line and the hour was late. So this is who we took."

A loud trill filled the air. From inside her cage Rose was singing a defiant song. It made Nell's heart ache and all at once she felt it. Felt a pain in her heart pulling her as if there really were an invisible rope connecting her to her mother.

"Look," Freyja gasped with a little laugh. "She sings her final song. Why, it is almost as if she knows her little life is ending. Save your song, little mother. I want to hear it when I crush the soul out of you."

Laughter erupted throughout the hall. Nell's whole body was trembling, and she looked at Max, her eyes filling with tears.

"It's not your fault," he said.

"I'm useless," she whispered hotly and put her arms over her face like a child hiding beneath the covers. There was a quiet thump as something flew out of her pocket and landed in front of her. Nell lifted her head. Max was staring in surprise at what he had just seen. On the floor before her was *The Fearless Travellers' Guide*. The book cracked itself open and the pages fluttered, moving as if blown by the wind until they stopped on a blank page. Ink raced across the page, forming a picture of an antique alarm clock, the round kind with hands and two large bells at the top.

Beneath the picture, it read:

TO FIGHT DARK DAUGHTERS

The dark demon sisters known as the Dark Daughters cannot be harmed by you, so do not attempt to fight them. They can only be destroyed by a council of Dreamers. The only hope is to stun these demons and make a quick exit. As time is their enemy, the proper way to do so is with a clock.

Remove this clock, and set the hands to 11.59.57.

Breathe deeply, pull the knob and throw accurately. When the clock goes off, the Dark Daughters will be frozen. You will have sixty seconds or more before they send one of their BEASTIES after you.

They look like this:

On the bottom of the page was a picture of a beastie. The creature was a horrible little monster that looked like a monkey covered in green lizard skin. His eyes were electric lights, his hands wielded enormous curved fingernails and his mouth was filled with razor-sharp fangs.

With *The Fearless Travellers' Guide* between her fingers, Nell felt her confidence flowing back. She wasn't just a twelve-year-old girl. She was a Fearless Traveller, and she wasn't alone. She glanced over at Max. She had help. The Dark Daughters had taken her mother, but they weren't going to get away with it. She might fail. She might flee. But Nell was going to fight and, without a doubt, she would find her way home!

"We're going to get out of here," she said, wiping the tears from her eyes.

"I know we will," Max reassured her. "What's the plan?"

"We need that trumpet as much as we need my mother. The trumpet case is on the table. I'll get Rose. You grab the trumpet, and then we'll both head for the exit."

"Then what?"

"I have no idea, but I think it's probably best if we don't get caught."

"Don't get caught?" Max repeated. "That's it?"

"Yes," Nell said, suddenly self-conscious. It had seemed like the right thing to say when it was in her brain, but now she wasn't sure.

"That the stupidest plan I've ever heard."

"Sorry," Nell said, slightly deflated, but Max smiled brightly.

"I love it."

"What?"

"Stupid plans are the best," Max said, "and they always work."

Nell turned back to the book and studied the picture. *Remove the clock?* She turned the book over, looking for a secret compartment, but there was none. It had to be the drawing. With a shaky finger she reached over and touched the illustration at the bottom of the page. Instead of being stopped by the page, her fingertips slid into it as if the page were a pool of water with something floating below the surface. The clock felt solid and metal. Nell grabbed hold and pulled it out. As it peeled off the page, it gained mass, filling out until it was a solid antique clock. The face was white and the numbers bright red. Nell turned it over. On the back was a piece of masking tape, and scrawled across it in marker were the words "Sparktondale Supplies".

Nell felt a pang of happiness, as though Badger were right beside her. Steeled for what was about to follow, she turned the knobs and set the alarm. "Whatever happens, don't let them have that case," she told Max.

Max nodded and, with a breath, Nell pulled on the starting lever. At once, the clock began to tick loudly, and boots began to shuffle as though they sensed approaching danger.

"Now!" Nell urged and shot out, followed by Max and Lefty. As she appeared from beneath the table, all eyes were instantly riveted to the big alarm clock she held in her hand.

"Clock!" a Dark Daughter shouted, pointing at Nell, who had her eyes fixed on the head of the table where Freyja Skoll stood, regal and furious. At the sight of the Dark Daughter queen, a red-hot rage filled Nell. It was unlike anything she had ever felt before. With a roar, she cocked back her arm and threw the clock, hurling it as hard as she could straight towards Freyja Skoll. As it sailed through the air like a hand grenade, the alarm rang out, loud, clear and utterly beautiful, instantly freezing every Dark Daughter solid as a statue. The clock sailed in a perfect arc and hit the stunned queen in the centre of her frozen face. The moment it did, Freyja Skoll's head vanished in a puff.

"RUN!" Max screamed.

Nell didn't waste a second before jumping on the table and running towards the cage. Max was right behind her. On either side of them, the Dark Daughters, some half-changed back into birds, stood still as statues, every part of them frozen except for their eyes, which followed Nell with venomous hatred.

By the time Nell reached Rose, the little bird was chirping wildly. "I am so sorry," Nell said, opening the cage door. She'd hoped that Rose would jump onto her outstretched palm, but Rose darted back towards the exit from the room. Nell understood completely. This wasn't the time for apologies.

"Now," Max said. He held the trumpet case and started running. With her heart racing, Nell followed Max and her mother, running as hard as she could along the table.

The alarm that was keeping the Dark Daughter frozen was getting weaker with each ring. Any second, the noise that was protecting her would end, and a flood of evil demons would be upon her.

As she got to the end of the table, it happened. The alarm ended. There was a blink of silence, then immediately the room filled with screams of agony as the Dark Daughter held their ears in pain. From their mouths, they began to spit great purple globs of slime. The globs hit the table and took form, springing up into scaly beasties the size of small monkeys. Chattering viciously, the beasties locked eyes on Nell and gave chase. As Nell reached the door of the banquet hall, she snatched her umbrella from the still-dazed Dark Daughter who was guarding the entrance.

Max had made it through the door, his hand tightly gripping the wooden case. Nell wasn't so lucky. Before she could make it through, a dozen beasties jumped over her head and turned, blocking her way. Nell was about to swing her umbrella and see if she could really use it when Lefty scurried beneath her legs and curled himself into a fist, giving the beasties hard punches in their squealing faces.

"Thanks," Nell said to the hand as they both fled into the hall, shutting the door behind them. Max was already at the far end of the corridor, holding the doors of a waiting lift open with the wooden trumpet case.

"Come on. The doors want to shut!" he yelled.

"The stairs!" Nell screamed. She had forgotten to tell him about the Lift Dreamer. "We have to take the stairs!"

But it was too late. The door to the banquet hall burst open in a spray of splintering wood, and with deafening shrieks, the beasties flooded out by the dozens. If there was a stairwell, they'd never find it now. All that mattered now was getting away. Nell darted down the hall and shot past Max into the dark lift. The doors slid closed with slicing force, and a rain of thumps pounded against the metal. It was a small, wood-lined little room with a brass handrail along the wall and a crystal chandelier hanging from the ceiling. For a moment there was silence and then the hum of the lift moving.

"What were you screaming?" Max asked.

"Take the stairs," Nell said.

"Why?"

"Because in the Dreamlands, the lifts don't go between floors but through realms and realities. There is no telling where we might end up."

"Sorry," Max said as suddenly the lift sped up. Nell could feel her stomach drop and her voice snatched from her throat. A distant roar shook the walls. Overhead the chandelier swung, the crystal chiming. Whether they were falling or flying, it was impossible to tell. All they could do was clutch the handrail and jerk to a stop. Nell's heart began beating like a drum in her chest.

"It's going to be okay," Max assured her. Nell nodded silently as the doors opened slowly, revealing a vast wasteland of dark concrete cracked by the beating sun.

"Where are we?" Max said.

One look told Nell the truth. "The Wicked Places," she whispered.

CHAPTER 24

The Maze Dreamer climbed out of the cauldron and stood before it, looking around and blinking her eyes like she had just awoken from a deep slumber. The long-dead Dreamer, newly risen, was a beautiful woman. She was a giant, as all Dreamers are, and was dressed in an opulent, hooped and bejewelled dress of pristine orange silk with puffed-out lace shoulders that looked as if a powerful Renaissance queen had worn it hundreds of years ago. Her dark hair was swept up, woven into a complex stack that showed off her long neck. Her skin was pale as bones tumbled by the sea, adorned with a tattoo on each cheek. The ancient markings were perfectly round mazes with an intricate Celtic design. And along her sides were not one but three pairs of slender, silk-covered arms.

She looked around and sighed, happy to be once again in the Dreamlands. One pair of arms was busily brushing away wisps of smoke that still swirled around her like harried attendants. Another set of arms was delicately putting lipstick on her thin lips, while the final set of arms was taking off her long white gloves and stretching like a fighter about to step into a boxing ring.

"Shouldn't we be running?" Speedy asked. For as beautiful as this woman was, she radiated a sinister menace, a punishing sense of evil. The drawings of Druid mazes on her face began to glow the incandescent orange of molten metal.

"We will not run," Badger answered with the grave knowledge of one who had been through this before and barely survived. "As far as you could get right now, running as hard as you could at your fastest, you would not escape. There is no escaping the Maze Dreamer now. Once inside the maze, the trick is not to run, but to face the confusion before you with calmness."

"Maybe your problem is you just don't run fast enough," George said.

"No one runs fast enough to escape the Maze Dreamer," McShank responded.

"Sorry," George said, "but that's loser talk."

"We must stay together," Badger said. "If we get separated, you won't return."

"But you'd find us?" Speedy asked.

"That's kind of what you do," George pointed out. "The whole Fearless Traveller thingamabob?"

"I would hunt for you for as long as it took, as is my vow," Badger replied, "but by the time I found you, you might be ninety years old."

"Not the most positive guy, is he?" George said to Pinch.

"That was positive," Pinch replied.

"It could take a thousand years," McShank moaned. "I'll lose my whole life lost in the maze. Aye. There's nothing worse than the maze."

"So don't move?" Speedy said, trying to be clear on what he had to do to survive.

"I didn't say that," Badger snarled. He pulled a small copy of *The Fearless Travellers' Guide* from his back pocket.

"You're going to read now?" George moaned. "Save it for the library, man."

"I thought you gave that to Nell," Speedy said.

"I always carry an extra," Badger grunted and opened the book, scanning the pages until he found the one he wanted. At the top of a page was a pen-and-ink drawing of a mountain-climbing rope. He stuck his fingers into the pages. They slipped inside as if submerging into water, and from the paper he pulled out a rough length of cable. Working quickly, he tied climbing clamps onto the rope and had the boys wrap its length around their waists and through the clamps until Speedy, George, Pinch and Badger were all attached like mountaineers battling a windswept peak.

"What about me?" McShank said, left out of the line and desperately pulling at the rope like a man grasping for a lifeboat.

"What about you?" Badger said. "This is your doing. You are on your own, McShank."

"You can't let me be lost!" He was crying now. "Never see my poor mother again."

"You don't have a mother," George reminded him.

"I meant brother. I have eight brothers. Helpless they are."

"Criminals!" Pinch said with scorn. "Each one worse than the others."

"Come on," Speedy said. "Give the leprechaun some rope."

"He sent your sister in alone to meet Freyja Skoll!" Badger bellowed.

"I'm sorry," McShank snivelled. "So sorry. I was scared. I made a mistake."

Speedy undid his section of rope from the clamp.

"What are you doing?" George said, kicking the leprechaun, who winced but did not react. "Not next to me, you're not."

"Don't do it, boy!" Badger warned Speedy. "He is a Nightmare. He gets nothing."

"Sounds wrong to me," Speedy said. "Everyone deserves something." He undid the rope and, without further explanation, pulled McShank beside him, wrapping the rope snugly around both of them so they were now joined side by side.

"Nell would want me to," Speedy said as if trying to convince himself.

"No, she wouldn't," said George.

"We'll ask her!" Speedy roared, losing his temper and suddenly transforming into a large bear.

"We can't, because of *him*!" George said, turning into a rat, fangs bared.

McShank let out a frightened yelp.

"BOYS!" Badger said, smacking them both with spirit stones. Instantly, they both reverted to humans. "Hold tight. The Maze Dreamer begins her dream!"

"Good evening," the Dreamer said, raising her head to all the birds pressed together in the street. She took a deep breath. "The night air. My goodness, that is delicious. You never forget how good fresh night air feels when you are in the Dreamless Place."

She spoke with a cold calmness, like a strict substitute teacher who had come to explain to her new class the way things will be run. The kind of teacher who makes it clear just by the way she moves and talks that any hopes you had of slacking off should be immediately forgotten.

"Now. Here is what's going to happen. Actually, it has already happened. But I want to explain it to you anyway, because fighting against it will be quite painful and will assure you endless wandering. I say this because I am not a Dreamer

234

who inflicts pain. I merely am the maze. In mazes, there is a way in and a way out. Though none of you shall be getting out, I'm afraid. I mean, it is possible, but my dear friend Freyja Skoll woke me to ensure that all of you are trapped in the maze. You see, the fewer of you in the dreams of others, the weaker your Ravenhead is in the land of Dreams."

Birds began to squawk in confusion. They knew they should fly away, but they couldn't flap their wings. Just as the Dreamer said, what was going to happen had already begun. They were trapped by her powerful magic.

The Maze Dreamer's body buckled and shivered. The tattoos on her cheeks glowed bright orange, making her pale face appear as if bathed in the light of a roaring flame.

"Oh dear," she said with a surprised laugh at the force of the dark magic that was coursing through her body. "Here it comes…"

The Maze Dreamer spread her six arms wide, and each of her six palms began to glow a deep amber. Then suddenly something sprang from her palms like webs from a spider. But instead of webs, they were walls, each one six metres high, one metre thick, and made of old grey castle stone. The walls unfurled from her palms like long ribbons, spraying in slithering curves that shot off in every direction across the night. Some of the walls climbed in waves towards the stars, shattering through the branches of the trees above, which fell to the earth in large clumps. Other walls landed on the ground in ear-shattering thuds, and others charged forward in rigid lines. In seconds, the streets of Crypt were no longer streets but the corridors of a maze. Large walls of stone separated one side from the other, twisting in a relentless expansion, turning the world into an endless labyrinth.

The Maze Dreamer swung her arms around like a conductor leading a thundering symphony, and the great walls that flew from her palms spread wildly.

"Dreams are the only truth," she said. "One night, you dream and find yourself alone in a dark wood. One night, the rooms of your house never end. Sometimes you find yourself in the corridors of your school or the place you work, and all goes on and on and the truth is clear. You are lost. You are lost. You are lost. All come to the maze in the end," she said tenderly, her voice a near lullaby. "Don't believe hope. Don't believe in escape. None will be found."

In the trees was a dizzying *rat-tat-tat* of flashing lights – thousands of bright, white-hot pops of illumination, like camera flashes, as people across the world awoke from this awful dream, shivering and moaning. No one realized it was actually happening in a realm beyond their own, in a place they visited but never knew was real. For the birds there was no waking up, no getting out. Trying to fly above the wall would not help, for the walls would always be there, twisting, turning, blocking them from leaving.

Badger held tight to the rope, pulling hard, as the boys, scared by the noise and the orange sparks of stone walls hitting the ground and spreading like octopus arms, tried to run.

"Let go!" George screamed.

"Steady," Badger said, swiping a match on the ground. The blue tip sparked to life and shone like a lighthouse in a fog.

"Here it comes," Badger barked above the din, digging his heels into the ground as a large wall of stone headed straight for them. It was a colossal, towering sheet of heavy, bone-crushing granite. It moved fast, speeding along what had been a main street, but would never be again. The wall would crush and destroy anything that stood in its path, but still Badger held his group in place.

"What are you doing?" George yelled, straining to get free.

"We must choose correctly," Badger said, staring at the oncoming wall as calm as if he had been inspecting cakes in a bakery. Chunks of asphalt spewed into the air as the massive wall carved its way towards them with explosive force. Badger's eyes calculated, his nose twitching as he took in the scents in the air, and he mumbled to himself.

"He's going to KILL US!" McShank screamed, yanking at the rope. "He's crazy!"

Suddenly, with a burst of power, Badger pulled hard, moving the group to the left as the rumbling sheet of perfectly piled stone slid past, close enough that they could feel the wind of it shooting by on their faces.

Instinctively, they made to run as far as they could, but Badger pulled them in as another wall rushed by with the ear-piercing wail of a high-speed train. All around them were birds, flying in great flocks towards an escape that they would never find. Their wings kicked up a great storm of blinding dust, and through it all, the light of Badger's match never once dimmed. He told the boys to watch its glow. He knew if they focused on it and felt the rope, they'd know they were connected to something and not alone.

"How do we get out?" George asked as the dust cleared, his voice quiet, for this was truly the most frightening place he'd ever been. On either side of them, rising three metres high, were walls of stone, freezing to the touch. The walls stretched in either direction for a hundred metres before they split and turned, leading in two or three directions to places they couldn't see.

"That depends on where we are," Badger said.

"Where we are? We're nowhere. That's the whole point!" George was starting to lose it.

"Easy there," Speedy said, putting his hand on his brother's shoulder and giving it a squeeze.

George knocked it off in despair.

"There is no such place as nowhere," Badger said. "Especially in the Dreamlands. And now we will find out where we are." All around them, the walls of the maze began to transform. The blank grey bricks of stone suddenly were covered with striped wallpaper, adorned with circus animals and antique wall lights that gave off a rosy glow. Every metre there was an identical mirror in the shape of a moon and a framed French poster of a man on a unicycle. George and Speedy glanced at each other in stunned silence. The looks in their eyes reflected shock and horror.

"What is it?" Badger said.

"This is our house," Speedy mumbled in amazement.

"Are we home?" George whispered hopefully.

"You should hope not!" McShank said.

"Familiar mazes are the most deadly," Badger explained.

"Filled with hidden things," Pinch added.

"Our house isn't deadly!" Speedy protested.

"But this isn't your house," Badger explained. "Not really. It is a Nightmare's version of your house."

"What do we do now?" Speedy asked.

"What he means is, how do we escape?" George added.

"When lost in a maze, walk forward," Badger said, and he began to move slowly. They all followed behind, still joined at the waist by the rope. Badger kept his hand on the wall, moving his fingertips along, fluttering them as though playing a piano.

As he walked, he explained. *"The Fearless Travellers' Guide* tells it all better than I can, but the long and short of it is this. The Maze Dreamer is an ancient Dreamer, one of the first of all Dreamers, which is why even cavemen drew mazes. As time passed, her power grew, and she became so powerful that she began to secretly take control of the world. All wars, all madness are mazes. It was why all the other Dreamers had her banished to the Dreamless Place. The Maze Dreamer is many things, but above all else, she is a liar. She says that in the maze, there is no hope, but that is not quite true. Because inside all the walls is a river – a roaring, golden river. It is the only hope you need. Find the river, and you can sail through the walls to escape."

Badger stopped as though he had located the spot he was looking for. He tapped on the wall and looked at Pinch. She put her large, dark head against the wall, listening intently. Her tail twitched, her nose moved. She stuck out her tongue and licked the wall.

"I think I speak for everyone when I say *yuck!"* said George.

"This is the spot," Pinch said confidently.

Badger pulled out his *Fearless Travellers' Guide* once again. He held the small, weathered, leather-bound book in his hands and, grunting, gave it a hard twist until he had bent it into the shape of a cone.

"What are you doing?" George asked.

"Listening. For beneath all the confusion of the maze – the darkness, the endless halls, the unbreakable stone – beneath what you think you see and where you think you are, hope is there, waiting for you."

Duke Badger put the small opening of the cone to his ear and the other opening to the wall. He nodded and motioned for the boys to take a turn. They each put their ears to the listening side of the cone. The sound was nearly imperceptible, but it was there. Soft and slow, a *drip, drip, drip* of water drumming on stone.

"The river. It's not strong enough here," Badger said. "We must keep walking until we find it rushing."

Walk they did. For hours, they trudged single-file through a hall that George and Speedy had known all their lives. Flocks of frightened birds shot around them with angry caws, and they had to cover their heads so as not to be cut by their razor-sharp talons. Winds sometimes hot, sometimes cold blew, fluttering their clothes around them. Unlike their own house, which was a comforting and clean place, the walls of this endless corridor were sad, dreary and filled with an evil strangeness. Spiderwebs hung from lights, and the wallpaper was stained with blotches of mould.

"Look," George said as they passed a familiar family photo that hung in the hall.

"Weird," Speedy said as he studied it. And weird it was. The people in the pictures looked not so much like them, but like actors who had been hired to play them. It was unsettling and gave Speedy the feeling that he couldn't remember what he or his family really looked like.

But that wasn't the worst. Worst was the toys. Every time the maze turned, they'd see a new batch. Some of their favourites from childhood, broken, burnt and torn, with stuffing falling out of the holes. Dogs, bunnies, raccoons, pink elephants, the ones they'd slept with and loved and hugged through endless nights, creatures that they needed now more than ever, would see them and scuttle away like roaches at the snap of a light, disappearing down another corridor.

"Buddy!" Speedy yelled after a beloved stuffed Jack Russell terrier of long ago. The dog was missing both her eyes.

"What kind of name is that for a dog?" McShank asked.

"What kind of name is McShank for an idiot?" George said. "Oh, I know. A good one."

And all the while they walked on, not resting, and Badger studied the wall of the maze, stopping here and there to lift the cone to his ear and listen for the river he claimed flowed inside the stone. Finally, he stopped. "Here," he said.

Badger unhooked himself from the line. The wind had picked up and was whistling briskly down the corridor. The smell of a distant fire hung in the air.

"This is going to take a while," he said. "Whatever happens, don't move. When the river appears, you dive in. Don't think. Don't ask how. Just dive into the water. Understand? Any questions?"

George raised his hand.

Badger nodded. "Yes?"

"Please tell me we don't have to see you in a bathing suit."

"Just keep your mouth shut and your eyes on me."

"So you have some dynamite to blow a hole in it or something?" George said, nodding at the wall.

"Something like that," Badger grunted as he pulled out a handkerchief from his back pocket and tore it into strips. He took the strips and began wrapping his knuckles, like a boxer before a fight. He worked slowly, keeping his eyes focused on what he was doing, concentrating on what was about to come. Finally, he turned to the wall, nodded at Pinch, and stood, legs firm. With a deep breath, he let loose a powerful punch to the wall. There was a dull thud and a jump of dust. He quickly followed with a second punch. *Thud.* And another. *Thud. Thud.*

Thud. Hitting the wall in a slow, steady rhythm. The wrappings offered little protection, and with each punch, Badger winced, teeth gritted against the pain. The more he hit, the more the wallpaper crumbled away, revealing the dead granite blocks. Then, a tiny bit of the rock began to crumble in places, and beneath it, a golden spray of something rushing behind the wall was clear. A river. A river buried beneath the stone!

It was slow, painful work, and Badger breathed heavily. Sweat poured from his face. But not for a second did he stop pounding the wall. And all the while, with each punch, he muttered a single word to keep up his spirits. "Yes," he grunted quietly, almost secretly. "Yes."

While Badger was breaking through the stone, Speedy made a mistake. Even though he had been instructed not to turn, to keep his eyes forward, he couldn't get the thought of Buddy out of his head. How he had loved that little stuffed dog. From the corner of his eye, he saw something dart through the darkness. McShank was also watching.

"You see a dog?" Speedy whispered.

"A little white one, you mean?"

"Yeah."

"Saw her right round there," McShank said knowingly.

Speedy gave a quick flick of his head and there it was, a tiny flash of white darting around the corner.

"It's Buddy!" Speedy said, but no one was listening. All eyes were on the hole Badger was opening in the wall. The passage in the stone was almost big enough to escape through, and behind it, a golden river was rushing past with a singing hum.

"Hold the line!" Pinch instructed. "A few more punches, and we can dive through."

There was the sound of barking: the scared, mournful bark of a lost dog begging for a way home.

"Get her," McShank instructed, grabbing Speedy's arm, his green eyes blazing with tears. "Go on and get yer little Buddy. You saved me, boy, and I'm paying back the favour. You can't leave her here. Get her quick, before we leave this place."

Speedy nodded at the wise leprechaun and, without thinking, he unhooked himself and darted into the inky blackness of the maze.

It was like diving into a lake. From the moment he left his friends, all was utterly dark and silent. Speedy's heartbeat pounded in his ears. Turning the corner, he found himself before the door to his very own room. A puddle of light was flowing through the crack at the bottom. A soft bark was coming from inside.

"Buddy!" Speedy said, overjoyed to be reunited with his old lost friend.

Speedy opened the door and, standing there, framed in candlelight, was Fenn. Of all the things Speedy had expected, this was not one of them.

"Hello," he said in confusion.

"Goodbye," Fenn said, revealing a set of pointed fangs. Like a coiled snake, she darted forward, biting him on the shoulder. Her venom slipped into his blood and instantly his head began to spin.

Speedy screamed. Above him, he could hear the wicked laughter of McShank, who hopped onto a passing bat and flew away, calling, "Enjoy the maze, boy. You'll be stuck in it forever."

Before Speedy knew it, he was down on the ground, Fenn standing over him, her boot on his throat. She held a small, curved knife in her hand and was screaming, "Where is she? Where is my bird?"

There was a deafening roar, and the enraged Fenn turned, too late, to see Pinch, who smacked her away from Speedy with one strong paw. The force of the blow bounced Fenn to the floor, and before she could rise, Pinch had pinned her massive jaws around the small girl's terrified face. Quickly, Pinch snapped a pair of handcuffs onto Fenn's tiny wrists.

"Bring them both!" Badger yelled from the wall, continuing with his work. "The river appears."

Speedy was blinded by the pain. Nothing made sense. Where was Buddy? On one end of the hall was the stairs, and at the other end was their mother's bedroom. They were in the stretch upstairs between Nell's room, the room Speedy shared with George and a bathroom, but they never reached the rooms at the end of the hall. It was maddening. They would come close to a room, and the maze would suddenly turn and the room would disappear into the distance. The world was a complete blur. But then his little brother was beside Speedy, helping him to his feet. The only thing he knew for sure was that his shoulder felt like it was on fire and dripping blood.

"Come on. We have to move. You can do it," George said, pulling his dazed brother by his hand as Pinch nudged the shackled Fenn forward. They reached Badger, who inspected Speedy's wound.

"You're going to be fine," he said, but his eyes said different. "Hold your brother's hand. Understand?"

Speedy nodded.

"You got him?" Badger asked, turning to George.

"Yes," George said.

"That's right," Badger said. "Keep saying that."

Badger unlocked one of Fenn's handcuffs and hooked it onto the collar around Pinch's neck.

"Get me off this dirty cat!" Fenn yelled.

"Correct me if I'm wrong, but as far as I know, Dark Daughters can't swim," Pinch said. "I'll let you go, but then you are on your own."

Fenn looked into the coursing golden river streaming behind the last thread of rock, and her already pale face got whiter still. She lowered her head and said nothing.

The wrappings on Badger's hands were ripped, ragged, and stained with blood. Another punch seemed one more too many, but one more was what was needed. Badger quietly murmured the Fearless Travellers' motto, reared back, and gave the wall a final punch. He grunted against the pain.

The last stones fell away. Golden light shone over them.

"Yes!" Badger shouted as the roar of a raging river filled their ears. Spray danced across their cheeks. The boys readied themselves to dive into the coursing rapids, but there was no need for that. It was not a river you dived into but a river that took you. With the speed of a bullet, a hand as tall as Badger made of river water shot out, wrapped its wet fingers around their bodies, and yanked them inside with great force. The breath left their lungs as they disappeared into the golden river.

PART THREE
THE WICKED PLACES

CHAPTER 25

Nell and Max stood alone beneath a gunmetal-grey sky in a desert of black asphalt, taking in where they now found themselves. In the distance was a place that was at once familiar and deeply confusing. Rising up before them, far into the sky, was the closed head of a rose. It was the mirror image of the city of Dreamdon. Yet, unlike Dreamdon, the rose was made of rusted iron.

"What's that?" Max said, trying to comprehend the towering flower.

"The place we need to go. We're in the Wicked Places," Nell whispered.

"That doesn't sound good." Max studied the dark city in the distance as the ground began to rumble beneath their feet. A great screeching of metal on metal rang out across the asphalt plains as the iron flower began to open, twisting slowly. The massive rusted walls bowed down, stretching across the desert floor, revealing a sinister metropolis inside.

The skyline of the wicked city before them wasn't just the skyline of one particular city, but the shape of every oppressive city from the beginning of time. Heartless skyscrapers of glass and chrome, towering factories spewing smoke, rotting wooden mansions covered with vines, forbidding castles encased in their own green mists and spiralling prisons from a far-off future made of flickering neon beams of light, all woven together in one perfectly balanced shape, as though the sinister city weren't a collection of buildings, but a single living entity of evil.

Suddenly Nell and Max both felt a hard pull on their chests. They were flung forward, and the world around them began to blur with passing speed. It lasted less than a blink, and then they were deep inside the city. The pavement they now stood on was bustling, filled with a lively mob of humans and animals in different costumes from different eras going about a busy work day, much like they had in Dreamdon, except for one terrible difference. Everyone and everything was a skeleton.

"What is this place?" Max whispered.

Nell saw a rusted metal sign that stretched across the broad avenue and pointed. The sign read "Boneville".

No skeletons took any interest in them, yet still Nell felt scared. She petted Rose with her finger and gave her a kiss on the head. The softness of her red feathers steadied her, and her smell gave her hope.

For a few hours Max and Nell wandered through the twisting streets of the city looking for something that would lead them to Vazencrack. Some clue. Some direction. Anything. On every street stray skeleton dogs trotted along looking for food, filling Nell with sadness.

"Look," Max said, nodding his head towards a poster on a bus stop. It showed a few skeletons in winter gear standing before a sinister black mountain. The poster read:

VISIT VAZENCRACK
HOME OF THE BLOODY MOUNTAIN

TAKE A GOYLE BUS!
BUSES LEAVE DAILY FROM BONEVILLE

Max suddenly leapt back as a large knife fell between them. The fat blade plunged into the pavement at their feet, vibrating with the power of the fall. Nell and Max both looked up, expecting to see a knife-throwing Dark Daughter overhead, but all they saw was an innocent-looking grey cloud. Suddenly, another knife came hurtling towards them. A glinting cleaver with a razor-sharp blade swooshed down, nearly slicing the tip off Nell's nose.

The noise startled Rose, who darted from her perch on Nell's shoulder into the air.

As she flew, another knife, identical to the last, fell right past her wing. She turned and tweeted as another knife zoomed past.

"It's raining knives!" yelled Max. The skeletons on the street had all run into shops. There was a loud clatter as blades hit those skeletons that were too slow. Their bones scattered like sheets of broken glass.

"MUM!" Nell screamed as Rose zigzagged in the sky, dodging blades. Another knife sliced so close to Nell's hand that it scraped her. "Ow!"

Max glanced at her. "What do we do?" he asked as a knife plunged close enough to rip a line in his leather overcoat.

Nell didn't even think about what she was doing, but quickly reached behind her back and pulled out her umbrella. She planted her feet and tried to hear the whisper of the Night as Badger had instructed. For a moment, all she heard was the clatter of metal on the pavement, but then behind that she realized there was something else – a distant hum of flowing energy. The noise rang in Nell's ears, and with a yell she swung her arm. This time, with a loud, satisfying *THWACK,* the umbrella opened.

"Get under," she said, grabbing Max and pulling him close. Lefty leapt onto Max's shoulder as he scooted in beside Nell. From beneath the umbrella's dome came a warm shaft of blue light. Above their heads was the sound of thuds hitting the top of the umbrella, but no blades poked through. They both watched in silent horror as Rose wove her way between the knives, finally reaching Nell's shoulder and letting loose an excited trill as the storm broke wild.

All around them, the knives fell and clattered, sticking into everything. The noise was tremendous – a sea of humming blades slicing the air and crashing in metal cascades against every surface.

"This is a really good umbrella," Max said.

"You have no idea," Nell answered with relief.

As quickly as it began, the storm ended. They remained under the protection of the umbrella for a few moments more, just to be safe. The air was still buzzing with the vibrating clang of all the fallen metal. Finally, Nell and Max stepped out from beneath the umbrella. The black dome resembled a porcupine, with gleaming blades sticking out all over. Nell gave it a SWING. The knife blades flew off as the umbrella closed with a THWACK. Nell put it carefully over her shoulder.

"You're good with that thing," Max said.

"We need to find the bus station," Nell answered. "Before it starts to snow pigs."

"Don't worry about the bus station. Lefty's got it," Max said with confidence. "He can always point out the way."

The hand leapt from Max's shoulder, touching the ground with the nimble grace of a gymnast. The second he hit the pavement, he was off, scuttling down the street through skeletal legs and bony feet.

"He's better than a bloodhound," Max joked, grabbing the wooden trumpet case with his one good hand and hurrying after the disembodied other.

As they walked, the sun peeked through the clouds. The knives that littered every surface began to evaporate, first becoming limp and spongy and then disappearing altogether. Soon, they came to a large, crumbling building. Lefty pointed to a pink neon sign above the door, which buzzed with the words "Goyle Bus Route".

"Told you he was good," Max said proudly.

Inside, the station was nearly empty save for several wooden benches and a ticket window. A few skeletons in suits and dresses were seated or wandering around, talking on phones, reading newspapers or watching the slowly clicking departure board. On the walls were advertisements that showed skeletons doing all sorts of things: playing tennis, eating burgers, driving sports cars and utterly enjoying their skeletal lives.

Nell saw the ticket window and approached. A skeleton wearing a green plastic visor and a waistcoat on his bony shoulders turned to Nell.

"When does the next bus to Vazencrack leave?" Nell asked as politely as she could.

"Next bus leaves in three hours. But I wouldn't go."

"Why not?"

"Clowns. They're on a rampage in the hills. Stopped six buses last week. No one saw the passengers again."

A shudder went up Nell's spine, and in her mind's eye she saw Venom Shivers's cruel painted face sneering at her. Instinctively, she turned towards the exit. No way. There was no way she could see that clown, or any clown, ever again.

"Where are you going?" Max asked.

"I…" was all Nell could say, the fear so strong now she could hardly breathe. She sped out of the station with Rose on her shoulder. The *clip-clop* of horses' hooves filled the air. Nell looked towards the skeletal horse driven by a mournful ghost, a woman with long white hair, a flowing dress and a tearful face. Coming up beside her was a band of ghosts playing a funeral march. A scream rattled the air, and then came the sound of broken glass. Somewhere a fight was unfolding.

Nell took it all in and knew the truth. There was nowhere else to go. They were in the Wicked Places now; evil and fear would be everywhere.

"Nell!"

Nell turned. Max was standing at the entrance to the bus station. He held up his good hand and pressed his index finger to his thumb, making a circle, and then flipped his arm up and placed it to his eye so he was looking out of it.

"Nothing can hurt us when I have my safety monocle," he said.

Nell smiled as Max made a goofy face and pretended to be a fancy gentleman. It was just what she needed. Not to hear "it's going to be okay" or "don't worry", just a reminder that they had found each other again, and as long as they were together, they'd help each other no matter what.

Max's stomach let out a loud grumble.

"Sorry," he said.

Nell reached into her pocket and pulled out the chocolate bar Badger had given her.

"What's that?" Max asked.

"Chocolate."

"Is it magic?"

"It's chocolate," Nell said, carefully unwrapping the golden foil. Her stomach rumbled. She hadn't realized how hungry she was. She snapped off a few squares and handed them to Max and then broke off a few for herself. The bar was smooth and rich and melted gently on her tongue.

"Man," Max said, closing his eyes. "That's good."

They talked about saving some for later, but they continued to eat. Nell offered Rose a square, but the little bird would not even give it a peck. In a few minutes, the bar was gone and both Nell and Max felt better.

They slipped back inside the bus station and purchased their tickets. Nell had found a few pounds inside her *Fearless Travellers' Guide*. Having time before the bus left, they found a place on a bench beside a large skeleton who began snoring. Nell and Max both looked at each other and suddenly they began to laugh. It was one of those fits of laughter that comes on quickly and is unstoppable. They laughed until they cried, until their sides hurt, and Nell clamped her hands to her mouth. And the moment they regained their breath the skeleton snored again and their laughter would tumble out of them like a bag of marbles falling down a flight of stairs. When finally it ended and they regained their breath, Nell was struck with a thought.

"Isn't it weird?" she said in wonder.

"This place?" Max said, shaking his head. "Yeah, definitely."

"No. Everything. Don't you ever think about it? Like it's so weird we have bodies and walk around."

"And eat toast."

"Yeah. Toast is weird and awesome," Nell agreed.

"Exactly. Like this place. The Dreamlands is weird, but isn't everything strange? School. Bicycles. Pizza. Phones. Tennis. Someone made it all up. It all came out of someone's brain."

The thought that life itself was just as strange as the Dreamlands was soothing, and Nell felt hopeful that perhaps they could make their way through the danger that lay ahead. Nell felt her body growing tired. She hadn't been sure if you could sleep in Dreamland, but soon she discovered that you could sleep, and sleep well, though you did not dream.

Three hours later, the loudspeaker squealed. "Bus to Vazencrack now boarding!"

Nell woke up first. She was leaning against Max, her head on his shoulder, and Rose was snuggled up inside Lefty, who lay like a kitten in Max's lap.

"Time to go," Nell said, gently shaking Max awake.

"I'm good!" Max yelled, bounding up with a start. Lefty fell to the floor with a thud and shook himself like a dog. Rose flew around Nell's head and landed on her shoulder.

Together they exited through the rear of the station to greet the bus, and both Max and Nell stopped short. It was not like any bus they had seen before. Instead, it was a nightmarish version of a bus, which did not move on wheels but was strapped with thick metal bands on the back of a snow-white wolf, large as a house, with blazing electric-red eyes. Two skeletons in crisp Goyle Bus Route uniforms were nervously pushing a set of steps up against the side of the standing wolf as another skeleton was fuelling him, throwing bits of raw red meat into his massive, chomping jaws.

CHAPTER 26

"There is nothing to worry about," Nell said as they got in the queue to board the bus that would take her and Max to Vazencrack, where the Dark Daughters were holding Ravenhead under their spell. The bus was one thing. The dangers they would face once they got there were another story.

Take it one step at a time, Nell told herself. *Right now,* she reasoned, *all we need to do is get on a bus. I won the dice game, I can ride a bus. So what if the bus might be on top of a giant beast? It is still a bus, and buses are nothing if not safe.*

Suddenly, the wolf turned and ripped the arm off the skeleton that was feeding him. Its horrible screams filled the air as the pale beast crunched slowly and small flecks of bone rained out of the sides of his jaws.

In a flash, Max and Nell shot up the wooden stairs of the walkway, taking the steps two at a time, and entered the bus. A skeleton in a bus driver's cap, blue shirt and dangling tie sat at the wheel, gazing through the front window that looked out over the top of the wolf's white head.

The driver glanced at Nell's umbrella and gave her a nod. "Always happy to have a Fearless Traveller on board."

Nell felt the colour rush to her face. She glanced at Max, who seemed impressed. She liked his look of admiration, of being proud to be with her, and didn't want it to disappear by explaining that she wasn't part of the ancient order. If the driver wanted to think she was a Fearless Traveller, there was no harm in that. She fixed her toughest look on her face and winked at the old skeleton.

The bus was quite old, and they walked down the aisle to find bright green vinyl seats, wooden luggage racks overhead and oval windows lining the sides. Skeletons of all sizes, dressed in suits or dresses, filled up nearly the entire bus, and Nell and Max found seats near the back.

Clearing his throat, the bus driver pulled down a round chrome microphone from overhead and spoke. "Welcome to the Goyle bus from Boneville to Vazencrack. This is a non-stop bus and I don't expect any delays."

"What about clowns?" a skeleton in a T-shirt and jeans yelled obnoxiously, much to the delight of the friend sitting next to him.

"All Goyle bus drivers are trained to handle any situation, but according to my sources, we have some extra protection here today. Riding on our bus in the back is none other than a Fearless Traveller."

The driver pointed at Nell. A gasp of excitement went through the crowd as all the skeletons turned their skulls and looked at her.

"Maybe," the bus driver continued, "she'll give us a little demonstration with her umbrella."

All the skeletons stared with their hollow sockets, waiting for Nell to say something calming, something that would guarantee them safe passage through the land of clowns.

Oh no, Nell thought. This was followed by her thinking herself stupid and replaying in her mind her tough guy wink.

Idiot, she thought, but out loud she mumbled, "I'm not," as her nerves took the words from her mouth.

"Not scared of clowns?" someone said.

"Maybe she's not a Fearless Traveller," another added.

"She'd better be," a large skeleton blubbered, "or we're all doomed."

Everyone was staring at Nell and waiting for her to say or do something, but she simply felt frozen. She looked at Max. "Help me," she whispered.

"The book," he said after a moment. "Read something from the book."

Yes, Nell thought and took out her *Guide.* Something she could say to the passengers to calm them.

"Don't worry," Nell said pushing the words out quickly. "As it says in our book…"

"Stand up," Max whispered. Nell awkwardly rose to her feet, holding *The Fearless Travellers' Guide* in her hands. She opened to the first page, hoping there would be something wise written inside. To her horror the page was blank, but she remembered what to do. Think but without trying to think. As she concentrated on the emptiness, black letters formed. She read aloud what they said as they formed.

"The … Fearless … Travellers … are…"

The rest of the words came all at once and she read them quickly.

"…an illegal organization."

There was a cheer and an explosion of laughter. She didn't understand. "An illegal organization?" But nonetheless it worked. Nell had said the right thing.

With a loud growl, the wolf leapt forward, and soon the bus was moving across a lonely landscape of dry, weedy fields and lonely farmhouses. The ride was bumpy, but not as jostling as Nell had imagined, just a steady, whispering bounce. Instead of engine noise, there was the insistent huff of a running animal and the rise and fall of pads across the earth. Occasionally, the wolf would leap and the bus would sail high in the air, and for a split second, the noise outside would cease. A silence, like the jolt of diving off a high board, would overtake the bus, and then, like a body plunging into water, the wolf's paws would hit the ground and the huff and gallop would resume.

With every leap, Nell felt something stir deep inside her. Something wanting to burst out and run alongside the wolf, to shed all she knew and be nothing more than a creature, wild, terrible and free. The pull was deep and very real, a physical tug at her chest that made Nell grip the back of the seat before her in pain.

"Are you okay?" Max asked.

Nell was growling – it was the deep, low growl of a fierce and untamed animal. Her mouth was clenched tight as though she dared not open it, but her eyes were blazing with fear.

"How can I help?" Max asked. Nell needed to tell him about the spirit stones but dared not speak.

"Is that a real bird?"

Nell looked up. Standing before her was a small skeleton, a girl of about five in a pretty red dress. She was staring at Rose, who was perched on Nell's shoulder. For some reason, the sight of the little girl broke the spell, and the change dissipated.

"You want to say hi?" Nell asked, finding her voice.

The little skeleton nodded with the grave, respectful silence of children who can't believe their sudden good fortune.

Nell breathed in to whistle, and Rose hopped down from her shoulder and flew into her open palm, cocking her head at the diminutive skeleton.

"Give me your hand," Nell said, gently taking the skeleton's tiny hand in her own. It was so light, so weightless and the bones so brilliantly white. In Nell's world, skeletons were things in dusty cases in science rooms or plastic Halloween decorations. They were discarded things that she'd rather not touch. But now Nell felt like she was handling a jewel. All the little white bones moving together like the inside of a clock. The sight of them filled Nell with a sudden mixture of joy and sadness. Joy for the intricate loveliness, and sadness for what was missing around them – the skin, the nerves, the blood, the life.

"Look," Nell mouthed silently to Max, who was watching her with the strangest look, and she felt her cheeks redden.

Rose jumped from Nell's hand into the little girl's and sang a bright, chirpy song. The small skeleton let out a quiet giggle.

"She likes you," Nell confided as Rose jumped from the girl's hand to the reed-thin bones of her shoulder. As Rose sang, two warm brown eyes appeared inside the dark hollows of the little girl's empty eye sockets. They were beautiful eyes – gentle, curious, happy to take in the entire world without thought or judgment. They stared at the golden bird on her shoulder with complete amazement.

"Eyes," Max whispered.

Nell nodded silently, not wanting to talk, as if the eyes were a pair of rabbits who had poked their heads out of the brambles in early spring looking for food and would be easily startled.

The wolf stopped suddenly, and the little girl was thrown off balance and tumbled in the aisle. The eyes that had appeared in her sockets vanished, leaving dark hollows, and with a frightened yelp, she turned and hurried back to her parents. Nell and Max gazed out the window at the dark forest. Instantly they knew they were in a different place, and without question a more dangerous one. It was a grim, shadowy realm of enormous burnt trees, black volcanic rocks and bushes of burr and thistle.

"It's all right, folks," the driver said. "She's just stopped to sniff out directions."

"What were you staring at before?" Nell asked. "You had the weirdest look on your face."

"Nothing," Max said and looked away, embarrassed.

"Do I have something on my face?" Nell tried to see her reflection in the window and rubbed her forehead.

"No," Max said, trying to find the words. "You're just so…"

"So what?"

"Nice," Max whispered, as if the word itself were a timid thing that might dart off at any moment.

"Nice?" Nell repeated, feeling unsure of what Max was getting at. "Is it bad? Am I lame?"

"Being nice?" Max smiled. "Lame? No. It's really cool, actually."

"Thanks."

Max was silent for a moment, but Nell could see that he wanted to ask her another question.

"Go on," she said.

"Do you still see stuff? You told me once that you sometimes see things that other people can't."

"Inner animals," Nell said, her voice equal parts proud and suddenly shy.

"How's it work?"

"I don't really know. My heart starts beating fast, and suddenly everything gets quiet and slows down. Everything is clear and bright. Badger told me, 'What is fake falls away, and what's real comes to the surface.' He said what I'm seeing is the truth of the situation. Mostly it's just kind of freaky."

"It's not freaky," Max said, shaking his head in admiration. "It's important. No one cares to think about who people really are any more, you know? People create a character for themselves every day. They wear a costume and do everything just so they can post pictures. So everyone can agree they are that character. That fake thing. It's like we've all become fast food. We're easy to identify. You know what you're getting. You don't have to waste time deciding if you like it or if it's healthy; you just pick the character. We're all just empty calories. But you get to see the real stuff inside people. The stuff people hide from themselves or are embarrassed by. You know who people really are. That is kind of awesome."

The single squeak of a rubber horn rang out with a chilling *HONK!* A skeleton screamed in alarm. Nell grasped the seat in front of her. It felt as if she had been punched.

"Let's try to stay calm, folks," the driver said.

Another horn sounded outside, loud and mocking. This was followed by the thump of something heavy landing on the metal roof. Footsteps creaked across the metal, cutting through the horrible quiet that now filled the bus.

HONK!

"No," Nell muttered. "It can't be."

"CLOWNS!" a young woman screamed.

"Don't panic, folks," the driver said, his voice trembling. "They ain't coming in."

HONK!

Nell turned towards the window in time to see a clown pop up. He had a double chin and a tiny moustache. His face was painted a pale white and lined with red and blue streaks like war paint. He opened his mouth and smiled, revealing a set of yellow fangs.

Nell grabbed Max's hand as the front door opened and another enormous clown entered. He was a tall, powerful man. He wore a Civil War-era coat, wool trousers, and heavy boots, and around his neck was an iron chain from which hung the skull of a large dog. From his belt hung a curved dagger. His face, like his companion's, was painted without care. Dripping streaks and violent scars of bright colour were slashed across the clown's corpse-pale skin.

"Stay back!" the driver said, standing up. "This is private property."

"Clown property now," the clown grunted. With a hard shove, the clown forced the driver back into his seat. Then he turned towards the passengers and held up a bullwhip, swinging it around his head and snapping it with a piercing *crack*. "Everyone out!" the large clown snarled.

The old woman skeleton in the seat behind them leaned in and spoke quietly and quickly. She handed Nell a round black hat with a small brim. It was an old-fashioned bowler hat. "I was bringing this to my son," the woman said. "But you have it. The inside is lined with steel. Put your bird inside, and don't let them see her. They eat them, you know."

"Thank you," Nell whispered, taking the bowler hat from the woman.

"MOVE!" the clown snarled, cracking the whip again.

"No," a large skeleton said and raced towards the clown. With another piercing crack the whip came down upon the skeleton's spine. It was as if the thread that held all the bones together was snapped. With a clatter all his bleached white bones tumbled to the floor of the bus, where they remained for a few seconds before turning dark and feathery. The large clown knelt down over the blackened bones, which still held their shape. All the other skeletons on the bus watched, riveted. They knew. They knew what was next. The big clown drew a great breath and blew out. The black bones exploded silently into a dark cloud of ash. The ash blew through the cabin. Nell and Max covered their mouths. Nell quickly put Rose inside the bowler and put the hat snugly on her head. For a moment, Rose fluttered around inside, but Nell gave the side of the hat a few taps and Rose got the message that she had to be still.

Instantly, all the skeletons got up, as if the idea of refusing or fighting didn't exist, and began marching towards the door.

"I'll fight them off," Max whispered protectively. "You escape into the woods with Rose."

"Don't get all hero-y," Nell answered. "I can handle this. But we need to think it through."

"All right," Max said.

"You two. Move it!" The clown cracked his whip at Nell and Max. They ducked, and the whip hit the window behind them. The glass shattered. They dashed down the aisle and out through the doors of the bus.

The clowns were seated on rundown velvet couches in a train carriage whose walls had been removed and whose roof had been replaced with a pointed antique circus tent of red and white stripes.

"These aren't normal clowns. They're slave traders," the driver said through clenched teeth, nodding towards the front of the train carriage.

Up ahead, there was no engine to turn the large, steel train wheels. Instead, the wheels were hitched to two lines of creatures shackled in thick metal chains. The slaves were a mixed lot: people, animals, robots, oversized objects and those that were combinations. It was a terrible sight that made Nell's heart ache. "Imagine if this is where your Sleeper came every night when you closed your eyes. A slave in a dark forest, owned and abused by the most foul creatures. No wonder so many people are unhappy," Nell said, feeling she had just unlocked one of life's great mysteries.

"What?" Max said.

"The slaves. During the day you could seem to have everything, but if you are a slave in your nightmares, then how can you ever feel right when you wake up?"

"Unhappy dreams, unhappy life," Max said.

HONK!

All eyes turned towards where the sound came from – a figure hidden in the shadows. He was sitting on the couch in the train carriage, gazing down at the row of skeletons lined up before the bus, like a king surveying his feast.

"And they say the bus is the safest way to travel," he said, sneering.

The voice made Nell gasp. The clown stood, and Nell felt sweat dampen her forehead and her heart begin to pound as Venom Shivers jumped down from the train carriage into the light.

"Not today it ain't," one clown yelled.

"Not today it ain't?" Shivers repeated as if he couldn't believe he had been interrupted. Reaching into his long, weather-beaten leather coat, he took out a fluffy pie. He turned to the clown with the sad face.

"I'm sorry, Venom. I didn't mean to interrupt," he mumbled at the sight of the creamy dessert.

"Stand up and honk your horn, please," Shivers said without emotion.

The clown jumped down from the couch and stood before his leader. He nervously gave his horn a tiny honk. Suddenly, the frothy cream on the pie burst into a hot flame. The clown's eyes grew wide, and then in a flash, Shivers pushed the flaming pie into the clown's face. There was a sizzle of flesh. The clown jumped off the train, ran off screaming, and disappeared between the trees, much to the delight of the remaining clowns, who roared with laughter. In the distance, a splash was heard as the clown found a murky pond.

"Anyone else want to interrupt?" Shivers asked the passengers. "Here's the fun stuff," he continued. "All of you are going to be sold as slaves to the Spider Dreamer. Some of you will be saved to pull our rig. We always need pullers. Those who put up a fight will be fed to our dogs. Any of you have anything to say?"

Nell was hiding behind Max. It was dark and maybe, just maybe, Shivers wouldn't see her.

The bus driver stepped forward and cleared his throat. With a nervous but proud voice, he spoke. "This is a Goyle bus, sir. We guarantee safe passage to all our passengers. Bus jacking is a violation of the Night Transport System's treaty of safe passage through lands both Sweet and Wicked."

"Is that so?" Shivers said, rubbing his chin and tilting his head as if it were the most interesting thing he'd ever heard.

"Yes, sir," the driver continued through his fear. His hand bones were shaking, but he held them up in a friendly manner. "Now, here's what I'm going to do for you fellas. Since we have protection on board, I'm going to let you off. You just be on your way and leave us, and we'll forget any of this ever happened. If not, I think you shall be sorry."

"Protection?" Shivers said, feigning fear. "Oh, dear."

"Yes, sir. We have the aid of a Fearless Traveller."

Nell felt her stomach clench. Perhaps she had heard wrong.

"A Fearless Traveller?" Shivers said with a mocking laugh. He turned and scanned the crowd for the one who carried an umbrella.

HONK!

Shivers honked his horn and let out a coyote howl that shook the branches of the leafless trees above. "Well, look who it is!" he screamed in delight as he spotted Nell in the crowd. "Nell Perkins! Evening, Ms Perkins." He pursed his green lips and blew her a kiss.

"You know him?" Max whispered.

"Long story," Nell said.

"And she'll fight you to the death," the driver continued. "It's her job."

"I'd have it no other way," Shivers said, staring at Nell, and he removed his knife from his belt.

CHAPTER 27

A ll was silent. All was golden. The five bodies – two boys (one small, one large), a man and a panther with a little girl chained to her – were underwater, lazily floating beside each other, suspended and surrounded by the coursing, honey-coloured river. Pearls of air escaped from the sides of their mouths. They were all dazed at having been so suddenly robbed of breath and lost beneath the surface of the powerful current, but none realized they were beneath the water. All they knew was they were floating in a warm, beautiful place, and none of them wanted to leave it. They shared a single, peaceful thought – this was a place to silently drift off to sleep, to escape into a deep, restful slumber. And suddenly, almost simultaneously, they all had a second thought. *I am drowning.*

Badger noticed it first. His body snapped into action, and he pointed violently towards the surface.

"To the surface!" he mouthed silently. "UP, BOY. UP."

George shook his head wildly. He couldn't move. Now his lungs were burning. He was trying with all his might to hold Speedy's mouth shut. His brother had passed out, his eyes were closed, and George feared he was dead. Kick as George might, Speedy was too heavy. He was sinking, and George was sinking with him. George kicked furiously and then lost his grip. Speedy was ripped from his hands, his motionless body drifting with the current. George lurched for Speedy and felt a hard thud against his side.

Next thing he knew, Badger had him and his brother under his powerful arms and was holding them tight. Badger gave a few strong kicks. With a gasp, they reached the surface.

The warm, golden water fell from their eyes and drained from their ears. George looked first at his brother, who was coughing. He was alive. George was so happy that he punched Speedy on the side of the head.

"I'm okay," Speedy said, but his own voice sounded strange in his ears. Then he was struck silent by where he now found himself. Last thing Speedy knew, he was in the dark maze with the demon Fenn standing above him, her smelly boot to his throat, her ragged teeth snarling. And now? It was hard to understand exactly where he was. This place was unlike any place he had seen.

They were floating, the five of them, borne along by a strong current in the middle of a rushing river of water, golden in colour, as if the water were lit from below by a hidden sun. The river was flowing inside an old underground tunnel. Above them, the curved ceiling was carved out of bone-white stone. On either side of the golden river were places. Wonderful places. Glorious places. They would pass through one perfect place and drift to the next.

They were in a Buddhist temple and a towering Gothic cathedral. They were in a mountain forest drenched in moonlight and a hidden, sun-speckled jungle at the break of day. They were in the streets of New York City at the turn of the century and the gleaming avenues of a city far in the future, a place made of grid-shaped buildings of neon light.

They were inside a teepee. They were on a screened-in porch, with cat-tail marshes dotted with fireflies rolling lazily beyond. Each world was layered on top of the last as if they were all painted on transparent sheets of plastic that were rotating past like carousel horses. One world coming into view for a moment and then slipping away as another took its place. And like on a carousel, the air was filled with music. Intense, beautiful music that made you want to scream with delight as if you were holding glowing sparklers and running as fast as your legs could carry you down a green hill.

"Where are we?" Speedy asked George, who was floating in the water next to him.

George looked at him strangely, and Speedy realized that his words were jumbled. What he thought he had said hadn't come out. Not in English, anyway. George tried to answer, and his words were equally scrambled and useless, sounding like the sad flop of a fish on dry land.

"Phap gurlapaga ott?"

"Rickadrumcracken shom."

The brothers looked first at each other in confusion and then at Badger, who shook his head and screamed, "YES!"

They heard that word clear as a bright, happy bell.

"Yes!" Pinch added. She nodded at the boys, encouraging them to do the same.

"Yes?" George said quietly, and when he did, a feeling of intense relief filled his entire body as though he had been holding a swarm of bees in his throat and had finally realized all he had to do was open his mouth and let them fly free.

"YES!" he screamed again, and nodded at Speedy, who understood.

"YES!" Speedy shouted.

And now they were all shouting the single word above the music.

"*YES! YES! YES!*"

All, that is, except for sour-faced Fenn. The tiny Dark Daughter was holding her unchained hand to her ear and screaming as though a rabid dog had bitten her. She was screaming the only thing she could think of: "NO! NO! NO!"

Badger waved his hands in the air, coaching them, pushing them to scream louder. "YES. YES. YES."

With each scream, the many worlds that lined the walls of the secret tunnel began to fade, like a dream upon waking. The cities and towns that lined the banks disappeared. The broad avenues and quiet lanes faded, and the outside world came into focus. The walls turned misty. The music dimmed, replaced by the sounds of a night time forest, and with a final chorus of shouts, the golden river evaporated completely. Speedy and George, along with the two Fearless Travellers and their prisoner, found themselves outside, lying on their backs in a grassy field filled with bright yellow dandelions.

It was late afternoon. The sun was sinking below the crags of a distant mountain. For a moment, no one said a word. They all just listened to the sound of their own breath, happy to be free of the maze and astonished by the simple word that had made it happen.

Finally, George spoke. "I'm more of a *no* man, myself."

"Yes!" Speedy said. "I mean no. I mean yes. That's true."

"Don't be," Badger said. "In the darkness of this place, trouble begins when you say no, when you run, when you turn away from the truth of who you are. This world is a shape-shifter, an ever-changing show, a place where what appears real is fake and what appears fake is real. Here, you always want what you don't have and always have what you don't want. So to survive, you must say yes to all that appears. Being scared is okay. It is expected. But don't let that stop you from what you must do. And what you must do is never say no. Fearless Travellers charge forward, taking whatever comes. That is the secret. Say yes. Be yes. It is the only way to get back home."

"Say whatever you want. Your sister is going to die," Fenn snarled, yanking at the chain that connected her to Pinch. She pointed her skinny little finger at them viciously. "The Dark Daughters will find her," Fenn said coldly. "Find her and destroy her."

"Not if we find her first," George spat back. He turned to Badger. "We can find her first, right?"

"Once we get the *Compass*, she is as good as found," Badger said, pointing to the sky overhead. Above the field loomed a large, dark cloud lit by the setting sun. The breeze was blowing, slowly pushing lavender ribbons of vapour across the sky. There was something behind the clouds, something huge and hidden. As the dark-lavender wisps of cloud raced away, what was concealed became distinct. Floating in the dark night, with legs crossed, eyes closed and arms resting across his lap, was a towering chimpanzee, tall as a ten-storey building. In his hands, which were cupped together on his crossed legs, was a large circular ship of rust-brown metal.

"NO!" George yelled. "No way! No more things."

"Things?" Pinch said.

"We want to find Nell!" Speedy agreed. He understood what George was feeling. They were tired. They were scared. They missed their mother and sister very much, and no matter how hard they tried there was always another thing standing in their path.

"No more things!" George yelled as he threw himself on the grass and folded his arms in a gesture of defiance. Speedy sat down heavily beside him and folded his arms as well.

"Yell all you want," George said. "We are not going on your stupid ship. Just do some Fearless Traveller magic and get us there."

Badger said nothing. Instead he knelt down on one knee and looked the boys right in their eyes, which were wet with tears. For a moment he was silent. When he did speak he didn't yell or snarl. In fact, for the first time his voice was soft, gentle.

"The only magic is persistence," he said. "This Dream, the one we are all sharing, is not filled with challenges. The dream we all share is *made* of challenges. Challenge is the fibre that weaves it all together and gives it all its shape. You are here to meet those challenges, whatever they may be, and Fearless Travelling is the way you will meet them. I have no doubt you are up to the task. Just remember: you will make mistakes, but don't let them stop you."

"The Dark Daughters will stop you," Fenn said and spat at them. "We will stop you and burn you to bits."

Pinch turned and snarled at Fenn, showing a full set of fangs, and the little girl's eyes grew wide and she said no more.

The boys were silent. They watched thin purple clouds drifting around the towering monkey.

Finally, George spoke. "Please don't tell me the monkey is alive," he begged. He was not a fan of apes. Not in the least. "Just say it's a cloud."

"He is very much alive," Pinch said. "Alive and beyond life itself."

"He's the Monkey Dreamer."

"What happens when he meets the Banana Dreamer?" Speedy asked curiously.

"Don't ask stupid questions," George said and then paused. "All right, what happens?"

"They are good friends. What he does not like is people trying to take the ship he has been given the task of guarding. So we must board it and escape without waking him," Badger said.

"What happens if you wake him?" Speedy asked.

"About what you'd expect to happen when you wake a 35-metre-tall spirit from his sleep while stealing the thing he has sworn to protect. He goes ape," Badger said. "The trick is to approach without making a sound. But not to worry. I've called upon an old friend who knows the secret. He's on his way."

There was nothing to do now but wait for Badger's friend to arrive. They sat in silence. They lay on their backs, looking up at the Monkey Dreamer. Badger produced a deck of cards and they played hand after hand of Go Fish until Badger caught George cheating.

As George jumped up to defend himself, the ground began to tremble and the dirt started to churn. Something was tunnelling its way out beneath them. Everyone stumbled away as two gloved hands poked themselves out of the soil, followed by a mop of bright yellow hair. A giant and handsome young man with bright green skin jumped out of the hole in a single leap. He shook off the dirt and appeared before them sparkling clean. Upon seeing Pinch and Badger, he revealed a large smile of perfectly white teeth.

"Duke! Pinch! This here's a night, ain't it?" He had a Southern US accent, and his voice was soft and filled with a syrupy excitement, as if he had a secret he was dying to share.

"Thanks for coming," Badger said.

"My pleasure. Who are these folks?"

"This is Speedy and George."

The boys nodded politely.

"And this, boys," Badger said. "This is the Dandelion Dreamer."

"Nice to meet you folks. Is that Fenn over there?"

"Come near me, and I will bite your head off, you dirty flower freak," Fenn snarled.

"Actually, that's her prettier, nicer sister," George said.

The Dandelion Dreamer smiled at the joke and glanced again at the sky. "So you need a boost up to Marty, huh?"

"Marty?" George laughed. "The monkey's name is Marty?"

"We need to reach our ship," Badger said.

"I can get you there, but if you wake the ape up, y'all are on your own."

"I would be in your debt," Badger said.

The Dandelion Dreamer stretched his neck and his arms, then slapped his hands together and blew into them, warming them up. When he was done, he turned to Speedy and George. "You're not Sleepers; you're humans?"

The brothers nodded.

"That's great," he said. "Earth's the place for love. That's for sure."

"Whatever," George muttered.

"Listen," the Dandelion Dreamer continued. "You kids ever sit in a field in the spring and blow on a dandelion?" He gave them a searching look with his intense green eyes.

"No," George said with horror.

"Yes," admitted Speedy.

"Well, those little fluffy white things? They're the seeds. You may or may not have noticed this, but dandelions always release their seeds into the air the same way every time."

"I don't watch flowers," George said, as if that were a strange way to pass the time.

"Really? You should. You'll learn a lot. Well, here's the quick lesson."

George was about to make clear he did not want to learn anything about flowers when he caught Badger's gaze. Badger made a *cut it* motion, moving his hand across his neck, and George knew it was time to do the thing he hated most – pay attention.

"This is the Dreamlands," the Dandelion Dreamer explained. "When the seeds escape and fly into the sky, it's always the same. They move in a pattern. A spiral. If you watched it slow, you'd see that at the end of the spiral is a seed I like to call the true. This is always the last seed to release itself, sort of like a captain on a sinking ship. It clings tight until all its brothers and sisters are off on their journeys. In this dream, the dream of riding dandelions, the one true seed is all that matters. Once the seeds begin to break apart, you'll need to find the true fast. The true is what continues to float up while everything else has fallen away. Find it, and you can travel forever."

"How do we find it?" Speedy asked.

"You don't. It will find you."

"Find me?" Speedy worried. "What if it doesn't?"

"It always does, as long as you don't panic. It is there, I promise." The Dreamer turned away to prepare.

"That's it?" George sputtered in irritation at an answer he considered full of equal parts mumbo and jumbo.

"I'm sure Badger told you that in this place your breath is your guide. If you feel yourself starting to panic: breathe. Just know you'll be okay." He smiled. "Now y'all spread out," he said, his voice now slipping into that of commander. "Don't make a single sound. Just jump onto your pod when I give the signal. All you have to do is drift upwards. I'll blow you there. At this distance, with this wind and this moon, I'm figuring your pod *will* start to collapse about halfway."

"When you are above the ship, leap down," Badger added.

Badger nudged George and Speedy. They spread out along the dandelion field, each finding a spot with a metre around them. The brothers looked at each other and glanced at the monkey high in the clouds.

"I hate to be the one to break it to you folks," George said. "There is no way that those teeny, tiny flowers are going to do anything for anyone, except maybe an ant, a very small ant."

The Dandelion Dreamer ignored George and took a deep breath, sucking air into his lungs until his eyes bulged. When he was full, he pursed his lips and let out a long, steady blow of icy wind. And magically, around their feet, the dandelion heads closed up against the cold. The Dandelion Dreamer blew again; this time the air was a warm spring breeze, and now the closed dandelions began to open, and from them grew large, fluffy white pods. The pods hummed softly as they rapidly expanded, growing like balloons filling with air, until before each of them stood a delicate, perfectly round white pod, three metres across.

"Step inside your pod," the Dandelion Dreamer instructed.

Speedy and George each pushed their way through the soft stems into the middle of their own pods. Badger was in another dandelion pod, and Pinch and Fenn in the last. It was like stepping inside a forest made of feathers. George wasn't happy. The puffy, cloud-like ball didn't seem strong enough to hold anything, much less a person. The arrangement of the delicate, willowy branches that rose from the seeds formed small, diamond-shaped windows, and through them they watched the Dandelion Dreamer take another big breath.

"Get ready to fly," Badger cautioned.

George wasn't ready for this. But ready or not, a quiet breeze rustled the fluff around him, and suddenly the pods began to rise. With a jerk, they were lifted softly and noiselessly into the night sky. Up they flew.

The ride was gentle, a tender drift on the wind. In a few moments, they were high above the field, four giant dandelion pods dancing, bright white orbs floating silently in the silver moonlight. All faced east, away from the giant ape, and the passengers took in the world that stretched out beneath them. It was a sinister world, a nightmarish land of ancient forests that rolled on for many kilometres. Behind the mysterious forests was the outline of a blackened sea shrouded in fog. The dark silhouettes of long, oddly-shaped ships slid between the fog breaks. Behind them, far in the distance across a snow-swept plain, lay the knife-sharp tip of Vazencrack, the Bloody Mountain, above which a dark cloud roiled.

"You're doing fine," Badger said to his fellow riders as they drifted slowly towards the cloud.

"That was a lot of blah, blah for nothing," George said, enjoying the ride much more than the lecture about flowers and keeping still. As far as he could see, the pods were pretty solid and moving fast. They'd make it to the ape in no time.

"Hold tight," Badger said. "Breeze is coming. We're about to break."

"Break?" George said as the stems of his pod began to rustle – softly at first, but then, as if a rope had been snapped, the stems began to shiver wildly. Beside his face, the first stem plucked itself from the base of the pod with a deafening *POP* and flew into the air with the rapid explosive power of a missile firing. "Hey!" he screamed in surprise as another stem exploded, knocking him down as it shot out into the night. Forgetting his instructions, George quickly jumped to his feet.

"George! Don't move!" George could hear his brother's voice between the quickly escalating explosions as all around him the seed stems ejected skywards. With each lost stem, the dandelion started slowing down until it wasn't rising any longer but plunging towards the hard ground with the distinct whistle of a falling bomb. The whistle filled George's ears, and a cold, cruel wind slapped against his cheeks. Now he understood that what the Dandelion Dreamer was saying was true. His tiny craft would never hold. It was born to break.

"Oh, no," he muttered as a series of stems shot out in all directions, above him, below him, on either side. It felt as if he were in a war zone.

"Stay still, boy. Stay still!" Badger directed from above.

Glancing up, through the haze of fluff, George could see the bottoms of the other dandelions moving quickly away from him towards the ape. He looked down. Below, the ground was coming up quick. The full forest of stems that had surrounded him when he entered the pod was now gone, and his pod looked like the head of a bald old man.

"Stay calm. You know what to do," he told himself. "Find the one, and don't move. Stay still." But how could he? How could anyone, with the wind whistling in his ears as he fell towards his doom? George's heart pounded wildly. He studied the stems and narrowed in on one that looked larger than the others.

"The one," he said and grabbed the thick trunk, clenching it tight. It was a rough, bristled length of plant, grizzled as a sail rope. The moment he wrapped his fingers around it, the stem was ripped from his hands by the wind, slicing open his skin as it shot into the air.

"YOWWWWW," George screamed in pain and looked at his hands. They were the small, pinkish, blood-speckled hands of a rodent. Without even realizing, he had transformed into his rat form. Instantly, scents and sounds by the thousands poured into his ears and nostrils. Calculating and sorting with the speed of a computer, George knew at once that each seed stem had its own scent, as individual and distinct as spices. And all were rustling in the plunging wind, but each vibrated at a different speed. It seemed the stronger the smell, the slower the flap. Where those two things came together, the true would be found. George grew still, letting his mind calculate as two more stems shot past him, leaving only two more. If he didn't choose correctly *right now*, he would be smashed to bits.

The last two stems detached from the base of the pod and, like a crack of lightning, George suddenly knew which stem was the true. He leapt for it, taking hold as it shot up like a rocket. The moment he touched the rising stem, he transformed back into a boy, and the white canopy opened as wide as a parachute. Below him, the pod hit the dirt with a deadly *bang*, kicking up dust.

He had done it! He clung to the stem as it rose quickly through the warm night.

In a few moments, he was floating past the massive white feet of the giant sleeping ape and getting his first look at the *Compass*.

The metal ship was a perfectly round disc of burnished silver with four jutting prows, where north, south, east and west would be on a compass. Each prow was shaped into a head. There was a beautiful woman to the north, a laughing skull to the south, a fierce eagle to the east and a knowing whale to the west. Standing on the flat metal top of the ship were Badger, Speedy, Pinch and their prisoner, Fenn.

Badger was swinging a rope over his head. "Catch the rope. I'll pull you in," he called.

George got ready. Badger released. The rope sailed through the air and hit the boy's hand with a stinging smack.

"Nice," Speedy said.

Badger and Speedy pulled the rope and guided George to the metal deck of the ship. He touched down and let go of the seed stem. It shot off into the night.

"Thought we'd lost you," Badger admitted.

"I'm tough. Rat tough," George exclaimed, filled with a sudden unexplainable happiness as he realized how well he had done.

"Welcome aboard the *Compass*."

For the first time, George glanced around at the massive rough white hands that held the ship as though it were a fragile thing. All the enormous paws would have to do was simply close up, and they'd all be crushed like flies beneath a mallet. George shivered and looked at Speedy for some sort of reassurance, but his brother could offer none. All he could do was point upwards with his thumb. George's eyes followed the dark, fur-covered wall of solid ape to the beast's massive head, where its eyes twitched in a deep dream. The hands that surrounded them seemed the least of their worries now. The truth was clear. The ape was not a statue or a cloud in the shape of a monkey but an animal, massive in size and very much alive. Being crunched between the hard teeth of a monkey who was as big as a skyscraper was not the way George wanted to die. Now he had only one question: "How do we get inside?"

"Very quietly," Pinch said, her eyes flickering to the round metal hatch at their feet.

Fenn's eyes lit up. Sensing a chance, she lunged for the latch but was caught by Speedy, who grabbed her in his big arms and held her tight.

"Let go of me, you nasty pig," she snarled, but Speedy did not.

Quickly, Badger pulled the handle of the hatch. A loud siren wailed out. Above them, one of the monkey's massive eyes opened in sleepy confusion.

"Inside, children," Pinch warned. "He's waking. Quick now. Down the hatch."

There was a clatter of footsteps, and the children followed Pinch down a metal ladder. The small passageway was dark and the ladder only as long as an adult. It was hard to tell where they were. Above them, Badger shut the metal latch, a light was switched on, and all became clear. They were in a small, black, metal anteroom. Badger pulled a lever on the wall, and two black doors opened, revealing the ship's bridge. Badger and Pinch wasted no time. Badger rushed over and grabbed the ship's large steering wheel as Pinch slapped a few levers. They moved with the confidence of those who'd done this many times before. Lights and machines hummed to life, and from down below came the whirl of engines revving.

"Everyone hold on to something," Badger screamed.

A large, curved piece of metal in the front of the cabin slid away, revealing the outside world, and at the moment, it was not a happy place. A roar from above rattled their teeth. No doubt about it, the Monkey Dreamer was now awake.

"Am I powered?" Badger asked.

"We are online," Pinch answered calmly. "In five. Four. Three…"

Suddenly, the ship was rocked forward with a massive wallop. On the window outside was part of the monkey's hand. The monkey was awake and trying to rip the ship in two.

"Two," Pinch said.

"Hold on!"

"One!"

There was the deafening *WHOOSH* of rockets firing as the ship sped forward, deftly avoiding the monkey's lurching arms, and zoomed into the night.

CHAPTER 28

Nell, Max and the skeletons stood in the forest in a straight line, as the clowns had instructed. The air was bitterly cold and absolutely silent, save for the scratchy rustle of the leaves on the trees. The bus was gone now – the wolf had been set free and chased away with a few stinging lashes of the large clown's vicious whip.

Hours passed. Nell's legs ached. She could feel Rose curled on the top of her head inside the hat. As long as she slept, she was quiet. Nell didn't dare move. She didn't even want to hold the *Travellers' Guide*. Even turning a page might wake Rose, so she did nothing but stand. Max, on the other hand, thumbed through the mystic book, his face fixed with a look of awe.

Shivers had not moved for the longest time, but stood perfectly still in the darkness, his red eyes staring intensely at Nell, who looked at the black ground to avoid his penetrating gaze.

"The book," Max said, turning his head and whispering in Nell's ear.

Nell knew was Max meant. The book hadn't failed her yet. *The Fearless Travellers' Guide* would have the answer or a weapon – some way to fight clowns and win.

Nell thought about what Badger had said about the Minder. About jumping into the darkness, leaping into the unknown, and suddenly an idea came to Nell. It was a long shot – a ridiculous, crazy plan. In fact, a stupid plan – and, as Max had said, stupid plans were the best. To make it work, she'd have to act as though she had not a care in the world. Running it through in her mind, she steeled herself and began. She lifted her head casually to the clown as though they were about to play a friendly game of tennis and asked, "Did you bring your rule book?"

"Book?" the clown spat as if the word was poison.

"Not a book. A *rule* book," Nell said brightly. "I only fight to the death using the Dreamlands rules established by the Death Fight Dreamer. If we are using the Wicked Places rules, I'm going to have to check my own book."

"There aren't any rules in a death fight," he said, sneering.

"No rules? You can't have a fight without rules. I told Freyja Skoll you'd say that." Nell shook her head and bit her lip at the thought of the headless queen.

The sound of Freyja Skoll's name made Shivers tense. Without a sound, he walked closer to Nell, as if he didn't want to be speaking about the queen of the Dark Daughters too loudly in case there were spies in the woods. "What does she have to do with it?" he asked.

Nell knew at that moment that she had him. The clown had fallen for it. She had laid the trap, now all she had to do was reel him in. She shook her head as though what she was about to say was painful, almost too horrible to recall. *Keep it realistic,* Nell told herself. That was the key to making a lie sound convincing.

"And thanks to you, I won the token to the Ghost Stew at Crypt," she said. "We were on our way to see Ravenhead, but we were too late. Freyja Skoll had put him under her spell and was taking his body with her to Vazencrack. But of course you knew that."

"Taken Ravenhead?" Shivers said. His sneer seemed to reveal that he didn't believe it, but his eyes said differently. They darted to the trees as he realized something that had been nagging him.

"Yes. Look around," Nell said with authority. "Not a lot of birds out lately. They're disappearing, and when Ravenhead dies, they'll all go. You won't even remember they existed. Your favourite meal, gone forever."

Shivers touched the necklace of bird skulls around his neck softly and, without thinking, ran his blue tongue across his lips. Nell continued spinning her plan, feeling a growing confidence that not only would she have a chance to look at her *Fearless Travellers' Guide*, but that it alone would save her.

"As you know, Freyja Skoll had turned my mother into a bird, and I was hoping Ravenhead could break the spell. But she caught Max and me. And then, that little girl of hers, Fenn, she separated Max's hand from his body."

The clown stared at Lefty, who was perched on Max's shoulder.

Max understood what Nell was doing and joined in. "She used a rusty blade," he said, recalling the pain.

"For me, she wanted a punishment that was even more painful," Nell said. "She said, 'I'm going to keep your bird, but I have something better for you. Instead of twisting off your head now, I'm sending you through the forest to face the clowns. But then I told her how I cheated you at dice."

"Cheated?" Shivers said, his eyes narrowing. "You cheated?"

"And you fell for it. Everyone was in on it. Badger. The Moustache Dreamer."

"I knew it!" Shivers muttered, as if suddenly his loss made sense.

"Freyja said that while you were a fool, you were an okay fighter."

"Okay?" he snarled. "That's how she rates Venom Shivers?!"

"I told her I thought you were less than okay. And I bet her I'd make it through alive, and what's more, that I'd bring back a clown's nose."

"That so?" the sad clown roared in offence, jumping off the train.

Shivers shot him a look, and he froze in his tracks. "Go on," Shivers said to Nell.

"Well, Freyja Skoll said if I did return with a clown's nose, she'd let my mother go."

"Really?" Shivers snorted.

"But she told me I couldn't use any Fearless Traveller tricks. I promised her that it would be a fair fight with rules and to make sure we all agree I will read them aloud. So as soon as we check the rule books," Nell said, "we can begin."

"Well, we don't have no books!" the sad clown snarled.

"But I do," Nell answered brightly, trying to mask her glee at how this had all worked out.

"Of course you do," Shivers spat.

Nell felt a drip of sweat on her forehead. Shivers sounded awfully suspicious. *Maybe I'm wrong,* she thought. *Maybe he sees right through my plan.*

It was too late to stop now, though.

"Yes," Nell said, her voice tinged with a tremble. "My book will tell me exactly what we need to know."

"Then take it out!" Shivers boomed, his mouth foaming with spittle. "Won't help you."

A wave of relief swept over Nell. This was her chance. *The Fearless Travellers' Guide* would have an answer, maybe even a weapon on the page. It would save her the same way it had saved her from the Dark Daughters. As Max handed Nell the book, Shivers put his dagger back in his belt and took a small horn bulb from his coat. He gave the bulb a quick squeeze, and from it shot a long sword blade. He swung it through the air viciously, and the force of his swipe sent a threatening, cold breeze against their cheeks.

"Nice work," Max said in encouragement as Nell removed the ancient leather-bound book from her pocket and held it before them.

"It will be just like the alarm clock," Nell whispered. "There'll be a weapon or a spell or something to help. I know it." She cracked open *The Fearless Travellers' Guide*. The pages were blank. A warm light flushed her face. She had to clear her mind. To focus on what she needed, and then what she needed would appear. She closed her eyes and said to herself, "My name is Nell Perkins. I am surrounded by clowns."

In a flash, the blank page began to fill with a thin line of black ink. The line curled around and formed itself into a drawing of a witch's old, bent, clawed finger. The clawed finger moved slowly across the page leaving words trailing behind it, and as they appeared, Max read them out loud.

"Rules … for … Fighting … Clowns."

Max glanced up. All eyes and hopes hung on his every word.

"The rules for fighting clowns in the Wicked Places are strict and simple," Max continued, raising his voice so all could hear. "There is only one. The rule is this. There are no rules," he said, suddenly confused.

Nell stared at the book. No rules? It couldn't be. "That's wrong," she said nervously. "This is a trick."

More words were appearing, and Max kept reading, hoping that another answer would follow. "You will fight."

"No," Nell said. "No." But that is what the guide said, and as she had learned, it only spoke the truth. No one could save her from this dark place but herself. Fighting was the only choice, and it was no choice at all.

There was a *whoosh* as Shivers's sword smacked the book out of Nell's hand. It hit the dirt with a dry thud. Nell looked up. Shivers had the tip of his sword to her throat.

"You read your rules," he said, his smile malicious and full of glee. "Now take out your weapon, and let's see who loses a nose."

Nell felt sick to her stomach. As if sensing her agony, Rose began to flutter her wings beneath the bowler hat. Nervously, Nell put her hand on the side of the dark round hat.

Please keep quiet, she thought. Any noise would tip them off. The umbrella was pressed against her leg, the only weapon they had.

All the skeletons had backed away from Nell and Max, so they alone were standing before Shivers. Nell glanced back at the bus passengers. They smiled, and the little girl's mother whispered, "Thank you." All were holding out hope that any second Nell would unleash her umbrella and, with the legendary skill of a Fearless Traveller, send the clowns running.

"Go on," the bus driver said with encouragement. "Show them what you've been sworn to do."

"Nell!" Max was holding her arm. "Don't do this. You can't."

Nell hadn't any choice. She had taken a gamble and failed. If she tried to run now, she would be caught.

And though she didn't believe it, she patted Max's hand, shook her head and said, "It will be fine. If something happens, can you try to find my brothers and bring my mother to Vazencrack?"

"No!"

"No?" Nell sputtered.

"It's me," Max screamed at the clowns. "I'm the Fearless Traveller. Fight me!"

There was a crack of a whip, and a bright flash as the metal tip shot through the air like a bullet and slashed Max's face. He yelled and stumbled back in pain. Lefty pressed himself against Max's torn skin. Max was furious. He peeled Lefty off him in a rage. A red wound in the shape of a smiley face now lay across Max's cheek. The big clown swung the whip overhead menacingly, waiting to take a second shot.

"The girl!" the big clown instructed.

"I'm ready," Nell said quietly, stepping forward. Reaching behind her, she slid the tightly wound umbrella from its scabbard and turned to face the clown. Her hands were shaking, the umbrella shivering like a stick of liquorice. Max touched her arm. She looked up. The wound on his face was fresh with blood.

"Oh, Max," she said, sighing.

"I'm fine." He winced through the sting and looked into Nell's eyes, needing her to hear him. "Listen. The book said one more thing. It says when in trouble, remember, but when fighting, *forget*."

"Forget?" Nell said.

"I read this in the guide. I think it means forget the idea that the umbrella belongs to you. It doesn't. It belongs to the Night. Let the Night flow through you."

Nell nodded, remembering how graceful Badger had been when she had seen him fight, moving like the night spreading across the world.

In three steps, Nell was standing face to face with Shivers, nearly gagging from the rank smell that oozed off him. Mould and rot. A blue tongue darted out of his mouth and ran across his pointy teeth.

"Any last words?" he asked.

"No," Nell said, shaking her head, trying not to breathe. She tried to picture herself over a dark lake jumping into the known, but her mind was blank. All she could see were Shivers's horrible teeth. She already felt like a failure.

"Then prepare to die," the clown said. "On the third crack of the whip."

The big clown swung the whip over his head. *CRACK!*

Nell held tight to her umbrella. This was it. There was no choice now. It was time to leap into the unknown.

CRACK!

Nell took a step towards Shivers. As she did her heart raced and a rippling noise rang in Nell's ear as a current of energy flowed over her body and concentrated itself in the umbrella. Before, she had merely heard the sound, but now the sensation was real and it was happening.

Nell took another step. The umbrella began to heat up. A quick wisp of electric-blue light ran up the handle and crackled along the tip.

CRACK!

The third whip sounded, and Nell didn't think, for all thoughts had been drowned out, replaced by the sound of the Night crashing through her ears. It was a wild roar, a mad shout, a rush of wind, a clatter of rain. It was all she could hear and it was beautiful. Nell dashed at Shivers, red hot with anger. He saw her coming and sneered, bringing his sword down fast and hard, but Nell, following the slight tug of the umbrella, darted left.

From where Max stood, he could see Nell shrouded in a flickering cloud of tiny stars, bright and electric.

"The Night," Max gasped.

Nell felt it as well. She was fighting and moving and thinking, but another force was guiding her, being her, and she was being it. Her movements were no longer the movements of a child but the graceful curve of the moon rising.

The clown's blade missed Nell, coming close enough for her to hear it whistle past. Nell followed the tug of the umbrella again, pivoted and swung with all she had. The umbrella struck the clown's arm, a crackle of blue light slicing through his coat. He grunted in pain. But Nell did not stop, understanding the way of the umbrella, one with the Night, her energy flowing with the force of a current of water shooting down a mountain after a violent summer rain.

The fight began full on. The dark sky filled with the clash of weapons and the grunt and huff of the fighters, each looking for an advantage. But the advantage was all Nell's. Again and again she found a weakness, slashing the clown, burning hot holes in his overcoat and raising a few wounds on his face. Two more good shots, and his arms would be useless.

The two other clowns were throwing stones at Nell, and one stone slammed into her bowler hat. Rose let out a song from inside the hat, and her mother's familiar bird voice startled her. The light that was surrounding Nell vanished, her energy cut off. Shivers, seeing his opening, kicked her hard in the stomach with his dirty boot. Nell doubled over and gasped for breath as the pain of the kick blasted through her body like a bomb.

Anger replaced all her senses. Her ears rang with the rush of water flowing. The Night had awoken inside her once more. Deep. Powerful. Endless. Night. Roaring, Nell leapt up and charged, swinging the umbrella like a master swordswoman. Her skill was overpowering. Lines of blue light crackled from the umbrella's tip and trailed through the darkness in great arcs and swirls.

Try as he might, Shivers was no match for her and could not deflect any of her blows. Two more slashes to his legs, and he was defeated. He sank to his knees.

"You won't be needing that!" Nell said, giving a hard slash to his sword, and in a bright blue flash, the weapon melted. Great globs of metal hit the dirt before him.

Shivers's yellow eyes were wide in disbelief. He had been defeated by a child.

Nell was breathing hard. She held the sparking blue tip of the umbrella to Shivers's defiant face.

"Go on," he snarled. "Get it over with. Off with my head."

"I'm no clown," Nell said, not taking her eyes off him. "We're leaving now, and you and your friends are going to be our prisoners."

"Please," the clown whimpered. Nell looked into his eyes for a moment, wondering if the trembling clown was actually scared. If there was any real feeling hidden beneath his make-up. Could a Nightmare have ever known any sort of kindness or even imagine what it meant to try to save another?

"You don't understand." Shivers began to cry.

"It's okay," Nell said kindly, feeling sorry for him.

But Nell's kindness was her undoing. A large stone hit her on the back of the head, knocking off her bowler hat. It landed upside-down in the dirt. Rose peeked her bright red head out of the bowler and, quick as a wink, the clown's pale hand darted out and grabbed Rose, squeezing as though he was trying to snuff the life out of her. Rose chirped in pain, and the clown brought the bird to his face, opening his pointed teeth, ready to bite.

"STOP!" Nell gasped, holding the crackling blue tip of the umbrella at his face.

"Touch me and you'll burn up this little bird along with me," he said coldly and smiled wide, knowing he now had the upper hand.

"Give her back."

"I don't think so."

"Give her back," Nell repeated.

"Put down your weapon," Shivers said. "I'll trade you. This bird for your umbrella."

"The minute I do, you'll take me prisoner."

"That's right. But I won't kill you or this bird. I'll just sell you and all your friends to the Spider Dreamer. What he does with you ain't my business, but at least you'll live. For now, that is."

Nell looked at Rose in confusion.

"Better make up your mind," said Shivers. "This tasty bird smells delicious." A string of drool dripped from the clown's pointed fangs and splashed on Rose's head. He was breathing hard, his hand shaking at having the treat of a fresh bird so close to his lips.

CHAPTER 29

T he *Compass* was flying swiftly through an endless windblown desert of red sand. The vast, lonely expanse was visible through the curved glass of the ship, which stretched the entire length of the large cabin. Badger, seated in the cracked leather captain's chair, had his two hands firmly on the jet-pilot-style steering wheel. He eased the wheel with utmost precision, leaning the craft slightly as he slid between the rose-coloured outcroppings, thin as columns, that rose suddenly from the desert floor. As the columns spouted up, they'd take the form of horned demons and fallen angels, eyes flashing first in surprise and then in hatred before dissolving again into the sand.

"Wouldn't it be easier to fly over them?" George asked.

"The higher you go, the higher they rise, and the more alive they become," Badger explained.

"This height is perfect!" George squeaked.

Pinch sat in the co-pilot seat beside Badger, checking gauges and dials and slapping buttons with her powerful paws. The interior of the cabin was filled with dark wood, brass valves and leaded glass dials that housed shivering needles. There were endless rows of switches and blinking lights of red and green. It had the feel of an early submarine or a plane from long ago.

"This ship rules," George whispered to Speedy, who was too full of wonder to speak. Like many children their age, they loved ships and planes and spacecraft, things of wonder that combined nimble speed, brute power and intricate technology. This was a special place. Not just a means of transport, but also a well-loved and trusted ship, burnished by battle: a warrior that had seen it all, that had been piloted by many and had saved even more. The *Compass* had been a home on long missions, and it showed. In fact, it looked like an antiques shop where every object had a story: some triumphant, some hilarious and some too terribly sad to speak of.

Faded stickers, tin action figures, old colour photos of beautiful men and women were all jammed here and there along the dashboard. Bits of silver Christmas tinsel were strung above the window. A long, rectangular black-and-white photo of a group of stern-looking men and women in old-fashioned clothes was drilled above a small green radar screen.

A brass label on the frame of the photo said "Fearless Travellers, First Class". The year was too faded to make out. Everywhere they looked, there was something old and interesting. There were glossy postcards of places Travellers wished to go or had visited during time off, tiny hand-carved jade statues of long-lost Dreamers, football stickers from teams that were no longer in existence, an intricately woven chewing-gum chain, and on either side of the dashboard, as if watching over all, sat a blue sock monkey and a yellow stuffed duck. Each was very much alive.

"Who are these guys?" George asked.

"Duck's name is Uh-Uh. Monkey is Toots," Badger yawned.

"Engine six is losing power," Pinch said gravely.

Badger stood and turned to George. "Take the wheel."

"What?"

"Take the wheel. I need to check on a jam in the engine, and I'm taking your brother with me."

"Don't I need some kind of driving licence?" George asked.

"It's simple. Any idiot can do it."

"I know you can," George said, "but we're talking about me."

"Go!" Badger snarled and George scurried into the captain's seat. "Just hold on with two hands. Keep it steady, we're out of the time sands now, so all you have to do is keep it straight."

"Good luck, George," Speedy said, giving him a pat on the shoulder, which made George jerk the wheel and sent the entire ship tilting wildly to the left.

"Sorry," George apologized and righted the ship. It was easier than he'd expected, and this instantly made him feel better. He let out a quiet sigh. "Go on, I can do this," he said with growing confidence.

"Let me know when you get a reading on Nell," Badger instructed Pinch. The panther nodded and continued to work a set of dials on a green radar screen where a single line swept round and round, searching.

Badger led Speedy through the network of catwalks and corridors of dark metal and glowing, amber-coloured lights. Speedy walked lost in his thoughts of Nell.

"She sings," he said.

"Who?" Badger said, confused by the large boy's sudden declaration.

"Nell," Speedy said thoughtfully. "She tells everyone she can't sing and she never does, not when anyone's watching anyway. When she has to sing at school she doesn't even move her lips."

"Most people singing in a group are faking it," Badger agreed. "Unless you have one of those voices that make people stop and listen," Badger said as though he had met a few who possessed that gift.

"Thing is, Nell IS that girl and no one knows it," Speedy paused. "Except for me," he smiled with a secret. "Her room is right next to mine. And every night her alarm goes off at three thirty. I can hear her get out of bed, walk across the room to the window, and she begins to sing. Softly. All sorts of songs. She sings until three forty-five and then walks back to her bed and goes back to sleep."

Badger stopped. "Nell?" he said, smiling. Speedy nodded. "But don't tell her. She'll kill me."

"You have my word," he promised and asked, "Is she good?"

"Awesome," Speedy said, thrilled to be sharing his only secret with someone. "I used to imagine I had a magic singing bird living in the next room." No sooner had the word "bird" left his lips than he was reminded of Nell and his mother and the danger they were in.

Badger understood. He put his hand on the boy's shoulder and explained how they would find Nell in the vast region of the Wicked Places. "The only way she could have escaped Nevermore Hall is by the lift," he said. "The Lift Dreamer is a tricky one; she opens doors and rearranges realities. Sometimes she will bring you exactly where you want, and sometimes she will bring you to the place you fear most."

"That's not nice."

Badger stopped. He turned and studied Speedy to see if he was making a joke. Speedy's kind brown eyes were unflinching. He was not. "What makes you think that people should be nice?" he asked.

"I don't know," Speedy said thoughtfully. "I never really thought about it. I just think it's natural."

Badger looked at Speedy and laughed. A large, loud, hearty laugh.

"It isn't?" Speedy asked.

"Of course it is. But we're not talking about people. She isn't nice. And she isn't mean. She is a Dreamer. She sees things we cannot. She could have dropped Nell in Vazencrack, but it's more likely she didn't. She doesn't want to take anyone's side in this. But every umbrella is equipped with a homing device. As long as Nell still has it, once we get a reading on where she is, we'll set course and be with her in no time."

This gave Speedy a great sense of relief. He hadn't stopped worrying about Nell and Rose since he saw his sister disappear into Nevermore Hall.

As they neared the engine room, the hum and roar of the mechanisms inside grew louder. At the end of the corridor was a heavy steel door with a round window in the centre that was fogged with steam.

"The engine room is a dangerous place, understand? It is loud, so stay close and try not to get bitten," Badger warned.

"Bitten?"

Badger pulled the lever, pushing open the door. A thick wall of warm steam flooded over them. For a moment, Speedy was lost in a cloud of whiteness. Badger grabbed his hand and pulled him forward. Speedy could see nothing, but he knew they were not alone, because all around him was the huff of breath, the roar of an engine chugging and the occasional whinny of a horse.

"Hold on," Badger screamed above the din and hit a lever that activated a fan. There was a whirr, and when the steam cleared, Speedy got his first look at the engine that powered the *Compass*. Standing in a line before him, in stalls separated by bands of neon blue light, were eight enormous horses that appeared to be part animal and part machine. The front part of the animals – their heads, necks and chests – were horses, very real and very alive, but their bottom and back halves were motorcycles. One wheel in the front and two in the back. The creatures were beautiful, their coats made of brilliant, gleaming liquid chrome that pulsed with life and their eyes a fierce chestnut colour. The horses' gazes were wise and truly wild. They were animals, not robots: creatures that hadn't been built, but born.

"This is the Dreamland's only eight-Silverback-power engine," explained Badger.

The wheels of the creatures spun in a uniform hum over a rectangle of flowing blue light. Speedy gazed into the light, and a demon's face slid by. He jumped up.

"The Silverbacks run on Nightmares," Badger explained. "But they're trapped in the tank, so don't worry."

One of the horses, engine number six, was jammed up. The creature's back tyres were straining but not spinning. Badger walked onto the thin catwalk beside the struggling creature. Kneeling down, he studied the back wheel and immediately determined the problem.

"Here," Badger grunted to Speedy. "Stand in front of her head, and when I give the signal, lay your hands across her eyes."

"You want me to touch her?" Speedy said, peeping nervously at the massive silver beast. Even glancing at her caused her to snap and show a mouthful of sharp silver teeth.

"It's the only way we can keep her calm while I regroove her. You must do it quickly."

"Look, I'm called Speedy because I'm *not* quick. It's a joke, see? I only move fast at weird times. When I'm not thinking about it," he said. Then he quietly added, "Or if I have to use the bathroom."

"Perfect. Don't think."

"You say that a lot, you know."

"It's good advice in almost every situation."

"Just. Okay. But…" Speedy said, trying to think up another reason he couldn't help. One thing he definitely wasn't speedy with was coming up with excuses.

"No buts!" Badger yelled. "Do it quick. Hands over eyes. Once they're covered, she'll become as gentle as a lamb."

Speedy took a few steps until he was standing right before the creature. It snarled and snapped, hot steam snorting from its muzzle. "She's going to bite my face off," he said.

"On three," Badger said. "One, two, three."

As quickly as he could, Speedy snapped his hands over the Silverback's eyes. Instantly, the creature grew calm. The energy flowing through her was intense and sent a shivering vibration through Speedy's entire body.

As he held her head, Speedy saw something in his mind's eye coming into focus out of a whispering haze, and suddenly he found himself before a ragged-looking man in a long overcoat and black boots. His greasy, matted hair was bright orange and his face was painted pale white with a blue slash across his lips and red drips like splatters of blood along his cheeks. A clown. Not just any clown, but a dark Nightmare of a clown. And standing before the clown was Nell. They were fighting a duel in a dark forest as skeletons stood by, watching. The two fighters staggered through the darkness, slashing at each other with grunts and screams in a duel to the death.

"Let her go," Badger said. Speedy removed his hands from the silver creature's head, and the vision vanished. His eyes were wide, his face blank with terror.

"She's back on groove," Badger said, nodding to the Silverback.

"I saw Nell," Speedy said, dazed.

"Where?"

"She was in a forest, and she was fighting a clown," Speedy said with a shrug and even faked a little laugh, hoping that it was a strange imaginary vision, some side-effect of touching the Silverback that Badger would explain with an annoyed frown.

"Clown?" Badger asked carefully, as though the word was a bottle filled with acid he didn't want to drop. Speedy knew then that what he had seen was absolutely real. "Go on."

"It was in a forest. Skeletons were watching. I heard a word, too. 'Despairo.'"

"Despairo Forest, that's north of Boneville. It is a hideout for clowns." Badger turned and began hurrying back up towards the bridge.

"Engine six is back online," Badger said as they entered. He glanced out of the windscreen. The desert outside had been replaced by a dark landscape of a ruined city. A swarm of cow-sized bats swooped past the window, flapping their leather wings.

"I think I made a wrong turn," George said as he jerked the wheel to avoid a charging bat and flew through the window of a crumbling skyscraper.

There was a screeching, scraping *crash* as the eagle head on the ship's western prow hit the side of the wall and burst out again through another wall, which fell away like paper.

The sky was a cold blue-black and shimmered with stars. The *Compass* flew on into the night.

"You did fine," Badger said, grabbing the wheel and nodding for him to get up. They quickly switched places. "Nell is in Despairo Forest," he said as he guided the ship upwards above the clouds.

"Clowns?" Pinch asked, her eyes narrowing.

"Looks that way."

"We got a cloud of something coming towards us," Pinch said.

A long, bone-chilling moan rattled the ship, sending a stab of cold through the cabin.

"What was that?" George said nervously. "No. Don't tell me. Because whenever I ask, it's something messed up."

"Spiders," Badger answered.

"I said, don't tell me."

All eyes were now fixed on the windscreen. Streaking across the sky were what looked at first like black-tipped missiles shooting out dark smoke. Hundreds, maybe thousands of spiders the size of cars were headed straight for them. The first spider rocketed past. It was enormous, with a massive head the colour of tar. Its spindly legs worked furiously, moving like knitting needles as they rapidly pumped out an endless curtain of smoke-coloured silk that unfurled wildly in the night air.

There was something caught inside the dark silk.

"Don't look!" Pinch cautioned, but it was too late and impossible to turn away from the horrible sight of it. On the other side of the black curtain were Sleepers, thousands upon thousands of them, caught by the spiders' webs, tumbling helplessly upon each other.

"What are they?" Speedy murmured, his lips quivering.

"The Spiders of the Waste," Badger whispered. Finding his voice, he continued, "They inhabit the wastelands at the edge of Vazencrack and have never left before, but they're fleeing now. They're fleeing and taking their slaves with them."

"Why?"

"There is one possible explanation. But I thought I'd never live to see it."

"What?" Speedy asked nervously.

"The Red Egg," Badger said. "They sense it is about to break. Time is running out." Badger pushed a few buttons that made the ship rumble. "We must reach Nell before they do! Full speed ahead!"

Every metal surface conducted the explosive sounds of the engines and the rattles and thumps shut down the cooling system. The bridge was now a hundred degrees, as blasting waves of heat and a constant thunderous rumble poured through the vents. The bleat of an alarm filled the air.

"Dark Daughters!" Badger screamed above the wailing siren. "George, take the blasters on the whale prow. Speedy, take the eagle prow. Don't fire until you get the signal."

Speedy suddenly realized the implications of the command. "Awesome."

Pinch led the boys down a thin iron staircase, through a narrow, vibrating corridor to a chrome door on which someone had long ago painted a skull and crossbones. The door opened, revealing the cockpit. They crossed the threshold and were inside the large, silver, whale-shaped prow that jutted out from the western side of the ship. The small space had a leather chair, a two-handled blaster, and a small round window that looked out across the immense sky. Out of a bank of purple clouds flew hundreds of Dark Daughters racing towards them, on the backs of flying octopuses. The sight made things suddenly very real.

"Get in the chair and strap yourself in," Pinch said.

"You didn't say 'please'," George said, trying to hide the fear in his voice.

Pinch growled in response and raised her paw, pointing to a tall tube light. "That light will start to glow blue. When it turns red, fire. But do not even think of firing before it's ready, even if you're taking heat."

"Taking heat?"

"Being attacked."

"Which is no big deal, because the glass is totally blast-proof," Speedy added, tapping the round bubble window that separated them from the sky.

"Not exactly," Pinch warned.

"But it's going to be okay," Speedy said. "We're not going to leave you in here to be shot at?"

"That's exactly what we are going to do," Pinch said. "And we are taking *you* to the eagle prow to be shot at."

"And it's going to be okay?" Speedy repeated. "Dark Daughters are not really fighters, right?" The idea of shooting a blaster had seemed fun to him before he realized that people would be shooting back.

"I don't think so," Pinch said matter-of-factly. "Dark Daughters are fearsome warriors, crack shots and will fight until their enemies are dead."

"Well, that's just great."

"Indeed. But that is the situation," Pinch said directly, her gaze steady as a steel bridge across a river. "In the Dreamlands everything happens for reasons that you'll never unravel. Things change. Reality shifts. You don't have time to ask why.

'Why is this happening? Why am I here? How did it all come to this?' All you know is you are here and your moment to live it has arrived. And now our moment is a fight. A fight we might not win. That is the situation. We are overmatched and outnumbered. That we can't control, but we can control our fear."

"How?"

"By turning it around and using it."

"That's not helping," Speedy said quietly.

"It will when the arrows begin to fly."

"What if it doesn't?"

"If it doesn't, you won't survive. Now, Speedy, follow me."

Speedy gave his brother a pat on the shoulder and followed Pinch to the opposite side of the ship, where the eagle prow awaited. He followed her through the steel door and found an identical room. He strapped in silently. There was nothing left to say; he was going into battle, and blood would be spilled. Pinch pointed out the gun and the gauges, and Speedy nodded as though he was listening, but he wasn't. His big, kind eyes were fixed on the tide of Dark Daughters that were coming to kill him. The octopuses flew in one long line, their tentacles undulating smoothly in the wind.

Pinch slapped the telescope welded to the top of the gun and motioned for Speedy to look inside. Speedy put his eye to the cold brass.

On the back of each octopus was a leather saddle on which a single Dark Daughter rode. The women wore long, flowing robes, tall boots and necklaces of black flowers. Their faces were not visible. Each wore a mask of burnished silver, shaped like an animal head. Hounds. Snakes. Hyenas. Strapped to each Dark Daughter's back were her weapons – longbows and quivers filled with flaming arrows.

"Find your weapon."

Speedy removed his eye from the telescope and wrapped his fingers around the handles of the old blaster.

The first flaming arrow shot past the window, falling far short. A warning shot. The battle was coming.

"You can't kill a Dark Daughter," Pinch instructed. "But with a good shot you can stun them and knock them out of battle. Remember the blue light. Wait until we are at full power." Pinch snarled and darted out the door to return to the bridge.

The door slammed, and the small cockpit was silent except for the wind rushing against the glass. The thin pane was all that separated Speedy from the Dark Daughters. He peered into the sky. They were coming closer, a tidal wave of masked warriors growing ever larger. A few flaming arrows sizzled past the ship. They were too distant to hit the *Compass* just yet, but that would end any second. Speedy felt his heart pounding ferociously. The blue light grew brighter, the small tube filling up like a thermometer rising.

"GET READY TO FIRE!" Badger's voice crackled over the loudspeaker.

Speedy felt calm now. He tightened his grip on the blaster's handles. On the top of each was a red button for his thumbs. All he had to do was aim, point and press.

He put his eye to the scope. A single fighter in a hound-shaped helmet now led the vast line of Dark Daughters. She held a glowing sword above her head. Behind her, the line moved in military precision, their bows drawn and ready to fire their flaming arrows on her command.

"Ready!" Badger said over the speaker.

The leader brought down her sword, and the army let loose their arrows. Even from inside the cabin, across the distance of the sky, Speedy could hear the unison *ping* of the bows releasing and the *whoosh* of thousands of flaming arrows as they flew straight for the *Compass*.

"FIRE!" Badger shouted.

Speedy's thumbs pressed down rapidly on the buttons of his gun. There was a roar. A screaming flash of neon red exploded across the sky to meet the arrows head-on. Some were taken out, but many more were unharmed. Speedy watched in terror as a hail of flaming arrows came towards the glass. Suddenly, the ship dipped hard, dodging the assault.

Badger was a skilled pilot. He dipped and rolled the craft, sliding through assaults, and then he swung back around. He again gave the command to fire. Speedy shot, hitting a large Dark Daughter in a wolf's helmet. Suddenly, her octopus plummeted downwards.

The attack intensified. Arrows pelted the ship like rain. Some smashed against the window, sending shivering cracks across the panes. Speedy held his fingers steady on the gun. Blasts fired repeatedly from his gun and others. He tried not to think about George as arrows smashed into the ship. There was the sound of explosions and metal singed and tearing. *Fight*, Speedy thought. *Fight and don't think.* He blasted away, turning the gun to follow a Dark Daughter racing past. The sky was ablaze with smoke and screams and glowing blasts of light. All the while, the ship zoomed in and out of the cloud of flying fighters.

For a moment, the sky was clear, then a tall Dark Daughter wearing a golden helmet shaped like a shark's head flew out of the cloud and headed straight for Speedy. She moved quickly, and before he could react, she had landed her octopus on top of the eagle prow. With murderous calm, she walked towards the bubbled glass of the gunner's cockpit. Speedy's heart beat wildly. The barrel of his gun shot out, but not directly up. He could not reach her. She stood over him, staring into the bubble of glass, silent and still. Without taking her eyes off him, she removed a flaming arrow from her quiver and placed it in her bow. She slowly drew back on the string and aimed straight for Speedy's heart.

"No…"

Speedy tried to undo his seatbelt and escape, but it was locked. He was trapped. The Dark Daughter watched him struggle for a moment and then nodded as if to say, *It's over.* She released the arrow with a vicious *ping*.

A loud explosion violently rocked the ship. The arrow shattered the glass beside Speedy's face and sank into his seat right beside his neck. He glanced up at the Dark Daughter. Calmly, she pulled out another arrow, fixed it in place, and drew back her bowstring.

"Don't…" he said. "Please, Miss…"

The Dark Daughter smiled slightly and shook her head. "Too bad. It's too late. Your dream has come to an end," she said almost sweetly. But her eyes weren't sweet. They were dark with murder. Mercy would not be shown today or ever. It was time to die.

Speedy closed his eyes in fright, when suddenly the ship plunged, diving straight down. The Dark Daughter lost her balance. Her feet slipped and she pitched over the side of the prow into the sky below.

Speedy leaned over and gazed into the telescope.

The Dark Daughters were retreating.

"YES!" he shouted. "YES!" He was ecstatic. They had done it.

"Stand down," Badger commanded. "We got them on the run. Let 'em go. We need to save power. Lock your weapons and return to the bridge."

CHAPTER 30

Nell had been beaten. She knew it and dropped the umbrella. The clown smiled. He puckered his green lips and gave Rose a kiss on her red head. She tweeted defiantly and pecked at his fingers. The clown grimaced in pain and tightened his grip.

"I'll bite your head off right now," he snarled and squeezed harder.

"Stop," Nell begged.

He stood, never taking his eyes off Nell, and scooped up the weapon. "I've always wanted one of these."

"Give me my bird."

The clown laughed wickedly.

"We made a deal!" Nell sputtered in disbelief, her face hot with embarrassment at her own stupidity.

"What deal?"

There was a flash of blue light as the clown swung the umbrella at Nell's face and burned a slash beneath her eye. Nell screamed, and suddenly she was a silver fox. She charged at the clown, her fangs bared. A crack filled her ears, and the whip was around her throat, strangling her. She tumbled to the ground, struggling against the whip. The big clown held tight to the lash, yanking it in vicious jerks and, as she began to lose air, Nell turned back into herself.

Shivers put his dirty boot on the young girl's chest. "Now surely a Fearless Traveller knows never to trust a clown."

"Give her back," Nell croaked, her voice sore and tattered.

"This bird is going to be roasted and devoured, but if you are a good girl, I will let you eat the skull."

"You're disgusting!"

"Thank you," the clown said. "But before you go complaining to your friends about how terrible I am, what a liar I am, remember this: I will keep part of my promise. You will live. At least until we reach the spiders. Now, join the others while we get the fire ready." And with that, Shivers gave Nell a parting kick in her side with the sharp tip of his boot and walked to the edge of the clearing, where the big clown was building a fire pit.

"You were amazing."

Nell looked up into the kind face of Max, who was standing over her. She felt woozy. Her eye throbbed, her side ached, and her throat burned as if she had swallowed glowing coals.

Lefty was on Max's shoulder, holding a small glass bottle filled with a honey-coloured liquid. Max took it from Lefty, popped the cork, and handed it to Nell, who sat up with a groan. Pain shot up her side. Ribs were broken. "Drink this," Max commanded.

"Where…" Nell tried to say, but the pain was too great.

Max knew what she meant. "The book. *The Fearless Travellers' Guide*. On a page for medicines and tonics. Actually, that book is pretty handy."

Nell put the warm liquid to her lips. It tasted of honey and herbs from a sacred forest. The medicine tingled as it slid down her throat. She coughed raggedly. Her eyes popped. But then she was healed, simple as that. Her throat no longer burned, the ache in her ribs had disappeared, and the cut below her eye had vanished; in fact, she felt wonderful throughout.

"Thanks," Nell said, taking Max's outstretched hand, and he quickly helped her to her feet. Nell followed Max back to where the skeletons stood, waiting to be led through the forest and given over to the spiders.

"I tried to convince them to run. They had a chance, too, while you were fighting. I said I would distract the other two clowns. But not one would go."

"Why not?"

"They didn't want to leave you."

Nell turned away. She felt a wave of shame and failure. "I lost Rose," she said to Max. "They should have run. I lost everything."

"Not yet."

The thump of branches being thrown into a pile shook the ground. Nell turned. The clowns were ripping branches from a tree to build an enormous fire.

"I have a plan," Max said.

"I hope it's better than mine."

"Shut up. Okay. Just shut up," Max nearly shouted. "Your plan was amazing, Nell. You saved us all and you beat an evil clown. You won, only he cheated."

"I should have known."

"You will fail," Max said.

"What?"

"That's what the book says. The motto."

"I know the motto."

"You don't. Listen," Max said as he repeated what he had already memorized, a motto that he now realized wasn't just a simple saying but a map and a weapon carved out of words.

"You will get lost. You will be afraid. You will fail. You will fight. You will remember. You will rise. And without doubt: You will find your way home.

"You see," he stressed. "Everyone fails. We're in the land of Nightmares! What else could we do but fail? It's kind of what this place is all about. Failing is part of the plan. But what's next? You will learn. See, from failing, you learn. And as you were fighting, I did learn something. The book doesn't say without *a* doubt you will find your way home. It doesn't promise anything. It says *without* doubt. *Without doubt*, you will find your way home. Don't you see? It's up to us. We can get out of here as long as we think it's possible, and we will, I swear it."

"Thank you," Nell said, suddenly so grateful that Max had appeared in this world. To be here in this dark forest with this person whose body was tossing in a bed somewhere in another world, dreaming he was here helping her, was more strange and wonderful than anything else.

"You don't have to thank me. I'm your friend," Max said.

Impulsively, before she could think about stopping herself, Nell, the unhugger, gave Max a quick hug.

He held his hands up awkwardly. "All right, calm down."

"What do we do?" Nell asked, trying not to feel embarrassed about the hug.

"Glad you asked. Remember when we were on the bus and Rose began to sing to the little girl skeleton?"

"Her eyes," Nell said, realizing what he was getting at. "Her eyes became real when Rose began to sing. Music does something to them."

"There are twenty big men over there," Max said, nodding to the skeletons huddled together. "As skeletons, they're useless, but as men – maybe we could fight the clowns. Twenty versus three. Plus a one-handed kid and a Fearless Traveller."

"There isn't a Fearless Traveller," Nell said.

"You, Nell," Max said. "I mean you."

Nell felt her cheeks redden. She agreed the plan was perfect until she realized that Max might expect her to sing.

"I can't sing," Nell said in a tiny voice, her cheeks suddenly hot with embarrassment.

"I know," Max said.

"What do you mean, you know?" Nell huffed.

"I would always watch you when we had to sing in school. You never move your lips."

"And why were you watching me?" Nell demanded. She didn't like to be watched, especially when she was trying not to be noticed.

Now it was Max's turn to be embarrassed.

"Why do people watch people?" Max said. "Because…"

"Because what?"

"Look, " Max said, avoiding the question. "You don't have to sing. I play the trumpet. If this Ravenhead's trumpet is as powerful as they say, we could use it to transform the skeletons into humans. Give them bodies, and we'd have a small army."

For a moment, neither of them spoke. Rose was now tied to a stick that was jabbed into the dirt. The big clown who had been given the cooking duties was sprinkling her with spices, rubbing his thick fingers across her soft golden feathers and streaking them with clumps of rotten butter.

"I want her burnt to a crisp," Shivers snarled.

From her stick by the fire, Rose was warbling, singing a defiant song as if she knew that Nell was on her way to save her. Hearing her mother alive and safe, Nell felt so happy she feared her heart would burst. She whistled an answer to Rose, and the small golden bird responded in kind.

"QUIET!" snarled the big clown. Behind them, the trees the clowns were trying to cut fell down. "Finally," the clown said, turning to the slaves. "Get that over here and light it up."

"Let's go," Nell said to Max. As the slaves built a large, roaring fire, Nell approached the skeletons. They were sitting on the ground in defeated silence, having given up any hope of getting free. Nell and Max spread out and explained the plan to them, and the dark hollows of their eyes watched them with rapt attention. When Nell and Max played the trumpet, the skeletons would become human again and attack. The idea took hold.

"You really think it will turn us into people?" the bus driver asked.

"I hope so," Nell said. "But that means it will hurt if you get hit."

The skeletons smiled, laughing quietly together.

"What?" she asked.

"Darling," the old skeleton who had given Nell the bowler said, picking up a large stick, "nothing hurts worse than feeling nothing. To be alive again, just for a moment, I'd take a hundred lashes from that whip."

"He ain't going to lay a hand on you, Mum," a large skeleton said.

"I know, Sonny," she replied, "because I'm going to lay two on him."

"Everyone needs to grab a weapon," Nell instructed. All the skeletons watched her with their hollow eyes. "When the change comes, we all must attack and not stop until the clowns are gone."

The skeletons agreed. While the clowns were busy

watching the fire grow, the skeletons wandered around in the darkness, hiding at the edge of the woods and waiting for their moment.

Nell walked over to Max. He bent over the case and quickly slid the button on the latch. The latch clicked, and slowly the lid opened. Inside was an object of pure beauty: Ravenhead's trumpet. The trumpet was pure gold and embedded with hundreds of tiny eyes made of jewels that glimmered in the moonlight. For a moment they were speechless. Finally Nell found her voice.

"Can you still play?" Nell said.

Max knew what she meant. The hand he used to finger the keys was gone, taken by Freyja Skoll. "If you help me," he said.

"Help you?"

"I taught you once before."

"I was terrible."

"You were fine. Hold out your hand."

Nell did, and Max took it in his. He opened her palm and shook each of Nell's fingers as he talked.

"Remember? This finger is number one, this is number two, this is number three. When I start to blow, you push. One. Three. Two-three. One. One. Two-three. It's a simple song, but it's all we've got."

"All right." Nell nodded, listening intently. She could hear Rose letting out a desperate chirp. She turned to look at her, but Max shook her hand.

"We're going to save her," Max said. "But you need to focus. Say it to yourself, and move your fingers."

Nell did as she was instructed. "One. Three. Two-three. One. One. Two-three," she said.

"And back to the beginning."

"I want my BIRD!" Shivers roared, tossing the whisky bottle into the fire.

"Coming, boss," the big clown said. As he ran towards the bird, one of the skeletons threw a large stone that hit him in the head.

"Hey," he snarled, turning towards the skeletons, knife drawn.

"Now!" Max said. He put the trumpet to his lips. The mouthpiece was cold and smooth. Its jewelled eyes seemed to be staring at him. He took in a deep breath.

Nell stood right beside him and placed her fingers on the cool pearl pads of the keys. Max nodded and began to blow. As he did, Nell counted to herself, pushing down on the buttons. The eyes on the side of the horn came alive as a loud and glorious noise, like the trumpeting of a thousand geese, blasted out of the horn.

The song was a quickly changing kaleidoscope of sound. It was a moan and a shout. It was the squeal of joy at a midnight dance hall, the broad cheer of a parade and the rising charge of an approaching army. It was every sound they'd ever heard hidden inside one, but above all, it was music. Beautiful music, soft and sweet.

The clowns stood frozen for a moment, heads cocked as they listened to the music – unexpected in a place where usually the only sounds were the scratch of leafless trees, the howl of beasts and the screams of wounded victims. They had no idea what to make of it. It produced nothing in them but anger.

For the skeletons, it was different. The music fell upon them, tearing loose long-buried memories of another life. Like rain upon parched earth awakens sprouts of fresh grass, the skeletons became new. Blue, brown and green eyes filled hollow sockets. Soft skin of every colour rushed over hard bones. Hair, long and short, curly and straight, sprouted from bald skulls. In a matter of seconds, this sad band of walking dead became human beings, bursting with life, warm and beautiful. They looked at each other, laughing and weeping and shouting with joy, and all at once, they remembered what they needed to do. With shouts they charged. It was more than an attack. It was a celebration.

The clowns were taken by surprise. Stones rained down on them, clubs swung. A big skeleton, now a large and fearsome man, snatched a burning branch from the fire and swung it with a shout. Seeing their evil master clowns were being attacked, the slaves broke their chains and joined in the fight to destroy them.

As the former skeletons fought, Nell ran over to Rose and set her free. The small bird, suddenly unbound, darted forward, chasing the clowns, pecking at their heads before doubling back and landing on the umbrella, which was still stuck in the dirt.

Shivers knew he had lost, but he alone did not run. "All right," he snarled, swinging his sword at the line of men and women approaching. "I'm gone. But don't think I won't see you again." He sneered at Nell. "If you ever find yourself in the Wicked Places again, I'll be waiting for you."

Max gave the trumpet a hard blast, and Shivers's top hat burst into flames. With a yowl, he threw it down and ran off into the darkness of the woods.

The former skeletons cheered, and for the next few hours they wouldn't let Nell or Max stop playing. They blew into the trumpet and played song after song as the former skeletons and slaves danced into the night. The former skeletons delighted in their skin, in their strength, in the smell of the fire. They passed the little skeleton-turned-human around, kissing her giggling head of golden curls as she thrilled in having a body, although she was too young to even remember what it had been like. Rose was petted and whispered to all night by the old lady, who kept calling her "baby".

As one song ended, Nell's eyes were drawn to a flash of light streaking across the sky. The entire forest shook as a bright light shone from above, blinding them all and, with a hum, a large flying ship landed in the clearing beside them.

CHAPTER 31

The ship shone its warm light upon the crowd. All watched as the hatch opened. Speedy and George ran outside. Speedy threw his arms around Nell, and George punched her lovingly on the arm.

"You remember Max," Nell said.

"Hey, Max," Speedy yelled, full of enthusiasm, and gave Max a big hug.

"Hey, Speedy," Max said, wriggling free of the boy's arms. George ignored both his sister and Max. He stared at the disembodied hand.

"Hate to break it to you, Nell," George said, "but your boyfriend has a hand on his shoulder."

"He's not my boyfriend," Nell said and felt her cheeks redden.

"Glad you made it, kid," Badger snarled. Lefty leapt off Max's shoulder to shake Badger's hand.

"That's Lefty," Nell explained. Badger shook the bodiless hand without hesitation. Suddenly, the air filled with distant shrieks. The sound, one of pain and stark terror, rattled them all deeply. For a moment, everyone was silent.

"Time is running out," Badger said. "Come, Nell, onto the ship."

Nell said her goodbyes to the former skeletons who were still celebrating around the fire.

"Thank you," the bus driver said. "Give my thanks to your whole organization."

"My organization?" Nell said.

"The Fearless Travellers," the bus driver said.

"I'm not–" Nell started to say, when Max cut her off.

"She means, you're welcome," Max said, nodding at Nell.

Nell and Max followed her brothers and Badger into the *Compass,* and the hatch closed with a muffled WHOOSH behind them. Nell looked around, astonished at the ancient machine. Everywhere she looked there were coloured knobs, blinking lights, control screens and interesting trinkets.

Pinch took the controls, barking orders to Speedy and George, and with a loud countdown, the ship rumbled to life and lifted into the sky.

Badger twisted a heavy valve, and two deep brown leather chairs rose from the floor. He pulled down on a lever and a metal pipe with a round fire pit descended from the ceiling. Inside the pit, a small fire was already blazing. Badger nodded for Nell and Max to sit and handed them two steaming mugs of Travellers' cocoa.

"We need to go to Vazencrack," Nell said. "To save Ravenhead."

"Yes," Badger said. "What else did you find out?"

Nell and Max sipped the warm liquid, and all the cold vanished from their bodies. As they drank, they told Badger the whole tale of their escape from the Dark Daughters in Crypt and their encounter with the clowns. When they explained about the trumpet, Badger's expression changed. He typically did not show much emotion, but it was clear he was beyond stunned.

"Is that the trumpet?" Badger asked.

Max nodded.

"May I see it?"

Max nodded again and opened the lid.

Badger stared into the case and shook his head in astonishment. "Forget the fact that every time you play it, there is a good chance you will burst into flames … or worse. Do you have any idea what a powerful weapon this is?"

"Burst into flames?" Nell shivered.

"You might as well have been carrying around a ten-tonne nuclear bomb. This is the trumpet of Ravenhead. Played correctly, this instrument has the power not just to change creatures into other creatures, but to alter the entire landscape of the Dreamlands. It can twist time, bend fates, raise the dead, snuff out Dreamers and snatch things from Earth. This is not just an instrument. It is a weapon of the gods. Played correctly, it is devastating; played incorrectly, the results are even worse."

"Hello, Nell." A voice rang out over the speakers. It was Fenn, her wolf-like ears able to hear through walls. "Smells like you brought the handless boy. Thank you. I've been waiting to take the other hand."

"No," Nell murmured, her body trembling. "Why is Fenn here?"

"She is our prisoner," Badger explained.

Lefty jumped from Max's shoulder, ran across the bridge to the door, and began to pound on it, anxious to attack. Badger scooped up the wriggling hand.

"And Fearless Travellers treat our prisoners with compassion," he told the hand. "It is our first rule."

"But before I take his hand, first I'll take my stinking bird back. You stole it from me, Nell, and now I'm going to pick

off her feathers one by one. That will teach her to run away!"
Fenn's voice, cold as ice, crackled over the speakers.

Nell put her hands over her ears.

"Make her be quiet! Please!" she whispered. Even being on
the same ship with the little Dark Daughter made her stomach
hurt. After all Nell had been through, all she had seen, Fenn
filled her with a deeper dread than she could explain.

"She patched into the speakers somehow," Pinch snarled.

"Go and check on our prisoner, George," Badger said.
Carefully, as though he were holding a newborn, he put the
trumpet back in its case and closed the lid. "And remember,
George, don't talk to her or listen to her. Just check that she's
not up to mischief."

"Got it," George said, giving Badger an excited salute.

Badger turned to Max and Nell. "Here is our situation," he
said. "A spell prevents Fearless Travellers from entering Freyja
Skoll's castle. It will have to be you, Nell. You'll have to enter
and find Ravenhead."

"And me," Max said.

"And me," Speedy added.

"And me!" George said.

"Yes. All of you will need to go. But the most dangerous
thing that awaits you is not the Dark Daughters. It's that
trumpet. As dangerous as it is, I'm afraid you're going to have
to play it again," Badger said to Nell.

"Even though it could kill us?" Nell said nervously.

"Yes."

"Why are you saying that?" Speedy moaned.

"Because it's true. The trumpet is the only way to wake
Ravenhead."

"I bet I could wake him," George said. "A good flick on the

beak would do it. No one can sleep through that."

"Go!" Badger commanded, pointing to the door. "Check on our prisoner."

"All right," George huffed. He exited the bridge. Everyone listened for a moment as George's curses echoed behind the closed door.

"Sorry," Nell shrugged.

* * *

George soon ran out of curses, and he was immediately engulfed in the quiet hum of the engine. The noise vibrated off the metal of the long corridors and stairwells. George didn't like being alone down here. Walking along the narrow corridors of the ship, the dread grew until he reached the room where Fenn was being held. As George approached, he could see thin tendrils of yellow smoke escaping from the crack under the door.

"What on earth do you think you're doing?" George asked, turning the heavy lever and letting himself into the room. He coughed. The small room was full of thick yellow smoke. Half the room was a cell. Behind the thick bars, Fenn stood on her bed. She was mumbling in a deep, guttural language, her small chest rising and falling with each yowling word.

"Moartea. Intunericul. Mintea. Moartea. Intunericul. Mintea!"

Yellow smoke poured out of her nose like from a dragon. The acrid vapour smelled of burning plastic and burned George's eyes.

"Stop it!" George said, struggling to breathe. Fenn chanted louder and louder. The smoke grew in thickness, and the sounds from her body became more demonic. The smoke made George's head spin. His legs went numb, and he felt himself slipping. Everything seemed to be happening in slow motion. He tried to talk but his mouth didn't work, and before he knew it, he hit the ground. He struggled to rise but could not, his arms like jelly. All around him, hot globs of iron hit the ground and sizzled through the floor. Fenn was melting the bars with her breath.

"Now. You will all die!" Fenn cried, jumping off the bed and walking through the hole in the bars.

With all his might, George stuck out his hand and grabbed hold of her leg. Fenn turned and let out a stream of scorching yellow smoke that burned his hand. He screamed in agony and lay on the ground, clutching his hand, as she walked out of the door. George tried to speak, to call out for help, but his mouth was frozen shut. Even if he could speak, no one would hear him. The ship had run into a storm and was heaving and shaking.

* * *

On the bridge, all eyes were staring out of the window at the sky, trying to comprehend the evil that awaited them. They had passed through a wall of dark purple clouds and were now flying low over the ice forests of Vazencrack. It was a dead, windswept place of leafless trees dripping with jagged icicles that sent up hollow chimes as the *Compass* passed. Soon the forest grew thin, turning into an empty snow-caked plain that led to a single mountain of black ice, which watched over everything like a merciless prison guard. At the top sat Dark Dawn, Freyja Skoll's castle, encased in fog.

At the moment, no one was looking at the wasteland of ice or the desolate mountain but at the towering blood-red egg that hovered over Dark Dawn. The egg appeared to be as large as the mountain itself. Its shell shivered with hot, electric pulses of energy. Suddenly the *Compass* began to shake. The engines groaned.

"We're losing power!" Pinch screamed. "The egg is draining us. The engines are dying."

"Dying? How can we fly without an engine?"

But for the moment no one was thinking about the engine. All eyes were staring out the window at the great Red Egg floating above Freyja Skoll's castle at the top of the icy mountain. An ear-piercing *crack* rang out, shaking the air around them as in the distance the eggshell shattered, and millions of jagged pieces violently rained down upon the *Compass* with spitting hisses. As the fog of shells cleared, what had hatched took their breath away.

Floating above the castle was the Plague Dreamer. He sat cross-legged and completely still. His long, thin face was bone white except for his lips, which were the pale blue of a drowned man. His hair, long and scraggly, hung down to his shoulders from beneath a crown made of human skulls. His clothes were ragged, but his arms, folded in his lap, were powerful. At first he seemed to be shivering, making his whole body look hazy and out of focus. As they got closer a piercing buzz filled the air and it became clear that the Plague Dreamer, skin, clothes and all, was made of a black tide of insects. It was just as they had seen in their visions in the diner. When he finally stood and walked across the Dreamlands, that tide of insects would be unleashed and devour everything in its path.

Rose sat on the brim of Nell's bowler. She flew to the window and let out a loud tweet of alarm, trying to understand the sheer size of the beast towards which they were speeding.

"How can we stop it?" Nell asked.

"You can't. Once my mother crushes the soul out of my little bird and the Eclipse potion is all nice and poison-like, a needle gets sticked into Ravenhead's heart and we'll all watch him burn. He'll light up the sky as he flies screaming right up into the Plague Dreamer. That will wake him."

Everyone turned, shocked to see Fenn standing in the doorway with a foul grin. "I tricked all of you stupid idiots," she giggled happily.

"She's not your bird!" Nell said. "She's my mother!"

"Not any more," Fenn said and sucked the air into her lungs and then blew a plume of yellow smoke from her thin lips. The sulphur cloud engulfed everyone in a hot, stinging fog that choked and blinded them.

Badger screamed, unleashing his umbrella, though he could no longer see it. Through the fog, sparks of blue light flashed in sharp pulses, and the little silhouette of Fenn was visible for a few seconds as she shot this way and that through the chaos, her vision alone clear.

"The bird is MINE!"

"Grab her!" Badger shouted.

Whoosh! Nell felt a small body run past her through the blinding smoke. Rose was chirping wildly, sounding an alarm, and Nell felt her leap from her shoulder. "Rose!" she shouted. Her eyes felt as though they were melting in her head. Soft feathers fluttered past Nell's cheek, and she held out her hand to grab her mother, but Rose was confused by the smoke and did not stop.

"MINE!" Fenn cried.

"Get off," Max grunted. He had Rose in his hand, and he and Fenn were fighting.

"Max!" Nell coughed through the blinding smoke. "Where are you?"

There was a *swoosh* of metal moving through the air. Then Max let out a scream of intense pain, and Rose burst into a string of desperate squawks as Fenn grabbed her in her sharp fingers.

"MAX!" Nell screamed again, spinning her head in every direction, trying to find her friend in the blinding fog. Fenn gave a long, high whistle, calling for something that came instantly. There was a crash and the shatter of glass. The smoke was sucked out of the broken window, draining itself from the bridge. All eyes, tearing and stinging, went to the slimy octopus that the Dark Daughters rode, which had entered the ship. It was slithering across the floor with writhing tentacles.

Fenn stood over Max. The boy lay on the floor, moaning in agony, an ivory-handled knife stuck into his chest. All were watching but none could move, the paralysing poison from the smoke now fully in their blood. Fenn held Rose in her dirty, nail-bitten fingers.

"Hello, Gleipnir," Fenn said, kissing the bird on the head.

"Don't!" Nell pleaded, for she knew what was about to happen and also knew she couldn't stop it. Nell tried to become calm. She looked into Fenn's hate-filled eyes. "Don't take her, Fenn. Please. She's my mother. You have a mother who loves you?"

"I do," Fenn said and smiled, a little girl's hopeful smile. "And I'm going to make my mummy very happy." Then, moving with the explosive speed of a wild animal that had been pent up in a cage, Fenn darted across the bridge, dived onto the back of the octopus and shot out of the window, the shrieking Rose clenched tightly in her hand.

The air was clearing and, as it did, their minds and limbs came alive once again. Nell couldn't yet process that her mother had been taken. First they had to deal with Max, who lay on the floor of the ship, a knife sticking out of his chest. Nell rushed over to his side. Lefty was touching Max's forehead. Nell was on her knees beside him.

"I'm waking up…" Max said in disbelief as his Sleeper began to be pulled back into his human body. "I don't want to go," he moaned.

"It's okay," Nell said, trying to comfort him. "You're going home."

"I'm waking," he repeated, unable to believe what was happening. "You're fading."

"I'm right here," Nell said. She turned to Badger. "Help me. Help me. What do we do?"

Badger just sadly shook his head. "There is nothing we can do, Nell."

"Shut up. Shut up and help me. Please! You're a Fearless Traveller! There must be something in the book!"

Nell got out the book and frantically started flipping through the pages, but it was all blank.

Badger's hand fell upon hers and closed the book softly. "The book won't help this time. He's waking," Badger said tenderly, looking into Nell's eyes. "His Sleeper is leaving the Dreamlands and returning to his body."

"PLEASE!" Nell screamed. She threw the book across the room. "Help me!"

"All wake in the end. It comes to every Sleeper. All wake back in their human bodies and forget almost everything that happened to them in this world. That is life. Dream life. Brief and beautiful."

"Nell," Max said weakly. His body was growing translucent. Fading away. Lefty waved goodbye. It was a sad wave, the wave of leaving, of those boarding trains to far-off places from which there is no return. Max grabbed hold of his friend with his good hand, not wanting him to go, but even he could not stop him from fading.

POP! A bright flash of light exploded, and in an instant the hand was gone.

"Lefty. No. No," Max moaned in horror. He turned to Nell, his eyes wide and his voice growing weak. There was no stopping it now. He was waking, plucked from this world where his friend Nell remained. "Take the case," Max said. His voice was growing fainter, as if he were falling. He touched the trumpet case, but saw with terrified eyes that the case was disappearing with him.

"Where am I?" Max gasped, his voice far away. "Where am I?!" His body was becoming as see-through as glass. "It looks like the hospital?"

"Shh," Nell cooed, holding back the tears that were filling her eyes.

"I'll come back," Max said, coughing blood. "I'll travel through the Dreamlands and the Wicked Places and find my way back to you," he said with his final bit of strength as a bright flash of light engulfed him with a sizzle. When Nell's eyes adjusted, Max and the trumpet case had disappeared.

The ivory-handled knife clattered to the floor. Nell stayed for a while on her knees, staring at the place where Max had been. Her friend was gone. So suddenly, so completely, in just a flash of light, he was no longer in this world. And now she realized Rose was gone as well.

"Gone," she snarled. "Gone" – the word itself so terrible

and final, no different from the slam of a door or the close of a coffin lid. Nell turned to Badger and without warning ran at him with her fists curled.

"AHHHHHH!" she screamed and punched him in his chest.

He looked at her in surprise. "I'm sorry, Nell."

"Don't talk to me!" Nell shouted. "None of you talk to me!" She walked to a chair and turned away from them.

For a moment no one spoke. Finally, awkwardly, as if for no other reason than to break the terrible silence, Speedy asked, "Why did the case disappear?"

"It belongs to the last person whose lips touched it," Badger said.

"What are we going to do now?" George asked Nell.

Nell didn't answer. She stood and wiped her eyes. No one spoke. The only sound was the wind rushing in from the broken window. Finally, she shook her head, steadfast and defiant. She was not going to just sit by and do nothing. She let out another scream, bursting with anger, raw and wild.

"AHHHHHHH!!!!"

"Nell," Badger said calmly. "Listen to me. We will fix this!"

"What!" Nell snarled, facing him. "Don't scream? That it? Why not? GIRLS CAN SCREAM! We don't need to be polite! And we don't need to wait for someone to fix it. No one needs to help us! We can FIGHT back and that is what is going to happen. I am going to get Mum and take her home."

Badger walked forward and put his large arms around Nell, and gave her a hug. He held her by her shoulders, his expression full of pride and wonder. "Of course you will, Nell Perkins. Of course you will. Now show me how you scream."

Nell smiled and let out her loudest scream. She looked at her brothers and they joined her. For a few moments they all screamed. Screamed in anger until they felt ready to take on anyone and anything.

But it all came to an end when the engines groaned mournfully as the entire ship began falling.

"STRAP IN!" Pinch screamed. "We're going to crash!"

Everyone scrambled into a seat. The *Compass* bounced and jostled through the air as it fell from the sky, and with a tremendous *WHAM,* it smashed into the hard-packed snow and slid across the ice, downing trees and sending great plumes of white into the air.

For a moment, all was very silent and very cold. The impact had stunned them all. Nell's ears were ringing, her vision blurry. In a few seconds, sensations smashed upon her like a wave.

"Is everyone all right?" Badger asked.

Nell felt okay. No worse off for the crash. She looked at Speedy. He nodded. "We're fine."

"Go and find George," Badger instructed Speedy. "Pinch, start checking on the damage."

"I can already tell you we're down for a while."

Badger thought for a moment until the solution became clear. "They'll go by Silverback," he said.

"By Silverback?" Pinch repeated, confused. "How in the world do you plan to do that?"

"You know how. I'll have to feed him myself."

"No, Duke. You can't," Pinch commanded.

"We don't have a choice."

Badger said no more and began to pack up a few things.

After a few silent minutes, George walked into the bridge.

He was a little banged up and his hand was burned. Badger applied some ointment, quickly healing it. Following Badger's instructions, the three children exited the ship. They were in a desolate place. A lonely and terrible place. There was nothing save for the rush of cold wind blowing across a vast ice-bound land.

"I knew this hunk of junk couldn't fly," George said, his body shivering.

With a crisp THWACK, Nell opened her umbrella. Her brothers huddled under the warm light. Nell kept touching her bowler, hoping to find Rose, but there was no trace of her tiny feet or soft feathers. It felt so strange not having Rose with her now. She felt naked. Alone. How she missed her little red head and excited cheeps.

"You think Mum's okay?" Speedy asked.

Nell said nothing. She kept her eyes steady on the Plague Dreamer floating serenely over Freyja Skoll's towering castle of black glass, waiting to awaken and spread disease through this world and the next.

"She has to be," she said, staring straight ahead. "She has to be."

A hatch in the back of the *Compass* opened, and Badger and Pinch carefully led a Silverback down the ramp by a leather bridle. The half-horse, half-motorcycle was without power, dark and soundless. The heavy tyres made thick tracks across the snow. It was the first time that Nell and George had seen a Silverback. Even now, powered down as it was, it radiated a deep power and seething menace.

"What is that?"

"It's a Silverback," Speedy said. "It's one of the engines of the ship."

"Go on," Pinch insisted and nodded towards Badger. "Say your goodbyes."

Nell turned to Badger, who was adjusting the Silverback's saddle.

"Does she mean you?" Nell asked, her stomach fluttering. "Why won't we see you again?"

Badger did not answer the question. Instead, he gave instructions. "You three must make it to Vazencrack. You must climb the mountain, make your way inside the castle and save your mother before Freyja Skoll uses her to kill Ravenhead and awaken the Plague Dreamer. I can't tell you how to do it, only that you mustn't fail."

"Stop it!" Nell said hotly. "Just answer me. Why won't we see you again?"

Badger reached out and took Nell's hand in his own. He looked deep into her eyes and gave her a sad smile.

"The ship is dead. We'd never make it on foot. The only way is to ride across the wastelands on the Silverback. We can only give power to one Silver, but that is fine. It can carry all three of you. But in order to run, it needs fuel. It runs on Nightmares," Badger explained.

"Nightmares?" Nell repeated, confused.

"That's right."

"I don't understand. What does that have to do with you?" Nell said.

"I will be the fuel," Badger admitted.

"What? How can you be the fuel?" Nell said. "It takes Nightmares."

"When I was young, I made a lot of mistakes. I was shaped accordingly."

Badger pulled a small vial from his boot and popped the

cork. A medicinal scent perfumed the air. With a steady hand, he lifted the vial to his lips and drank. His body clenched. His eyes closed, and he screamed a violent scream, as though something elemental was being ripped from his body. Spidery webs of energy crawled over him as he began to transform. Before their eyes he became a creature, shadowy and electrical, with sharp red eyes, long, razor-sharp claws, a human's body and the head of an animal. A badger – fierce and terrible. And Nell knew at once that she was no longer looking at a man but at something else entirely.

"You're a Nightmare!" Nell gasped.

"No. I was a Nightmare," he growled, his voice rough and terrible. "I found the Night and was reshaped into a Dream. But my past can't ever be completely washed away. I've learned to control the Nightmare inside me. And right now I need to summon it," he roared as his body became a great black fog. The fog swirled violently, a mini tornado that fluttered the children's clothes and swept over the dead-eyed Silverback, entering its ears and mouth and disappearing inside. The creature's dark eyes glowed red as it came to life and let out a loud whinny.

"Get on," Pinch said, not wanting to waste any time.

"Badger is a Nightmare?" Nell asked in disbelief, her eyes wet with tears.

"Don't cry," Pinch said. "Years ago, he left that all behind and wandered alone in the darkest, most lonely places, searching out the wisdom of the most ancient Dreamers. He remembered who he was and became what he was born to be: a Fearless Traveller. And now it is your turn to be yourself. You won't let us down, will you?"

"No." Nell sniffled.

"Who are you?" Pinch asked.

"A girl who is trapped in a Wicked Place, has messed up everything, lost her mother, and is afraid."

"If that's who you think you are, that's who you will be. Now stop feeling sorry for yourself. You've come this far. So tell me, who are you?"

Nell took a deep breath. The wind was whistling softly all around them, and in the distance the Plague Dreamer rumbled.

"I am Nell Perkins!"

"And you won't forget it." Pinch nodded.

"No," Nell whispered.

"And you will find your way home!" Pinch snarled.

The three children climbed onto the Silverback. Nell sat in front, holding the reins. Speedy sat in the middle, holding the umbrella, protecting them from the punishing cold, and George rode at the back.

"How do I ride it?" Nell asked.

"You don't," Pinch said. "You just hang on tight. It will do the rest. Just tell it where it needs to go."

"You can't come?" Speedy asked.

"My duty now is to protect the ship."

"But we need you."

"You've come this far," said Pinch. "You'll be fine."

Nell lifted her eyes to the vast, snowy plain that stretched out before them and the awful Plague Dreamer that reached across the sky. There was no turning back. Her mother was there in the castle, and if Nell failed to rescue her, not only would the Perkins children lose their mother, but Ravenhead would die, the Plague Dreamer would wake, and everyone would be plunged into never-ending terror.

"Take us to Vazencrack," Nell said to the creature.

At first, the Silverback didn't make a sound. But suddenly its wheels began to spin, spraying snow into the air, and with an explosive rumble it shot off across the ice towards all that lay ahead.

CHAPTER 32

For an hour, the children rode across the immense plain of ice, chased by massive black hyenas. Drawn by the umbrella's warm light, they darted out of the darkness like phantoms and ran alongside, filling the air with their horrible yapping laughter. Their snapping jaws menaced the children, but the loping beasts kept their distance from the Silverback, who charged forward in unnerving silence, red eyes ablaze, a trail of vapour escaping from its mouth.

At the beginning of the ride, Nell had tried to talk to him, to see if Badger could hear her beneath the chrome skin. More than anything, she wanted to hear her friend's gruff, reassuring voice.

"Badger," she whispered. "Badger. Can you hear me?"

The creature heard, but Badger did not. Badger was gone. Nell felt this fact like a punch to an already bruised and tender place. This was the way of the Dreamlands. That much Nell knew, for she had learned the fact first-hand. Who they had been before was quickly forgotten, discarded. The Silver wasn't Badger any more than she was. The Silverback was what it was, and that was a silent and solitary creature on the border between good and evil. When a hyena got too close, the Silver snapped its head, quick as a viper, and bit off its ear. Maybe it should have reassured Nell that they were riding on such a fearsome monster, but it did not. It only made her feel more alone and made the task ahead seem more difficult, because Badger would not be there to guide them.

The sky opened up, and a hot, hissing rain began to fall, leaving red splotches on the ice.

"It's raining blood." Speedy trembled as he watched the crimson splatter in the snow.

"Just stay under the umbrella," Nell said.

The storm passed, but as they got deeper into the Wicked Places, others replaced it – fogs of bats, ghost gales and a hail of flaming eyes – yet through every tempest, the umbrella shone its warm light upon the Perkins children, protecting them from each new blast of dark magic and through each new storm. And all the while, the Silver never slowed his steady pace.

As night began to fall, they reached the base of the mountain. The storms had stopped. All was quiet save for the electric cracks of energy that raced along the body of the Plague Dreamer.

A simple stone gate marked the entrance to Vazencrack, and they passed through without trying to hide their arrival. Nell swung her umbrella overhead, closing it up with a THWACK, readying herself for a fight. Nestled at the base of the mountain was a small town made of winding cobblestoned streets and darkened gingerbread-style houses of grey stone. It was abandoned, the streets empty, the entire town silent, unpopulated except for a few sad old women who sat on oversized black toadstools. They watched the Silverback pass with knowing eyes, but said nothing.

The main avenue ascended a winding mountain road that was muddy and deathly thin, and the higher the Silver climbed, the louder and more frightening were the crackles of electricity in the sky above and the danker the smell all around.

"Don't look up," Nell warned. Not heeding, George and Speedy both did exactly that and felt fear, like a frigid wind, blow over them.

"Don't tell people *not* to look up if you don't want them to look up," George said.

"Sorry," Nell replied, eyes scanning the streets for attackers. But soon she realized they were alone, and this was just as unsettling.

The Silverback kept up a quick pace, his tyres squealing on the very edge of the cliff. Many times, Nell heard George gasp and Speedy gulp, but no one spoke. Freezing winds pounded their bodies, and soon even the warmth of the umbrella could not protect them.

The Silverback came to a stop and communicated with Nell for the first and last time, nodding his head in the direction of the entrance. The message was clear. Nell, Speedy and George were to enter, and he would stay outside. Silence fell upon the children. This was it – the end of the road. Here they would either save their mother and free Ravenhead, or they, along with all of the Dreamlands, would be plunged into an endless Nightmare.

"Listen to me…" Nell said as they all climbed off the horse-like creature, her chest tight, her hands sweaty. They wouldn't want to hear this, but she had to let her brothers know something.

"And listen good. If either one of you wants to stay and wait out here, you must. Don't worry about anything. Don't think about if it's right or wrong or anything else. The only thing that matters is that we're safe. Something might happen in there. And whatever happens … I mean, if we don't make it out … I just want you to know that I'm sorry."

"Sorry?" Speedy said.

"This was all my fault. I messed up. I could have caught the kite and pulled her down. If I hadn't ducked, they wouldn't have taken Mum. I got us into this. Got all of us into this."

"And you'll get us out," George said, giving Nell a punch on her arm. "You'll get us out."

"Not yet."

"But you will. Okay? That's what's going to happen, Nell!" Speedy shouted. The boy who was hard to upset was furious. He would hear no more of it. "End of story."

"But–" Nell tried to protest. Speedy shook his head and, taking the umbrella from Nell's hand, pointed to the gates.

"You heard the man," George said. "End of story."

Nell gave each of her brothers a quick hug and looked into the Silverback's eyes a final time, waiting for Badger to shine through somehow, to give her some sign that he was here with her and understood all they now faced. The Silverback did not respond but stared off across the cliff's edge, sniffing the wind and ignoring Nell and her brothers.

"Thank you," Nell said anyway. The creature had got them there safely, and right now that was enough. She turned and her brothers turned with her, and together they faced the ancient iron gates clad with gargoyles and stargazer lilies. No creatures were standing guard, so there was nothing to do now but walk through. Nell felt for *The Fearless Travellers' Guide* in her pocket and, finding it secure, took the umbrella from her brother's hand and gave it a mighty THWACK. A warm blue light shone down. There was nothing else to do now, so they walked forward.

As they passed through the gates, they found themselves in a large, moon-swept meadow alight with swirling fireflies. Beyond the meadow was the castle, but it was hidden in a curtain of fog, which only added to the inexplicable beauty of the field.

"Whoa," Speedy said, expressing the wonder they all felt.

As they walked through the tall grass, the tiny flickers of amber light flew towards them in welcome. The delicate bugs zigged and zagged in looping circles around their heads.

"You bugs are in the wrong field," George said, swatting his arms.

"Don't you dare!" Nell warned, feeling she needed to protect the tiny creatures.

"Have you found my mother?" a teeny spark of a voice called out. The sad voice stopped Nell in her tracks.

"Are you going to bring her back?" another voice murmured.

"It's the fireflies," Speedy said. "They're talking."

The tiny creatures began to land, coming to rest softly on the tips of cat-tails and hollyhock and the other tall plants that lined the meadow. In no time, a thousand pearls of flickering light had settled and lit up the entire field.

"She has red hair," a tiny voice squeaked.

Nell bent down, expecting to see a small firefly, but instead she beheld a child no larger than a beetle. It was a human girl, who looked about six years old. Her miniature body was glowing brightly, but beneath the light she was wearing a nightgown and had a look of inconsolable sadness.

"They're Sleepers," Nell said to her brothers.

"A cloud took her," the girl whispered. "She hasn't come back."

"Mine too," said a little boy sitting on the tip of the next plant. Soon all the fireflies began chattering, pleading, begging for help.

"Quiet," Nell said tenderly, trying to calm them. "One at a time."

"She's in there," the little girl said.

"Where?" Nell asked. A slight breeze fluttered through the field, and the fireflies were borne away. The gust cleared the mist at the field's end, and Nell saw what was awaiting them all.

Before them stood Dark Dawn, the ancestral home of the Dark Daughters. The castle was built in the shape of an enormous thundercloud and was made completely of dark stained glass and sheets of enamelled metal. All was in constant motion. Sheets of metal and flowing glass rode upon each other in rumbles and screeches as ribbons of energy crackled in spiderweb bursts along the edges.

Nell and her brothers crossed the remainder of the field in silence.

"Shhh!" Nell cautioned as they approached an unguarded door that led inside. With a *whoosh*, Nell closed her umbrella tight and readied it for fighting. They had yet to see anyone, but still, caution was necessary. Noises meant people. People meant weapons. Behind the door, any type of Nightmare could be waiting for them. Nell put her ear to the door and felt a vibration on her cheek. Beneath the metal, she heard another sound – the frightened chirps and squawks of thousands of imprisoned birds.

"Birds," Nell whispered. "There are birds inside."

"Mum," Speedy and George said simultaneously. They raced to put their ears to the door. The boys' collective weight swung the door open, and both tumbled inside, Speedy landing on George.

"Nice going," George hissed, pushing his brother off him. "Real smooth."

"It was an accident."

"You're an accident."

Nell quieted them and gazed around in disgust. They were hidden in the shadows of a vast warehouse with towering walls and a high ceiling. The cavernous space was filled with square metal birdcages that lined the high walls and were stacked in large mechanical towers. Thousands upon thousands of birds of every type were stuffed into cages that had nothing to do with their size. Giant birds were cramped into tiny cages, while scores of tiny birds were darting endlessly around immense cages.

Nell felt the meanness of it and felt sick to her stomach. This had all had been done without the slightest care for the suffering creatures. The only thing that seemed to matter to the Dark Daughters was that their prisoners made no noise, for all their beaks had been bound shut with wire. Some twisted so tight that they were caked with dry blood. A few of the birds had broken the wires off, and from their bloody beaks came continuing cries of fear and pain.

Overhead, a red light flipped on. A buzzer sounded, and the cages began to move, rumbling along a mechanical track. The cages rolled up the columns, along the sides of the wall, and out through a hole in the far end of the warehouse.

"Follow me," Nell said, walking quickly through the maze of stacks.

She followed the conveyor belt across the cavernous room to the far wall, where, beside the hole through which the cages disappeared, a door was cracked open. Nell put her eye to the crack and let out a gasp of fright.

"What is it?" Speedy asked.

Nell said nothing but slowly opened the door and showed her brothers what lay on the other side. Before them stretched a vast, sterile factory that went on for a thousand metres. Hundreds of slave workers sat in rows before a long conveyor belt that snaked through the room in neat aisles. Running along the edge of the conveyor belt were thin metal sinks of running water that Nell imagined was for drinking, but she did not see any cups. The slaves were human, animal, demon and robot, and there were many human children among them. All wore dark uniforms and had the haunted expressions of the imprisoned, alone and confused. Sentenced to life in a place from which there was no escape. For even though they woke in their beds, every night they would return here again.

Every slave was silent, staring blankly at the conveyor belt as if waiting for instruction. Each held a device shaped like a hammer, except that the top of the tool was not curved metal but the head of a small, bald demon. At the base of each device was a translucent tube. The tube ran up towards the ceiling and was connected to a glass tank the size of a blue whale that hung above the factory floor. A glowing liquid filled the tank, bathing the room in an eerie light the colour of burning embers.

A loud, hollow bell rang out, and the conveyor belt whirled to life. Nell felt a shiver of dread. She knew without question that nothing good was made here. This was a terrible place, and they were about to witness something horrible. Badger had said the *devilartkia* would be thick, and now she knew what he meant. A low growl escaped her throat, and a few silver hairs sprouted on her arm. Her throat began to close up. Her breath quickened, and she could feel her teeth beginning to morph and sharpen.

"I am Nell Perkins," she snarled, stamping her feet. Suddenly, Nell had the feeling that something had changed. A shift had occurred inside her, and now the slipping away, the uncontrolled change that had haunted her all her life, was replaced by a feeling of control.

I am Nell Perkins, she repeated confidently, not saying it out loud but deep in her mind, and just like that, the wild-animal tingling vanished and her skin returned to normal.

There was a second bell, louder and harsher. From out of a dark hole in the wall, birds in their antique cages began to appear one after the other on the conveyor belt. Starlings, swans, finches, pigeons, jays, robins, egrets, herons, eagles, ospreys, warblers. And on and on and on, each one more beautiful than the last. Unlike the birds of Crypt, these were familiar sizes, the regular birds of Earth. The poor creatures stood silent in their cages, their eyes filled with fright. When every slave working the line had a bird before them, the conveyor belt stopped and, in unison, the cages vanished with such speed that the birds could not react. In that instant, every worker brought down their hammer on their bird's head. As the tool sped towards the unsuspecting birds, the little demons at the top opened their mouths and took a bite into the feathers.

No noise escaped from their beaks and no slave missed, but two things happened. Instantly, shafts of ember-coloured light shot up from the top of each bird. Inside the column of light were the flickering ghostly frames of young women, their faces frightened and confused, as if suddenly waking from a nightmare.

"It's all the mothers," Nell gasped, realizing what was happening. "All the ones who've been stolen from the world and turned into birds by the Dark Daughters."

"So many," Speedy said.

The stolen mothers gazed around in confusion as if awoken from a dream. Some screamed, some cried. No one answered and as quickly as they appeared, they disappeared. The mothers' ghostly forms were sucked into the little demons' mouths on the top of the hammers, pulled up through the tubes, and emptied into the giant tank above.

Inside the tank, the liquid burped and roiled with the new influx of mothers. Terrified faces and desperately swimming forms swirled behind the glass, trying to escape, but from the depths below sprang whirling octopus arms that sped across their mouths or lashed around their throats and dragged them down into the murk, where they were not seen again. After a moment, the liquid became calm.

The instant the ghosts left the birds, the spell was broken and the birds were transformed into hollow china statues. *WHACK!* The noise sounded in efficient and deadly unison as the slaves simultaneously brought their hammers down upon the hollow birds' ceramic heads, shattering them to dust. With cold sweeps of their hands, the slaves pushed the dust into the gutters of running water that lined the conveyer belts, and the shattered pieces were borne away.

All three children felt a great pain in their hearts. They knew that they had witnessed something truly evil, and fear, like freezing fingers, crawled over their skin.

George, in a tiny voice choked with rage, said what they all were feeling. "I hate these people."

"They're not people," Speedy spat. "They're Nightmares."

Nell's mind was racing. Her gaze returned to the great glowing tank of ember-coloured liquid. A spiralling glass tube snaked up out of the tank and disappeared into a hole in the ceiling. Nell was certain that wherever that tube came out, they would find Ravenhead. She turned to her brother.

"George. Do you think you could turn into a rat?"

"I don't know. I never – I mean, it always just happens."

"You can do it. You can control it." Nell spoke quickly. "It's the secret of all Fearless Travellers." She explained to her brothers that they had to give over to it but keep part of themselves holding on.

"Remember who you are – who you really are. Let the rat thoughts come and go, but keep remembering you are George and you will be both, a Dream and a boy, together. Understand?"

George nodded and began to murmur, "I am George. I am George," saying it until it became one word, a nonsense sound that made total sense, as if it were unlocking a deep secret. His mind picked up the rhythm of the sound, and he stopped speaking it, letting it reverberate inside.

"You see that tube?" Nell said, pointing to the glass tube that rose from the tank of glowing liquid floating overhead. "Follow the tube and find out where it goes. That is where we will find Ravenhead."

"What about me?" Speedy asked.

"You are going to help me smash this machine."

"As a bear, right?"

Nell nodded and turned to George. "Ready?"

"Yep."

"Good luck."

"Stop being so nice," George said.

"What am I supposed to be?" Nell asked.

"An animal." George smiled and tried to say, "I am George" a final time but only got so far as "I am", before his whole body began to shiver and shrink. In an instant, a large rat stood before Nell and Speedy. The rat looked up at them with his large, dark, knowing eyes, sure of who he was, and with a wiggle of his whiskers, he winked and darted away.

CHAPTER 33

George ran, and the clear shapes of the world melted into blobs. As a rat, his eyes were useless, but his nose was alive with an ocean of scents that showed a picture clearer and more detailed than if he'd had X-ray vision. The scent of the mothers' souls inside the tank and rushing in hidden pipes throughout the factory was overpowering, a deep and wonderful scent of honey and spring and warm sun on soft grass. It was easy to follow. In his mind's eye, he saw the tube moving up through the ceiling and leading to another room above. He had to get closer and, without thinking, he ran up a slave's head, leapt onto the long tube, and scurried up with such speed and grace that no one noticed. He leapt again onto the floating tank. The face of a young mother came to the glass, and he almost lost his grip and fell to the factory floor far below.

"Help me," she mouthed silently, air bubbles escaping from her mouth, before a long tentacle dragged her down into the darkness.

"I am George. I am George. I am George," he repeated. From the top of the tank, he got a picture of the vast factory floor, and he could smell the metal of a stairwell. In his mind's eye, he saw that the stairwell led to a door, and behind the door was where the stream of liquid was flowing into a second tank. George scurried down again, leaping from tube to tube until he hit the floor. Moving swiftly beneath the conveyor belt and the legs of the seated workers, he came to the stairwell and darted up the steps.

The smell of souls was stronger as he ran, and behind it was another scent: the dizzying smell of birds and a billion Dreams. It was so powerful that it hit George like a club. He let out a loud squeal of pain and, forgetting his chant, suddenly turned back into a boy.

Nell had lost sight of her brother, but at the sound of his squeal, she turned and saw him at the top of the metal stairs at the far end of the factory. "There." Nell pointed to George. "That's the way," she said, absolutely certain Ravenhead was in the space at the top of the stairs. Before they could follow, they had to stop this infernal machine.

Nell's eyes scanned the factory and caught sight of a hulking Dark Daughter who sat on a stool pulling a lever that worked the conveyor belt.

"I'm going for the handle," she said to Speedy. "You break the belt. Anyone comes for you, you fight and don't hold back. Remember who you are."

"I'm Speedy," he said.

"That's right."

Speedy repeated his name to himself, whispering. The change took hold, and he turned into a large grizzly bear. He dropped to all fours and took off, roaring across the factory floor. The thump of his great pads echoed throughout the vast space.

Nell followed. The fight had begun. Grabbing the umbrella off her back, she charged forward and felt the Night rushing through and all around her as the umbrella seethed with energy. Hot silver stars, electrical and shimmering, sparked from the umbrella's tip.

The Dark Daughter turned and saw Nell coming, her body encased in stars as the force of the Night surrounded her. The attack was a complete surprise, and she dived out of the way as with a mighty swipe Nell brought the umbrella down, slicing through the fat iron lever as though it were butter, rendering it useless.

Nell turned. Speedy stood on his hind legs. He raised his great and powerful paws into the air and brought them down upon the conveyor belt. It broke like a ribbon. A great crash of grinding metal rang out as tiny pieces of machinery rained across the factory floor.

At first, the slaves scattered, surprised by the attack. But now the massive Dark Daughter struggled to her feet and shouted orders. The workers, demon-headed hammers in hand, charged towards Speedy. Speedy stood up on his two hind feet and with one great paw, he scattered them as if they were bowling pins.

A few slaves charged Nell, but they were no match for her and her umbrella. The blue tip melted the hammers, slashed arms, and crippled hands with fierce burns.

"Here!" George screamed from above. He had recovered from the overpowering scent and was trying to get their attention. He screamed again, his words drowned out by the blaring alarm that had been sounded.

Dozens of Dark Daughters holding swords, bows and knives poured in through a doorway. There came the *ping* of arrows. Nell turned. The mob stood between them and the stairwell. An arrow grazed Speedy's shoulder, and he snarled in fury. He turned his head towards Nell and roared again. Nell understood the message. He would get them through. She ran to her brother and jumped on his back. With a final roar, the bear charged, head down, towards the mob. He smashed through them easily and bounded up the stairs. George had disappeared through the doorway but was at the top, calling for them. It only took three or four leaps and Speedy was through the darkened doorway. The moment he was through, Speedy collapsed, and Nell tumbled to the ground, hitting her head hard. Pain rang through her skull. When she stood up, she found herself in a large, ornate temple, lit by candles and burning fireplaces.

The ceiling was curved in waves like a cloud and through the sheets of glass, the Plague Dreamer's body could be seen hovering. And even more horrible was the stone table in the room's centre. The great marble slab was at least nine metres long, and laid out upon it was Ravenhead. The great bird filled every centimetre of it and was bound to the top by golden chains that tightly crisscrossed his chest. His eyes were closed, but his chest was rising and falling. He was under a spell, but he was still alive.

A hypodermic needle as large as Nell herself dangled over Ravenhead's heart. The stun of the fall and the shock of seeing Ravenhead laid out on his deathbed passed, and Nell remembered her brother. She looked on the ground. Speedy had returned to himself and was on the floor, moaning. Nell ran over. An arrow had hit the large boy in the arm, which was bleeding badly.

"I'm shot," he moaned, clutching his arm and trying to stem the blood.

"Don't worry," Nell said, though her heart was racing. *The book,* she thought. *The book will have some medicine.*

"Nell," George grunted. "Give me the umbrella?" His voice was trembling. As he stepped out of the shadows, she saw why. Fenn was standing beside him, holding a knife to his throat.

"Give us the umbrella," Fenn said.

"All right," Nell said calmly. "Just let him go."

"Yes, Fenn. Let the boy go."

Freyja Skoll had entered the room, dressed in a beautiful blood-red gown that was embroidered with hundreds of tiny bird skulls, each encrusted with diamonds that glittered in the candlelight. In her hand, she held an all-too-familiar cage. And imprisoned in it was Rose. Sensing Nell, Rose began to chirp wildly.

"Mum!" Nell blurted out.

Fenn released George. He scrambled over to Speedy. The sight of his brother's ruby-red blood turned his face white.

"He's shot," George said, his eyes wide in fear.

"He's going to be okay," Nell tried to say calmly, but her voice betrayed her nervousness. Rose was chirping wildly. Nell quickly took out her *Fearless Travellers' Guide*.

"I doubt it," Freyja Skoll said as she walked across the room and stood over him. "He's most certainly going to wake. Excuse me. He's going to die. On any other night, he would be a Sleeper and he'd wake back in his bed, but he took it upon himself to enter my world as a human. So, dead here, dead there."

Rose began to chirp furiously in protest.

"Nell," Speedy moaned. "Is that Mum?"

"Yes. She's fine. Hold on. I have medicine," Nell said.

"Hurry," George pleaded.

"Please. Stop whining. He's going to die," Fenn said, sneering and kicking him hard in the side.

Speedy screamed in anguish.

"Let him die in peace," Freyja Skoll said, as though she were doing them a favour.

Nell tried to ignore the fact that the queen of the Dark Daughters was standing over her, holding her mother in a cage.

"Go on. Look through your book. It won't help you here," Freyja said, gazing up through the window at the Plague Dreamer floating above. "Nothing can help you now."

With shaking fingers, Nell flipped through her *Fearless Travellers' Guide*, looking for medicine. The pages were blank, white as the ruthless plains of ice that led to the castle.

"They're empty," Nell said.

"Why are they empty?" George said in disbelief.

"I don't know," Nell shouted, feeling as though a cruel trick had been played on her. It was this place. This evil place. She couldn't think straight, and it was affecting the book. "Do something!" she pleaded, turning to Freyja Skoll, the one person who had the power to save her brother and make the pain stop. "Please!"

"In a moment, I am going to do something. Something wicked."

Freyja Skoll's head suddenly faded away, so all that stood over Nell was the queen of the Dark Daughters' elegant dress and headless body. The body turned and walked towards the table where Ravenhead lay. Nell couldn't believe it. She was having a moment. Now. After all this, in this place, she was having a moment.

"I am Nell Perkins," she whispered. "I am Nell Perkins, and I am going to get my family out of this place." She blinked. Freyja Skoll's head was back.

A warm beam of light drenched Nell's face. She turned. The book was illuminated. The glowing page was filling with a drawing of a small vial. Medicine. Nell reached in and pulled it out. Inside the glass vial was a bubbling green liquid. With trembling hands, Nell popped open the cork and poured it into Speedy's mouth. Before their eyes, his wounds shrank and vanished. He was healed.

Nell glanced up. Freyja Skoll was standing over Ravenhead, holding Rose's cage in her hand. This was her chance. Nell grabbed the umbrella from the ground and charged Freyja Skoll.

"The Gleipnir," Freyja Skoll whispered to the enormous bird. With two hands she opened the great bird's beak. She ran her finger along the razor-sharp edges and winced. Her finger was cut. Blood beaded the surface. She licked the blood off with relish and reached for the small door of the cage.

"Don't!" Nell commanded. Freyja Skoll turned slowly and discovered Nell standing before her, holding the umbrella at her heart, the blue tip crackling with electric power.

"Give me my mother!" Nell shouted.

"Why, dear girl, didn't Badger warn you? These are the Wicked Places and we are the Dark Daughters. Forgetfulness and confusion are the base of all our spells. I couldn't change that if I wanted to. This bird is now a bird and nothing more. Even if you were to return her to human form, her memory is gone."

"She will remember me," Nell said. "A mother always knows her children. She couldn't forget if she tried."

"She won't remember you. I promise you that. But you're not stupid. You know what is going to happen. I am going to stuff this ugly little bird down Ravenhead's throat. He will be injected with the Eclipse potion and he's going to burst wonderfully into flames. I assure you it will be quite exciting.

He is going to fly up, straight into the heart of the Plague Dreamer, who – having been asleep for thousands of years – will go ravaging across the Dreamlands, destroying it all."

"Give me my mother!" Nell demanded once again.

"I'm afraid not," Freyja said and, faster than a bullet, she gave Nell a quick kick in the chest.

Pain seared through Nell's ribs as she went reeling to the floor. Her entire body hurt.

You will rise, she thought, remembering the Fearless Traveller motto. *You will rise.*

"All right," Nell said softly as she struggled to her feet, trying to catch her breath. Freyja threw both her arms into the air. With a loud CRACK, both arms turned into swords. Swinging them in powerful swipes, the hideous queen of the Dark Daughters marched towards Nell.

Nell's body was tingling. Fear, hot and electric, surged through her. Every sweep of Freyja's arms sent a *whoosh* through the air. Nell's heart pounded furiously. She gripped the wooden handle of her umbrella tightly and let the sound of rushing water fill her ears and calm her mind. Freyja continued to march towards Nell and then suddenly, with blinding speed, attacked. One of her swords headed straight for Nell's throat. Nell ducked, and the sword flew overhead. Nell pivoted and countered, catching it on her umbrella. Metal hit metal. Sparks flew in a dizzying spray. It was like battling two fighters at once.

* * *

Fenn was pointing a bow and arrow at Speedy, daring him to move, and suddenly he did, grabbing her tiny hand. The bow shot wildly, shattering glass overhead, and still, he held tight. While she was distracted, George flipped through the book.

"Help me. Help me. Help me," he whispered. Never in his life had he felt so lost, so alone, so in need of help. As the sound of the fight filled his ears, George whispered again to the book and then watched in shock as black ink slowly filled the pages.

The words said:

> Help is always here for those who ask. When all is lost, The Fearless Travellers' Guide is here. Call forth any Sleeper or Dream to assist you, and what you need will be delivered. All Fearless Travellers know that there is no such thing as lost, only the waiting. The waiting to be...

A picture was being drawn on the blank white page, an illustration of a large diamond. Beneath it was one word:

FOUND

With trembling hands, George reached into the book and took out the large glittering jewel, unsure of what it meant or what to do with it. It was the size of a golf ball and brilliantly clear, like ice from a mountain on which no one had ever set foot. He glanced up. Two fights were going on now. Nell and Freyja Skoll, and Fenn and Speedy. Nell let out a scream of pain. Freyja had slashed Nell's arm with her sword. Her skin was visible beneath her hoodie; a line of blood ran above her elbow.

"Trumpet," George whispered to the diamond. It was the first thing he could think of and he wasn't even sure what it meant. "Trumpet," he said again.

"Give me that," Fenn said and lurched for the diamond, grabbing George's wrist. The large diamond tumbled from his hand, but did not fall to the floor. Instead, it floated up, and, with a hum, a beam of white light shot straight down from the brilliant jewel. Inside the beam was the silhouette of a figure.

"Max," Nell said in surprise as she saw her friend step out of the beam of light. Max had made it. Someway. Somehow. He had found his way back into the dream, and in his hand was Ravenhead's trumpet. Rose let out a wild cheep of recognition.

"What are you doing with that?" Freyja Skoll said, her eyes trained on the trumpet Max held in his one hand.

Nell, catching Freyja Skoll off guard, brought her umbrella down hard across the evil queen's knees. She screamed and sank to the floor. As she fell to the floor, she brought both her sword arms down on Nell's umbrella, and it shattered with a loud pulse of energy. Nell knew she no longer needed it – what she needed was something else. She darted across the cold marble to her friend and stood close beside him. He had the trumpet. All they had to do was play, and Ravenhead would awaken.

"You remember," Max said.

"Yes," Nell said. "We could die."

"That's true, but that's not what I meant. Do you remember how to play?" He demonstrated. "One. Three. Two-three. One. One. Two-three."

"Yes," Nell said, so happy she wanted to scream it.

Max put his lips to the mouthpiece and began to blow. Freyja was already up, racing towards them in fury. She opened her mouth, and out shot a flaming tentacle. It slithered towards them as sound exploded out of the trumpet like a chorus of millions all singing one beautiful harmony. The wave of glorious noise shrivelled the tentacle, snuffed the candles and doused the flames in the fireplace and, with a *whoosh*, the room went completely dark.

The gloom was overwhelming but only lasted a moment, for a light appeared, growing stronger and stronger as Ravenhead's body began to glow until it was encased in a golden radiance.

Then the great bird opened his eyes and yawned. The chains that bound him snapped as if they were made of paper, and he jumped off the table. When his clawed feet hit the ground, the weight of him shook the room.

Freyja Skoll and Fenn stood frozen in fear. Max and Nell stopped playing. No one could speak.

"My trumpet, please," he said to Max and Nell, his voice a deep, raspy rumble. The bird reached out his long black wing and took the trumpet from Max. At his touch, the trumpet grew until it was large enough to press against his massive beak.

All the while, Freyja Skoll said nothing. She stood frozen. Her eyes flickered towards the door and window as if calculating her escape, but it was too late. Ravenhead was already holding her still with the power of his presence.

"Whose doing is this, Freyja Skoll?" Ravenhead's voice boomed like a cannon. "I don't need to punish all of the Dark Daughters, only the one who is responsible."

Without missing a beat, Freyja Skoll stared at Fenn. "It was my wicked daughter, Fenn, my Lord. I tried to stop her."

Fenn, shocked and confused, looked at Freyja Skoll with great hurt. "Mama?" she said clearly.

"The child is nasty. Not really a Dark Daughter at all. Demon spawn," Freyja Skoll said, turning away from the trembling Fenn. "Do as you wish to her."

"Mama?" Fenn repeated, her whole body trembling. And suddenly she was no longer a murderous Dark Daughter, but a child frightened, alone, and in need of her mother.

"How could you?" Nell snarled at the cruel betrayal that seemed worse than all she had done so far. "It was you!"

"Of course it wasn't. This was all Fenn's doing," Freyja Skoll said haughtily. "Please, my Lord, whatever punishment suits you. Kill the child if it pleases you."

"If it pleases him?" Nell screamed. "It was her! Freyja Skoll."

"No," Fenn babbled. "Please. No. Mama. Don't let him hurt me."

"Goodbye, Fenn." Freyja smiled. "The end comes to all of us."

Ravenhead nodded as if this were true. He lifted his wings and put the trumpet to his beak and began to play. Unlike before, the music was soft and beautiful. Freyja's expression began to change at once. Dark feathers began racing up her and Fenn's skin.

"NO!" Freyja Skoll snarled in protest. "I am Freyja Skoll, Queen of the Dark Daughters!"

She wasn't done for yet. From deep inside her, she let out a string of curses in her native tongue. The sounds sizzled in the air. "You!" she screamed at Nell. "You did this to me!"

In her fury, she reached her hand to her head. In it, she held a long, silver needle. "You think you can be free of me? I am the Dark Daughter. Your mother…" she said, growling as her face turned into a beak. "Your mother belongs to me!" She screamed and threw the needle. There was a flash of silver streaking across the air, and then Rose let out a squawk of pain and was silent. The needle had hit the small bird directly in the chest.

"*NO!*" Nell's scream filled the room.

Freyja Skoll let out a final cackle as she and Fenn were completely transformed into small black birds. They tried to fly, but could not. Ravenhead scooped them up and deposited them in the antique cage that held Rose and closed the door.

Nell was frantic. She raced over to the cage and carefully took Rose out. The little bird was still breathing, but the needle was stuck in her chest, and a drop of blood dampened her feathers.

"Fear not," Ravenhead said gently. "I won't let anything happen to her. But this is not the place to restore her." He brushed Rose's chest with the tips of his feathers. The needle fell to the floor and the wound closed, but still Rose lay asleep in Nell's hand.

"We must go to a place where I can break the spell. What was your mother's favourite place?" he said, picking up Nell's burnt and broken umbrella with his foot, and as he did, an electric charge coursed along its shaft and it became new again.

"The beach," Nell said immediately. Her mother had grown up in a little cottage by the ocean, and she had always said it was her favourite place.

"Then that is where we shall go."

CHAPTER 34

Nell, Speedy, George and Max followed Ravenhead downstairs through the factory. All the slaves and hundreds of Dark Daughters were waiting, frozen in fear. Their queen was defeated, and they didn't dare try to escape. Ravenhead moved through the crowd, dwarfing everything. He didn't hop or skitter like other birds but walked in powerful strides, and as he did, he shot off bright blasts of his trumpet.

"I lied about not punishing them all." He chuckled and kept playing. Puffs of foul-smelling green smoke exploded as one by one the Dark Daughters were changed into mosquitos and buzzed away.

"Stand back," Ravenhead said. He had stopped below the giant glass globe of ember-coloured liquid and blew on his trumpet again. *CRACK*. Fissures spread across the glass and then shattered, showering down. The liquid hit the floor and rushed to the door in a great wave, smashing it off its hinges.

Outside, the wave washed across the grass as fireflies danced overhead, and suddenly from out of the river of liquid, rose the mothers. Hundreds and hundreds of them. The fireflies circled around them, and there were shouts of joy as the fireflies found their own mothers and transformed back into children. The mothers scooped the children up in their arms and hugged them tight, and the moment they did, in a great flash of light, they would both disappear, fading away. Awaking back in their homes and beds. The great nightmare over.

All of this filled Nell with joy, but then a sudden rush of sadness poured through her. She wanted her mother. Her own mother. She wanted her back and couldn't wait another second. Ravenhead seemed to understand.

"Climb onto my back," he said. George hopped on first, followed by Speedy. Nell had taken off her bowler hat and put her hoodie inside, resting the sleeping Rose in the makeshift nest, her tiny chest rising and falling.

"Go on," Max said kindly. "I'll hold her."

Nell nodded. She was too tired to speak. Max held the bowler, and Nell climbed on. He handed back the hat and jumped on behind Nell.

"All set, chief," George said, patting Ravenhead on the head.

With a flap of his massive wings, Ravenhead rose into the sky, passing the Plague Dreamer. Ravenhead let out a loud *caw*, and from wherever they had fallen, the shattered bits of great red eggshell that had housed the Plague Dreamer flew towards it and took their places. Like an infinitely large puzzle, they fit themselves together and reformed, encasing the monster once again. With another *caw*, the massive Red Egg was torn loose from its mooring atop Freyja Skoll's castle and floated off lazily into the clouds.

"Will he stay inside there?" George asked.

"For now," Ravenhead answered and flew away from Vazencrack.

The air was freezing, so Speedy opened the umbrella with

a *THWACK*, and its warm light protected them from the wind and cold as they flew across the wasteland.

"How did you get here?" Speedy asked Max.

"I don't know. I was in the hospital, then all of a sudden this light shot down from the ceiling and fell over me. In a second, I knew everything that had happened and what I needed to do, and when I stepped out of the light, I was with you."

"Cool," Speedy murmured.

"Look!" George said.

Down below, racing across the snow, was the Silverback. He lifted his head and let out a whinny. Ravenhead dived down so he was flying above the horse-like creature.

"Meet us at Neptune Beach," Ravenhead said. The Silverback nodded in acknowledgement and sped off as Ravenhead rose higher in the dark sky.

As they passed over the *Compass*, the great bird let out another CAW and all the lights on the downed ship hummed to life.

The ride was a blur to Nell. It might have taken hours. It might have taken minutes. Nell did not know. All she knew was that her mother had to be okay. The spell had to be broken, and she had to return home again.

Soon it was morning. They landed just before dawn in front of an old house by the beach. The *Compass* was parked on the sand. After they touched down on the boardwalk, Ravenhead took human form. He was a handsome, intense man, and he wore an ancient black suit. The door of the house opened, and Badger and Pinch walked out onto the wooden porch.

"Badger," Nell said in surprise and relief. She wanted to hug him and thank him, but his face was grim, set on the task ahead. And this, more than anything, made her legs tremble.

After all, it wouldn't be easy, and there was no guarantee it would work.

"Are you okay?" Nell asked. "I wasn't sure you would be able to change back from a Nightmare."

"Neither was I," he smiled.

"It's all ready," Pinch said and added, "You did fine, Nell."

Nell nodded, now too nervous to do anything else.

"All right," Ravenhead said. He turned to Nell. "Can I have Rose?"

"Where are you taking her?" Nell said, holding the bowler hat protectively. Even though she knew she must, it was hard to give her away.

"I am going to heal her, but the spell will release some very vicious Nightmares. It is far too dangerous for you to watch."

"I want to come," Nell protested.

"Nell," Badger said calmly. "We have to let Ravenhead do it his way."

Nell and her brothers each gave Rose a tender kiss and watched Ravenhead disappear into the house with their mother.

For hours they sat on the porch, watching the sea. From inside the house came the sounds of screams and animals snarling and occasional trumpet songs that filled them with sadness. Out of the chimney, ghostly monsters escaped, looking around before darting off into the air like prisoners on a jailbreak. Her brothers, restless of waiting, wandered down to the waves, leaving Nell alone.

"Nell…"

Nell turned. Badger and Ravenhead in his human form stood by the door.

"She's awake."

Nell's heart began to pound. Her mother was okay. It had worked!

"The spell has been broken," Ravenhead said. "She is human once more."

Nell leapt up. "Can I see her?"

"Nell," Badger said. "Remember what I said all along. The spell was strong. The strongest one Ravenhead had ever seen. Because Rose herself was unlike any other mother."

"Yes," Nell said, not understanding what Badger was trying to say.

"I did my best," Ravenhead said. "But her memories are gone."

"Gone?"

"I'm so sorry, Nell," Badger said. "She remembers nothing."

Nell couldn't believe it. Pain gripped her stomach. She took a deep breath and tried to muster every bit of bravery she had.

"She doesn't remember you or anything else," Badger murmured tenderly.

"Can I see her?" Nell whispered, trying to be strong.

Ravenhead nodded. "She's in the garden."

Nell walked through the house. At first she tried to walk calmly, but she couldn't. She broke into a run, out the door and into a sunny garden bursting with flowers. And there she was. Rose, bending over to smell a honeysuckle. Hearing the door open, she turned. She was wearing the same dress she had worn the day she had been taken. She was a person! A real live person, and she was as beautiful as ever!

"Why, hello," she said politely. It wasn't the voice of someone greeting her own child. Nell froze. And for a moment, neither Nell nor Rose said anything. Rose stared at Nell, her face troubled and confused. It was clear. There was something about the girl before her that meant something, but she didn't know what.

"Don't you know me?" Nell finally asked – though she knew the answer. Nell's heart felt as though it were being smashed and shattered and stamped upon by Freyja Skoll and every Nightmare at her command. She had lost. Her mother was her mother no more and never would be again.

"Know you?" Rose said quietly, startled by the question. Nell couldn't take it. And all at once, she didn't even care. All she wanted to do was what she had wanted since the moment her mother was snatched from her: to wrap her arms around her once again and hug her. Without waiting, she bounded down the steps and threw her arms around Rose, hugging her hard. The tears streamed from her eyes. All she wanted was her mother back.

"Nell," Rose said tenderly. "Nell. My sweet Nell."

"You know me?" Nell said, stunned, as she looked deep into Rose's happy eyes.

"Of course I know you," she said, laughing and crying at the same time. "A mother could never, ever forget her child."

Rose showered Nell's face with kisses, and Nell let her, welcoming each and every one.

"The moment I touched you, smelled your hair. It all came back. You saved me," Rose said, her voice raspy with tears of joy. "How did you do it?"

"Your daughter is a Fearless Traveller."

Badger was standing by the door.

"A what?"

Before Badger could explain, Speedy and George raced

down the steps and threw themselves at their mother, and all four fell onto the warm grass, together again at last.

CHAPTER 35

Night came. On the beach, they held a party. Ravenhead wanted to thank Nell and her brothers for saving him. Tomorrow he would have to deal with the Maze Dreamer and get his birds back, but tonight a few who had survived had come to celebrate. In fact the beach was filled with human-sized birds dressed in their finest clothes.

"Without you children," he said, "there would be no more birds in the world, and a world without birds ain't much of a world at all."

A bonfire burned, and a long table was laid out with food. As the ocean crashed in the background, everyone ate and raised their glasses and made toasts. After dinner, Ravenhead played with his band and everyone took turns dancing. Nell danced with a large owl and a crane. Rose danced with Badger and then Speedy. George shook his head and said, "Not a chance" when anyone asked him, until finally Pinch snapped him up and made him dance. Max didn't dance but watched Nell the whole time, unable to look anywhere else, until Badger dragged him onto the sand.

"The boy wants to dance with you," he said to Nell, making clear that it was an order.

"All right," Nell said. She smiled at Max, suddenly feeling shy. The truth was she liked him very much, and while they were going through everything, it had seemed easy, but now that he was back, she didn't know what to say – only that she wanted him to stay.

Before they had a chance to dance, Ravenhead stopped playing and gazed down at the crowd. He turned towards Nell and her brothers. Rose walked over and put her arm around her daughter, squeezing her tight. And even though her mother was right beside her, Nell kept looking out for the little golden bird.

"One dream comes," Ravenhead said, his deep, gravelly voice full of warmth, "another goes. And another one comes. That is the way of humans. But birds see it differently. To a bird, day and night, dream and light are all the same. For those who fly high enough, it's all one dream. So for us, there is no goodbye."

He picked up his horn and began to play. Nell watched as a large wave came towards them and, from it, a train sped out of the sea. On the front was the large, beautiful face of the Night Train, her eyes shining bright.

"I am the Night Train," she said. "Welcome."

The train dashed past them, and the next thing Nell knew, she and her mother and brothers, along with Badger and Max, were inside the train that was charging forward at a blinding pace.

"Where's Pinch?" Nell asked.

"Pinch must stay and tend to the ship, but she wishes you well," Badger said.

"Will you tell her thank you?" Nell added.

"Of course," he said.

George added, "And buy her a can of cat food for me."

"Watch it, boy!" Badger snarled, though both knew he was amused. "The Night Train is making a special stop for you."

Moments later, the train exited the rushing waters of Mist Falls and was barrelling down the streets of the sleepy town, its iron wheels sending up sparks like fireworks. They passed a darkened hospital building, and Max disappeared from the seat across from Nell.

"Max?" Nell said in confusion as her friend vanished. Instantly, a light went on in an upstairs window of the hospital, and Nell could see Max there, standing at the window, just as surprised that he had been transported. He gave Nell a wave with his left hand. It had returned. He was healed. Max watched them as the train sped around the corner.

The Night Train cut through the town as though it knew every street and came to a jolting stop in front of their house.

"You've arrived," Badger said.

Nell and her brothers walked off the train with Badger. Nell gazed back at the woman's face at the front of the train. A soft summer rain had begun to fall, and the drops misted down through the two beams of light pouring from her eyes. Nell wanted to look at the hypnotic sight forever, but she couldn't, nor could anyone, for the moment they stepped off the train it sped off down the street, turned the corner and vanished completely.

Nell looked at Badger, who had his face towards the sky and was letting the drops fall on his cheeks. Her brothers had already darted off into the house to turn on the television. Rose thanked Badger with a final hug and followed the boys inside, for she was exhausted and wanted to be in her bed, but Nell didn't want to leave. Not yet.

"Do you want to come in?" Nell finally asked.

"No," Badger said with a rare smile. "I need to go back to the shop and get some things, and then I will find my way back to the Dreamlands. The ship needs a lot of work."

"All right," Nell said. It was the end of a long journey, and, as hard as it had been, Nell felt sad that it was ending. Badger seemed to understand what Nell was feeling, and perhaps he felt it a little bit himself.

"You know why most people never remember their dreams in the morning?" he asked.

Nell was about to shake her head and say that she didn't when she realized that she did know why. "Because they don't think they're real."

"And what do you think?"

"It's all real," Nell said, watching as an owl glided past through the rainy night sky. "Everything."

Badger smiled again, pleased. "Do you still have your *Guide*?"

"Yes," Nell said. Reaching into her pocket, she moved to hand it to him.

"Keep it. You earned it," he said. "You're a Fearless Traveller now."

"Really?"

Badger nodded. "Of course," he said. "You're Nell Perkins."

The rain was coming down harder now. Badger took his umbrella off his back. Before he could open it, Nell touched his hand. "May I?" she asked.

Badger gently handed the umbrella to Nell and, taking a deep breath, she swung it around her head. It opened with a mighty *THWACK* and the reassuring warm blue light shone down from underneath its dome.

"That's some umbrella," Badger said.

"You have no idea." Nell smiled and handed the amazing weapon and protector back to him.

"Well," Badger said. "This is where all journeys end."

"Home," Nell said, understanding that now this was goodbye. Nell felt a terrible sadness wash over her and tears well up in her eyes, but then she felt a warm hand on her shoulder and heard a familiar voice.

"Come on inside, sweetie," Rose said. Nell turned to see her mother's bright smile and all at once felt so happy to be in that moment, so happy they had all returned home, even though things weren't the same. She certainly wasn't.

"All right," Nell said, but before they went inside, they watched Duke Badger, the Fearless Traveller, wander down the street as the summer rain fell around him, his body untouched, protected by the warm glow from his umbrella.

"Goodbye," Nell whispered as he turned the corner and vanished into the deepening storm.

Nell changed into her pyjamas and lay down in her bed, which seemed like the most comfortable thing she had ever felt. Rose climbed into bed next to her and stroked her hair. On the bedside table was *The Fearless Travellers' Guide*.

"Tweet, tweet," Rose said with a yawn. Nell laughed sleepily. "Do you want to go to bed? Speedy and George are already sleeping."

"No," Nell said with a large yawn of her own. "Let's stay awake for a while."

"All right," Rose said, her eyes fluttering.

Nell smiled as her own eyelids grew heavy and the room around them disappeared. The next thing Nell knew, they were running through an endless sun-soaked meadow together: a silver fox, a grey rat, a brown bear and a beautiful golden bird with a red head.

"Follow me," Nell said. She knew exactly who she was and where she was going. "Don't be afraid. It's beautiful here."

PETE BEGLER *lives in Los Angeles, USA, with his wife and two daughters. He writes for film and television, including the drama Chance, starring Hugh Laurie.*

For more exciting books from
brilliant authors, follow the fox!
www.curious-fox.com